someone else's
ocean

KATE STEWART

Cover by Amy Queau of Qdesign
Formatting by Champagne Book Design

dedication

For my dear friend, Donna Cooksley Sanderson, thank you for setting your coffee down to become responsible for me.

For my ASL teacher, Billy, thank you for showing me the beauty of a soundless language.

And for the people of St. Thomas.

Note to reader

For the purpose of being mindful about the nature of American Sign Language and the perception of the deaf culture, I'm writing my personal experience with personalities of those I've known, while incorporating my own knowledge of the language. While I do have a formal education in ASL, in the way of interpreter training, I do not claim to be an expert on the language nor the culture. Please keep in mind that the ASL communication in this book is between two individuals with years of experience interacting with the other, therefore leaving a broad avenue for *interpretation*.

Thank you, and I hope you enjoy it.
Kate

prologue

Ian

"**I**an."

I turned to face my ex-wife as she moved toward me at warp speed. "Where is she?"

"In X-ray. She's got stitches from a large gash in her arm and suffered a nasty break in her right leg."

Her shoulders slumped as she exhaled a stressed breath. "Are the other girls okay?"

I slipped my hands in my slacks. "Just bumps and scratches. Ella got the worst of it."

Tara looked at me accusingly. "You couldn't go with her to X-ray?"

"She didn't want me to. She's still in the midst of claiming her independence."

She pursed her lips. "You're the parent."

"Right, so you keep reminding me. Yet I was here first."

"I was working," she hissed, a ready defense on her tongue.

I raised a brow. "So that's what you call it these days?" Tara was an assistant to her new boyfriend, or rather, an old boyfriend that she'd taken up with after our divorce. He was a commercial builder based in Houston.

"I'm sure the boss will have no issue giving you time off considering your duties last long past the five o'clock whistle."

She rolled her eyes and crossed her arms, her sundress lifting enough to see the six-hundred-dollar cowgirl boots I bought for our last anniversary. "If I didn't know better, I would think you were jealous."

"But you know better," I said, sounding as bitter as I felt about the situation which had nothing to do with who she was with. It had everything to do with our custody agreement and the fact that I was expecting her to dispute it any day to suit her new 'professional' situation. And if the law saw fit, that meant my daughter would leave Dallas because of a man her *mother* was crazy about.

She gave me a wary glance. "Can we not do this now?"

"Fine. That was petty. I apologize. Ella lost some blood, and they had to give her a transfusion."

Tara's face went pale.

"She's fine," I assured her. "Thankfully she had been keeping up with her meds, so that helped. I didn't know her blood type. I felt horrible. How could I not know that? She's anemic for God's sake."

"We only just discovered it when she got her period a few months ago. Don't be so hard on yourself." Tara swallowed and stared at me with wide eyes. "By the way it's—"

"Type B, I know now of course." I moved to sit next to her as she studied me carefully. She was looking for anger. I knew it from years of being with her. What would I be angry about? She flinched as I took the cracked blue plastic seat next to her. The hospital's bones were dinosaur, but the healthcare was top-notch. It was the only reason I wasn't crawling out of my skin with worry.

"So, they did a blood test?" she asked quietly, her eyes cast down.

"Actually, I asked for a few tests just in case something like this arose again. The doctor said it's a good precaution with her condition."

Tara began shaking next to me, her fearful eyes meeting mine briefly before they flit away.

"What is it, Tara?"

"Ian, I—"

"Mr. and Mrs. Kemp?" The doctor interrupted and we both stood. "She's going to be fine. We've ruled out surgery, managed to set her leg and have given her something mild for the pain."

I blew out a long breath of relief. "Thank you."

Tara spoke up. "We were supposed to leave for vacation tomorrow. We're driving to my parents' house in Houston. Will she be able to travel?"

"She's going to have some discomfort no matter what, but it's a short trip and as long as you're equipped to care for her there, it should be fine."

"She can stay with me—"

"That's ridiculous," Tara scoffed. "The whole point is for us to spend time together."

"I thought the whole point was to spend time with Daniel?" I challenged.

Tara glanced away briefly in an attempt to hide her agitation before producing a fake smile for the doctor. "We'll be fine. Can we see her?"

I was being a dick, but I rather enjoyed it at her expense. Tara had a way of getting under my skin by her presence alone.

The doctor's eyes bounced between us. "They're finishing up now, but you can go back."

The walk down the stark white corridor was hell on earth. I was thankful the injuries weren't severe and said a little prayer of gratitude. No feeling in the world had ever been worse than that phone call from the paramedics.

Ella perked up when I walked into the room behind her mother. Her eyes wide and lingering on her bright purple cast before she gave me a weak smile. She lifted her hands as I leaned in and kissed her forehead. I beat her to the punch, signing to her.

Had to go and break a leg, brat?

She grinned. *You're such an asshole, Daddy.*

Does it hurt much?

Not too bad.

Who was driving?

She lifted her hands reluctantly. *Jessica.*

It was my worst fear as a parent. Most kids don't pay much attention in driving school—I know I didn't—and did the bare minimum just to get their driving freedom. Unfortunately, all you needed as a sixteen-year-old to get a license was decent eyesight and a little confidence to obtain that independence. With her friend Jessica being deaf and a new driver in a car full of deaf friends, she was already at a disadvantage. Sirens from speeding ambulances, warning sounds from car horns, and skidding brakes were forever silenced. Add youth and the fact that the girls relied solely on their hands for communication and it was a recipe for this father's worst nightmare. There were plenty of deaf and hard of hearing drivers on the road. I knew Ella would be a responsible and defensive driver when she got her license, but it did little to ease my nerves. She was still a year away from driving on her own and I was selfishly thankful for that blessing. My relief was cut short when I found out Ella had plenty of friends already behind the wheel. I had all but begged her mother to keep her away from the shitty clique of impressionable girls who were too old for her to hang out with. Tara hadn't taken my pleas under consideration. It was another reason for my irritation with her that day. Ignoring the surfacing anger toward her mother, I spoke to my daughter to keep the peace. Still, I couldn't help my hands.

You're fourteen. You don't need to be hanging out with sixteen-year-old girls.

Ella guffawed audibly and rolled her eyes.

I'm not that much younger. I turn fifteen next week. And I don't need a lecture. It was an accident.

Don't roll your eyes at me. And you'll get lectures until I'm dead. What happened?

I could see in Ella's hesitance to answer that the accident was Jessica's fault. And though it might not have anything to do with her disadvantage, her slow hands reluctant to respond told me different. Reading my face, Ella stiffened, her anger simmering. She was a lot like me and hated to admit when she was wrong.

I don't want to talk about it. I'm hurt and sleepy. Go back to work, Daddy.

Okay. I'll let you get to sleep. FaceTime me every day while you're in Houston. I'll miss you. Be good for your mother. With the sign of a P, I rubbed my hand over my chest. *Promise?*

Promise. Love you.

Love you, brat.

I looked over at Tara and signed while I spoke. "Stay safe and have a good trip."

Tara nodded, a distant look in her eyes, her porcelain skin tinted red in anger or embarrassment from our earlier exchange. I'd broken free from the responsibility of figuring her out when I left her a year ago. Her behavior was strange, but then again, we'd been strangers for years. Tara was good at reinventing herself every new moon, and I'd spent enough of my life figuring out who she'd decided to be with each moon that passed. I blew her bullshit off as a reaction to Ella being hurt. Taking my leave, I moved a few steps toward the door when Tara's earlier question began to gnaw at me.

"So, they did a blood test?"

A new sort of awareness plucked at my spine as I opened the door and froze. Sweat gathered at my temple as I turned to see my ex-wife had been staring at my retreating back. I stood statue-still as my daughter read my posture.

Daddy? What's wrong?

My gaze drifted over Ella—she had pale skin to my olive complexion, light hair to my dark, and deep-sea blue eyes to my gray.

In an attempt to mask the fear racing through me, I forced

a smile worthy of an Oscar as my gaze drifted to Tara. If it was guilt etched all over her face, if I was reading her right—which I'd become a pro at over the years—*every-fucking-thing* was wrong.

Ella raised her hands, a frightened look on her face. *What's wrong?*

I glared at Tara who sank in her chair confirming my worst fear. Apparently, there was a feeling worse than what I felt just hours ago.

Ella waved frantically for my attention.

Daddy, what is it?

It's okay, sweetheart. I just need a minute with your mother. Tara, I need to speak to you outside.

I walked the hall quietly, trying to steady my heartbeat with even breaths as she followed slightly behind me. I made it to the garage barely able to handle the rattle under my skin from the rage that threatened.

I turned on Tara abruptly and she stopped just short of hitting my chest. She was beautiful. At one point in time, I thought she was the most beautiful woman alive. At one point in time, I couldn't imagine a life without her. At one point in time, I would've taken a bullet for her, no questions asked. She had been my life. She had been my purpose, my meaning, my everything. Seething, I fisted my hands at my sides and tried to hold my bite, but it was impossible. I prayed I would owe her an apology for the thoughts that surfaced.

"I've always given you credit for being more intelligent than

xiv | KATE STEWART

you actually are. But by the look on your face, you're frightened about something that can't be true."

Tara stared at the stripes on my necktie.

"Look at me."

Her eyes shot to mine and were full of fear, tears threatening.

"Because in order to determine paternity, it would require more than a blood test."

"Ian—"

"I know my damned name. Fourteen years I was your husband, and fifteen her father. Tell me now, Tara. Right. Fucking. Now. Tell me my suspicions are ridiculous. Tell me Ella belongs to me in every sense. Tell me."

"Ian—"

"Tell me!"

Fear and trepidation marked every inch of her as all the anger dissipated out of me in one breath and devastation took its place.

Don't ask her, Ian. It doesn't matter. Don't ask her!

I pointed behind her. "Tell me that's my little girl in that room that calls me, Daddy, not *his*. Tell me I didn't lose my life to your selfish fucking whims. Tell me!"

Incredulous tears fell down my face as my heart bottomed out.

"Tell me she's mine, Tara," I croaked, my face soaked, my heart obliterated. "Don't do this to me. Please, I'm begging you. If you ever loved me at all, tell me she's mine."

"She is your daughter," she offered weakly.

"But I didn't father her, did I?"

one

Koti

I don't always feel like a failure, but as I picked up the iguana crap from the side of the pool, a small glimpse of the life I left behind hit me in a flash—sipping a designer martini with a killer view of the city from the thirty-fifth floor, a healthy bank account, and the feel of a new pair of heels.

"Freezing your ass off in those heels," I muttered, studying my chipped blue toenails in the flip-flops I wore.

"Pardon?" Mrs. Osborne asked as I removed the 'excrement' that she had called about fifteen minutes after I thought I'd finished my day.

Holding the warm crap in my hand, I studied Mrs. Osborne lying in a lounge chair covering herself with thick glue-colored sunblock while inside the house, Mr. Osborne scoured the five-bedroom rental opening every single cabinet and drawer. "I think we're all set."

Half an hour prior, I'd been in my plush sun chair on my porch with a freshly corked pinot when I got the call.

"At Ease Property Management, Koti speaking."

"Koti, this is Stephanie Osborne."

"Hi, Mrs. Osborne, are you enjoying your stay so far?"

"I am, but we have an issue." I took a well-deserved sip of my wine as I prepared for the worst. I loved my job, but there was always

that one guest that could make said job a living hell. The Osbornes had only checked into their villa three hours prior. One call was typical from a new guest, even with the inch-thick notebook that was on the counter, filled with every single piece of information they would need. It was her fourth call since I left them.

"How can I help?"

"Well, there was a large iguana next to the pool."

I choked down my laugh. "Yes ma'am, it's common on the island."

"I understand..." she said hesitantly, "and that's fine. He gave us a fright, but that's not the problem."

"No?"

"Well, it seems he decided to relieve himself next to the pool."

I sat up in my chair. "In the pool?"

"No, next to it."

"I'm not following."

"There's iguana excrement next to the pool."

I was already downing my wine and took my final swallow before I braved a reply. "Okayyyy."

"I was wondering when you would be by to pick it up?"

And there you have it. My new life in a nutshell—sans new Jimmy Choos and Christmas at Rockefeller Center—now the proud owner of an anorexic bank account.

I threw the poop in the trash can and inhaled a calming breath as I scanned her three-million-dollar view which consisted of deep blue to aqua surf and the neighboring island—St. Johns.

Nothing bad happened here, at least not in my private universe. The universe I created when I left my toxic life in New York and retreated to the one place I remembered being happy.

If the island could cure me, I was sure after a few days it would work wonders on Mrs. Osborne.

"Can I help you with anything else while I'm here?"

With curious, crinkled eyes she looked up at me from where she sat. "Do you really make your own electricity here in St. Thomas?"

"Actually, no, we buried a giant extension cord below the ocean from the States."

It was my best friend Jasmine's line for people who weren't smart enough to believe differently. I had never used it until I was forced to pick up iguana crap.

Mrs. Osborne—a seven-day refugee from Long Island—sat with a magazine on her lap, mouth open, her eyes on the surf while she pressed her brows together to try to make sense of it. I bit my lip to keep my laugh hidden. She was old money and hadn't earned a cent and it was painfully obvious. She'd clearly ignored the thousands of solar panels set up all over the top of the mountains as she was chauffeured in.

What was even more ironic was that I used to spend hours of my life on the phone with women just like her, answering endless questions and catering to their every whim much the same as I was at that moment, but for a much larger paycheck. Watching her ungreased wheels turn was entertaining, but I had a breathing bottle to get back to. "Well if that's all, I'll leave you to it."

The announcement of my departure led to another set of questions. "Is it true we will be bathing with rainwater?"

"Yes, Mrs. Osborne, as I explained when you arrived, we *do* use the rainwater since there are no real alternate water sources. The rain is captured by the gutters and then drained into a filtration system underneath the house. It's completely safe. I've checked your water level and it looks good for the length of your stay but feel free to give me a call if you need some delivered." Studying the excess amount of skin around her eyes and the sagging lady flaps underneath her arms, I was sure she wasn't worried about the pH of the water affecting her skin. Still, she was a beautiful older-looking woman. I had to give her credit, she put in a ton of effort when other women her age wouldn't.

"You'll deliver water?"

Please, God, I just want to go to my happy place.

"Absolutely."

"Okay, well as long as we won't run out."

"Have a good night."

I was halfway to the sliding door that led to my exit and the waiting bottle of wine when she spoke up behind me.

"Wait. Is it safe to drink, *you know*, or is it like Mexico?"

"Get the Osbornes settled?" I could hear the smile in Jasmine's voice—she must have known when she took the reservation they would be a pain in the ass. I drove along the mountainside enjoying the breeze and glanced over the cliff to see a cruise ship had come in while I was at the Osbornes'.

"Shit."

"What?" Jasmine asked through the speakers in the cabin of my Jeep.

"The cruise ship came in while I was dealing with shit, like literally. Now I'll never get home."

"What?" she asked absently.

"What to which part? I just picked up iguana crap. In fact, I was summoned to pick up *iguana crap*. Thanks, boss."

Jasmine's laugh belted out while I navigated through a thousand tourists. Shipwreckers walked around like new babies with their cell phones, arms up in selfie poses clicking away at the scenery while risking their lives in the rush of traffic.

"The ship never shows up this late. Damnit, I'm going to

miss the sunset." Routine was crucial to my well-being and the sunset was often a focal point of my day. For me, it was a finish line of sorts.

Parked in traffic, I surveyed the sparkling water next to me. It would never get old. Even when I got gray and ceased grooming, and had grown my own pair of lady flaps, I would enjoy the same view.

"All you do is complain, Koti."

I shoved a fistful of French fries from my brown-bag dinner into my mouth. "Liar. I hardly ever give you grief. I'm the best employee you have."

"You're the only employee I have, so there is no comparison."

Swallowing my food, I laid on the horn as a van veered slightly toward the median. In the rearview, I saw a lady whose attention seemed to be on anything but driving, her phone hanging out the window to get the perfect picture of the surrounding bay.

"Hey, lady, pay attention to the road!"

Jasmine ignored my shriek. "What are you doing tonight?"

I filled my mouth with more fries to keep from answering.

"Oh… let me guess. Nothing. *Again*," she chided. "Come join me, I'm at the wine bar."

"No," I cut her off quickly. "No, no. No, lady, no. Last time we did ladies' night, I ended up flashing my thong to a hundred people."

And it was the best night I'd spent in St. Thomas, but I wasn't about to tell her that. If there was one thing I'd learned, it was that you can't repeat the same good time twice. And the only reason I partook in that night was because I was half-drunk before we got to the bar.

Jasmine's infectious laughter was welcome amidst the chaos that surrounded me. "That was a great night. And if you would act a little more twenty-nine than eighty-nine we could have more of them. Besides, I only took one picture. *One.*"

"If that picture even exists." She was forever threatening me with evidence she never produced. "I'm fine with being a home-body. You know I prefer it." I laid on the horn again just as an old Cadillac cut off my progress. And seconds later, as if some cosmic force decided battling traffic on a ship day wasn't enough, a chicken—lady flaps spread wide—appeared on the hood of my Jeep and came straight for me.

"ARE YOU KIDDING ME!" I swung my arm out in a knee-jerk reaction. "Shoo!"

"What? What's going on?" Jasmine asked, more amused than concerned as I took up the inch of space between me and the car in front and tapped on my brakes to try to get the bird off my hood. The stoic chicken didn't budge.

"A rooster just jumped on my hood!"

"You are shooing a chicken?"

"Is there chicken-speak etiquette?" Apparently, there was, because the chicken came toward me like it knew I had a freshly plucked, chopped, deep-fried and wrapped relative in the brown sack next to me. "It's attacking my windshield!"

Honking the horn, I stood on my brakes as the rooster closed in. It would have been an easy jump into the open cabin of my Jeep. I was in full-on panic mode as the bird bobbed and weaved like we were in a Tyson fight. I might as well have put hot sauce on my ear because that bastard was ready to brawl and take a piece of it.

"What do I do?"

"It's a chicken," Jasmine cackled, "Shoo it away."

"You are such an ass*hole*," I screeched, as her laughter filtered through the speakers. I rarely ever spoke on the phone while driving. Car accidents were the most notorious killer. And my Jeep just so happened to be a deathtrap as well. But the Jeep didn't actually belong to me. It was on loan like much of the rest of my life. I had no choice but to drive it around the mountainous terrain of St. Thomas. The cloth hood made zero difference in safety. I'd checked. Being able to drive the SUV at all was my first milestone in the many I'd conquered in the last year. I wasn't about to throw them all away for a psychotic chicken.

I had to keep calm.

I looked for anything I could throw at the real-life version of an Angry Bird to keep it from making the easy leap into my passenger seat, then realized all I had was my dinner. The bird seemed satisfied with intimidation at that moment until I laid on the horn. Apparently, the sound was the chicken's trigger.

"Oh, come on!" The light I sat at had changed three times and I was in gridlock battling a psychotic rooster. "FUCKING SHIP DAY!" I screamed, hurling the bag at Tyson who let me have round two and jumped off the hood.

"Atta girl, blame it on ship day." Jasmine was still laughing as a group of people next to me applauded.

"I just nailed it with a chicken sandwich. How twisted is that?"

"I would give my left boob to see what just happened," she bellowed.

"Is there something you need, *boss?* Because I'm off the clock, and I really don't like you right now."

"No, you love me. You okay?"

And that was Jasmine, a friend first, boss second, but that wasn't the order we started in. She'd picked me up off the side of my quarter-life crisis and we'd been inseparable since. "Yes, I'm fine. Just really freaking done for the day. I love you too, you *jerk.* See you tomorrow."

She hung up as I battled cars, traffic, and new tourists for another half hour to get home. I managed to sip my pinot right as the sun met the water setting off an endless trail of diamonds too elusive to be captured by anything other than the naked eye.

I inhaled and thanked the God I hoped existed for the gift of it.

I dug my toes into the sand as Bon Iver's "33 GOD" drifted through the speakers off of my porch and melted the rest of my day away.

two

Koti

"At Ease Property Management, this is Koti." The next morning, I sat behind my two-inch desk as Jasmine waltzed in with a handful of coffee for us. I mouthed her a 'thank you' as she placed the cup in front of me and took the desk opposite of mine.

I listened to Mrs. Osborne ranting and saw Jasmine waiting for me expectantly, a devious smile on her glossed lips, a fresh story on the edge of her tongue. Jasmine was gorgeous, from the tip of her silky long hair to her dark-skinned toes. She was a bit older than me, but you couldn't tell because of her exotic looking features—caramel brown eyes bordering gold, a heart-shaped face, and ebony hair. She was curvy, and that day had poured herself into a loud yellow sundress that would look ridiculous on anyone else. Oversized sunglasses sat perched on the top of her head, a clothing staple for her. We were night and day in the looks department. Where she was dark, I was light. My mother had gifted me with silver-blue eyes and her body. I was the pint-size version of her. Where she had made millions with her frame, I was a bit more conservative in my dress. My mother kept her signature blonde locks even as she aged and though I'd inherited those as well, I'd razored them short after I landed in St. Thomas.

Blair Vaughn had been one of the first supermodels and

ended her reign on her own terms before she married my father. My parents' Fifth Avenue penthouse was a shrine to her illustrious career. Every room was covered in framed magazine covers she was featured on. She had owned Manhattan in her day in the way I had hoped to in my own. What she conquered with her breathtaking smile and figure, I'd attempted to master with my father's business sense.

My mother's smile won, and my smile was erased by reality. So, I created a new reality, where pavement was scarce and there was always a soft place to land. A place where I didn't have my mother's high expectations weighing me down.

Annoyed I was in my own headspace with my mother and even more so with the woman who'd called me every hour since seven o'clock that morning, I assured Mrs. Osborne, again, that she wouldn't run out of water.

"Koti, I find this disturbing," she yapped on the other end of the phone as if she was now existing in a third-world country.

"I'll go ahead and send a truck." *You really need a hobby, lady.*

"I'd appreciate it. I just think with what we've paid for this rental we shouldn't have to worry about necessities like *water.*"

"I completely understand." *You old, flappy bat.*

Once I'd put her at ease—though I refused to assure there would be no more visits from the pesky iguana who lived there because she was ridiculous—we hung up.

"Mrs. Osborne?" Jasmine checked her lipstick in a compact she produced from her purse. No matter the time of day, her makeup was flawless. She gathered her hair into a self-adhesive bun. "Cinco de Mayo is coming up," I joked, as she curled her lip at me. "Should we celebrate with a margarita?"

The first time I met her, in fact, the first time anyone met Jasmine, they assumed she was Mexican or of Spanish descent, which always led to her favorite line, "I'm *half* filifuckingpino."

Jasmine was raised in 'bumfuck'—her words, not mine—Minnesota and sounded like one of the cast of *Fargo*. There were a lot of ya's for yeah's, soda was pop, etc.

St. Thomas was an eclectic mix, even with the natives the accents were different, including the neighboring islands. Jasmine had moved to St. Thomas with an ex-fiancé and stayed after he decided he wanted to return to the States, without her.

"You know it was Mrs. Osborne and she's a pain in the ass," I said, typing a note on the property file. DO NOT RENT TO THESE PEOPLE.

"That commission is worth it," she scolded, before I reluctantly backspaced my note with a single finger, one key at a time. I added a death glare in her direction for good measure.

"You're checking them in next time." Curling my lip at her, I picked up the phone to fetch Mrs. Osborne her water.

"So, I had sex in a tractor last night."

With a raised brow, I paused my hand on the number pad and looked above my screen at her. "A... tractor. How is that even possible? How many tractors are on St. Thomas that you could have sex on?"

"At least one," she said, sitting back in her seat. "I feel a little dirty about this one, I will admit."

"Really?"

She stood and walked over to the coffee pot to refill her cup. "No, not at all. No regrets, my friend. And now that I think about it, I'm sure it was a backhoe."

I shrugged. "Well, as long as it was a backhoe."

"Exactly," she turned to me, hands propping her up on the counter behind her. Our office was a shoebox, but Jasmine insisted we rent a small space when we managed enough properties to make us more "official." Yet we never met any of our renters in the office and no one had ever occupied the two chairs we had waiting for clients. Jasmine claimed having a place to show up to made us more accountable. I agreed to a point because if I had it my way, I'd live as a happy recluse and work within the confines of my beach house. She started the company herself, heartbroken and determined to survive in St. Thomas without the man that lured her here and left her to fend for herself while licking her wounds. Our work hours could be grueling at times but, she paid well and after a year of being out of corporate hell, I wouldn't dream of doing anything else.

"Will you be seeing this one again?"

"Meh, I don't know." She pulled up her skirt to show me her thong clad, purpling-brown ass. "But man, is this a sign of a good time or what?"

Sighing, I held up my hand to block the view of her tan globes. "It's 9 a.m. Do I really need to see your ass this early?"

"I'll sing you the "Thong Song," come on." She giggled, flexing her cheeks to make them bounce.

"Oh, you just go straight to hell."

I grabbed my phone and purse as she resumed her seat and gave me a wink. "Best video ever."

I stopped in my tracks. "You have video?"

"Just remember I love you, and I have only good intentions for keeping this."

Panic raced through me as I thought of the night I'd let all my inhibitions go and I mean *let go*. The slow spreading smile on her lips revealed she was playing with me. There was no video.

"Where are you off to?"

"I'm getting new neighbors today."

"Oh, right. The Kemps' are booked, I forgot."

"Yep, two weeks. Newlyweds." I was excited about the idea of newlyweds. My parents and the Kemps bought our neighboring houses within a year of each other when I was five. They both purchased the properties for vacation houses/investment rental homes. And while the Kemps still rented theirs out, my parents were stuck with a daughter who had fled to theirs from New York costing them a year's worth of profits. While my dad insisted the house had paid for itself tenfold and it was mine as long as I needed it, my mother kept her tongue idle. I knew it would eventually become a bargaining chip. I always felt guilty about taking away some of their retirement income, not to mention the small fortune they wasted on a degree I no longer used. While my mother was no stranger to money, Ryan Vaughn had been a scrapper and worked hard for his fortune.

But in a way, even with my mother's grudge about my current situation, I think they knew that house had saved my life.

Or at least, helped me find a new one.

"Take it easy out there," Jasmine chimed, as I refilled my coffee. "Careful of those chickens, though we both know you could use a little cock."

"Classy," I said, rolling my eyes. "You aren't off the hook. I want to know what could have possibly led to backhoe sex."

My phone rang, and I cringed while Jasmine smirked, but it quickly disappeared when I silenced the call. Mere seconds later the office phone rang. Jasmine narrowed her eyes as she picked up the phone. "Good morning, Mrs. Osborne."

With the back of my floorboard full of clanking wine bottles, I pulled up to my piece of paradise, which was the second to last of two identical cottage-style houses on Vista Lane. To the right of the Kemp house, large boulders crowded the beach giving it an intimate feel, and to the left of my cottage lay a large stretch of silky beige sand and an endless view of the ocean.

The builder had only erected two of the three planned houses before the Kemps intercepted and bought the last available lot for more privacy. Aside from the residences on the neighboring cliffs, I basically lived on a private beach, which was the richest real estate you could find on St. Thomas. And though the houses weren't as modern as others—built in the eighties—they were equally as inviting. Between the two-story twin dwellings lay a wide sand path which was convenient for me.

I parked my Jeep between the two porches cutting off Bobby McFerrin singing to me "Don't Worry, Be Happy," hopped out and grabbed the flowers and wine before I dug for the last bottle lodged under my seat. I cursed my timing as I heard tires on the gravel behind me.

Crap, they're early.

I had no idea what condition the house was in and prayed the cleaning lady had done a decent job. Finally getting a grip on the loose bottle, I pulled it out along with the flowers and caught a glance at the retreating cab before I was motored over.

The bottle I'd retrieved hit my chin and I landed on my ass with a soundless thud. Large hands gripped me by my bare shoulders and I was instantly pulled back on my feet. A man dressed in a power suit stared down at me with shattered features and tortured gray eyes. Recognition of his pain was instantaneous, and I felt despair leaking from every part of him. Through thick black lashes, ready tears threatened to spill as he assessed me to make sure I was in one piece. It was a split second before he righted me on the sand and released me with a quick and barely audible, "I'm sorry," before he rushed away. I looked down at the crushed flowers on the ground and mourned them briefly along with dashed hopes of happy new neighbors.

If that man was one of my newlyweds, I was in for a shit two weeks.

I looked around for a bride to follow the groom and came up empty.

Shit. She left him at the altar!

My phone rattled in my pocket as I made my way toward the Kemps, my eyes in the direction of the groom, chin burning. He was standing at the edge of the water, shoulders slumped, hands in his suit pockets. Even from yards away I could see his devastation.

Poor guy. What an evil woman. How could she do that to him? Why do people do that? How do they leave someone standing at the altar thinking they are about to start the rest of their life and not show?

Even though I had made it out of New York a laughing stock with my peers, I got away with only a slightly jaded heart. And even that shit hurt. I'd been in the dating neighborhood, browsed but never decided to buy. I still had plenty of years to find Mr. Forever.

When it came to me, renting was a better option, and even with that decision, I hadn't bothered to act on it. It seemed the ideal thing to do when one goes flying off the handle, only to abandon her life and live in a new one. I was a work in progress and love could wait.

I tried to give my jilted groom privacy as I made my way to the porch of the Kemps' house and opened the door. It was spotless and up to standard; which was a relief. I doubted the guy would give a damn about the state of the house. I threw the broken flowers in the trash and stuck one of the wine bottles in the fridge as I eyed the window. My phone rattled again just as I pulled it out of my pocket to shoot a text to Jasmine and saw she was calling.

"Hey."

"We have a problem," Jasmine said without a trace of

humor. That tone meant we had a serious problem.

"Oh, I can assure you we do. I'm staring at a jilted groom."

"Jilted groom?"

"My new neighbors. It looks like the bride was a no-show."

I'd managed to land us the Kemp account last summer when they had come to stay for a weekend before heading further south. I adored Rowan and William Kemp, they were worldly wise, extremely kind, and more than happy to hand the business over. I was sure I'd pissed on someone who had managed their rental for years, but I needed the commission. I loved the house, it was warm and inviting much like mine with subtle differences in décor. So far, the house had brought in a steady commission and was rented for every week of the summer.

"*No*, your bride and groom are about to pull up."

"*No*," I spoke slowly. "He's *here*, she's *not*."

"Tall? Late thirties, dark hair?"

I squinted in the afternoon sun. "Yeah."

"That's Ian Kemp. Mrs. Kemp has been calling all morning to see if he might have shown up there."

"Ian?" I walked out onto the porch and studied his back. "I haven't seen him since I was seven. Well, I saw him for a few seconds when I was seventeen—"

"Babe, that's all fine and dandy, but we have a bride and groom whose ETA is *now* and we have no place to put them."

"We can relocate Ian." Even as I said the words, I knew there was no way I was walking up to that man and asking him to leave. The look in his eyes alone would haunt me for weeks. He stood statue-still as he stared at the aqua glass water.

"Something's wrong."

"Uh, yeah," Jasmine said, as I took another step forward. I had the overwhelming urge to go to him, but I was sure he wanted his space. His posture confirmed as much.

"No, I mean with Ian."

Jasmine cursed before she growled into the phone, I could hear her frantically typing in the background. "Every place else is booked. We are going to have to put them at Margulis Mansion."

"No, you can't! That's a twenty-two-million-dollar rental with nine rooms!"

"We're going to have to make up the difference. At least for the night. I'll call and see if anyone has something we can swap."

"Crap," I said, staring at the back of Ian's suit. "I needed this commission."

Jasmine sighed. "You and me both."

"This sucks!" I may have said it a little loud, but Ian didn't move. Not an inch. He was searching for answers. I knew that feeling. I'd done the same thing.

"Well, hell, why not a hotel room?"

"And risk a shit review? We're trying to build the business. These are newlyweds. Can't do it." Jasmine sounded pissed which was rare, but I understood it. We were going to lose a ton of commission.

"There is nothing else?"

"Nothing," she sighed over the line, defeated.

"Okay, text me the address. As soon as they get here, I'll divert traffic."

"K. Call me when you get home. Fucking ship day."

"That was yesterday, Jasmine."

"If you can use it, so can I."

three

Koti

After waving to the taxi driver like a bird trying to take flight, I threw the two newly discarded suitcases back into the taxi while I spoke rapidly to a confused bride and groom. After escorting them to their oversized mansion for two, where they repeatedly looked around with a "No shit? This is ours? No way!" I made my way back across the island to check Mrs. Osborne's water—at her insistence—and scoured the porch for any poop before I turned two more rentals. When my workday was done, I pulled up to my house and pressed my forehead to the wheel. I had an ass full of sand, thanks to my new and unexpected neighbor.

A chuckle escaped me as I trotted down the alley to my porch where my serenity waited and paused when I saw Ian. He was still standing in the exact place I left him *hours* earlier. From what his mother had told me last summer, he'd been married and had a daughter. They lived in Dallas and were doing great. The Kemps had emigrated from South Africa and moved to the States. Ian had told me as much when we were kids. Smiling, I recalled the first time we met. It was just feet away from the water he was transfixed on.

Treading on the surface, I looked at my newly designated play-mate. My mother saw fit to entertain our new summer neighbors with strict instructions that we get better acquainted. "You talk funny." I stared at the brown-haired boy with bright eyes and a chipped front tooth.

"I lived in South Africa until last week," he defended.

"Where did you move?"

"Texas. Dallas. A dreadful place surrounded by dirt. No weekend safaris. I hate it. Now—"

My giggle cut him off. "You're so... proper."

"Do you want my help or not?"

I jumped the wave that rolled through us to keep from getting another mouthful of water. My feet barely touched the sand and we were neck deep. The water was warm, and I could feel the sunburn on my back and arms even with the floaties my mother made me wear.

"I think I have it," I said, lowering my mask and biting the mouthpiece.

"You don't have it," he challenged.

"You don't have it," I repeated in the worst imitation of a South African accent ever.

"Fine then. You're on your own now."

"Fine then," I mocked with widening eyes through my mask. Ian laughed before he gripped my shoulders. "Don't worry if it trickles in a little. Let the pressure of the water keep the mask to your face, even when you think it's safe not to breathe, breathe anyway."

The truth was I'd been out there for the better part of an hour panicking before he swam in, barking orders. I'd watched Jaws the night before with my father's permission. It was the one time I regretted talking him into letting me get my way. I didn't want to go anywhere near the water. No matter how many times I told myself it was just a movie, I heard the du-nuh every few seconds.

"Okay," I said with false courage. "I've got it."

He shook his head as if he knew I would choke. "All right, give it a go."

"You sound like The Crocodile Hunter."

"He is Australian." He rolled his eyes. "And you sound ignorant. Now stop stalling."

"Don't be rude, crocky pants," I piped.

Ian shrugged, pushing his dark hair off his forehead. "You're scared."

"I'm not scared of anything."

"Well then go on, miss."

"I'm six years old. I'm not a miss."

"You sure don't have tits enough to be called a miss."

His eyes sparkled with his laugh.

"Pervert alert!" I yelled at the top of my lungs.

Ian cringed. "I was just joking."

"My father says any time a boy says a word about privates in front of me to tell."

"I'm not a pervert. And I'm too old to be babysitting you."

Offended but too terrified to be alone in the water, I shrieked when the next wave got the best of me. I was too far out in the surf and I knew I was about to get in trouble for it.

"I'll have tits one day," I promised, unable to think of anything else to say. Ian rolled his eyes as he pulled me by my floaties closer to shore. Choking, I pushed my hair out of my face. "I know you aren't a pervert." I smiled the way my mother did when she wanted her way. "I was just joking too."

Ian squinted at me as if he was trying to decide if I was being truthful.

"I want to be your friend. I'm sorry, Ian. Please don't leave me out here."

He grabbed hold of me then and pulled me to where I could safely stand.

"It's okay, little puffer fish." He lined my mask up for me. "All right. You can do this. I know you can. But," he looked behind his shoulder and then back to me, "no one said you had to."

"I asked for the mask and flippers for my birthday. I'm gonna be seven next week. I'm not afraid." I was lying. And he knew it.

"Are you scared of what you'll see under, then? Give them here." He took the mask from me and peeked underwater before he pulled up and shook his head. "Nothing to see but a few fish."

"Okay." Taking the mask from him, I pulled it over my eyes and nose and he became harder to see when the lens fogged up.

"No big deal." He knuckled the top of my head and I glared at him before I went under. Within seconds, a needle nose fish swam a centimeter from my mask and I began choking as I surfaced. "Holy shit!"

"Koti!" My mother shrieked from shore. She had the ears of a Doberman.

"Sorry, Mom, there was a fish!"

She stood in a bright red bikini and I saw Ian's eyes float her way with interest. My mother had 'tits' in abundance and a whole lot of everything else. Curves from head to foot, I could see Ian deduce she was the ultimate miss. Even as a retired supermodel she commanded the eyes of everyone she sauntered past. "Young lady, I better not hear that language again."

"Yes, ma'am." I could feel the blood rush to my face. Ian shook his head and nudged his chin forward.

"Try again."

Embarrassed, I shrugged. "I don't want to."

"Mad? Humiliated? Scared? That's when you should do things anyway. It will always piss the other guy off." He grinned at me with pencil point freckles dotting his nose. "Have fun anyway, Koti. I'll keep a lookout for you."

I knew a little about the boy inside the man I watched. The boy who had put together my first s'more, laughed with his whole body at the surprise in my eyes when I tasted the toasted marshmallow, a product from a fire which he, himself had built. While Ian was allowed freedoms like that, I was allowed very little sugar and spent an hour bubbling marshmallows and smashing them between graham crackers and melted chocolate. I could still remember Ian's amused reaction as I gorged. He was a firecracker then, about to turn fourteen, but he took me under his wing that summer.

There wasn't a trace of that boy in the man who stood in a puddle at the edge of the sea.

Life was funny like that. For a moment in time, a few weeks in the summer when we were both just a couple of naïve kids, I called Ian Kemp a friend. Earlier that day he had treated me as a stranger. It was the summers after that turned us into nothing more than a few memories.

But those few memories turned significant.

Ian Kemp had introduced me to my comfort food. He'd also given me the confidence to smile to spite my mother when she got the best of me.

And for those memories, I felt a little indebted. A little bit more familiar to the stranger on the beach.

I made my way back to my house, my gaze fixed on Ian until I was forced to unload my sand-filled panties. A hot shower and a loofah scrub down later, I poured another glass of wine from my already corked bottle and took residence on my porch chair overlooking the calm sea. In an attempt not to screw up my routine, a routine I carefully followed to the letter on most days, I lit my hurricane candles on my porch as Novo Amor's "Faux" drifted through my speakers and out to sea.

I learned much too late, ambiance was the key for me. Music, wine, and candles created my safe haven. These little things made me feel like I was in the midst of something, instead of looking forward to something else. I had spent way too much of my life looking forward to things.

Those things rarely ever came the way I'd imagined them.

Certainties were pap smears, head colds, and flat tires. But the feeling you got wrapped up in a good book, the perfect song, surrounded by candlelight could be repeated over and over. Endless self-made memories that no one could screw up? *Yes, please.*

Because when you date yourself, there is no one to disappoint you. Jasmine didn't get it. But me and my hesitant libido understood. I'd gone through an entire year without missing men. I'd go through another if I felt like it. But it wasn't about setting restrictions on my life. It was about the way I felt about myself.

I'd come to the island anxiety-ridden and the blue water was my prescription. I'd set goals to forget my old ones and shed my skin for a better fit. One that bled life without calculations and bred alternate possibilities. I basked in the smell of the ocean—a new necessity—and marveled at the swirl of different shades of blue that hit the slightly rocky shore.

Several healthy sips of wine later, and much to my dismay, my bottle was empty.

As wrong as it was, I glanced over at Ian who remained in the same spot on the beach and then over to the Kemp's house, where I knew an expensive bottle was chilling in the fridge.

As the sun began to fade behind the new Armani-clad statue in the neighborhood, the ocean and surrounding mountain islands behind him, I tiptoed over to the house. In record time, I had the bottle in hand and walked out of the Kemps' ready to step lightly back to my side of the invisible fence. I shrieked when I saw the dark cloud that waited on the other side of the door and dropped my keys on the porch between us. Ian peered down at me as I scrambled to retrieve them.

"Shit, I'm sorry. Ian, hi, do you remember me? Koti?" He remained mute with no recognition on his face. "Well, it's good to see you. I was… just making sure the place was ready for you. I manage this property now, I don't know if your mother mentioned it?" Ian stood silent, his hands in his pockets. He was pale, his stubble-covered face was slightly bloated. Red-rimmed eyes were a sure sign of the day he'd had, and his full lips didn't move with a single tell.

Ian glanced at the bottle of wine with indifference before he sidestepped me, plucked the key out of my hand and went through the door shutting it soundly behind him.

"Well, that was good, Koti," I muttered, taking a step away when he sounded through the door, his South African tongue slightly faded, but much more masculine.

"It was awful, actually. Terrible liar. But then I guess that's a thing with you women."

"Wow, uh, geesh. I'll replace your wine tomorrow," I said through the closed door. "Sorry, for… sorry."

What in the hell was I apologizing for? He'd just thrown women into a collective group and labeled them all liars, insulted an entire sex because of my slight alcoholism on a Tuesday night.

The nerve.

Stomping across the sand, my cell phone rang. Already on edge, I shrieked in surprise before I pulled it out of my pocket. I'd forgotten to turn it off after my shift and it was Jasmine's night for after-hours calls. I blew out a breath as I looked at the lifeless house behind me while dusk set in. He hadn't turned on a single light. Reluctantly I answered. "At Ease Property Management, this is Koti."

"Hi, Koti, it's Rowan Kemp."

"Oh, hello, Mrs. Kemp."

"Koti, I insist you call me Rowan. Is Ian there? Is he still at the house?"

"Yes. He uh, showed up about six hours ago."

"Oh, thank God, okay..." I could hear the fear in her voice. "Koti, darling, I need a huge favor," I swore when the woman spoke to me she could make a simple sentence sound like a song lyric. Ian's father was all-American, but his mother was where the South African roots lay.

"Sure, you know I'll help any way I can."

"I'm sure the rental was booked for the week, correct?"

"Yes, ma'am. Actually, it's booked almost every week for the next several months. We had to spend a small fortune relocating the guests today."

"I'll cover all of it, double your commission. I really need your help."

"Okay." I was up for anything that had me in electricity and wines that didn't taste like syrup. Living hand to mouth had been a refreshing change when I first moved to the island, until it became a burden. Maintaining island life took work and a lot of it. "What can I do for you?"

"Watch him."

I pressed my phone closer to my ear. "Watch him?"

"Yes. He's just been through the worst divorce. Almost a year of fighting. He left home without a word to anyone. His father and I were frantic. He won't take my calls. Just please check in with him each day. Make sure he's okay."

I lived in the house next door, there was no way it would be hard for me to check on him and the commission alone had me speaking up. "Of course."

"I'll send the money right away. Whatever he needs, invoice me. If he stays longer than a few weeks, we'll be down."

I highly doubted Ian wanted a visit from his parents, but it wasn't my place to say so. "Yes, ma'am. Can I ask... actually never mind." I had to admit I was curious, the image of his tortured gray eyes flashed through my head.

"He wanted the divorce, he asked for it. I'm not sure what happened."

"I'm sorry, I didn't mean to pry."

"Ian is a good man, a very good man. I've raised an amazing son. This… running away is not like him." I thought back to a year ago when I showed up to my parents' sanctuary with nothing but the clothes on my back, my purse, and my passport.

Back inside my house, I sat in my living room, opened the table side window and listened to Simone as she began to sing her lullaby. "If any place can make him feel better, it's this place."

"I'm so worried." She was crying now as I gripped the phone tight, hearing my own mother's voice from a year ago. *"Koti, you can't just run away. You need to face this head-on."*

Thinking back to the worst day of my life, I spoke from experience. "This island frees people, Rowan. I promise I'll look after him."

"Thank you, Koti."

"Call me anytime."

four

Koti

"**W**hat the fack!" In the midst of a foggy, wine-induced dream, I snapped to and looked at my bedside clock.

4 a.m.

Groaning, I grabbed my body pillow and cradled it between my legs as I heard repetitive banging in the house next door.

Everything went quiet for a few minutes before I heard another enraged growl. Pulling myself from the bed, I moved to my window where I saw every light in the Kemp house had been turned on.

"Okay, Ian, have your freak out and go to bed." It was going to be a long night if he had insomnia.

Another loud clatter had me jumping away from the glass, while his growls grew louder.

"What in the *fack*! Eish!" It seemed his native tongue made more of an appearance when he was angry. "Fok hierdie plek!"

He stormed onto his porch with a broom in hand looking back at the house and tilting his head as if he were straining to hear. I moved out of sight before I turned my light on as he slammed his way back into the house. Another series of bangs had my head pounding. I moved to my kitchen and grabbed a bottled water when I heard the repeat thwack of his back door. Realization dawned, and I began to laugh when the door slammed again.

"Oh Simone, you've got yourself a new victim." I grabbed a new pair of noise-canceling plugs from my nightstand and marched over to the porch where Ian paced. With a heated glance my way, he didn't bother with pleasantries. "The facking smoke alarm is broken. I'm..." he tapped his forehead. "Gatvol!"

"Gat what?"

"I've had it! Never mind. It's the alarms, we need to have them checked."

"No..."

Ian, still in his slacks and undershirt, glared at me. The porch light illuminated us in weak shadow. He was a beautiful man, even with a vampire tan and the slight bulge around his waist. His thick, gelled, dark-brown hair was scattered from a day of running his hand through it and feathered over his brow. He'd grown up pretty... and pretty *bitchy*.

"Don't tell me no. I've been listening to the screech for hours. I've dismantled them all!"

"Ian," I said carefully, as I closed the few feet between us like I was cornering a very angry six-foot-plus mouse. "It's not the smoke detectors."

He scrutinized me in my shorts and thin halter top, sans bra. "Brilliant, just brilliant. You manage this property, right? How does anyone get any sleep here?!"

"If you will just listen—"

"Are you *mad*, woman? I have been listening! I'm certain it's the alarms."

"It's not—"

He moved toward me his lips upturned. "Listen—"

"No listen, Ian, it's—"

"Shush!"

Pressing my lips together he craned his neck until his eyes widened. "Hear it? Don't tell me that's not an alarm!"

I stood with my hand on my hips, cupping his remedy—the earplugs—in my palm. Shrugging, I made my way off his porch. "Fine, it's the alarms. Good luck with that."

Marching into my house, I slammed the open window and turned on my AC. Even with the added white noise from the unit, I could hear the frog, who'd taken up residence in the thick brush behind the Kemp house, begin to sing. Simone, my sweet Coqui Frog, who I'd lovingly named after Nina Simone, appeared to me on one of the plants next to my porch after a three-week fight. Simone sounded very much like a smoke alarm with dying batteries. But Ian and his head-biting ass would just have to find out the hard way.

Welcome back to St. Thomas, Mr. Kemp.

Some horses you could lead to water and they would still walk straight through it believing it was a mirage. Such was the case with my angry new neighbor.

Still, angry was better than sad. And if Ian was about to fight the good fight, he needed that fire.

I fell asleep a few minutes later to a more muted, "What the fack! A frog?!"

"I don't give a rat's ass, Kevin! This is unacceptable!"

I opened one eye and groaned before I pulled a pillow over my head.

"Rubbish! And she made sure of that!" Ian was growling into his phone and must have decided his back porch was the perfect place to vent. I looked at the bedside clock.

7 a.m.

I pulled myself from the comfort of my cloud and made my way outside, slamming my screen door and eyeing him from my porch with my hands on my hips, in hopes that would be enough to stop his tirade.

"Oh, bullshit! That's bullshit!" He paced on the sand yard purposefully ignoring my presence and plea for peace.

"Excuse me," I whispered on the wind. I needed to grow some balls and fast when it came to moody Mr. Kemp. I didn't do well without my sleep. Years of sleep depravity in New York followed by a year of rested bliss had changed me.

"This is inexcusable! What I want, what I want? I want you to do your facking job!" Ian's accent had turned into a strange mix of pissed off Texan with a lash whip of South African. He stood in boxer briefs pacing as he ignored me. He was tall, disheveled and shirtless. The extra weight he carried did little to take away from his appeal. On any other day, I might have enjoyed the testosterone-filled man parading in front of me.

"So facking wrong! Eish! All of this is wrong!" More silence, then, "That should have been brought to my attention a year ago!"

Ripping my eyes away from his muscular thighs, I found myself screaming along with him. "Hey, take that brawl inside, crocky!"

Ian glared at me and I swore he bared teeth as he made his way up his porch steps. I was dismissed as he began his pacing on the faded wood giving me a view of his muscular back.

"A little louder, I don't think everyone on the island is awake yet," I muttered as he continued his rant.

"Fine. I want a call within the hour." Ian ended his call and threw his cell on one of the porch chairs before opening his screen without glancing my way.

"Hey!" I interjected as he paused his retreat and glanced

my way. "Look, buddy, I'm all for getting a point across, but can we not do it at seven in the morning while our neighbor is sleeping?"

"Fine. Right." He slammed the door behind him.

"I accept your apology!"

His voice drifted through the open windows in his living room. "I didn't offer one, miss."

"Koti. My name is *Koti* and you damn well know it. And from what I remember you were all about formalities and manners, Mr. Kemp, so how about showing some common courtesy?"

The only way to get privacy between our two houses was to shut them up *completely*. Even then, without a little white noise, you could hear a lot.

Fact: People have a lot of sex on vacation. A lot of sex.

The rumble of Ian's voice drifted through the air. "It's rude to listen to other people's conversations."

"As if I had a choice!"

"Who's screaming now?"

"Well, we're both up now anyway, thanks to you."

He stayed mute as I growled from my own porch.

Koti Vaughn, you need this commission.

Minutes after my first sip of coffee, I found my calm in the crash of the waves on our shared beach. Ian made his way onto his porch dressed in his slacks from the day before, his own cup in hand. Wrinkled and wrecked were the best words to describe him and I couldn't help the tug of recognition of the state of his distress yesterday. Mustering up some patience, I made another effort to extend the olive branch. "I'll be by with your groceries at noon. I didn't get a chance to check your water levels so let me know if you're running low. My phone number is in the book on the counter, text me if you want me to pick up anything else for you."

His reply was a curt nod.

"Okay, well, I'll see you at noon."

"That bad, huh?" Jasmine's eyes surveyed me in my zombie-like state. I managed to throw on a sundress and applied some sunblock and deodorant before I made it out of my house. I left the state of my wet hair up to my Jeep.

"Nice hair."

"Bite me and he's a nightmare. He's hurt, but hard to sympathize with. He spent half the night putting holes in his ceiling and the morning screaming into his cell phone."

Jasmine filled a fresh cup of coffee and put it on my desk. "Is he hot?"

I sat back in my chair and winced due to the building throb in my skull.

"He's a headache."

"A hot headache?"

"He's handsome, I guess."

"Handsome? Who says handsome?"

"I just did." I rolled my eyes as I logged into my desktop. "I know what you're thinking and trust me, you don't want to meet the ass. The first thing that came out of his mouth was that all women are liars."

"So, he's handsome?"

"Very handsome, and *very* pissed off. He taught me how to snorkel when I was six. He was cute then. He's handsome now and completely standoffish."

"Hmm." Jasmine chewed her lower lip and scrutinized my face. "Sounds like an opportunity."

I ignored her by typing an email reply to a new renter.

"Koti." It was a demand. I met her soft brown eyes over the screen. There wasn't a trace of humor anywhere. "You've barely dated since you've been here. Don't you miss sex?"

"I told you... I fooled around enough in New York. I'm happy with being alone. It's what I want for the moment. And my angry neighbor is *not* the one to saddle up with." She planted her ass on the edge of my desk and covered my busy hands.

"I worry about you. You are completely anti-social. No TV at home, what do you even do?"

"I read, I take long walks down the beach, I drink wine, I attempt to play the piano, and I get a lot of sleep. I'm fine." It was the truth. The absolute truth. I'd found calm. I wanted to keep it.

"Fine, but a little flirtation wouldn't hurt."

"Trust me, he's not the one to flirt with. He's either yelling or grunting. Anyway, I spoke to Mrs. Kemp. She's going to double our commission and cover the difference of the Margulis mansion."

Jasmine perked up. "Really?"

"Yep, the only stipulation is that I have to keep an eye on him and it looks like I have my work cut out for me."

Jasmine bit her hot pink lip. "Do you think he would... you know," her eyes bulged, "hurt himself?"

I bit the edge of my nail and she slapped it away, it was a peeve of hers. "The way he looked yesterday... it was awful. But no, I don't think so. Not after the fight I saw in him this morning. He seems as angry as he is hurt. He's divorced, but his mother said he was the one who wanted it. I don't think it has to do with his ex, but who knows."

"Huh," Jasmine said as she looked at me thoughtfully.

"He probably just needs a break. I'm bringing his groceries

in a few hours and I intend to tread lightly. I'm going to make sure we get this commission."

She lifted a brow. "Going to get creative?"

I shouldered my purse as she gave me a suggestive wink. "You are such a backhoe."

five

Koti

I parked my Jeep as Banion came out of his flower shop to greet me.

"Hey yank, you still look fresh from the boat."

"Liar!" I accused, as he opened my door. "I passed the one-year mark. I'm officially a *local*."

"Yank-*key*," he said, adding more charm to the word with his thick island accent. "What ya need today?"

"Three bouquets please, we have a busy day."

"Maybe four?" He looked over at me with a knowing smile. "One for you."

"Perfect." Ushering me inside he began to gather the bouquets, taking stems from various buckets he kept in a small cooler. He had the roughest looking florist shop in St. Thomas but made the most beautiful bouquets. I always told him if I ever struck it rich, he would be my lone investment. He was highly underrated and undervalued due to the state of his shop, but the locals knew. And though I'd spent six summers in St. Thomas over the course of my life, I could honestly say I was becoming an expert at navigating the potholed pavement.

"When are your parents coming, yank?"

"Thanksgiving, I pray."

"You have not spoken to them?" He peered at me over a handful of orange and purple stems. One desperate and lonely night when I had first arrived on the island and just gotten my job with Jasmine, I'd spent a few drunken hours with Banion spilling the events that led me to St. Thomas. He hadn't let me forget the night of verbal diarrhea, nor the physical vomit I had christened the floor of his store with. Not my finest hour, or week, or month.

"We talk."

"But do you *really* talk?" Banion was ridiculously tall to the point of being intimidating. His charcoal-colored skin and dark eyes were only softened by the sincerest of white smiles and a smooth voice.

"We talk. They still badger me to go back."

"And you want to stay?"

"I'm staying," I insisted, adding a few pink sprays to the mix. Banion shook his head. "No, the green." I pulled a few green stems from the basket as he wrapped the leaves around the flowers and tied them without a binding.

"Beautiful," I said, amazed at his handiwork.

"One day, when you have the time, I'll show you how to tie the flowers." He pushed the bouquets into my hand as I handed him the cash. Banion was old school, person-to-person was his motto. It was also one of the reasons his flower shop wasn't as widely known. But I understood it. My motto was very much the same. In fact, if you googled Koti Vaughn, you would see closed social media accounts. Being connected used to be the bane of my existence.

Years of conditioning—prep school, followed by a five-year stint in college to get my masters—had been wasted. I was one business move away from making myself immortal before I choked. Well… before I got a reality check. And in the Virgin Islands, on one of the mountains, surrounded by sea, I was a property manager dolling out bottles of wine and Banion's bouquets to the ones who had gambled and won.

One day-*poof*. Dream job, *gone*, swanky apartment, *stripped away*. I went from being the real estate wolf of Manhattan to the black sheep of St. Thomas.

My piece of the Big Apple had a worm in it.

Like Ian, I spent the first day in St. Thomas staring at the ocean in the safety of my parents' rental house.

Life was fucked in New York.

But in St. Thomas…

"Don't forget yours," Banion said, handing me another armful of beautifully tethered stems.

Thankful to be jerked out of the debilitating cold of my past life, I hugged him before I stepped out into the warming sun.

I set the bags down on the porch one by one before I knocked and got no answer. "Ian?" Knocking again, I pressed my face to the living room window. The house looked abandoned. "Shit." I gripped an extra key that I'd taken from the office since Ian had stolen mine the night before and let myself in. Aside from a crumpled blanket on the edge of the plush white couch, the place was empty. In hopes that Ian was somewhere wandering the beach, I began to unload the groceries and replaced the bottle of red I'd stolen and added an extra. I skipped the customary liquor bottles to avoid a drunken tirade. The man was already off the rails, I wasn't about to add strong alcohol to the mix.

I was a hypocrite of sorts. I drank like a fish when I arrived on the island in ashes. I added a few things to the list to keep Ian fed and put out several items I knew he hadn't brought with him—shaving cream, a razor, deodorant, body wash, shampoo, and extra toilet paper. Just as I'd finished unloading, he walked through the door with several shopping bags in hand. He paused when he saw me standing next to the counter.

"Hi."

Eyes averted he spoke low. "Seeing as how my parents *own* the home, I won't be needing your services, Koti."

"Well, this request came directly from your mother." I surrendered the last rental key on the counter. "And I told you I'd be by with groceries."

"And I rather hoped you'd left by now."

I bit my tongue as he moved past me and set his bags down. I eyed the contents and saw several shirts and pairs of shorts with tags. I hid my excitement that he was staying. Not because he was ideal company, but because of the financially worry-free months ahead of me.

"I'll leave you to it. Just let me know if you need anything."

Gray eyes met my blue briefly. "I won't." Devastation. It was clear as day. Anyone who looked at the man could never question what he felt. His eyes were a window, though his features remained stoic.

"You know, Ian, I came here about a year ago a complete mess—"

"I'd like some privacy, please."

Swallowing my pride, I walked out the door without another word.

Thwack.

Thwack.

Thwack.

"Fack!" It was another one of the hundreds of curses that erupted from the Kemp kitchen.

With wide eyes, I watched the wood fly across the porch and onto the sand and heard another loud crash as I stalked the house next door with my phone pressed to my ear.

"So how is my son?" His mother asked as I saw more of Rowan Kemp's kitchen fly over the railing, off the porch, and into the sand. "Is he adjusting well?"

"Damnit! Oh, fack your motha," Ian's voice rang out in frustration. Giggling, I covered the mouthpiece of the phone as another cabinet door hit the sand. He'd been at it for a few hours. It started with an explosive phone call that I managed to avoid, mostly due to my taking cover in the shower and ended with a bang.

"He... is. It looks like he's remodeling the kitchen."

In a flash, Ian stood on the porch only in shorts, his chest heaving, a bottle of the red in his hand. He studied the wood in the sand before he glanced at my house. I ducked out of his line of sight and answered her before more banging started. "He's fine."

"Oh, that's wonderful news. Maybe you could put him on the phone?"

More growling ensued and then a clear, "Damn you! EISH!"

"Well, at the moment, I think it would be impossible, he's in the midst of demolition."

I cringed at the ripping sound and poked my head out of my screen door just as he hurled more wood over the railing.

"You know he's always been so good at things like that. He built his father a beautiful bookshelf for his study."

"That's wonderful," I said, as Ian unloaded an entire can of lighter fluid on the discarded wood. I raced around the bottom floor of my house and collected every fire extinguisher I had before I sat them next to my front door. Seconds later I heard the whoosh of the wood go up in flames. The rising inferno seemed to fuel him as he added more of his mother's kitchen to it piece by piece.

Rowan went on, speaking of her pride and joy. "From boy scouts all the way through college, my boy excelled at everything he did. Honor student, swimming, tennis. I had to beat the women away with a stick."

Ian chose that moment to snap another cabinet door in half over his knee and used his empty wine bottle to bat it into the burning pile.

"You don't say."

"Oh, yes, he was such a ladies' man before he met Tara, his ex-wife."

Only mildly prepared, I walked out onto my porch at the same time Ian returned to it. He had several photo books in his hand. Rowan whispered in my ear as if he could hear her. "I was never really that fond of her, she seemed a little cold compared to his warmth."

Ian pulled pictures from the books and began to burn them one by one. Something in my chest split as he walked around Rowan Kemp's burning kitchen cabinets, tossing away what I was sure were irreplaceable pictures.

He had lost his shit. It was, without a doubt, Ian's doomsday.

"Don't!" I screamed from where I stood.

Ian ignored me as he tossed an entire book into the fire before shaking another so that the pictures fed the flames.

"Koti? What is it?" Rowan said anxiously on the phone.

"Oh nothing, I was just…"

"Is everything okay?"

"Oh, fine," I said, as I paced the porch watching her son destroy his mother's memories. He must have found the pictures in the linen closet. The Kemps had very few of their own things in the house.

"Rowan, I'm going to ask him if he needs any help."

"Okay," she said hesitantly. "But please ask him to ring me."

"Will do." I was already running toward the small bonfire just as Ian tossed another picture into it.

"What are you doing!?"

"Privacy," he said through thick lips. "That's all I asked for."

"Kind of hard to ignore you, Ian. Since you've gone all Tom Hanks *Cast Away*—*me man, me make fire!*" I reached for the picture in his hand as he tossed it in. I watched it burn. It was a shot of a woman in her wedding dress who I assumed was Tara. She looked beautiful as she smiled at her groom. I was only able to admire Ian in a well-fitted tux for seconds before the fire engulfed the photo.

Jesus, what could have happened?

"Ian, if you want to talk about it…"

He picked up another book and took a few pictures out shoving them into his pocket before he tossed it into the pile.

"Leave."

"Please stop. You don't understand what you're doing."

Blazing eyes scoured me before he looked back at the fire. "I know exactly what the fuck I'm doing."

Sweat pooled on his forehead. He was covered in splintered wood. Ian Kemp had cracked, and he wasn't coming back until he was ready.

Way too far into his headspace, he ignored me standing next to him.

I walked back to my house and watched him dismantle years of memories as he stared at the fire until it went out.

And then the house next to mine went completely quiet.

SIX

Ian

I sat in the dark living room staring out the window at the brightly lit ocean. Thousands of stars littered the night sky as the sea swept the shore. No matter how hard I tried, I couldn't temper the anger. I couldn't bring myself back to some semblance of the man I was just days before. It was a new beginning I didn't ask for—that I hadn't planned on—but I could feel a part of me coming to the surface, a part of me that I had ignored for years. The selfish part.

The last fifteen years of my life had been a series of compromises, and mostly on my part to be the man I was raised to be—a good husband and doting father. The things I swore I wanted. Another crack deep within bled freely when I thought of all that time I spent believing my family was a gift and purely my own. The irony is my ex-wife had been lost to me for years, a stranger before I left her and asked for a divorce. And my daughter... I scrubbed my face as I fought the threatening explosion within.

I would give anything to take those minutes at that hospital back. With everything in me, I wish I would have played dumb, instead of recognizing Tara's guilt and figuring it out. Not only did I have the knowledge that Ella wasn't mine, her mother was now threatening to tell her the truth. Threatening to reveal to my little girl she didn't belong to me in the biological sense. This was no doubt Tara's plan in an attempt to transition her boyfriend into being a family man. I didn't need a paternity test to know that Daniel was Ella's sperm donor. Tara had been dating him her whole life up until the month we met. It seemed as though their relationship didn't end when ours started.

Rage boiled again, refusing to let me feel anything else in that moment. If the look on Koti's face when she watched me unravel the last few days was any indication of my well-being, I was safer sitting in the dark dealing with my temperament alone.

I left a loveless marriage for the sake of all three of us. Though Tara fought the divorce and claimed to love me even after the papers were signed, I still cared for her enough to set her free to find something more than the shackle of obligation we felt.

I wouldn't let my daughter suffer another needless argument. I refused to stay together and set that horrible example for her. It wasn't blissful or comfortable. It was waged war and over the simplest things. Everything I'd ever done, including the dissolution of my marriage, had been for Ella. I had no woman waiting.

But that was now the case. I had a little woman waiting. I had to go back. I had to go back and fight for what was right for Ella, but I had nothing inside me but hate and the taste of betrayal coating my tongue and clouding my vision. I would not abandon my daughter, but she would not recognize the man I was now.

As starlight struck the water and twilight hit, I couldn't see the beauty. I couldn't fixate on the awe-inspiring light, I only saw the darkness in-between.

Soft music drifted from Koti's bedroom as I slapped the water away from my eyes. I moved to the kitchen to see her bedroom clearly lit. On her stomach with a book in hand, her knees bent and bare feet up, she swung them back and forth to the melody. In that moment I envied her ability to live only for herself and the freedom that came with it. I wanted that. I'd just been granted that freedom in the cruelest of ways by Tara's confession. But I could never embrace that freedom because of the loss I would surely suffer. Still, the idea of it appealed to me more than anything. Not the loss of Ella but the need to do things differently, to finally make my life my own, about me. Anger blurred my vision as I sat back in the shadows of the house. The dark would have to do for now.

seven

Koti

A day went by without a glimpse of him, and then another. I spent a good amount of time staring into the darkness watching for any movement, a trickle of light, but came up empty.

I tried to muster up any excuse to check on him but had none. He asked for privacy and I had to admit when I arrived on the island, I wanted the same.

Rowan called nightly and I assured her with a false update that her son was fine.

But after a third day, I no longer felt safe in assuming the best. When my alarm went off that morning, I grabbed some clothes and made my way to the house next door. After my knock went unanswered, I began to pound. "Ian?"

Nothing.

Fear crept through me as I stood on the porch for a solid five minutes knocking. Desperate, I glimpsed through the window and saw him lying on the couch with his eyes to the ceiling. "Ian. Open the door, please." His eyes drifted to mine and my heart skipped a beat. Reluctantly, he moved to get up and a few seconds later, we were face to face. His jaw was covered in dark stubble, his hair a scattered mess, expression unreadable. I scoured him from his sad gray depths to his shirtless chest, to his bare feet. He was fine, aside from looking completely desolate.

"What is it, Koti?" It was a different tone, equal amounts of defeat and exasperation.

I lifted my folded clothes. "I'm out of water and running late for work." It was a lie but a damned good excuse. I peered into the house behind him, before I made my case.

"Can I please borrow your shower? I'll be quick."

He let out a long breath and opened the door stepping back to let me in. With quick appraising eyes, I looked around the war zone. The kitchen was torn to shreds, the wood splintered. On the floor of the living room lay several empty boxes, one for a laptop that sat on his coffee table. Curious, I braved a look at the screen and saw nothing but a generic screensaver. I decided I'd made a good call about the absence of liquor when I saw the empty wine bottles on the floor. Walking down the hall, I noticed the holes in the ceiling from his attempt to silence the alarms and bit my lips to keep from laughing before I closed myself in the guest bathroom and made quick work of taking a shower. Under the warm water, I decided I'd had enough of his intimidation. There were people worried about him who needed assurances directly from the source. I never made my parents wait for word from me, even in my worst headspace.

I had no idea what had unglued Ian Kemp, but I knew I wasn't the reason.

Fully dressed, I walked into the living room to see him sitting on his couch signing at the screen. His hands moved skillfully in conversation, the computer open toward him so I couldn't see who he was conversing with.

Fascinated, I watched him for a few seconds.

He flashed a beautiful smile and waved at the screen before he closed it. Gray eyes drifted to me.

"Yes, Koti?"

"You know sign language. Wow."

Cold eyes roamed over my damp hair and sundress before they landed on my face. "Yes."

"That's—"

"So, you're showered."

I was being dismissed *again*, and just as rudely as the first time. I balled my fists, the New Yorker in me was ready to rip him to shreds. I pushed her aside for the moment to reason with him.

"Would it kill you to be decent to me? I know you're going through a rough time, but would it hurt you so much to say one kind word?"

He pushed his computer off his lap and resumed the position he was in when I knocked on the door. Several seconds passed, I looked him over expectantly.

His lips barely moved. "I apologize."

"You should," I said without missing a beat, "sincerely and repeatedly."

He lifted his head from the couch. The circles underneath his eyes ran deep. I doubted he'd touched a thing in the fridge. He'd drawn most of the curtains in the living room, so sunlight was scarce.

What happened to you, Ian?

"That's none of your damned business."

I'd said it out loud.

Crap.

"No, it's not."

"If that's all…"

"Actually, it's not. I'd like to extend a dinner invitation to thank you for the shower."

His answer was immediate. "And I'd like to decline." Moving to sit, he planted his feet on the floor while his hands gripped his hair.

"I'm sorry, Ian."

He ripped his head free of his hands and turned to look at me.

"I'm sorry for whatever happened to you."

He kept his eyes connected with mine as I took a careful step around the debris. "But your mother is worried, to the point she will probably show up here unannounced if you don't call her."

He frowned. "Tell her I'm fine."

"But you're not."

"Again," he said standing. "None of your business."

"I get it, okay. I didn't come here to fucking snorkel either."

Surprised by my venom, he stayed mute. It seemed I had the floor for the first time since he arrived.

"A year ago, I showed up in the same shit shape as you."

"You have no idea—"

I waved my hand in the air and cut him off, giving him a taste of his own medicine. "And that's your secret to keep. I had my own reasons. Reasons that were just as personal to *me*." People are selfish with their pain, but not their anger. I got it. I'd lived through it.

"I understand you right now more than you know, so just take a step back, okay? I'm not the enemy. I'm waving the white flag here. The dinner invitation stands. Seven o'clock. I'm a shit cook, but it's better than staring at the ceiling."

I made my leave without another word, relieved that he was capable of at least faking a smile for whomever he was on screen with.

Halfway to my Jeep I pulled my buzzing phone from my pocket and answered on the first ring. "Good morning, Rowan."

Ian stepped out onto the beach in my line of sight before he disappeared down the shoreline.

"I just spoke to Ian. I invited him for dinner. I think he may come."

"Oh? That's wonderful news."

"I was just at the house. It looks like the remodel is coming along." Another lie. The next question was purely selfish. "He was on his computer signing with someone?"

"Oh good. He was speaking to Ella. His daughter, my granddaughter. She's deaf."

"Oh." The smile he gave her was genuine.

"Okay, love, thank you. I was just checking in. I hate to bother you so much." Her voice was sincere and apologetic.

"It's fine, Rowan. Anytime."

"Thank you, Koti."

I inhaled the sea air as I gazed at the rolling waves. It once renewed my faith. I had no doubt they would work their magic on Ian.

eight

Koti

I sat that night with candles lit all over my deck, freshly broiled fish waiting in the oven and a crisp salad spoiling on the porch. Ian was a no-show. I was surprised at my disappointment when he stomped on my white flag and even more flabbergasted minutes later, when the sound of a woman's laugh filtered in the air before I heard the rumble of Ian's voice. Hopping to my feet as the sun set, I blew out the candles and dashed inside in an attempt to save face from his rejection. From my upstairs porch, stretching my neck and body, I peeked over the side of the house to see Ian ravaging a woman in our large sand-filled alley. He was dressed in slacks and a light button-down and she was plastered to the siding, hidden under his tall frame. I heard her moan underneath him before her head tilted up heavenward, her eyes tightly shut as he whispered to her before lifting her skirt, his hands working beneath. Too intoxicated to look away, I watched him devour her as she gasped under his touch.

Face flushed I looked on, silently scorning the total pervert I was and felt a slight twinge of... something.

Jealousy?

For Ian? No, he was a dick.

A total and complete dick.

So much for s'more loyalty.

Mentally I picked up my battered white flag and tucked it back in my pocket.

Was I jealous of the attention the woman was getting?

Definitely. It was one thing to go without, it was another thing entirely to have it tossed in your face. I loved a good kiss, the whisper of a man's lips on my neck. I was beginning to miss sex, but that was the most of it. I'd done long-term without the happy ending, short-term with the abrupt record scratch ending and more one-night stands than a girl should admit to. When you referred to the last guy you were intimate with as the one with the black-checkered tie, as I did, desire took a back seat to self-worth. I wanted the relationship with the next man to be a little more meaningful, but that would require commitment and I'd just gotten myself together.

Everything about my life in New York went fast.

My new focus was slow and meaningful.

Fighting with myself to look away; instead, I chose to drink in the scene below. Accusatory gray eyes met mine when I glanced back down at the couple and my face lit up in embarrassment. Ian ripped himself from her, his eyes still on mine. He was clearly drunk and staggered into his house with the woman in tow, slamming the door behind them.

I threw the untouched fish in the sink and grabbed a pair of silencing plugs from my nightstand. It was going to be a long night.

The next morning, Ian sat on the beach in nothing but swim trunks as I made my way out of the house for work. He barely glanced my way which was fine with me. I had nothing to say to him. At least I didn't have to worry about false reports to his mother because he had finally joined the land of the living. Despite my best efforts to block Ian out, I was up half the night hot and cold, tossing and turning, with body aches.

I knew what was coming and had the pissy mood to match.

In a freshly purchased pair of flip-flops, with an iced coffee in hand, I walked toward my Jeep to start my day when he spoke.

"Have you talked to my mother?" He wiped the sand off his swim trunks as he stood. Ripping my eyes from his profile, lit by the early morning sun, I continued walking to my Jeep without a word.

"Oh, you are going to play hurt?" He barked at me. "I declined your dinner invitation. I was pretty clear."

I bit the inside of both cheeks and kept my feet moving.

"Could you at least tell her not to come?"

"Tell her yourself," I said, throwing my purse into the passenger seat.

"Favor for a favor, Koti. I lent you my shower. This is not a difficult request."

Facing him, I crossed my arms. "Why are you so afraid of your mother?"

Hypocrite.

I barely answered my own mother's calls. My failures looked horrible on her face and were no less daunting over the line. Her "in my day" speeches suffocated me and had my whole life. The less we spoke the closer we got to middle ground.

Ian took a step forward. "She's a mother. She asks too many questions."

"Seems like you had no issue talking last night." A single brow rose while he studied my face.

"Dirty boy, aren't you? Tell you what. Why don't you take your spoiled ass inside that house and call your own damned mommy."

Screw babysitting, I would make it work. If Ian left, spoke ill of me to his mother, if I lost the commission, I would beg Jasmine not to fire me while I rallied for another property.

Ian took an aggressive step forward. "Not that it's any of your business but I haven't had sex with anyone but my ex-wife in fifteen years so I guarantee you if I sleep with anyone, it's a well-deserved fuck."

"Well, I hope you wrapped it up tight because we don't need you multiplying your kind of crazy around here."

His face turned to stone and his jaw ticked. "What in the hell did you just say?"

Ah, the angry South African Texan had returned. I'd done a fine job of ruining my twenty-four-hour truce. My father always told me before I entered any argument to go in with three justifiable points, or the battle wasn't worth it.

Where Ian was concerned, I was good to go. "News flash buddy, number one, I've made more allowances than I should for your rude behavior. You have not once thanked me for the trouble I've gone through on your behalf to keep you in that house. Number two, which by the way, was fully booked when you decided to show up with your shitshow circus and has made my work days harder. Number three, not only that, I've lost more nights of sleep since you've been here than I have in a year! I *said* call your own mother, burn her house down, starve to death. I'm done watching over you. You aren't worth the trouble!"

"What's your problem, Koti. Are you jealous? Do you fancy me?" He asked, his tone unmistakably mocking as he took a step forward and then another until I was pinned to my Jeep. "I noticed you watching us."

Feeling the blush creep up on my face, I chose to ignore the fact that he busted me.

"Jealous?" I scoffed as ice gray eyes slanted down and

stunned me. "Do I *fancy* you? You think an invitation to dinner is a request for sex? Man, you *have* been out of the game for some time, old sport. You were an arrogant ass as a kid, but you've got one hell of an ego on you now, don't you, *crocky*? What in the *hell* would I possibly have to be jealous of? Drunk sex with a hyena? I bet you can't even remember her name."

He glared at me openly.

"What did you call her when she left this morning, barstool number five with big breasts?"

Ian's eyes instantly went to my chest before he glanced up and raised a brow.

"Oh, you're disgusting."

"Fine. I'm disgusting. AG Man!"

"What is that, more South African sailor?"

This time he jerked his chin back. "What?" He rolled his eyes in understanding. "It means—go away. And mind your own damned business."

My eyes were trained on his lips as I pushed at his chest. "Stay on your side of the fence, asshole!"

"Fine by me." He turned toward the beach and my feet began to move on their own accord as the last of my patience flew away.

"What is *wrong* with you? You can be civil enough to some lady at a bar to get her into bed, but you can't show me any common decency? We were friends once."

He barely glanced over his shoulder. "I hardly knew you."

"Still, what in the hell is your problem with me? Because it has to be specifically with *me*, right? I mean you can smile for your daughter!"

His turn was sharp as he leveled me with one single look. The man was pure venom and anger and he was dragging me down with him. I could feel the panic in me start to rise and blew out a breath.

"Forget it! Just keep the noise level down on your side of the fence. Screw half of the island for all I care. But I *live* here. Remember that. I'm not leaving, so deal with it."

His broad muscular back to me, he muttered his reply. "Not like I have a choice."

My brain didn't bother to tell my hand to stop when I drew wet sand from the beach and formed it into a ball, my limbs didn't bother to slow at all as I tossed it full force at the back of his head.

PMDD. Premenstrual Dysphoric Disorder and sleep deprivation. When the two get together, sand bombs happen.

Ian stood with his back to me several seconds before he turned to look my way, his face covered in disbelief. I had a ready middle finger stretched out in front of me, the only *sign* I knew before I stomped back to my Jeep. He was still glaring at me from where he stood in the sand as I sped off.

nine

Koti

The next few weeks were much of the same. The Kemp house was quiet. Too quiet. I never saw flashing TV lights in the living room or heard any more of his ranting. He would disappear for a few days on the weekends, which I assumed was when he went to see his daughter. Despite my resolution to give him his space, I knew he wasn't improving. But I was gone during most of the day, never really having any idea what he did when I wasn't home.

"You're thinking about him," Jasmine said as I took a bite of my salad. We were on the sun-covered porch of the Oak Hotel. They had the best salads and an even better view of the bay.

"I just keep wondering what happened."

"Cheating."

"No, he wanted the divorce. That doesn't make sense." I forked some chicken and looked out at the water. "God, I love days like this." It was hot, but not to the point of being miserable. The breeze blew off the surface of the sparkling water yards away. Jasmine eyed the man who sat alone next to us and he smirked our way over his paper.

"God, you're terrible," I noted, glancing his way. His eyes met mine and I gave him a weak smile.

"I'm thirty-nine and single," she said a little too loudly as I sank in my seat. "I want to live a little."

"Oh, you've been living," I said just as loudly and the guy belted out a loud bark.

She glared at me. "Just because you decided the house was your new convent doesn't mean the rest of us are hanging it up."

"I've been thinking about that a little lately and maybe it's time to give dating a chance." The man Jasmine had been eyeing was suddenly at our table. I looked up to him as he plucked his wallet from his back pocket. "Pardon my eavesdropping, but I'm actually glad to hear it." He set down a card in front of my plate and I winced at the sun-filled sky behind him trying to get a better look. He was beautiful, with thick coppery brown hair and a strong jawline. I couldn't make out his eye color. Casually dressed in slacks and a polo, he looked down at me with curious eyes.

"Patrick." He held out his hand and I took it, stunned. "Koti." Patrick looked to Jasmine with a smirk, which she countered with one of her own. "I'm Jasmine."

"Nice to meet you both. Koti, I would love to take you to dinner some time."

"Okay, Patrick Roberts," I said eyeing his card. "But it will be expensive." He bit his lip and winked. "And she brings me a doggie bag," Jasmine chimed in.

He leaned down slightly, so I caught the amusement in his eyes—which were blue—and a hint of some intoxicating cologne. "I look forward to it."

We both watched him disappear, fully confident in his walk. The man had an ass and swagger to boot.

"That was bold. I bet he's packing in the penis department."

I choked on my water as she looked at me and shrugged. "And I'm just going to say right now, I totally thought he was staring at me. I may need my eyes checked."

"He's the one that's blind," I said, eyeing my best friend in her signature red dress. I'd been surrounded by beautiful people my whole life, but none of them shined quite as bright as the woman who held out her hand to me and picked me up when I was at my lowest.

"Stop doing that," she said, popping a piece of bread in her mouth.

"Doing what?"

"She was beautiful, I'm sure, but it's okay that you are beautiful too. Stop downplaying your looks to appease your mother. She's not here."

Mouth gaping, I jerked back in my seat. "Whoa, are we on the couch, Dr. Gersch?"

"Koti, I don't think you realize how much you do it, but you are gorgeous. Case in point, that hot ass man wants to take you on a date and do the dirty."

Our waitress grinned as she set the check down between us. "Sorry, I walked into that, but if I can be of any help to you, he had a black Amex. You really should call him." The waitress made her leave as I stared at Patrick's card.

"See," Jasmine said with the nod of her chin. "Rich too."

"I've dated rich and entitled. I'd rather date a man who has to work hard to buy me expensive wine."

Jasmine tilted her head. "Why?"

"Because that would mean he would have to *work* for me, obviously."

"Oh, as opposed to giving it away." She threw her napkin on her plate.

"Don't. This isn't about the way *you* do things, it's about what I want for myself."

She darted her eyes around the table, a rare sign of the guilt she inflicted on herself for her random hookups.

"One day I *will* get over him."

"You will," I assured. "It's okay to enjoy yourself."

Jasmine chewed the inside of her cheek. "What if I can't love another man?"

"Then we'll love each other."

She looked at me with gleaming eyes and asked in a shaky voice, "Promise?"

"Promise. You're my person, Jasmine Ann Gersch. You don't ever leave your person."

She smiled, but it was weak. Even though it had been a little over a year since her fiancé had abandoned her in St. Thomas, her issues remained. It wasn't rocket science. We both knew why she wouldn't commit or even attempt to. She had been badly burned.

"You can talk about Steven, with me, if you want. You know that."

"I think I'm over that phase, but I appreciate it. My sisters won't even let me say his name. He's the reason I'm here and away from them and their children. My sisters are having babies and marrying their princes and I'm not even a part of their lives."

"Then go see them."

"I will. I want to, but I was too busy trying to get the business off the ground. I felt like I had something to prove to a man who doesn't give a shit about me." She took a sip of her water to cool the emotion budding on the tip of her tongue. "I just don't understand how I can feel so much after all this time and know he doesn't feel anything at all."

"You don't know that. And he's an idiot."

"That doesn't help."

"You had sex on a backhoe."

She chuckled as she pursed her lips. "What is *wrong* with me?"

"You got your heart broken and won't give it to anyone

else," I stated. "You need more time."

She wiped underneath her eyes and whispered across the table. "How much more?"

"Until you and your heart are ready."

"What about you, Koti?"

"I'm holding out for the first time in my life. I'm not in a hurry. I just need my body to cooperate."

My abdomen chose that moment to start screaming. Jasmine saw me wince.

"It's starting."

"Okay," she said shooing me away. "Go home. Text me later."

When I didn't move, she looked over at me. "I've got this, Koti."

I lowered my eyes. "Everyone's checked in, we shouldn't have too many calls."

"So, you check out." She gripped my hand across the table. "It's okay."

Frustrated, I tried to ignore the deep throb in my center. "I can make it through the rest of the day," I said, starting to inhale and exhale deeply. "This is ridiculous."

Jasmine squeezed my hand. "Go home."

On my deck wrapped up in a blanket and freezing, even with the day's heat, I popped a pill from my prescription bottle, my jaw shaking from the onslaught of cramps. It felt like two tiny men had cut their way into my abdomen and were playing the bongos. I lay in my hammock in a ball as I listened to the waves in an attempt to ignore my treacherous body. My insides screamed and I braced myself for the worst. I'd been diagnosed with endometriosis a few years before I left New York. Clustered with severe mood swings and my anxiety, for several days of each month, I was a ticking time bomb. I did what I could to kick the mood swings with workouts that had me crawling toward a hot shower and relaxation techniques my therapist had taught me. Nothing helped but drugs and time. Though I'd been managing the clusterfuck for years, it still felt like a small Armageddon every single month. I was lucky enough to have a best friend as a boss who allowed me to slip away for a few days until the worst of it subsided. A shock wave of pain coursed through me and I tensed when another set of cramps hit hard.

Some time later, with my eyes tightly shut I sensed I wasn't alone.

"Koti?"

I wiped the tears from my face and pressed my chin to my chest to hide them.

"Go away."

Ian stood to the side of my hammock. I could feel the day's heat coming off him. Lifting my eyes, I noticed his skin had slightly bronzed from the sun. For the first time, I was able to study the solid wall of tattoos that covered his right pec—Semper Fidelis ran in a bold cursive pattern in the middle of two crossed swords on his bicep. He'd been a Marine. He'd also lost some of the weight around his middle in the last few weeks. If I wasn't so engrossed in my pain, I might have noticed how long his eyelashes were and how they were so dark they looked wet and spread out in a beautiful pattern over his cheek when he looked down at me. If I wasn't in complete agony, I might have noticed the fullness of his lips and the small white scar in a subtle divot on his chin where stubble refused to grow.

"You've been crying for hours."

"I'm fine. Sorry about the noise." I wrapped my arms

around my stomach and bit my lip to keep from moaning. He scanned the porch and pulled the prescription bottle from the table and eyed it. I was too wrapped up to give a damn. Inside my body was unleashing hell.

"What happened? You're hurt?"

"Ian, what do you want?"

Meeting his gaze, I saw eyes filled with concern. It was completely ironic.

"I'm fine." Even as I said it, my voice shook and fresh tears leaked out of my eyes.

He looked at me pointedly for a believable explanation, but I wouldn't bring myself to tell him I had the most painful periods in the history of womankind. And every month I cursed Eve for her treacherous act because of that tempting apple.

Ian opened the bottle and handed me another prescribed pill along with the bottled water I'd left on my table. I took the pill and swallowed it, overwhelmed by a fresh wave of cramping. I bared my teeth and grunted as it hit hard.

"Jesus, Koti, what's wrong?" It was odd seeing his concern for me. We'd remained complete strangers in his first few weeks on the island, yet I had felt the need to protect him from his own hurt. Maybe he was beginning to remember that for a few weeks, and endless summers ago, we *were* childhood friends.

"It will pass. I just want to sleep."

"Okay." He stood watching me shake for several moments before he reluctantly made his way off the porch.

Hours later I awoke in a sweaty heap. The sun had set and the only light was the moon's half glow. When I tried to shift in the hammock, I realized there was an arm wrapped around me. It tightened as I moved to get up.

Ian's smooth voice rumbled behind me. "Feeling better?"

I wanted to ask him what in the hell he was doing. I wanted

to fight him and throw his comforting efforts away as he had mine, but in truth, it felt amazing being in his arms. Suddenly, I was aware of his breath on my neck and the gentle stroke of his fingers on my stomach. The breeze covered us both as I laid mute, too exhausted to argue instead embracing his rare gift of comfort.

"I'm sorry I've been such a bastard," he whispered, his apology sounding sincere. "Sleep."

I eased back into his strong hold as he took small liberties with his fingers. The weight of his body behind me was a reassuring reprieve from the constant ache. He pulled me tighter as the ocean breeze drifted over us. I pressed myself further into him and gripped the hand that stroked me as another debilitating wave took hold. I breathed through it as he murmured into my hair. Body tense, I cried quietly in his arms until I slipped back into an exhausted sleep.

I barely stirred when the hammock moved some time later and when I woke up, I was alone.

A few days later, I emerged from my house feeling as if I'd been through a war. Ian had knocked on my door twice, but I couldn't bring myself to open it. As I walked down the steps to get to my Jeep, I saw him unload a handful of wood onto his deck, his eyes intent on me. "You're better then?"

"Yes, thank you."

Ian's eyes lowered to my sandals. "I see you are still fond of those dreadful gold sandals, but they suit you."

I smiled at him and he back at me.

"Oh, I remember you, puffer fish. And your tacky sandals."

I rolled my eyes. "Well, I'll ignore that snarky comment,

seeing as how you aren't being a *complete* ass today."

In our short summer together, years ago, he'd poked fun at my sandals when I refused to take them off. As a six-year-old, I was convinced my few wardrobe staples in life would be my father's Fruit of the Loom white T-shirts that fell below my knees, gold belt, and matching sandals. I had a thing for Greek mythology, especially Aphrodite and I hadn't really grown out of it.

I shrugged, looking down to admire my new sandals. "Some things don't change."

"But some things do," he said carefully, studying me closely in my spaghetti strap white sundress. The morning sun's effect paled in comparison to the current of heat that swept through me as our eyes locked. Ian broke contact first, pulling a hammer from one of the bags on the porch. With the way he swung that hammer, I felt like I had my very own Greek deity, my own Sucellus in front of me.

He paused his hammer briefly when I ripped my eyes away and moved to leave. "I apologize again," he offered, a small smile on his freshly licked lips, "repeatedly."

"You're forgiven," I said, watching a drop of sweat from the tip of his chin drip down to his navel and disappear below his waistband. I'd never wanted to be a drop of sweat so much in my life. "I'm off to work. If you need anything…"

"Koti, I'll take it from here," he said softly. "Thank you."

"You're welcome."

I lingered in hopes of more conversation, but Ian turned his back and grabbed a box of nails. "Have a good day."

"You too."

Inside my Jeep, I stared at the ocean that lay beyond our houses.

Decades of life separated the two of us and I was more curious than ever of what his years held.

Nine hours later, I came home to a ripped and colorful sky. I went straight from my Jeep to the rocky shore and put my aching feet in the water. I glanced over my shoulder to see the Kemp house was dark. It didn't surprise me in the least. Ian was still struggling with his hurts and didn't want to share them. Pain didn't disappear overnight. He needed time. He had wounds to lick. Another few days of silence between our houses confirmed as much.

ten

Ian

She had to be the most beautiful woman I'd ever seen in my life and that was saying much. I'd been on every continent and to places most human eyes had never seen and even the most exotic-looking women couldn't hold a candle to her. It wasn't just her soul-filled eyes, perfect face, or full lips, her body was every man's dream—petite, toned, curves, day-long legs, and perfect feet. She was a wet dream and the kicker was, she had no knowledge of it or at least didn't use it to her advantage. From what I could tell she hadn't a clue of just how attractive she was. Holding her that day in the hammock, her pained cries had been agony for me. I ended up taking too many liberties with my fingers. I knew how soft the skin of her stomach was. I'd traced the curve of her hips and reveled in the way she fit inside my arms. After hours of studying her beautiful face partially covered by sun-bleached hair, I had to get the hell out of that hammock. I was there to comfort her and grew unbearably hard as the minutes passed. The need to touch her more intimately had my skin on fire. She was in a great deal of pain and though it bothered me to see her in such a state, I had no idea how holding her that way would affect me. And it had, so much so that I couldn't stop fantasizing about her days after.

I slammed the hammer down as I tried to reason with

myself. She looked so beautiful this morning in that dress with freshly glossed lips. My first instinct was to close the space to rid her of it and smear that gloss with my lips and cock.

I wanted her and that was dangerous. I was in no position to offer her anything at all. I simply wasn't ready to begin to trust another woman after what Tara had done to the rest of our relationship. Though it wasn't Koti's fault, I was too angry, too bitter, too unsure of my feelings at that point that a friendship would be pushing it. What was worse, and from what I could tell, the attraction was mutual and she had no idea that just moments ago, I was seconds away from pushing any moral thoughts aside and ravaging her. I discarded the hammer on the porch and laced up my takkies. I needed to clear my head.

Koti had zero place in my life, nor I in hers. I had absolutely no desire to start anything, whether it be sexual or more, with any woman. Keeping my distance would be the only way to avoid a disaster and I was good at that. She'd granted me the space I asked for. In an attempt to wipe thoughts of her away, I began to jog down the beach. I wasn't a teenage boy, I could handle attraction. It was nothing more than appreciation for the beauty that she was. An entanglement of any sort with me would only hurt her. With distance, I could rid myself of the ache to touch her.

I sped up as Koti's lingering gaze flashed through my head. *Fuck.*

Koti

"What in the fack? Koti!"

I hid in my bedroom with repressed laughter as the puppy squealed with cries. As soon as I saw her, I knew who her rightful owner was. It wasn't a man's dog, by any means, but Ian needed a friend and since he was opposed to the human kind, I'd taken it upon myself to get him a suitable companion. As soon as I put her down on Ian's porch in a box she couldn't climb out of, she began to howl bloody murder.

"Just look at her, Ian." I urged in a whisper spying their first meet from my window. I heard the thwack of his back door and a brief pause of silence. I was sure they were staring at each other. More silence followed, before the boom of a loud knock on my door.

"Koti!"

The pooch whimpered in his arms, still traumatized for being a fifteen-minute orphan.

"I'm not dressed," I yelled from the safety of my bedroom.

"Then get dressed!" he ordered.

"I have to shower," I called out toward the door before slipping into my bathroom.

He knocked again ignoring my lies. I went and took an unneeded shower to give them a chance to bond. When I emerged from my room minutes later, all was silent. I peered through my living room window and saw no sign of either of them. Curious, I peeked out of my back door to see if the coast was clear.

"I appreciate what you're trying to do," Ian said with a lifeless voice sitting on my wicker loveseat with the tiny puppy in his lap. He slid thick fingers through her fur while her pink tongue darted out and rewarded his other hand in kind. "But this is the *last* thing I need."

I squared off and stepped onto the porch. "I disagree. Everyone needs a best friend."

"I can't take on this responsibility." His tone was distant, cold, his head down as he stared at the nameless dog.

I spoke up, far too uncomfortable with the pain that still radiated from him. "I was thinking Disco, for a name. She looks like a Disco, doesn't she?"

"Koti," there wasn't an ounce of humor in his voice. Murky gray eyes trailed over my romper. For a flicker of a second, I had his attention and it felt way too rewarding.

"Just give it a week, okay?"

Ian stood from my love seat. Disco was dwarfed by his size, engulfed in his large hands. I inhaled his scent as he towered inches above me, his stubble had grown out slightly, but he never went more than a few days without shaving. In a little over a month, he'd settled nicely into the beach bum look. I was tempted to brush the unruly dark hair away from his brow. I felt inexplicably drawn to him while he stared at Disco as if she were going to speak. Rows of curly white and beige hair made up the most of her. She weighed no more than a few pounds. Her dark chocolate eyes stared back at him before she let out a squeak.

I caught the subtle smile he tried to hide.

Come on, Ian. Can't you see she loves you already? She can give you a thousand of those smiles.

I saw his decision before he spoke. "Again, I appreciate the gesture, but—"

"I'm allergic." *Lie.* "And I couldn't bear to see her homeless." Another lie. I'd paid a fortune for her.

Ian studied me with ill-tempered eyes. It seemed he was immune to my bullshit.

"No."

"Ye-es." I said in a sing-song voice. "She won't be any trouble. Besides you've already entertained a hyena." I grinned cheekily.

He looked confused until he realized I was talking about

his booty call. "Cute."

"What was that hyena's name again?"

Ian rolled his eyes as he gripped Disco and brought her to his face. Nose to nose they assessed each other before she licked him.

"You will get along famously," I cooed, itching to run my fingers through her hair.

Ian sighed and stretched Disco out in front of him. I began to scratch my arms as he held the puffy pooch toward me. "Sorry, can't. I'll break out in hives."

A moment of silence passed between us as we stared each other down in challenge.

"Koti, don't do this, okay? I don't need the hassle."

"You *need* her and she's helpless."

"Damnit, woman, just take her." When I shook my head, a furious Ian left my porch and walked back to his house slamming the door behind him.

Hours later in bed, I heard the puppy cry and cringed with every loud protest, afraid for her because of her temperamental new owner. Who would have thought a dog that little would have such an amazing vocal range? It may not have been the best idea, but it made him accountable for something besides himself. Disco had needs and he would have to meet them and maybe, just for a few minutes a day, it would distract him from that hurt.

Another agonizing hour later, the dog kept two houses on Vista Lane awake.

"Oh, for fack's sake!"

I withered in my bed as Ian's growl drifted between our houses. And then all went quiet. She was sleeping with him. I was sure of it.

Lucky bitch.

The next morning, I slipped out the front door of my house and didn't look back as I tore out of the driveway unable to face the wrath I was sure was coming to me. I was greeted by an equally sleep-deprived Jasmine as she walked through the door with two lattes.

"Double shots," she said, offering me my cup. I took it, grateful.

"How's the puppy?"

"She's adorable and very *vocal.*"

"Oh, no. That bad? You've been looking forward to getting her for a month." Jasmine laughed, studying my face. "Poor thing. You can bring her in tomorrow so we can keep her awake during the day." She took a seat behind her cluttered desk. "I love dogs."

"Yeah, my mom never let me have one when I was a kid. She always said no puppies in the penthouse."

"You've never had a pet?"

"Never."

"Well then, go get her now. You haven't shut up about her, I want to meet her."

"I can't."

Jasmine gave me a sideways glance. "Sure you can. I'll watch her here."

I shrugged as I searched through the schedule. "She's kind of in someone else's custody."

Jasmine pushed away from her desk and crossed her arms. "You gave her away?!"

"I loaned her out."

"To?"

"Ian."

"Really?" A wide smile covered her face. "You've got it bad for him, don't you?"

"Not possible."

"Oh, it's possible," she piped.

I sighed. "Jasmine, he's in the middle of a crisis. The puppy will help. It's no more than that. Maybe I'm just a little curious because, after a month of living next to him, he's still a complete mystery." Aside from the attraction I had for him, he was off-limits in every way. Emotionally unavailable and temperamental were far from on my wish list.

"I'm a little attracted to him. But you know crazy attracts crazy."

"You aren't crazy," she said sharply. "You're just a nervous nelly."

"I left New York and my career because I had a brush with death and now I have an instilled fear of dying. There's a big difference between having a breakdown in Target over the pillow selection and cracking up on *my* level."

Jasmine jerked out of her chair. "You *ass*. I'll have you know that breakdown was legit."

"If you say so."

"Target is the mecca of indecisiveness I'll have you know. That breakdown on *sheet sets* was well warranted."

"Forgive me, I forgot it was sheets. I appreciate you trying to relate, but a breakdown about bed sheets pales in comparison."

"You haven't had an episode in a few months though, right?"

"Yeah," I said thoughtfully. "It's been a little over a month, but that's a very long time for me." I looked her over. "Sorry, I'm sure it was traumatizing for you in Target. I didn't mean to be a jerk. I'm tired. I'm sure your breakdown was legit."

"It wasn't legit, it was PMS." She yawned. "I'm exhausted.

I got *no* sleep because of Chris. He's a sea captain and has a hooked penis."

I swallowed down my latte with a chuckle. "Oh? Do tell."

"And the man's got a thing for Mexican women."

"Please tell me you didn't—"

"Oh, yes I *did*. Last night I was Maria Valdez. I even went as far as reciting some old high school Spanish." She waggled her brows.

"That's wrong on so many levels." I shook my head. "Seriously, you spend half your time correcting people on your ethnicity and you mean to tell me you changed it for curvy cocked Chris?"

Jasmine wrinkled her nose. "Don't say cock, that's gross."

"And penis is clinical," I chided.

"Dick?" She offered as a middle ground.

That time I wrinkled my nose. "Better, but to me, that describes more of a type of personality than the actual body part."

Loud laughter erupted from the door as Toby, our water deliveryman, stood holding our weekly five gallons on his shoulder. "Never a dull moment in here, huh ladies?"

Jasmine didn't miss a beat. "Hey, Toby, what do you call your penis in the heat of the moment?"

I choked on a bite of bagel as he shook his head to ward off her question and switched the water bottles out.

I spoke up glaring at Jasmine. "Sorry Toby, I apologize on her behalf. She was raised by Mrs. Valdez, who ran a brothel in Mexico."

"Har, har," Jasmine snapped before narrowing her eyes at me. "And as far as *that* story goes, I grew up with my aunt in California who lived just over the border." Jasmine walked over to where Toby stood and I cringed. "I'm serious. Toby, are you married?" Toby turned to us with his hands on his hips. He was stocky and a little taller than Jasmine but not by much. He had a teddy bear's build and thick sandy blond hair. One side of his mouth lifted. "Married, no. And you really want to know?"

She nudged him with her shoulder. "Water cooler talk." Toby and I shook our heads fighting a laugh before he assessed Jasmine with a thorough once-over. "Depends."

"On?" Jasmine's voice was syrupy sweet, and I rolled my eyes at her as she looked on at Toby unashamed and entertained.

"On how dirty the sex is," Toby replied boldly.

Jasmine's dark eyes fixed on his lips as he spoke. "If it's dirty…"

Even I was leaning forward as Toby sucked all the air out of the room. "I mean if it's *really* dirty…"

"Yes?" we said in unison. He leaned over and began whispering in her ear. She nodded as she kept her playful brown eyes on me. My bagel became chalk in my mouth as the two whispered back and forth before I swallowed and demanded an answer. "Well?"

Jasmine's mouth dropped as he leaned in one last time and whispered to her suggestively before he gave me a departing wink and walked out the door.

Her impossibly tan face turned crimson.

"Well?"

"It's cock."

"One point, Koti. I *told* you."

"I think my breasts are sweating," she said, fanning her boobs. "Did you feel the heat coming off of that one?"

I was definitely feeling… *something.* "Is it weird that just made me hot?"

Jasmine shook her head and we both laughed. "Babe, I would be worried about you if you weren't. Phew," she picked up one of our brochures and used it as a makeshift fan for her sweaty breasts. "Who knew the water boy had it in him? Then again that is the basis for good porn."

"You are something else you know that? Get a grip, Gersch. Your escapades have turned you into a pervert."

"Cock…" she practiced shaking her head and wrinkling her nose. "Cock." She pushed her voice up a decibel. "Cock." She looked over to me. "It sounds weird, right? In no way, does that sound sexy coming out of my mouth"

"Maybe it's the Minnesota in you. It sounds more like you're saying caulk."

"Cock," she repeated, shaking her head again as I buried my head between my hands and pressed my forehead to my desk. Her voice was low as she spoke it again. "Cock." She practiced again and I banged my head on my desk. "Cock," she repeated until… "Nope, it's penis."

eleven

Koti

After work, because it had been a decent day and I felt I had the strength to handle it, I answered my phone as I was stripping down for a shower.

"Hi, Mom." I unbuttoned my shorts and slid them off before I laid on my bed in a sweaty heap.

"Koti, Troy Emerick wants to meet with you!" I ignored her attempt at getting straight down to business without greeting pleasantries and went on a spiel of my own.

"I'm fine. The weather is great. I think we may get some rain, which we need. Work is good. We're gaining clients daily."

"Koti." Her voice held that sharpness I'd grown used to but had also become immune to.

"This is Troy Emerick, you know he's one of the best agents in New York. He's agreed to meet with you as a favor to me."

"Thank you, but I'm happy here. I wish you hadn't called in that favor on my account."

"What you're doing with your life is not sustainable forever."

"I disagree," I said, turning to study my body in the full-length mirror. It was a far cry from the stick thin skeleton frame it was a year ago. The circles under my eyes had disappeared. I'd gained the twenty pounds I needed to resemble healthy. I wondered if for one second my mother would forget her ambitions for me and notice the difference if she saw the new state I was in, or if it would even matter. "Mom, I'm in my underwear ready for a shower, can I call you back?"

"No, because you won't." I gritted my teeth but held in my impatient sigh as she continued. "He can get you back in. You might have to—"

"Mother, I already sold my soul. New York has it, okay? I'm never going back." I took a deep breath in an attempt to ignore the stirring tension in my limbs.

"Okay, Koti, it's been long enough. I've talked to your father and we need you to come back to discuss your future." And there it was. I was sure it took a good amount of her strength to be a concerned parent first and put expectant on the back burner. Apparently, a year was her limit.

But she hadn't been there, not in the way I needed her. And though my father tried, he couldn't understand just how that day had changed me. I had a hard enough time coming to grips with it myself.

At that moment, I remembered running through endless faces in the freezing cold with a box full of my belongings in six-hundred-dollar heels, my face pouring defeat, my heart pounding out of my chest, passing stranger after stranger, the words 'help me' on my lips and not a single soul around who gave a shit. After wandering aimlessly around New York for hours without a future, I tossed the box that held my degree in the garbage and sat in front of it in the cold until my limbs went numb.

"Mom, I'm a little old for this talk of my future. If you're going to threaten to take away the house, I'm prepared for that, so go ahead and do it. I'm too old to map out my life, instead, I'm living it. Here in St. Thomas. This is my future. Whatever issues you have with my failure, you're just going to have to deal with it, like I have."

"Deal with it!? You ran away!" Her breathing was erratic. She had totally planned to play the house card. But how much of a threat would it be anyway if the stipulation was to return to New York?

"Are you taking the house away?" I pressed on, unafraid of what she would say. There was nothing she could do to me that the world hadn't done already.

"Of course not, Koti," she feigned offense.

I heard my father ask to speak to me. That card I wasn't ready for. He was still disappointed I lied to him with my promise to come home for Christmas.

"I have to go, Mom. I have a renter calling."

"Koti! We haven't seen you in a year! You're breaking your father's heart."

"I know, Mom, and I'm sorry. I've already apologized for that. I'm not ready."

"Koti." My father's voice was a mix of concern and growing impatience for both of us, I was sure.

"Dad, I'm sorry I can't talk now."

"Listen to me, you either get on a plane or we will."

"Dad, I have to work," I said weakly, his deep voice piercing my heart. "I can't just leave; my boss depends on me."

"No more excuses on either side." I knew his stern words were also meant for my mother, who I was sure was the reason my father hadn't already shown up in St. Thomas. I knew she was sure I would come running back for financial help, guidance, or both. Another disappointment for her.

"I need to see my little girl."

His words struck hard and I did my best not to let him hear it. "Soon, Dad, I promise. I love you both. I've got to go."

"Koti—"

"Dad, I'll call you back. I love you." I hung up as my

heartbeat sped up and my face flamed.

I lay back in bed panting, a tear rolling down my cheek. In and out. Breathe. *Nothing's wrong. Nothing's wrong. You're okay. You're okay.*

"Nothing's wrong."

One, two, three, four, five, six, seven.

Five. Ten. Fifteen minutes passed before I lifted my newly drained bones off the bed and submerged them in a shower. Twenty minutes and half a Xanax later, I was dead to the world.

Disco barked as I turned on my side and looked out the window toward the Kemp house before glancing at the clock.

2 a.m.

Unable to handle her yapping, I ripped myself away from the bed and slid on my flip-flops.

I could feel the tension behind the door before I knocked. Seconds later, a T-shirt clad Ian answered with wide, helpless eyes.

"Have you picked her up?" I pushed past him to see Disco in her box in the middle of the living room. "Ian, she can't see that you're here and that's why she's freaking out!"

"Well, she pisses and shats everywhere!"

"She's a puppy," I said, pulling her from her prison. "You have to take her outside every hour or so and reward her when she pees or poops."

"I'm well aware," he snapped. "So, you take her."

"I can't, I'm allergic," I said with a mock cough. He crossed his arms as I held the dog toward him. Disco whimpered and scrambled in my grip before she leaped at him. He was forced to catch her and when he did, I could see the delight cover his face. He was reluctantly smitten. He looked over at me with narrowed eyes. "You are conniving."

"Thank you, I do my best. This is a puppy we are talking about here," I said, looking at the dog with longing. "Puppy breath, puppy love. Seriously, don't miss out on this."

He raised a thick brow and looked down at my camisole top before he averted his eyes without a single tell. Had I gone over there in my skimpiest camisole on purpose?

Absolutely... not.

But my breasts were the elephant that now sat on the puppy at hand.

Disco lay quietly in his grip.

"See, she just needed some love," I said, feathering her soft fur through my fingers. I leaned down and kissed her forehead before I looked up at a surprisingly close Ian. "Disco needs you, crocky."

He rolled his eyes as I spotted a large dry erase board behind him.

"What's this?"

Ian cradled Disco in his arm and stepped in front of me to obstruct my view of the board. "Just something I'm working on."

I tilted my head. "Why so secretive? I've already seen you at war, Marine."

His lips twitched in amusement. "That was years ago." His eyes strayed down to his stomach. I saw his disappointment and felt my heart rip slightly at the degrading evaluation he gave himself. So he'd gained a few pounds since his service. No big deal. He'd already lost quite a bit of it in the month he'd been on the island. And I found it admirable that he served at all. Little love handles aside, the man was drop-dead gorgeous. He had to know that. But I wasn't going to leave it unsaid, I'd been a victim of self-image awareness my whole life. So, what did I do to make sure he knew he still had it?

"Ouch! What in the hell are you doing, woman?"

My hand burned as I lifted my reddened palm away from his firm ass and presented it to him, "Still got it, eh?"

Not my best move, but when Ian Kemp threw his head back and laughed, a wave of pure bliss washed over me.

Ignoring the urge to kiss his prominent Adam's apple, I shrugged as if I went around slapping men's asses on a daily basis. I sidestepped him as he kept Disco snug in his arms and looked at the board. There was a list of lecture topics and keynotes.

I nodded toward it in question.

"It's a course shcedule. I teach."

"Shcedule?" I grinned, and he grinned back.

"Right, you always had a thing for my accent."

"Doesn't every red-blooded American woman? I bet you cleaned up with the ladies *very* well in Texas." I gave him a wink and his answering grin didn't deny it.

My whole body tensed at the sight of his smile. Angry with my horny self, I moved to the defensive. "And your accent has faded a little, what a pity." He gave me that all-knowing stare again. The one that told me he knew my next words before I spoke them. I walked over to the board and felt his eyes on me.

"I blame Texas."

"South Africa to Dallas, what in the world made your parents make that move?"

"We went there initially to wait for my brother, the birth mother lived there."

"Your parents told me a little about him last summer, I forgot his name...?"

"Adam. He's adopted. My parents and I waited in Dallas for

the length of the pregnancy. They got acclimated. I hated it, but we stayed."

"Too hot?"

"I can handle hot," he said, looking over the list on the board before he took a step forward with Disco cradled in his free arm and erased one of the notes. "The academics were lacking. I was several levels ahead, and it was all very boring."

"I remember you griping about not being able to safari on the weekend. No chance of lions invading Dallas then?" He threw his head back at my shitty attempt at his accent. I felt like I was batting a thousand every time I heard that sweet rumble erupt from his chest.

"No, there wasn't much adventure for me in the concrete jungle."

"I could say different about where I came from. I suffered from overstimulation. What do you teach?"

"Linguistics and American Sign Language and sometimes I dabble in creative writing."

"Professor Kemp?" I mused, unable to picture him instructing a classroom. "You went from the Marines to teach?"

"Actually, it was my wife's doing. My *ex*-wife, Tara. When we discovered our daughter was deaf, I dabbled in speech, speech pathology, audiology, and linguistics. She pushed me in the direction of teaching. I used to write letters to her when I was stationed overseas. She thought I had a knack for it."

"So, you started it mostly for your daughter?"

He nodded. "I taught some classes at her school for a few years when she began attending."

"Sign language is fascinating."

He nodded thoughtfully and let Disco free. She ran straight toward me and jumped through my feet attacking my flip-flops.

"I agree. I spent years studying the language and the culture.

And with Ella's disability, it seemed a natural progression," he shrugged.

"None of this is impressive at all," I said sarcastically.

"Tara was more in tune with the Marine, I think. Her pursuit for me career-wise actually backfired."

"Did you see yourself in this career?"

"I didn't see myself as anything. I joined the Marines to buy time to figure it out."

"And just so happened to finish some of the hardest military training in the world?"

Ian shrugged. "It was either that or go to college for a useless degree."

"Touché."

"Pardon?"

"I agree with you. I am a proud owner of one of those useless degrees."

He winced. "Sorry."

"I'm not. I'm glad I'm not wasting any more time." I nodded toward his full erase board. "So, teach me something, professor."

"This doesn't interest you."

"Everything interests me." I scooped up Disco and took a seat on the corner of his couch. "Were you practicing in here?"

He scrunched his nose as if he smelled something bad. "Practicing? I don't need practice. This is a list of lectures."

"Where do you teach now?"

"Nowhere at the moment. I'm hoping for a position at my daughter's new school."

"So, teach me, here, in St. Thomas."

Ian bit his lips and shoved his hands in his pockets. "I know what you're doing. Did my mother put you up to this?"

"Yes, your mother prodded Disco to whine all night and forced me over here to snoop at your dry erase board. My education awaits, Professor Kemp."

"And what was your major?"

"I got a master's in business, got my real estate license, joined a firm and blew a $2 billion deal because I had a panic attack. I should have joined the Marines, it might have made a better woman out of me. Now, teach me something."

Ian looked down at me skeptically. "It's late."

"I'm wide awake," I said, eyeing the collection of books stacked on the TV stand. "If you won't teach me anything, how about we start a book club?"

"What do you read?"

"Everything. Lots of historical romance lately."

"Really?" His demeanor changed and his shoulders relaxed. He was no longer on the defensive.

"Yes, historical romance. What's wrong with that? You learn something *and* the boy gets the girl, but not before the widespread panic, famine, cannibalism, cholera, the Nazis, and of course, the hurdled forty or fifty life-threatening situations."

Ian tilted his head back again. The rumble of his laughter my new driving force.

"So, will you teach me how to sign?"

"Maybe," he said as he playfully squared his shoulders, "it depends, Mrs. Vaughn…"

"*Miss.*" I pressed my lips together wondering if he remembered his remark the day we met.

Ian's lips twitched. *He did.* But he had enough tact not to stare at my miss tits.

We shared another smile, this one was far more intimate. Awareness of the unwanted distance between us began to creep into my thoughts.

Was I crushing on Ian Kemp? If so, I was developing a crush on the *mid-life* professor. And that wasn't healthy for either of us.

"I should go. Thank you for the lesson."

"I taught you nothing."

"You don't give yourself enough credit, Professor Kemp."

"Koti." His voice was glum, to say the least. I paused my feet at the door and glanced his way. "If we are going to engage in any sort of conversation, for future reference, I want honesty over everything. That's important to me, all right?"

I stared at my toes. "All right." A beat passed before I could brave another a look at him. I'd become acutely aware of my body's response to his smile, his laugh, his voice. "Can I ask you something?"

"Sure." He took a step forward closing the space between us and my breathing picked up. I studied the sprinkle of hair on his navel that trailed down past the button on his shorts while I savored his smell—new leather and soap—and wished for a few moments we were back in that hammock so I would be surround-ed in it, in *him*. I blinked the thought away and cleared my throat.

Ian seemed eager as he studied my face. "What do you want to ask me?"

"Are you okay?"

I braved a look and what I saw wasn't the scorn or the ev-er-present bitterness he carried, it was genuine curiosity. And for the first time since Ian landed on my island, I felt like I had his undivided attention.

"Why are you concerned about me?"

I could have told him I was paid to be worried about him. But that really wasn't the truth. I was paid to keep an eye on him, but that was the extent of it. My concern stemmed from somewhere else. A place I recognized, a place I felt like Ian was drowning in.

The lump I tried to speak around kept me quiet for a few mo-ments. And then I gave him exactly what he asked for—honesty.

"Before I came here, I had a really shitty thing happen, the kind of thing that breaks people. I think you're familiar with that." He slowly nodded. "Well, I was alone—alone in a way no human should ever be—and I needed just *one* person to ask me that question. I was surrounded by thousands of people, but I just needed *one*. And I decided I wanted to be that person for you. Because I *do* want to know. Because I am worried for you and about you. Because you deserve to have that question asked. So, Ian, are you okay?"

He didn't hesitate a second. "No."

Tense moments passed as we stared at each other. "And what will you do with that answer, Koti?"

"I'll keep it in confidence. I'll respect your need for privacy and I'll ask you until you say you are, or you could be, or you might be someday."

Lost in his eyes, in the hurt they held, in the clench of his jaw, and the answer to his pain on his un-telling lips, he whispered to me. "I can't say those things."

"Then I won't stop asking you."

He hung his head and let out an audible breath. "It's not your job to care about me."

"See, this is where I disagree." I reached over and gripped his hand and gently squeezed it. He tensed slightly. "What made you lay next to me in that hammock?"

"I don't know." He bit his lip as he browsed through his thoughts. "You were in pain. You were crying. It was the most agonizing sound I'd ever heard."

"Okay, well what I saw in those eyes of yours the day you got here is the worst pain I've ever witnessed, Ian Kemp. And it's everybody's *job*, isn't it?"

I slid my thumb over the top of his hand. "I mean, we are all just extras sipping coffee in the background of someone else's life. But that could change at any second. If I wanted to, I could put my coffee down and become responsible for you. We are *all* responsible. We could all choose to take responsibility, couldn't we? Human compassion. What the hell happened to that?"

Ian pressed his brows together while I got lost in my thoughts.

I wasn't sure how much time passed before I finally snapped out of it and slowly pulled my hand away. Ian's twisted face was a thing of beauty. I felt the blush creep through my cheeks at my rant and then even more so by his close scrutiny.

"Never mind, I'm talking nonsense to you. Goodnight."

He opened his mouth to speak, maybe to address one of the hundred questions I saw in his eyes but kept them to himself and instead responded with a curt, "Goodnight."

Great, Koti, way to go. You sounded like a philosophical moron.

Taking my leave, I walked across the sand and back to solitude where I felt safer with my own ramblings. I felt his watchful eyes on me from where he stood on his porch. Maybe I should have been more embarrassed and a little more careful with the words I spoke. But in the last year of my life, I'd recognized my flaws and the depth of my narcissism while I licked my own wounds. After a hard look, I didn't like a tenth of what I'd become. I saw my flaws, my differences and discovered a few of my strengths too. I was done with certain parts of myself that were a product of expectation. And what was left was a woman who embraced vulnerability, her idiosyncrasies, her ticking clock, *and* treacherous body.

In a way, I was proud for speaking up, especially to a man who was afraid to show his own defeat and weakness. If I had to write the story of my life post-apocalyptic Koti Vaughn, it *would* be of a story of hope.

It would be human. And that's all I wanted to be. Striving for perfection had cost me enough sanity.

twelve

Koti

There's a name for human awareness and it's called Sonder.

The definition: the realization that each random passerby is living a life as vivid and complex as your own—populated with their own ambitions, friends, routines, worries and inherited craziness—an epic story that continues invisibly around you like an anthill sprawling deep underground. It's a pocket in time, where you may redefine life by the idea of the struggle of others.

My time in my own purgatory, battling my anxiety and the crumble of my planned future had taught me to reflect not only on my own mess but on the life of my parents and their triumphs and failures. And after that in-depth analysis where I had to forgive them and myself, I paid close attention to everyone I came in contact with. It changed me in a way I couldn't ignore. It was a deep, emotional cleansing and one that I could never take lightly.

Everyone, at some point in their life, gets lost in their own head, whether it be a low or high point where they are looking down at the path they'd chosen. This type of reflection led me to the train of thought that brought me to revisit my first substantial memory.

My first foggy recollection as a child was getting stung by

a wasp. I remembered being too small to open the door of my parents' Hamptons house and the relief I felt when my mother rescued me. I remembered her quieting my cries as she looked down at me with tender eyes and a soothing voice while she sprinkled powder on my bite to get the sting out. And I remembered very little after, just the lingering feeling that I was safe.

In searching through those memories, I remembered a bike ride on top of the handlebars and somewhere between that, a string of nights spent with my mother in bed when I got the flu. She'd kicked my father out of their room and slept with me. I could still feel her cold hands on my hot back. A few childhood friends drifted through my memories as well, not exact memories but words and gestures, indistinct moments in places I couldn't remember. One of my classmates had died of pneumonia. She had blonde curly hair and big dimples. When she passed, I was observed by the adults around me in such a way I knew I was expected to grieve. Because of that expectation, I pretended to cry, but the concept of death was lost on me. I recall feeling bad as the casket was lowered to the ground because I felt nothing and everyone around me wasn't pretending. Their tears were real. It was the first time I felt guilty.

Everyone had those moments, where those bits and pieces surfaced, and memories were triggered, some of them more significant than others. Some of them a mystery as to why they stood out from the rest. Three hundred and sixty-five days a year, twenty-four hours in a day. What would I remember when I was forty?

It seemed incomprehensible no matter how well you know another person, that you could never fully understand them, and what memories they kept and *why* they were significant. I had no idea what my friend's name was that passed away, no idea whose handlebars I was riding on, but I do know the most vivid childhood memory I held was the day I met Ian Kemp.

"Good morning."

Ian greeted me as I stood on my back porch sipping a cup of coffee in light cotton sleep shorts and the same cami I had on the night before. The waves rolled in and crashed against the rocky shore in front of me. I was far too deep in my reverie to do anything more than lift my cup and give him a low reply. "Morning."

"Listen," Ian said, stepping off his porch and making his way toward me, forcing me back into the moment. Delighted that his shirt was inevitably off, his newly tanned feet made good time between our houses. He stood on the bottom step of my porch, his back to the rail as he followed my line of sight and studied the waves with me. "Last night. You took me by surprise, but I want you to know I understood what you were saying."

"Okay." I rolled my eyes as I wrapped my arms around myself, still holding my cup as a buffer between us. No matter how determined I was to be unapologetic about my newly adopted philosophies, I still felt a bit self-conscious about sharing that new part of myself, about voicing my thoughts to those who might not be so receptive or understanding.

"There's no reason to get defensive."

I shrugged, looking down at my cup. "Sorry." I didn't want to reveal more than I already had, but I couldn't pretend I wasn't slightly embarrassed. "I haven't ever really said those things *out loud*. But if you are thinking I'm the weirdo hippie with healing crystals, who is walking around concerned about higher consciousness, you are barking up the *right* tree."

"You have no idea what I'm thinking," he said softly.

Unable to believe his sincerity, I defended myself. "I'm not some quack, you know. I lived years out there, in that world." I gestured toward the ocean. "And I decided to unplug. A lot of people are doing it and we all have our reasons."

"Again," he said, taking another step up. "You don't know what I'm thinking."

"I'm pretty sure you've labeled me the crazy lady next door."

"No," he said, taking another step and taking my cup away from me. "I don't think you're crazy at all. There is absolutely *nothing* wrong with doing a little soul-searching."

Soul-searching?

Soul-searching.

I'd spent the last year inside myself, and at times questioned if I was losing my mind.

In mere seconds he had simplified it so... *perfectly.*

Soul-searching!

I chuckled at how naïve I'd been to expect that no one else would understand what I was going through and felt a weight lift from my shoulders. Ian had just put it all into perspective in seconds.

In that moment, I wanted to throw my arms around him in gratitude. Instead, I watched him as he took a sip of my coffee. "Oh, man this brew could kill a horse."

"Like it?"

"Hell yes."

I grinned, and he grinned back keeping my cup in his hand. He glanced at me over the lifted cup before he spoke. "In my creative writing class, I deal with a lot of saturated minds and half of their problem is they want to expand those minds past the walls they built around themselves to become better people, better writers, but how do they do that? What tools could I give them?"

"You can't, right? They have to experience things for themselves, figure out how to open their own minds."

He nodded. "And that's exactly what I tell them. Unless they want their intellectual palate to be the size of the box of knowledge they already possess, they have to get out there and gain some real-life experience to add to that imagination. It's what makes the writing authentic and original."

"Can't write about a broken heart as well as a broken heart can?"

"Precisely. How do you ever really know true living if you do it vicariously?" He looked at me attentively. "And what if... what if that person sipping coffee in the background of your life, what if they," he said pausing to take another sip, "are the next chapter?"

My heart galloped as I stuttered through my next sentence. "So, w-what you're saying," I managed to mutter keeping my door opened for his invitation, "is that you get what I was saying."

He chuckled as he followed me into the house, and I pulled another mug from my cabinet pouring us both a fresh cup. We sat there wordlessly sipping for a few minutes. I glanced over at him, but his eyes remained fixed on the sea.

"This place," he said low before shifting his gaze to mine, "I never really appreciated how beautiful it was until *now*."

Heart hammering, I made quick work of changing the subject. Some part of me knew that I was seconds away from offering Ian more than coffee and small talk. The way he undressed me with his eyes, not only to my bare skin but deeper, had me squirming where I stood.

"You know, Ian, you said something to me when we were kids that stuck with me."

"Oh?" The twinkle in his eye was gratification enough, but I still paid him the compliment.

"You were only, what, fourteen?"

He nodded.

"You told me even if I was mad, or humiliated, or scared to

have fun anyway."

He grinned at the thought, surprised. "I did?"

I nodded. "You did. Pretty insightful for a kid who told me I didn't have tits big enough to be called a miss." Ian chuckled and it made my stomach flutter.

"You made a bit of an impression on me," I confessed, my back to him while I dug through my cabinet and threw the ingredients on the counter. Turning back to him satisfied, I saw his face light up in recognition.

"You're an addict," he commented as he saw the mass amounts of chocolate, marshmallows, and graham crackers I kept on hand.

"I told you, you didn't give yourself enough credit, Professor Kemp. You taught me well."

He gawked at the massive pile of chocolate on my multi-colored tile island. "So, are we dining on s'mores for breakfast, then?"

Disco chose that moment to raise the Devil's hell from her box in his living room. "Guess not," he said with the shake of his head.

"I would go get her, but I'm allergic."

"And full of shit. You are a terrible liar and that's a wonderful thing, Koti."

Ian put his empty cup on the counter and moved to free Disco from her box of shackles. He paused at my back door. "How about tonight? I'll set up one of our bonfires for old times' sake?"

"I was beginning to think you forgot."

His grin took my breath. "Quite the opposite."

My chest filled with warmth. "Okay, but how about you use regular wood this time?"

He gave me a guilty smile. "Agreed." He glanced around the

room and then back to me. "There are no crystals in here."

"Made you look though," I retorted playfully.

"Koti?"

"Yeah?"

"Thanks for asking me." Penetrating silver eyes stared me down and I had to force myself to speak.

"You really *do* get it, don't you, Ian?"

"I really do. I'll see you tonight?"

"See you, professor."

thirteen

Koti

I spent the day running around like a mad woman with Jasmine by my side. Her car had been vandalized at the grocery store where she had left it the night before to meet her date.

"Okay, I'm going to tell you about last night," she said with a sigh.

"You banged a bag boy?" I asked, glancing toward the grocery store.

She turned to me, her dark hair tied up in a bun on top of her head, clad in an electric blue dress. She was rummaging through her thirty-gallon purse. "Me and the captain's love affair is officially over."

"So soon?"

"You're judging me," she snapped as she searched through the massive purse in her lap.

"Do you check for dead mice in there from time to time?" Jasmine thumped my shoulder and I gripped it with a shriek. "Oww, that shit hurt."

"So did last night," she said, wincing.

"Oh Lord. The freak came out of him?"

She nodded, managing to pry three pairs of shades out of her bright red bag. She picked through them as I started the Jeep. "That's exactly what happened."

"Jasmine, it's nine in the morning. Can't I be spared until at least noon?"

"I promise not to show you my ass."

"That's your idea of mercy?" I glanced at her as I turned out of the parking lot and she pushed out her bottom lip. "Okay, tell me."

"The captain decided he wanted to role play."

"Oh?"

"Yes, and you know me, I'm down with that."

"Right up your backhoe," I said with a grin.

"Are you ever going to let me live that down?"

"Not likely, please continue."

"So, I'm expecting like dirty French maid and millionaire boss or something juicy like that."

"Okay."

"And I was right."

"Sounds good."

"Except what the captain really meant was a role reversal."

My eyes widened. "Oh?"

Her lips were trembling as she fessed up. "He came out in heels and a frilly frock."

"Oh, my God!" We both burst into hysterical laughter as Jasmine shook her head with her hands covering her face. "I had no idea what to do. I just stood there while his crooked penis poked out of the apron. I'm telling you as blunt as I am, I lost it. I completely lost the ability to speak."

"What did you do?"

"I ran. I picked up my purse and RAN!"

I pulled over at a gas station and face planted into my steering wheel. "You have got to be kidding me!"

"Nope. I walked it off until I could think to call a cab and went straight to the wine bar. There I met Mark and only let him get to first base before I passed out in his hot tub."

I couldn't contain myself, tears were pouring from my eyes as she wiped her own away.

I sighed, my laughter subsiding slightly. "Poor baby," I said, leaning over to hug her to me. "You are something else, lady. And you should have called me. I would have come to get you."

"I'll never be the same," she said mournfully.

"It's probably for the best."

"This is weird," Jasmine said, noticing the missing key from the lockbox at the Harper rental. "They should have left it at checkout."

She knocked on the front door and when she got no answer, she looked at me with a shrug.

"You don't have the master?"

"I haven't been home," she said sheepishly. "Or to the office, remember?"

"That's right, you were up late watching the Discovery Channel."

"Shut up, or you're fired," she snapped. "Crap. Let me see if I can hop the deck. This is my bad." We walked the side of the cliff house and I stood in the driveway as she made her way toward the upper deck. There was only a narrow margin for her to get her footing on the ledge.

"Don't! Not smart, lady!"

"I've got this." She tucked her cotton dress between her legs and scaled the deck like a pro.

"I give it a six at best. Sloppy landing," I piped as I saw her head pop up behind it.

She shot me the bird.

"Hurry up, it's hot out here!" I ordered. The sun was beating down on the top of my head and I moved to step into the shade when I heard Jasmine's blood-curdling scream.

"What's wrong?!" I yelled loud enough for the street to hear.

"Koti, oh, my GOD! KOTI!"

"What's wrong? What is it?!" I scrambled to the deck and tried to peek over.

"KOTI!"

"Open the front door, JASMINE! Please!"

"OH, MY GOD! Koti! Don't come in!"

Fearing for her life, I risked my own and leaped to the ledge of the deck holding on for dear life. My execution was far less graceful, I went over like an old maid clinging to the top of the railing before I landed on my ass. Jasmine was still screaming as I jumped to my feet, ran around the side of the house and came to a screeching halt at her back. "OH, MY GOD!"

Eighty-three-year-old John Harper lay in a deck chair spread eagle and naked as the day he was born, his dick standing at attention for all the world to see. I covered Jasmine's eyes. "I'm so sorry, sir. I apologize. We must have had our schedules mixed up." I turned Jasmine back the way we came as she ripped my arms away.

"What are you doing?" I bulged my eyes. "He's naked, come on."

With her next words, her voice got eerily calm. "I'll meet you out front, okay?"

"Ugh, the man obviously needs some privacy."

"Koti," she took my shoulders in her hands. "Honey, he's dead."

"Dead?" I glanced over my shoulder and saw his mouth was wide open.

"Oh, my God."

Jasmine was nodding slowly, weighing my reaction as my scrambled brain tried to process the sight before us.

"Are you sure?"

"Yes, honey, he's gone. I'll call an ambulance and meet you out front, okay?"

A towel lay a few feet from where he expired, and I picked it up quickly and covered his saluting soldier. My heart ripped at the sight of him. "Oh no, poor Mr. Harper. I'm so sorry."

Jasmine bowed her head. "I have to live with that image for the rest of my life."

"Jasmine!" I scolded as she pulled out her phone from her boobs and frantically dialed emergency services.

As she explained our situation, I took a seat next to Mr. Harper and took in the view he was blankly staring at. If that wasn't the way to go, I didn't know what was. He'd probably just taken a swim and sat down to dry off. In the distant water, a whale breached just as Jasmine came back into view, her shoulders slumped.

"You scared the hell out of me. I thought you were being attacked."

"All I saw was an old man's penis. It was horrific."

I glowered at her. "Can you please have a little respect here? This poor man just died."

"He was what, early eighties? And he died rich," she shrugged. "He definitely didn't read the warning on the Viagra box."

"Jasmine?!"

"What?!"

"I really can't handle this today." She made her way inside the house and raided the cabinets until she found a bottle of vodka. She poured herself a healthy cup as the emergency sirens sounded down the street.

She drank a half glass and then downed the orange juice in the fridge.

Crossing my arms at the sliding glass door that separated the patio and large kitchen, I watched her fill another glass of juice. "Hope it wasn't the OJ that did it."

She sprayed the juice all over the counter before she gave me the stink eye. "Now you've got jokes." She scrutinized me. "Wait, why are you okay?"

"I don't know. Just go with it."

She nodded.

I moved to again sit next to Mr. Harper. The silent blue water seemed appropriate for the cloudless sky.

Another whale breached in the distance. I saw the large fin as it flipped on its side before disappearing below the deep blue surface.

Without glancing his way, I spoke to him. "I hope you got to see them before you went."

The whole situation was completely depressing. John Harper might have been wealthy, but he was alone when he died. Alone with his fortune and his twenty-million-dollar view. Suddenly nothing about the water calmed me and my whole body broke out into a sweat.

Did he die knowing he was loved? Did he sit on that chair and mentally list his regrets? Did he call for help? I sat up as my throat began to burn. What if we could have helped him if we'd shown up a few minutes before. I looked over at his gaping mouth and sprang from the seat, my heart pounding.

"Koti?"

"I…" I held my chest as Jasmine crossed the deck to get to me. I stood mute as a wave of nausea hit. My chest tightened unbearably, and I looked to her in a full-fledged panic. "He was alone! That's not right. It's not right!"

"Koti," Jasmine said with a small shake in her voice. "Baby, you can't take this into yourself."

"What if we could have helped him?"

"It happens. This stuff happens," she said in a soothing voice as the sirens grew closer. "Try and calm down."

"You know I *hate* that! Don't tell me to calm down!"

"Okay babe, you're having a freak-out. It's cool. I'm here. Deep breaths." She got to me just before my legs gave out and gripped me tightly to her.

"No."

"It's okay," she said, gripping my hand. "Let's just breathe."

"Get away from me, please. I *can't* breathe."

"Koti, you *are* breathing. Come on, baby, just breathe. You can do this."

"He was alone!"

"I know. I'm sorry I made a joke. In... out. You can do this."

"I don't have my pills."

"You don't need them, you've gone all this time without them. It's just life. Let's make it through this. Come on buddy, breathe."

"Get away from me!" I shrieked, trying to pull away, but she held on tighter. The sirens blared outside the house as I began to melt down.

"Okay, Koti, listen," Jasmine said softly "everything is okay."

My body shook uncontrollably as I continued to try to yank my hand away. She stood undeterred. "Breathe, one, two, three..."

Pound. Pound. Pound.

"The door is open!" Jasmine yelled while she kept me captive in her stare and instruction.

"Please let me go."

"Can you walk over to the couch?"

I pulled away from her as the medic emerged from the patio door and eyed us.

Jasmine, still engaging me fully, nodded toward the chair that held Mr. Harper. The man rushed to his side as his partner looked at me. I averted my eyes as I breathed in again trying to calm myself.

"Panic attack," she mouthed to the second medic.

Instantly furious but unable to control my breathing or the shaking, I took steady breaths and let Jasmine walk me to the couch. "Sit tight, okay. I'll take care of this."

"It's my worse fear," I said, hot tears trailing down my face.

"I know."

She picked up my hand and kissed it before she gently pushed me back into the cushions.

"I'll be right back."

"Jasmine," I pleaded knowing I was making a fool of myself.

"I'll be right back, Koti."

I drew my knees up as my body quaked and took breaths until the fatigue set in.

fourteen

Koti

"**I**'m sorry," I said, staring at the mismatched houses that flew by us as Jasmine drove us to the office a short time later.

"Stop."

"I'm so embarrassed," I admitted.

"Stop it," Jasmine said firmly.

"Why can't I just make jokes like you or throw up like normal people?"

She let out a loud laugh. "You think I'm normal? Babe, please. My mother was a nurse. Her calm reaction would have made us both look crazy."

"I *feel* crazy."

"You are a little bit. That's how you deal with things. I make jokes. Who knows what other people would have done in that situation."

"Stop trying to make me feel better." My limbs ached. I could barely keep my eyes open. "Why do you even deal with me?"

"Trade-off, you save me right back. I'm pretty selfish. That's how this works."

I let out a long breath and turned down the radio she'd just turned on.

"Where did he go, when he died, where did he go?"

"I don't know."

"That's the worst part," I swallowed as the fear began to resurface, "we don't know for sure. We don't know, and even the truest of most faithful believers aren't certain there's a heaven or hell or just darkness. And if it's just darkness, are we aware of it? We get to know *nothing* except that death is every single living creature's fate. The thing I'm most afraid of in the world is the one thing that is inevitably going to happen to me and everyone I love. I get to know nothing else."

"We all have that disadvantage, no one knows for sure."

"But you aren't afraid to die. You've just accepted it. And you live every day of your life not worried about it."

"Give yourself credit, kid. You've done a damn good job curbing your fears this past year."

"I know, but then today this happens and I'm more terrified than ever."

She grabbed my hand and held it. "I wish I could say something that would change this for you, Koti, but I can't."

"I know," I said tearfully. "Some days I feel like our creator is the cruelest with the rules and some days I can't believe how amazing this world is. Ya know? It's like here, enjoy this life while I give it to you but be careful because at any moment I can take it away and you don't get to know what's next. And then there's religion and what if it's wrong, or if it's *right* and all the people who don't believe have this horrible fate because they are realists and need proof?"

"Deep breaths, Koti."

"Okay, okay, I'm sorry."

"Stop it. Don't be sorry. These are all valid questions. You aren't crazy."

"I *feel* crazy."

"You're human. You have thanatophobia. It wouldn't be a

phobia if you were the only one. There are millions of people with the same fear."

I swallowed and nodded.

"And your anxiety makes it worse."

I nodded as thoughts of the rest of our schedule raced around my head. "We have to open the Brewer house in five minutes."

"We'll make it."

She gripped my hand before I pulled it away.

"Stop, honey, stop beating yourself up."

"God, I'm so sick of this. So *sick* of myself. One step forward, a hundred back. This is bullshit."

Jasmine's next order was a plea. "Stop."

I turned in my seat to face her. "I'm so full of shit. You know I spewed off some crap last night to Ian about being proactive and taking care of other people. I'm such a spaz. Who the hell am I kidding?"

She eyed me for a long minute at a stop light. "That's who you *are* for me. You take care of me."

"I have all these ideas of the new and improved Koti Vaughn and then crap like this happens. I feel so out of control. My mother says it's all in my head."

"We all feel out of control most days. Especially on days like this, I really hate your mother for making you feel like that. It's anxiety and we all have it in different degrees. My sister won't leave her house. Trust me, yours could be a lot worse."

"Is that how you knew how to deal with me?"

Her shoulders slumped. "I'm not *dealing* with you, I'm being your friend."

I nodded as a hot tear slipped down my face. "Who's going to want me like this?"

"A *very* intelligent fucking man."

This time when she gripped my hand, I squeezed hers back. Jasmine was overly affectionate, at least that was my opinion when we first met. She was quick to hug and offer her sympathy. But over time, I learned to love it about her. In fact, it was what I loved most.

Even as I managed to get through our day, I still felt the dread course through my veins. I was thankful when I pulled up to my house and hit the pillow.

A knock at my back door had me scrambling from my bed. My chest and throat raw, I raced to the bathroom and cupped water in my mouth before I answered the door still half asleep.

Ian stood on the other side, his easy smile wiped the minute he saw me.

"Are you all right?"

"I'm fine. What's up?"

He drew his brows. "You forgot?"

"Forgot?"

"About our bonfire?"

Yes.

"No, I'm sorry. I must have drifted off."

Ian took a step back as I pried my eyes open further to see he was dressed casually in shorts and a T-shirt. It was a far cry from the suit-clad man he arrived as a month before. His thick brown hair had gotten slightly sun-bleached and a few blond hairs had sprouted out of the thick disheveled mess. Gorgeous gray eyes peered at me through thick black lashes. It was always on the tip of my tongue to tell him how beautiful he was.

"Koti?"

"Yeah?"

"Bonfire?"

"Yeah."

Ian patiently pressed his lips together to hide his grin.

"I mean, yeah. Let me wash my face, okay?"

"Must have been some nap," he said with a small smile. "I'll be out here."

"Okay. Do I need to bring anything?"

He paused again and cupped the back of his head with his palm. "Chocolate, graham crackers, marshmallows?"

"Right."

He frowned. "We can do this another time."

Snapping out of my haze, I finally met his watchful gaze. "Nope, I'm on it."

He turned to make his way to the beach as I admired the fit of his clothes. The man had swagger and it was dizzying. He carried himself as any military man would—with confidence and purpose.

Ian chose the exact moment I zeroed in on his ass to glance back at me. I didn't bother acknowledging I was caught. Instead, I shut the door and raced to my bedroom.

I spent short minutes showering and scouring my skin in a sugar scrub that smelled like juniper before I raced to my closet and threw on my favorite white sundress and gold flip-flops. With another minute to spare, I brushed some bronzer on my cheeks and glossed my lips. Feeling lighter from the shower, I grabbed a small bag from my pantry and threw my stash into it along with a few other provisions. I grabbed a bottle of wine and two plastic wine glasses. Outside, Ian was carefully crafting our bonfire. I watched him work with it for a few seconds before I ran back inside and turned on my beach mix. The first few notes of Mazzy Star's "Fade Into You" sounded as I shut my door and crossed the sand. Slightly nervous and still a little drained, I met Ian near the shore where he was setting up a pair of folding chairs next to his newly lit fire.

"This is perfect. I brought wine."

He perked up and eyed the bottle I pulled from my bag. "Looks familiar."

"Yeah, well, it's delicious." I pulled out a second bottle and we shared a smile.

"That kind of day?" he asked.

I slowly nodded as he took one of the bottles from my hands and I dug through the bag for my corkscrew. "We found a man lying dead in a lawn chair at one of our properties."

"Oh?" Ian said with interest. "We?"

"Me and my boss, Jasmine."

I held out an empty glass to Ian who poured generously into one and then the other. We clinked our plastic and took a seat.

Nervous laughter burst out of me. "He was naked."

His eyes bulged. "Wow."

"Yeah, nothing kinky. He wasn't tied to the chair or anything. He probably didn't expect to die naked on a porch. He was in his eighties." I felt the lump in my throat threaten and pushed through it. "He was alone. I hate that."

Ian took a sip of wine. "That's unfortunate."

"Yeah," I said dismissively though my voice shook. "Yeah, it was."

"Does he have family?" Ian asked.

"I don't know. I don't think so. Let's talk about something else. How is Disco?"

"She was asleep when I left."

"Oh well, she'll keep you up all night."

Ian rolled his eyes. "As she has every night."

"Got to get her on a *schedule*, professor."

"She sleeps with me now," he said affectionately.

Lucky bitch.

With a glass of wine in hand, we sat for several minutes simply enjoying the view, the sun slowly creeping down before us. The islands were becoming giant black rocks with twinkling lights as their canopy as each minute passed. I had so many questions but decided to start with the one I thought was the safest.

"How long are you staying?"

He paused before he answered. "I'm not sure."

"How long has it been since you've been here?"

"A few years after I got married. The last time I saw you was the last time I was here."

"You were leaving," I said, recalling the day he walked out of the Kemp house, keys in hand. I remembered pausing to look at him before I stepped out of my parents' SUV.

"You recognized me right away," I said with a grin.

"You had on gold sandals," he laughed as he studied my feet. "What is it with you and gold sandals?"

I shrugged and sipped my wine to hide my smile and pushed off my sandals to drag a lazy toe through the cooling sand. "Why didn't you say hi? You just took off."

"I was in a rush to get home," he said, taking a sip of his wine.

"And you couldn't say hello?"

He sank a little into his chair while an expression I couldn't place flit over his features. "I was late for my flight."

"Oh."

"Feels amazing out here," he said, his eyes flicking to the firelight.

"It does."

"You're really here for good?" he asked.

"Yep. No other place I want to be." Ian picked up our bottle and refreshed our glasses.

"Right now, with this view, I have no argument." I sank further into my seat as the sun set, a wine buzz, and the music drifted between us. I'd only ever shared my bubble with Jasmine. I felt strangely comfortable doing it with Ian. Because though the man in front of me was a far cry from the boy who chased me through the sand, he wasn't a stranger.

With a bottle between us and the false courage that went with it, I studied him.

"So, tell me about the Marines. Is the training really as hard as it's made out to be?"

"Worse," he muttered. "It didn't matter, I was up for it and I had already been training for months before I went in. But it wasn't a breeze by any means. God, that seems like another lifetime ago," he whispered almost inaudibly.

"So, you got out right away?"

"I served four years and I could have served more, but I had a baby coming, I wanted to be out." He pulled at his lip and nodded. "I didn't want to miss anything."

"How old is she?"

"Just turned fifteen."

"Wow."

He stoked the fire as I swallowed a little intimidation.

Ian had been married, divorced, and was raising a daughter. The longest commitment I'd had was with my Mac, who I murdered on my way out of the city.

I chuckled.

"What?"

"I was just thinking of how much further evolved you are than I am. You've already had a marriage and are almost done raising a kid."

He shrugged as he dug his feet into the sand. "What's the rush?"

"No rush, well actually, at this point…"

Prodding eyes flicked my way.

"I have no plans past today, and those are my plans tomorrow."

"I like your life. I wish I had it so easy."

"Trust me, I pay for it. My mother is pissed and my dad is utterly confused with my choice to stay here. I tell them constantly they should have had another child, at least then they could do that fun comparison thing. It's not my fault my mother was worried about her figure instead of procreating, and they were forced to place their hopes on one kid."

"Some pressure, huh?" Ian grinned. "I guess since my parents adopted I lucked out."

"Trust me, in regards to your mother, there is no disappointment in the slightest when it comes to you. Rowan is wonderful and thinks the world of you." I said with a smile. "We caught up briefly last summer, but I don't remember much of her when we were kids, but I do remember her banana pops. God, what was in those?"

Ian grinned. "I'll teach you."

"Really?"

"Yes," he said as he filled our glasses again. "If you fancy them that much."

"I definitely fancy them. I've been dreaming of those for years." I twisted in my seat and tucked my legs underneath me. "She was always smiling, I do remember that."

"She's an amazing woman. Both my parents are great people," he said fondly.

"Call her. She's worried. Okay?"

"I did."

"Oh? Good."

Ian chuckled, and I looked to him in question.

"Are you feeling a little loose then, Koti?"

I realized then I was rocking back and forth to the beat of the music. And I don't mean casually, I mean shoulders and head into it like the guys from *Night at the Roxbury*.

"Oh, crap." I pressed an embarrassed hand to my forehead. "I do it at the store too. It's in my genes."

"Your father is a musician, right?"

"No, he was a sound engineer, mostly for reunion concerts. He was the guy with the big soundboard in the middle of the crowd. He did a lot of reunion tours for seventies and eighties rock bands."

"Oh," he said perking up a bit in his lazy seat. "Anyone I would know?"

"All of them," I said without missing a beat. "I'm not kidding. *All* of them."

"Wow."

"Yeah, my favorite was Stevie Nicks. She is incredible."

"So, your father knew rock stars and your mother was a model. Some childhood you must've had."

"Yeah, their life." I shrank in my seat. "Not mine."

He smirked at me. "And you are the castaway."

"And loving it."

He raised a brow. "Right," he said as he lifted his glass, "to the castaways."

"To the black sheep."

"Baaaa," Ian belted out and we both burst into laughter.

"You look like you're shedding a little wool," I noted, glancing at his rapidly slimming physique.

"Yeah, and it's hell," he said, patting his stomach. "While you're clearing naked dead men from rentals, I'm hauling my ass down the beach regretting about a thousand fast meals I ate during my divorce."

"That bad?" I asked.

"That bad," he muttered tonelessly as he studied the fire.

I picked up the wine this time. "But it didn't kill you."

"No, no it didn't."

So, what did?

Just on the tip of my tongue lay the intrusive words but there was no way I was breaking up the carefree vibe. I needed a reprieve from my own shit, just as much if not more than Ian did from anything that had to do with his hurts and I wasn't about to stir things up. I'd watched him tax his troubles for weeks. And I considered every smile, every laugh that erupted out of him a small miracle.

"You know, professor, every day I woke up when I got here… I was just numb. I'd been blindsided. It took me weeks to truly see the ocean and feel the sun on my face."

"I'm there." We exchanged a long look before he spoke. "It's a shame it wasn't the flying sand ball that did the trick." He smirked before he took a sip of wine.

"Yeah," I winced. "Not my finest moment. I'm sorry."

"I deserved it." He hesitated. "I have to admit, I was a bit resentful toward you when I arrived."

I gawked at him. "What in the world for?"

He leaned in toward me. "You know."

"No clue. My great taste in music?"

"No, I kind of like your nightly concerts," he said pensively. "You just…"

"Yes?" I drew out the word.

"You were all sunshine and smiles, just so fucking *happy*," he said with slight humor. "I wanted no part of it, still don't. I'm allergic."

"How inconsiderate of me." Still, his words stunned me and inwardly I beamed at his confession.

He gauged my repressed elation. "I don't expect you to apologize for being happy, Koti."

"Ha!" I said remembering my episode earlier that day. "Please don't take this the wrong way but you have no idea what you're saying."

"I'm pretty sure I may sneeze if you smile any wider. I can count your teeth."

"It's the wine."

"You're *happy* here," he said looking back at our matching houses. "And I want some of that for myself."

I sat up in my seat, leaned over and gripped his hand. He flinched and turned to face me. "It's already yours."

He shook his head in disbelief. "You're so sure."

"I am. Trust me, okay?"

He pushed the hair that stuck to my gloss away from my lips. And it took every bit of strength I had not to lean into his touch.

"You sure about everything, Koti?"

Buzzed, I willed myself away from his lingering fingers. "Lord, no. I had an anxiety attack today when I saw a dead man on a sun chair. I'm afraid of my own shadow some days and I blur out the bad parts as quick as they come, but I know this island and it's magical healing powers. This has nothing to do with me. I don't have the answer to *anything*. But *here*, this place is where everything wrong can be made right."

"I'll just choose to believe you."

"Hmmm, you're a skeptic."

"Realist."

"Okay, tell me this. Of all the places in the world you could have fled to, why did you come here?"

Ian sat back and harrumphed. "I never thought about it."

"Because you remember being happy here."

"I guess so."

"Me too. I hadn't been back since I was seventeen. And now onto s'mores."

Ian chuckled. "Well, that's random."

"No, I'm buzzing, and this is s'mores. I take them seriously." I grabbed the metal skewers from my bag and divided the ingredients between our laps. With practiced precision, I loaded a skewer with marshmallows and stuck it in the fire. Ian waited with a loaded cracker.

"Here, spread that on one of the crackers."

"Nutella?"

"Yep, *and* chocolate. If I'm feeling wild, I'll use *Ferrero Rocher*."

"You do take this seriously."

I placed a bubbling marshmallow on his cracker and pushed it toward his mouth.

"Ladies first," he said pushing it my way.

"That one's yours."

I put my own s'more together in seconds and shoveled it into my mouth. I was ravenous because I'd missed lunch and dinner.

"Holy shit," he said with a mouth full of goodness, "that's delicious."

I waggled my brows with my own mouth full and chewed.

His full smile had my heart pounding.

I'd told Jasmine he was handsome.

I was such a liar.

Ian Kemp was beautiful at fourteen. He was gorgeous when he was twenty-five and stood on his parents' porch waving at me before he left me with a crush. At thirty-eight, he was devastating, sitting next to me watching me inhale my dessert.

"More wine to wash that down?"

"Please," I said extending my glass.

The breeze kicked up at that moment and neither of us saw the tide had come in until a rogue wave came through and wiped out our fire.

Ian leapt to his feet and swept me out of the chair just before the gasping flames licked my dress.

His hands were all over me as he checked to make sure I was unharmed. I squirmed beneath him as I saw the bag with my dinner began to wash out to sea.

"Damnit!" I dropped my shoulders, helpless as we both watched the tide's greedy retreat and I managed to reclaim my soaked bag.

Ian gripped the corked wine and brushed it off before he presented it to me with a wry smile.

"Well, grapes are in a food group," I sighed nodding at his offering. "Come on, I have more of them."

"You sure love your wine," he said following me up the stairs into my house.

"My only vice."

Inside my house, I lit candles and turned down the music. Ian stood unsure at my kitchen counter.

"What?"

"I hope I haven't given you the wrong impression." He glanced at the candles and then back at me.

It had been an eternity since I'd entertained a man sexually, it took me a second to catch on. "Yeah, uh, I light candles every day of my life." I clicked on a lamp. "It's an anxiety thing." I turned to face him head-on. "But, should I be pissed you don't want to make love to me with all this highly romantic ambiance?" I lifted my hands, palms up.

He sheepishly put the bottle on the counter and moved to find glasses.

"That's right, go hide behind the cabinets. I'm pretty sure they can't shield that inflated head of yours."

"You sure do know how to bust a man's balls," he muttered lifting two glasses from the cabinet.

"You shouldn't be so quick to assume I wanted your balls or any other part of your anatomy, professor. Besides," I said as I stood on the other side of the island while he poured more wine, "I'm sure your students are all too eager to play teacher's pet."

He grinned down at his wine glass. "Never went there. Had a few chances."

"Ah, that's right. You chose to break your gentlemen's virtue on the side of my house."

His head snapped up and my smile vanished as something passed between us. Three or four heartbeats later, he looked over my shoulder.

"You know you're living in a time capsule. No TV, no computer, what gives?"

"My sanity. Do you even remember life without cell phones?"

"I do. Barely."

"Well, I use them only when I have to. Do you have any idea how much time I got back in my day from putting that damn thing down?"

Still smiling he answered, "I can only imagine."

"So much time. So. Much. Time."

"I want to be you when I grow up," he said softly.

"I don't want to grow up," I whispered back.

"Suits me."

An hour later, we sat on my porch love seat after finishing another bottle of wine and listened to my latest mix as Neil Diamond sang "Love on the Rocks."

Throwing myself into the song I mouthed the words, using

my fist as my microphone and he chuckled and shook his head. A few minutes later, we were back to comfortable silence before he spoke up.

"God, this is so true," Ian whispered.

"What?"

"This song. It's so true. Every bit of it. You get so high off love and then it all turns to shit."

I laughed inappropriately at his bluntness and glossy eyes before I saw brief emotion flicker over his face. I sat up and winced. "Sorry."

He pulled up to sit and clasped his hands between his legs. "Don't be. I haven't been upset about my wife in years." He stood and looked over at me. "This was truly a great time, Koti."

"It was a unicorn type of night, right?"

"Most definitely."

He looked over to me with a warm smile. "Goodnight, puffer fish."

"Goodnight, crocky."

I stood and leaned over to blow out the first candle.

"Koti."

"Yeah?"

"Thank you."

I bit my lip and nodded before he disappeared out the door.

fifteen

Koti

Hours later, flesh burning from the wine, alcohol-induced insomnia had set in. I rose from bed still in my dress and washed my face in the bathroom. I cranked my AC unit up high and spent a few minutes in front of it, cooling my skin from burning thoughts.

Ian's eyes haunted me, and in being honest with myself, they were what kept me awake. His eyes, his voice, the way I felt at ease with him. He looked at me like I had something he needed. I wondered briefly if he saw the mess inside of me would he look at me that same way. I loved the heat of his stare when he thought I didn't notice, and in my wine-induced haze, I felt sexy when I remembered catching that gaze before it flitted away. I opened my porch door in the pitch-black night and shut it softly instead of letting it snap close.

As I tread across the sand, I glanced at the Kemp house where Ian slept. In the past few days, he unknowingly revealed so many truths about me and accepted them like no man in my life ever had. We'd been at odds a majority of his time on the island and in just a matter of days, he'd unearthed so much. I should have felt uncomfortable, instead all I felt was relief.

Holding my dress to my thighs, I walked through the cool water in a daze, splashing around to cool the inferno that was building inside with thoughts of him. Finally able to feel some relief from my Ian-induced heat wave, I was taken by surprise when an unexpected wave had me scrambling to keep on my feet. Over the breeze, I could have sworn I heard his chuckle and narrowed my eyes in the direction of his house. I couldn't see past his porch stairs, but I had the distinct feeling I was being watched. Before I had a chance to investigate, another rogue wave smashed into me and leveled me flat onto my back.

Choking, I snapped to my feet before I was yanked in by the undertow. Freshly sober and trying my best to clear my throat, I heard Ian's porch door and in seconds he stood in front of me as I made it to shore.

"I'm trying—really, *really* trying hard not to laugh. Are you okay?"

"Yes," I answered, shaking off the pain like a wet dog before I looked at him accusingly. "You were watching me?!"

Shirt-free, tousled and deadly sexy, Ian stood in front of me, his eyes hooded.

Wiping my hands on my chest, I discovered one of my breasts was peeking through the shoulder of my dress. I twisted my body and righted it as Ian's breath hit my face. "Isn't that what you wanted?"

"I was hot!"

"Fucking right you were, until you wiped out," he said playfully as he pushed a heavy wad of hair off my forehead. "It was a good start, shitty finish. If someone put a gun to my head, I'd give it a six out of ten!"

"What is it with the freakish waves today? That came out of nowhere!"

"Just obeying the moon, I suppose," he said with a chuckle as I righted my dress while his eyes lingered on my bare shoulder.

"Or their muse," I whispered inaudibly, but he caught it.

"Muse?"

"I have a thing for Greek mythology," I said defensively. "Nothing wrong with that."

"So that's it? That's why you walk around dressed like Aphrodite?"

I rolled my eyes though I wasn't sure he could see.

"Old habits die hard I suppose," he said before lifting the strap of my dress back to my shoulder. "You are a right mess, *Miss* Vaughn. I suppose it's good fate we ended up on this island together."

"Agreed. But you must admit, you're the victor of the mess this month."

"Not arguing with that," he said softly.

"Can't sleep?"

"Not tonight."

"Do you want to talk about it?"

"No, I don't. So please don't ask."

"Okay."

I didn't get a chance to blink before he turned the tables. "You tell me. What brought you here?"

"That's not fair."

"No, it's not." He took a seat on one of the smaller boulders nearby. "But you did offer."

"I did, didn't I?" I stood silent for several moments. It was hard to convey what happened to me, why I was there because it seemed so trivial to some. A few really bad days was the gist of it. A few *really* bad days was the sum of it. For a long time, so much of me believed my issues were trivial because I was told they were. I was *told* my attacks were just temporary setbacks. But they just kept coming. It had always seemed impossible to explain my circumstances to anyone other than my therapist. No one in my life, especially my mother, who heard about my condition gathered that my disorder wasn't anything other than someone trying to seek attention. Even my ex-boyfriend, Trevor, had downplayed my attacks and told me I just needed to relax.

I hated that word. As if it could really be so easily executed by a person with generalized anxiety disorder on demand. As if it was that simplistic. Relax.

That word was a hundred percent of the reason why I left him holding the bag of our new relationship in New York. It took me a few months to start liking Trevor enough to commit to him and only minutes for me to decide that commitment was a mistake.

"Trevor, I need you."

"Relax, Koti. Can this wait? I have a meeting in an hour and I need to concentrate. I'll call you back."

Everyone close to me in New York, even the best of my friends never could grasp the reality of the hell I went through just to be present for them. Ginger, my friend since grade school, had dismissed my anxiety the way my mother had. Anger surfaced every time I thought about the day I left New York and the last time I'd reached out to her. She'd answered the phone while entertaining a few of our mutual friends and before I could get a word out, I heard her excuse for taking my phone call. "It's Koti, she's having one of her *episodes*." I hadn't spoken to her since. And I probably never would again. So much of my life I'd left behind, the day I boarded that plane. Everything. I'd left everything. And though it had taken me some time to open up to Jasmine, I didn't have to force the words out for Ian.

I'd watched him implode when he knew I was his audience. His breakdown, though not the same as mine, had been just as unavoidable. We were both matches on an island of fire and couldn't be helped. For us, our ashes were all there was left to work with. But I wanted him to know there was something to be said for those ashes.

"My parents started me early. I went to the best schools, got the grades, had the friends, the life everybody wants. I really can't complain. It all worked out the way it was supposed to, mostly, but when it didn't that's when the trouble started."

Ian sat quietly perched on the rock and waited.

"I had my first panic attack when I was fourteen. I didn't know what was happening. And it was for the dumbest reason."

"Which was?"

"I couldn't get a stain out of my skirt."

Ian studied me briefly before his eyes drifted back to the sea. A spray of water pooled between us and covered our feet. I moved to stand in front of him. If he wanted to know my answers, I wanted his attention. He didn't hesitate, his gaze landed squarely on mine. Even in the dimly starlit sky, I could see the storm in his eyes. If my story were only a mild distraction, I would give it to him. The odd part is that I *wanted* to tell him.

He spoke low erasing my doubts. "Tell me. I want to know."

"The first time it happened, I blamed it on PMS, but they just kept coming. My mother was completely intolerant of my '*weakness*'. And I felt the expectation *every day*, her expectation. She set the bar so high, it began to choke me. It was both physical and mental, I just couldn't get to her kind of *normal*. But, oh, how I faked it, or tried to. I held it inside even though every day I struggled. I'd watch my friends and their reactions to certain situations and I would do my best to imitate, and then I would find a bathroom or a place to hide and have my freak out. There was no end to it. I just worked through it, all day *every day*, but worked as in an act of *labor*, I exhausted myself. I passed out a lot. I hid a lot, I faked illness, so I could hide and it would buy me just a few blissful days alone and away from the world. When I missed so much school, to the point of my parents being summoned by the headmaster, my father suggested therapy. My mother grudgingly agreed after years of telling me it was all in my head."

Soaked from my fall, I crossed my arms and gripped the tops of my shoulders as I shivered in the breeze, feeling heavy with my confession.

"My psychiatrist used to tell me to fold my fears into fourths. To mentally write down what I was afraid of and memorize and recognize it for what it was and then treat it like a piece of paper and fold it in half and then fourths and so on until it was so small I could put it in my pocket and forget about it."

"Your pockets overflowed," he said slowly as he picked up the hem of my skirt and rubbed it between his fingers.

I nodded. "I tried everything. I counted. I took the meds. I did the breathing exercises. All of it."

"Nothing worked?"

"No, because despite my mother's permission to let me get help, her expectations outweighed my progress. I couldn't keep up. I couldn't be the daughter she expected, *and* anxiety-ridden, so I scrambled, and I hid it the best I could. I pretended the medication helped, for her, for my father and eventually convinced myself that I was capable of handling it."

I moved to sit next to him but he caged me between his legs. "Go on."

"So… then…" Ian kept busy dusting the sand off the bottom of my dress. I felt the low burning fire stir up again with the accidental brush of his fingers along my thigh.

"So, I faked my way through high school and college, feigning progress up until the time I got my job."

He dropped the dress and wiped the sand on his shorts. "What did you do?"

"Real estate. Biggest firm in New York. I was one of their

best brokers."

"That's ludicrous. How did you manage that stress?"

"Sometimes I think I purposefully put myself into that mess to self-destruct."

"Did you?"

"I don't know. Probably. I was working so hard and to my own detriment, I didn't stop for anything. My parents were so proud while inside I was screaming. My health got so bad. It was *all. So. Bad.* I started drinking heavily and went from having an attack every few weeks to daily. I spent years conditioning myself to stop listening to my body, and in a matter of days all my fears came to light and I mean *all* of them. Everything was gone, every single damn thing I'd worked for since I was in grade-school up to that point vanished."

"What happened?"

"I was in the midst of setting up one of the biggest real estate deals in New York. I was showing a property to a slew of investors. It was a billion-dollar deal. My job was to sell a set of high-rise buildings that were going to be turned into high-value condos, posh, exclusive, that sort of thing. I worked on it for a year. The day before I was set to pitch I was doing a walk-through of one of the buildings and I got attacked by a squatter." I shivered at the thought of that day. "He pulled a knife on me."

"Jesus."

"I barely made it out of there with my life and that's no exaggeration. One of my associates walked in and that's what saved me. But that incident opened up a whole different can of worms."

"What do you mean?"

"Let's just say, I've done more research on the hereafter than most theologists."

"Fear of death?"

"Yes."

Ian grabbed my hand and I let him hold it between his.

"A majority of my anxiety comes from lack of control. I have to have things a certain way, not so much OCD but to the point where I know what will happen in my every day. I'm not a fan of surprises. Routine is crucial to me, I'd never experienced anything like I did that day. And as you can imagine the realization about death, well let's save that conversation for a rainy day or *never*."

I was shaking as I remembered the man on the beach chair that morning. Ian read my thoughts.

"Today, you had a horrible attack." It was a statement. "And you joked about it. That's what you do with everyone else?"

Tears sprang to my eyes. "Yes."

"I'm so sorry. I didn't realize."

"You couldn't have. It's not your place."

"My job as much as it is yours, right?"

He turned my palm up and slowly brought it to his lips, kissing it softly. A small moan escaped me, and I wasn't sure if he heard it.

"What happened? With the deal?" He rested my hand on his shoulder as if it was the most natural thing. I was itching to run my fingers through his hair. My breaths came out faster, his subtle seduction was wrecking my train of thought.

"What happened?"

"The next day I was expected to move on as if it never happened. Unsympathetic boss, the show must go on, that type of thing. Anyway, I blew it. As soon as I entered the building with the buyers, I had the mother of all attacks. I was fired because I'd potentially blown one of the biggest deals in real estate history, though we all knew the real reason why. I had my first public meltdown on what should have been one of the best days of my career, a huge milestone for me. With that deal put to bed, the possibilities were endless, my commission would have made me wealthy, I would have made a name for myself, yadda, yadda. But in the blink of an eye, it was gone." Tears blurred my vision as he looked up to me and I smiled. "In a way, it was the best thing that ever happened to me. I didn't see it then when I was racing down snow-filled streets with a box full of my shit, having the worst day of my life. I didn't see it hours later when I abandoned my apartment in New York, my friends, my boyfriend, my family and took a cab to the airport. And I didn't see it in the weeks after as I stared at this ocean, or a month after that when Jasmine discovered me cowering in a bathroom of a Mexican restaurant after another attack. It's now, *now* where I truly understand what a blessing it was to give up the charade. Instead of continuing to live a life I couldn't live, I chose me."

"You chose wisely."

"I did. But you don't understand, Ian. I *wanted* that life. I did, *so badly*, for myself, for my parents, but I couldn't be that Koti and I never will be. There's a difference between can't and won't. *Can't* sucks. And I was good at it. I was *really* good at it. I loved my job, *that* part of it was never a lie. I loved my apartment. I loved New York most of the time. This, living here, wasn't supposed to be my life."

"Koti," he said softly, "no part of you reeks of a mogul. Not that I don't think you were capable, but I just don't see you as that type. And your parents must not know you at all."

"My dad, he knew. He just let my mother do most of the parenting and I know it breaks his heart and my leaving New York broke the rest of it. He feels like he failed me, he thinks I'm punishing him, but I came here to save myself. I don't ever want to go back. I don't resent him. I'm not even that angry with my mother. All of it, everything that happened, even my brush with death was a means to an end. It was my one and only warning to rid myself of a life that was slowly killing me anyway. I obeyed. I yielded to that warning. And so, I'm here living someone else's life, in someone else's house staring at someone else's ocean." I sighed. "Anyway, it's over, I'm here. I've made peace with it and I'm not wasting any more time pretending to be someone I can't be."

Ian's body shook with an ironic laugh. "You really are a good muse."

"Glad you seem to think so." I sighed. "So, there's my five-minute sob story. Surprised?"

"A little," he said as he stared up at me from where he sat. We were close, very close to the point I was hovering above him. Even with that awareness, I didn't move.

"So welcome to the island of misfit-humans. It's pretty cool here. And, by the way, Ian, you aren't broken."

"No," he agreed quickly. "I'm not. I'm just really, *really* fucking mad."

"Whatever's wrong now, will make sense later. I hope you believe that."

"I don't." He stood then, forcing me to take a step back. Water sprayed our feet as we stood there getting lost in the other. Ian was the first to break the connection.

"Goodnight."

"Wait, Ian—"

"Don't invite me into your life, Koti, or your heart, or your bed because I'm a selfish man right now and I'll take you up on it without a second thought. If you move a single inch closer to me, I'm going to fuck you. And as much as we both want that, we both don't need it. I will use you and it's not because

I don't think you're beautiful, or intelligent or worth more. It's because right now, I'm incapable of being anything other than the man that uses you. And because I do think you are worthy of better, I'm not going to let it happen. So, goodnight."

I stood stunned as he walked away. I expected him to head back to the house, instead, he walked down the beach.

sixteen

Ian

I was so close to tasting her, but I knew I'd be forced to spit that taste out. And that was the part that made me walk away. I had restraint. I could give myself credit for that, but not much. I'd been so close to taking her into my bed and losing myself, that I practically had to run from her.

An entanglement couldn't happen. As beautiful as she was, as much as I loved the sound of her voice and the sight of her smile, my heart was completely out of the equation. I didn't think it had even made an appearance in the time I'd been on the island. Friendship... I was fine with that. And the wine hadn't helped the fact that I was dangerously attracted to her. My cock grew rock hard at the sight of her frolicking in the water. She was pure temptation, an itch I was growing desperate to scratch and unknowingly receptive to me. Tonight, I made her aware of it and I could see the same need in her eyes. We were in hazardous territory and in no way was there any outcome other than hurting her.

Beautiful, smart, intoxicating, and exhausting. Koti came with a string of issues I had no intention of helping with.

Selfish.

That was the point of my new crusade. I'd played my part for two other women and had no intention of auditioning for the role of lead in anyone else's life.

It was finally time for me to check off a few things on my own list.

Koti was right in the sense that the time was now. I had no obligation to anyone other than Ella. I needed to get back to my daughter, but I still felt the irrational burn every time I thought of her mother. I wasn't ready. And I wasn't sure when I would be but touching Koti would be a mistake.

My phone buzzed in my pocket and I cursed when I saw Tara's name. Thankfully, the wine hadn't worn off yet.

"Yeah."

"Ian?"

"Is my daughter okay?"

"I need to talk to you."

"Again, is Ella all right?"

"She's fine."

"Then we have no reason to be speaking."

"I feel terrible."

"Fuck you."

"Please don't say that to me." She was crying, and I couldn't muster a single ounce of pity.

"What do you want, Tara? Forgiveness would be laughable."

She sniffed, and I had the urge to snap my phone in half. "A chance to explain."

"Explain? Here's an explanation. When I was deployed, you fucked your ex-boyfriend and you had a fight or better yet, let me guess, he dumped you. So instead of telling him he's a father knowing he would be a dead-beat dad, you decided to tell your devoted soldier you were pregnant two days before he was set to re-enlist because he would do the honorable thing. Did I miss anything?"

"It was a mistake, one I regret every day."

"A mistake that you decided to let me pay for. And now that

we're clearing the air, maybe it's time I told you something."

"Whatever it is," she said her voice hoarse, "I deserve it."

"I never loved you. Not the way I should have. After a few years, your charms wore off and I realized then I was stuck in a marriage I didn't want. In fact, I grew to despise you as the years passed. You were annoying and needy and didn't have a selfless bone in your body. You weren't the kind of woman I could respect, let alone truly and deeply love. I spent years suffering at your hand because of my love for a daughter that wasn't mine. But here's the thing, you conniving bitch, you can't change her love for me. You can't twist it or turn it or direct it toward Daniel, no matter what you do. If you want to tell Ella, be my guest; but if you do, you'll get exactly what you deserve, her hatred. And she won't love Daniel more. He has to earn her love and affection the way I had to for the whole of her life. I dare you to try to piss away at the years I've built being a father, but let me repeat myself so we're clear. You will never, *ever* ruin what's between us. Ella and I are what true love is supposed to be. She and I were the best thing to come out of our marriage and it had *nothing* to do with you."

I was being vile, but it was the truth for the most part that she hadn't been kind enough to spare me.

"You never loved me?"

"No."

I ended the call and walked the beach until sunrise.

"Disco," I called out, rousing from sleep. I stood and stretched stepping into a fresh puddle of her piss. "Get over here, you little rat, it's time for our jog. Disco!"

I heard a muffled squeal of delight and made my way to my

porch. Staring out of the screen, I finally spotted my dog and her kidnapper. Koti was running the beach with the tiny beast in tow, her timid bark sounding rapidly as she chased at Koti's heels.

Disco's ears flew back as she tried to keep up with her captor's sporadic movements. She dodged the puppy left and right as the storm winds blew in and thunder sounded in the distance. The only rays of sun left shone through the clouds on our beach and lit them both up as they pranced around on the sand. Koti's smile and delighted laughter took my breath away.

She had on a pair of barely-there shorts that showcased the insane length of her toned legs. A thin top covered her gorgeous tits and tight stomach. The woman was radiant, so fucking beautiful, that it hurt to look at her. I couldn't imagine the life she explained to me where she wasn't in control. She seemed so at ease in both life, and in her skin, but apparently, that had taken her back-breaking, life-changing effort and I admired her for it.

She was the best possible muse and completely unaware of it which only made her more alluring. She'd always been a gentle soul, even when she was a little girl her strength remained hidden. I couldn't help my chuckle when Disco lost her footing and toppled over, ending up as a rolling ball of fur before popping up again. Koti's smile radiated in the space between us as I tried to catch my breath from the sight of her.

This. This is what happiness looks like.

I remembered her words from the night before. *"It's already yours."*

I was so far from the place she spoke of, but just for a moment, I hoped I would be able to navigate my way there. I knew that hope was dangerous. I wished for the same thing after gaining my freedom from Tara and so far, had been nothing but disappointed. I knew I had to give myself time to adjust from being a family man. I just didn't realize in leaving my wife, I might have lost my entire family.

Koti plucked Disco up from the sand and held her over her head before bringing her in for a kiss. The puppy lapped up every bit of her attention as I let my eyes feast. She was stunning. Silver eyes, full lips, and that killer body all taunted me from where she stood. I couldn't tear my eyes away.

Not only was she temptation. Not acting on the need to touch her last night was agony and she'd been so incredibly responsive.

Beautiful, stubborn, and full of quiet strength. I knew that about her even when we were kids. Back then she'd been nothing more than a distraction to pass the time with while I waited to get back to the States.

My parents had forced my hand the way they had hers to keep us occupied together and out of their hair for the summer. But even then, with our age gap and her temperament and squeaky voice, I liked her. She made the time on the island bearable. She softened me with her vulnerability. I could never forget the first time I saw her cry.

I found her sitting on the side of the house, her body shaking as she sat with her back to the siding, her knees drawn.

"Koti, what's wrong?"

"Go away, Ian. I don't want to play."

"Well, that's good then because I'm a little too old for a play date."

"You know what I mean," she sniffed. Her eyes watering even as her words came out in an angry huff.

"What's wrong?" I asked, taking a seat next to her.

"My mother is an asshole."

"You sure swear a lot for a little girl."

"I'm seven now," she defended. "I'm getting bigger every day."

"Yes, you'll be driving in no time." I laughed as she glared at me.

"Go away, Ian."

"Fine," I stood and brushed the sand off my shorts. I had better things to do, a Sega game on pause. She spoke before I'd taken my first step away from her.

"She's so mean."

"What did she do?"

"She found some Twinkies I snuck into my room and she went crazy."

"I'm sure she didn't mean whatever she said."

"That I was going to get fat? And that nobody thought much of a fat person because they looked like they had no self-control and that made them weak."

"Jesus," I sighed. "They are just Twinkies."

"Tell that to her," she said choking on another sob.

I squat down in front of her. "I just so happen to have some banana pops at my house. So much better than Twinkies, want one?"

"I can't, I'll be spanked."

"You're getting too big for spankings. And no one needs to know but us." I held out my hand. "Come on, puffer fish."

She looked up to me. "Don't make fun of me for crying."

"Never."

"Okay." She grabbed my hand and I sat her on my parents' couch with a banana pop.

An hour later, I had to scrape her off the ceiling. As it turned out, she didn't do well on sugar, probably because she was raised on a lack of it. Giving her those banana pops had been like giving her speed, but her smile had been worth it. The same smile she wore now as she collapsed on her back with the puppy in her arms before moving her gaze toward the sea.

I would have given anything in that moment to be kissing her breathless, before sinking between her legs on that sand. I closed my eyes tight as I imagined those legs wrapped around me while I slid my tongue against hers.

She sat up as if she'd heard my thoughts and glanced toward the house. I was sure she couldn't see me staring at her through the screen. Resigned that acting on my desire for her was still a terrible idea, I made my way to the bathroom just as my screen door creaked open and seconds later heard the pitter patter of Disco's feet.

seventeen

Koti

I gripped the phone to my ear while being browbeaten by the person on the other end of the line. "I paid for the rental months ago."

"I'm so sorry, Mrs. Tartar. We've arranged for you to stay—"

"I'm not having it, I'll just cancel the whole trip."

"I don't want you to do that," I pleaded, glancing at Jasmine, helpless. "Please just let me speak to the tenant at the property. I'm sure we can work it out."

"I want an answer within the hour. I've been planning this trip for months!"

"I completely understand. You'll have it."

I hung up the phone and let out a breath of frustration. "Do not book the Kemp house anymore until we know how long he's staying. I have to somehow get him to a hotel."

"Is he still pissing and moaning?" Jasmine asked, looking up at me from her computer.

"Nope, I mean yes and no. He's come a long way in only a month. He's gotten some sun. He's lost some weight. He loves Disco and he takes long walks with her. He's no longer catatonic and doesn't live in darkness, I would say that's progress."

Jasmine pulled her ridiculously thick hair through the tie on her wrist. "How observant of you."

"It's my job," I defended. "And he's a really nice man."

"Handsome, right?" She snickered.

"Beautiful," I whispered.

"Beautiful, huh? Ask him to sleep with you."

I rolled my eyes.

"I mean at your house. You have three spare bedrooms. Let him crash there for a few days so we can keep the commission. It's not like he's a total stranger. You knew him when you were kids, right?"

"Yeah, we spent a summer together." I chewed on the idea for a moment. "I think he's repaired the kitchen. He's been sawing nonstop for a week."

A week he had barely acknowledged me. But I promised him space and in turn, he stopped the sawing when the sun set and even offered me a friendly wave when I got home from work.

"Okay, so ask him."

"Nah, he can stay at a hotel."

"Do you have the money for a hotel? Because I sure as hell don't. We need the commission and you have the space."

I stood and went to grab some coffee. "He's the one imposing, *he* should pay."

"Koti."

I sighed. "Fine I'll ask him, but I doubt he'll go for it."

"You need sex."

"How many times do I have to explain this to you. Sex is mostly *painful* for me. My body doesn't like it." I pulled some Chapstick from my pint-sized purse and coated my lips before I lathered on a small layer of sunblock.

"Every time?"

"Almost. I suffer for days and hardly ever orgasm."

"God, that's horrible," Jasmine said, terrified at the thought.

"It's my life. I've been dealing with it since I lost my virginity at a Cheap Trick reunion concert."

"That's even more horrible."

"It doesn't bother me," I said before I gripped her around the neck and gave her a hug from behind her chair. "You are loved, my little filifuckingpino."

"You too," she said staring up at me. "I want so much more for you, Koti."

"And I'm happy where I'm at," I promised. Ian's comment last night by the bonfire made me smile.

"What?" she asked, trying to read my expression.

"He said I was happy."

"Who?"

"Ian."

"Well, if Ian says so," she smirked. "Bow chica wow wow."

"Shut up."

"You like him, it's okay to tell me."

"There's nothing to tell. Look, he's newly divorced and already had a revenge screw outside of my house. He's emotionally incapable and we are on two different planets. There's no potential."

Jasmine shrugged. "Okay, so he's not a commitment candidate."

"Not in the slightest. But, God, Jasmine, he's so hard not to look at. I'm seriously having a terrible time not staring. I forgot how pretty men can be."

"Yes, yes they are, and then they open their mouths and it's like playing the lottery."

"He's still got a bit of a South African accent, it's so sexy."

"I'll come over tonight and check him out," she said, inviting herself before she tested the waters by glancing my way.

I was already shaking my head. "No, you won't because I'm going to be nervous enough asking him to sleep with me... I mean to sleep there. At my house."

She shrugged. "So, I'll be a buffer."

"Not tonight, okay? I don't need you coming over and making him feel weird."

She stood in her hot pink sundress and thin scarf and puckered her full lips before she crossed her eyes. "I would do no such thing."

"Sorry."

"Fine, I have a potential date anyway."

"With who?"

"I'll let you know if it happens. But all I have to say is that when it comes to this one, my body is ready."

"All you do is talk about sex. I'm over it. Unless you can grace this office with something educational or a topic that doesn't consist of it, I'm closing my ears to you. No more penis talk." I reached in my desk and pulled out my earbuds.

Jasmine stood with her mouth gaping as I began typing. Twenty seconds later, I got a company email from my pest of a boss that was marked urgent. It was a YouTube video of talking cats.

eighteen

Koti

The Cranberries' "Zombie" blasted through my speakers down the narrow road home. Ian's rental, a large cab Ford, sat in the driveway. I ignored the small thrill that raced through me at the thought of having him at my house for a week. We'd barely spoken that morning, but I could feel his eyes on me while he stretched before he took off for his run. I turned off my Jeep and made my way straight to his back door.

I knocked twice, and to my surprise, he met me with a faint smile before opening the door and inviting me in. Paint was smudged on his fingertips and across his bare chest and the floor was covered in plastic. The paint fumes filled my nose.

"Looks like progress in here. Good for you."

"Yeah, thanks for telling my mother I was remodeling. She's making a special trip soon just to see it."

"My pleasure. And you should thank me, I was covering for your ass."

He resumed his work to hide his smile. "Thanks. So what's up?"

"Sorry to bother you, but…" Disco yapped from her box. I kept my eyes averted from a shirtless Ian and peeked over to see her bouncing off the sides for my attention. "Hey, baby. Want a break from the smell?" I picked her up and hugged her tiny body to me before I scanned his progress further. "It really looks great in here."

Ian had replaced the cabinet doors with glass paned frames and was distressing the freshly painted wood with metal wool. "Rowan is going to love it."

"Thanks," he said as he resumed rubbing wool down the side of one of the doors.

"You have a talent for this."

"I went through a few houses with my ex-wife."

"Well, she definitely brought out the artist in you."

Ian said nothing, so I decided to keep those comments to myself. "You were saying?" Briefly, I admired his budding physique as he lifted another door to fasten it in. He'd spent most of his hours since he'd arrived at the island working out and it showed. I had to catch myself to keep from being embarrassed when he looked back at me expectantly.

"Okay, so we need to talk." He stopped the working of his hands and turned to face me. His shorts hung at his waist and were dangerously close to falling down. He was rapidly losing weight and his newly bronzed skin made his gray eyes pop. I cleared my throat.

"I need this house. I've diverted four couples and sent them elsewhere since you've been here, but I have this woman—she's threatening us—and I kind of told her I would make sure her reservation was…"

He nodded in understanding. "I need to leave."

"Well," I pointed to my house as if he didn't know where it was. "It's temporary. But you can sleep with me if you don't want to get a hotel."

Ian raised a brow, his lips twisted into a small smile.

"I mean, you can sleep in one of my spare bedrooms."

Jesus, why was I so nervous? I shook it off.

"Will you be done with this today?"

"I should be."

"Okay, great."

He crossed his arms and studied me.

Get those balls out, Koti!

"Look, I'm sorry. Stay at a hotel or take one of my rooms. Either way, I need you out of here by ten in the morning. Okay? This isn't a request. I have a business to run and I can't handle the loss of commission."

Ian bit his lip.

"Well?" I prompted, waiting for a response, the shake in my voice making my demand seem ridiculous.

"Oh, I think you've made yourself quite clear, Ms. Vaughn."

Deflating I took a step forward. "I don't want to fight."

"I'm not going to fight. I'll take your room."

"Good, because you're exhausting."

His eyes narrowed. "Thanks."

"Just stating the facts. Okay, so here's a key to my place." I pulled it from my pocket and set it on the counter. "Feel free to come and go as you please but if you take wine, make sure to replace it." The second he took a step forward to retrieve the key, his shorts went.

Our eyes locked right before I let mine drift down.

Commando.

I was staring at Ian's cock. Ian was staring at his own cock. Disco's eyes were on Ian's cock and I quickly covered them to save her virtue. It took every bit of strength I had to look away but not before I took a mental picture. Ian cursed as he pulled up his pants and apologized.

I held up my hand surprising myself with a steady voice. "It's fine, it's nothing I haven't seen before." That was a lie, his dick was impressive and beautiful. I regrouped and reclaimed my tongue.

"But you should probably wear shorts that fit and underwear while you stay with me."

"Agreed," he picked up his wool and turned his back to me. "See you tomorrow then."

The next morning, I heard Disco squeak at the foot of my bed and pushed off my covers just as Ian raced in after her. "Sorry, I tried to grab her before she got... *fuck me*—" his eyes lingered on my chest and I looked down and realized I wasn't wearing anything but underwear and my cami. During the night it must have shifted above my *miss* sized tits. I laughed and pulled down my shirt to cover myself. "Now we're even," I yelled at Ian's retreating back.

"Hardly. My cock is pointing north."

"Still a Marine with that filthy mouth, huh?"

"I'll keep it clean, Ms. Vaughn."

I picked up a vying Disco from the foot of my bed. "Don't worry about it, Ian. Thousands of people have seen these tits, Mardi Gras, not to mention hundreds of concerts. Alcohol has a way of temporarily curing anxiety. A few times a year, I could be quite the party girl."

That was before you became a bohemian recluse.

I left that part out.

Ian's voice echoed from the guest bathroom. "How worldly of you."

"I'd like to think so." Disco barked. "And Disco agrees."

"Better take a Benadryl," he said, peeking into my room to make sure I was decent before he again called me out on the fact that I was not allergic to the puppy as I tossed her around on my bed. "You needed her," I said affectionately and unapologetically as I kissed her fluffy face. "And I wanted you to have her."

Ian opened the door fully, sat on the edge of my bed and watched us play. After a few minutes, his voice cut through my laughter. "You grew up beautiful, Koti Vaughn."

Our eyes met before I gave him a lopsided grin. "And you grew up so handsome, Ian Kemp."

His smile was a sledgehammer to my chest. "So, I've moved my stuff into the guest bedroom. I set up my board in the living room. Hope that's okay."

"Of course," I said, lunging after Disco as she tried to wander off the bed.

"Damnit, woman! Could you stop that?" He asked, pushing me back to sit upright and pulling my comforter firmly in place to cover me. "I know we're friends, but I'm still a man."

"Really?" I said with a chuckle before eyeing his crotch with a smirk. I was shamelessly flirting and couldn't have cared less. "Hadn't noticed. Besides didn't you hammer all that pent-up sexual frustration out with barstool number five?"

Ian grinned. "No, I failed at execution and accidentally passed out while I was taking a piss. I woke up with a couch pillow under my head on the bathroom floor. She did leave me a note to call her."

"You lied?"

"Maybe I liked seeing you jealous."

"I wasn't jealous and how very immature of you."

"I never said I was a saint, Koti."

My name sounded like heaven rolling off his tongue. His eyes grew dark as I gripped Disco tightly to me. "Why would it make you happy if I *was* jealous?"

Ian's eyes roamed my neck and chest before they drifted back to mine. "Are you hungry for breakfast?"

"Are you going to answer my question?"

"No," he said, standing abruptly. "House rules, no nudity."

"Hey, I'm not the one with the hat-trick trousers," I said in an attempt to mock his accent.

"That was actually pretty decent."

"I'm trying to get better." We shared a smile before I forced myself to look away. It had been a long time since I'd had any testosterone in my bedroom. I was seconds away from stripping down and begging him to use me. Instead, I spoke to Disco.

"Hey baby, want some bacon?"

"Not us, we eat turkey." Ian plucked Disco from my hold and I frowned. "She loves you more, doesn't she?"

"She better, I'm the one who's doing all the training. Plus, she loves our runs, we're going ten miles today."

"You can't walk her that hard!" I said getting out of bed and shoving my pajama pants on.

Ian looked away as I pulled a thin T-shirt over my head.

"I don't," he called over his shoulder as I followed him down the hall.

"What?"

He turned to me and cradled Disco in his forearm.

"You run with her like that?"

He nodded.

"Ha! I bet you get a ton of attention."

"She's my ace in the hole. I have an orange juice waiting every morning at mile five."

I looked at him skeptically. "Making rounds all over the island?"

He gave me a devilish grin. "But I'll be coming home to you tonight."

My heart skipped an odd beat before he disappeared out the door.

I spent my day getting three houses ready and the last of it walking Mrs. Tartar through the Kemps' spotless beach house. Ian's new cabinetwork opened the place up, made it seem light and a bit more… airy. It was truly beautiful.

"So you live next door?"

"Yes, but I would prefer you contact me by the number on the counter."

Mrs. Tartar twisted her lips in distaste before she rudely dismissed me. I wasn't looking forward to a week of her scrutiny. She had a definite bug up her ass. I was counting on my island to rid her of it.

Walking back to my house, I saw my porch candles were lit and my playlist was already on. I opened the door to see Ian in the kitchen. He was wearing a navy-blue T-shirt and loose sports shorts. His white smile greeted me. "Hey, didn't want to disturb your routine."

"That's very thoughtful of you, thanks."

"I wanted to cook tonight if that's okay?"

"Of course, smells good." I pulled a vase from the cabinet next to him and filled it with water before I slid Banion's latest creation in.

"You brought me flowers?" he asked teasingly.

"My friend owns a flower shop. I use him to make welcome bouquets for the rentals. Beautiful, aren't they?"

"They are," he said as he chopped up some figs.

"What ya' cooking?"

"Salad and very bland chicken."

"I'll take it," I said, snatching a fig from the cutting board and popping it into my mouth. I picked up a mason jar that sat next to a pile of vegetables. "What's this?"

"Pomegranate dressing."

"Wow," I said before I shook it up and brought a fingerful to my mouth. "Delicious."

"Yeah, my mother insisted she teach me a few things about cooking when I was growing up."

"That's awesome. I had to learn my cooking skills from Paula Dean and with your diet, I'll be hard-pressed to find a recipe suitable for you."

"No worries. I'm easy. I also bought some bananas," he said his deep voice pure temptation. "I'm making you pops for dessert. I figured I'd reward you for being such a good muse."

"Good muse?" I took a seat on the stool opposite of him. "How so?"

"You always have music going, it's always lit up over here. I think I might enjoy your bubble while I'm here."

"They *do* sell candles and docking stations everywhere. You could create a bubble of your very own."

He grinned down at his cubed figs. "I said *your* bubble. Should I get crystals too? Then my man card should definitely get revoked."

"Nothing wrong with wanting a little calm in your life."

"I've been off the tit for some time, Koti. I can handle it."

I took immediate offense. "Yeah cause *most* people can, right? They don't need a silly routine when they get home to cope with everyday stresses." I stood abruptly. "I need to go shower."

"Shit," regret was clear in his features as I glared at him over the counter. "I didn't mean that. I'm sorry."

"Rule number one of friendship, don't ever use something against someone that they tell you in confidence, especially a weakness."

"You aren't weak at all."

"Well, then you have a fucked-up way of delivering a compliment. Backasswards way, *friend*."

Stomping down the hall, I heard Ian whisper under his breath, "Swallow your tongue, asshole."

I kicked off my shoes in my bedroom and glared into my closet. My shower lasted fifteen minutes longer than usual, and I knew I was wasting water. I brushed my hair and threw on an old T-shirt sundress. When I rejoined Ian in the kitchen, another apology, in the form of a glass of wine was waiting for me.

Ian's eyes flit over my face before he snatched a towel off his shoulder. "It was insensitive."

"It's fine. I'm used to it."

He picked up the glass and held it out to me. "Well don't get used to it from me, all right?"

I nodded, taking his offered wine, while he grabbed the chicken out of the oven.

"This is really nice of you."

"Least I could do, since you're putting me up."

Ian plated up our dinner and took the cushioned seat next to me on the island. We sat in comfortable silence for a few minutes as we ate.

"This is delicious."

"It's the dish my mother taught me to make for my dates," he confessed.

"And here I was thinking you had skills," I said with the nudge of my elbow. "Still, it's impressive."

"My mother was always thinking of things like that. She made me a cookbook for quick reference in case there was a second date."

"Wow."

"She trained me well. She said she always wanted her

children considerate more than any other characteristic."

"I think I love your mother," I said with a mouthful. "Rowan is good people."

"So tomorrow, will I get a rain check on the dinner I missed?"

"Oh, I get it. This is a favor thing?" I turned to face him and felt the awareness of him shoot through every cell, every pore. He was temptation, his smell, his smile, his beautiful voice.

"In a way. But I was wondering what that dinner might have tasted like."

"Well," I said as I took the last bite of chicken off my fork. "I'm not a modest cook with truly mad skills. The fish will be dry, but the wine will be delicious."

We clinked glasses. "I look forward to it."

"I've got the dishes," I said grabbing his plate.

"I'll let you." He grabbed Disco and nodded his head toward the door. "Going for a walk."

I nodded as my hands shook in the dishwater.

This is not good, Koti.

Half an hour later, I was browsing through a painter's magazine of canvas templates and accompanying paints while Ian set up his computer.

"Shit, the Wi-Fi here is barely catching with next door."

"Waiting on a call from your daughter?"

"Yeah. I may have to go elsewhere."

The glowing blue light flashed in front of him and I saw his eyes light in recognition. He waved at the screen.

Uncomfortable with the intrusion, I gestured toward my bedroom. "I'll just go."

"You don't have to."

He signed fluidly at the screen. "Stay."

"Okay." I sat back down in my seat and he began talking with his hands. I watched fascinated.

"I'm telling Ella," he said as he flicked two fingers out and closed them at his heart, "that I'm staying at my neighbor's as the paint dries at her grandmother's house." He twisted the computer and I saw his daughter wave at me excitedly. I straightened in my seat and waved back.

Ella waved a hand over her face and closed her fist before she began frantically signing.

"She wants to know if you're my new girlfriend."

I shook my head and wound my index finger next to my ear and pointed at her father to let her know I thought he was crazy. She laughed on screen. Ella was a beautiful little girl with long blonde hair and deep-water eyes. I assumed she favored her mother. And then she spoke. "Dad, what have you done to her?" Her English was clear but tainted in the way where she sounded as if she spoke through her nose.

He mocked offense and then spoke. "Nothing. I've done nothing to her."

"Does she read lips?" I asked.

He looked between us as Ella spoke up. "Yes, Koti, I read lips."

I moved in so she could get a better look at them.

"He's lying to you. He's an awful neighbor. I only let him come here because of this." I lifted Disco up and heard her loud squeal. Though her voice wasn't completely clear and she had a slightly off point tongue, she had mastered her speech. "Oh wow. Please, Daddy, tell me that puppy is for me!"

"She belongs to Koti and you'll meet her when you come," he signed as he spoke.

"What's her name?" Ella asked animatedly.

"Disco," Ian and I both answered before sharing a smile.

"I love it," Ella said, beaming.

"I'm going to give you some privacy. It was nice meeting you." I told Ella directly.

"Nice to meet you," she waved. I was close to leaving the room when she spoke up again.

"Dad, she's *so* pretty. Is she why you haven't come home?"

I looked over my shoulder to see him jerk his head to cut her off. I made my way to my bedroom and plucked a book from my shelf. I was curious as to why his daughter would be encouraging him to date. And after meeting her, I was curious about far more than that. Ignoring the constant clench in my stomach and the new warmth that spread through me, I successfully immersed myself into the pages.

An hour or so later, there was a soft knock on my bedroom door.

"You decent?"

I was tangled in my body pillow. "Yep."

"Sorry, I don't want to make you feel like you have to retreat in your own house."

"This isn't my house," I said with a wink. His gaze moved from the book I was holding to the bare leg that gripped the pillow.

"Trust me, I'm good here."

"What are you reading?"

"*Outlander.*"

"Ah," he said with a smile. "My daughter loves those books."

"They're amazing," I said, sitting up.

"Well, I just wanted to say goodnight."

"Thanks for dinner."

"No problem."

"There's some extra pillows in your closet."

"I'll be fine."

"Goodnight."

nineteen

Koti

The next day after work, Ian wasn't home when I got there so I did the twenty-minute prep for dinner. Foil, almonds, salt, butter. Simple and delicious. I went to my bathroom and disrobed before I realized I was out of shampoo. Knowing my hair would be a rat's nest if I used soap, I wrapped a towel around myself and crept down the hall to Ian's room and knocked out of consideration, which I was sure he would appreciate before I walked into the bathroom to grab the extra bottle. On my way back through the bedroom, I saw an open letter on his bed. Against my better judgment, I peeked. It had Ian's signature on the bottom. I glanced around briefly before I picked it up.

Tara,

I used to be the guy that gave the other guys hell. You know the guys who whined about home. I was the ball buster so to speak and the perfect wingman, but hell on the family man. I was the one who swore the metal in his hands and his country were all that mattered.

In the mess hall tonight-if you want to call a tent in the middle of hell a hall-I finally figured out the issue with those sad bastards. They weren't sure if they would get to see the faces of the woman they decided on.

I get that agony. I'm living it now because I decided on you.

Sometimes I wish I hadn't looked your way when you smiled at me. Sometimes I think it would be better if I were out here with a clear heart and nothing to lose. But, the sweet agony, the burn of missing you, needing you, it feels phenomenal. And I get it. And I'm swimming in it, because I know without a doubt, what we have is as real as what the sad bastard next to me has.

I miss your laugh, your face, the feel of your skin, the little moan you give when our lips connect. I miss your shitty jokes and giving you the answers to your mid-term prep questions. I miss the feel of your breasts on my back and waking up to fight you for bedsheets.

There are so many things that a soldier looks forward to, a hot shower, a decent meal, a good night's sleep, Chapstick, and a day without a bullet whizzing past their head. But even in a third-world country, where these things really matter, when a man has the comfort of a woman's eyes to concentrate on, the soft feel of her lips and fingers, it's like a lightning strike of ache that can't be ignored. I took you for granted even before I left your side. I didn't stare long enough, I didn't kiss you long enough, I didn't tell you how much that smile mattered. Because it mattered. It's why I chose you.

For the first time in my life, I'm that sad bastard.

It fucking hurts, but in the way that lets me know coming home will be the end of it.

Please send Chapstick.

I love you.
Ian

"Koti?" Ian's voice sounded as he burst through the door with a barking Disco. I set the letter down exactly as I found it and was at the frame of the door as he walked past it. He stopped abruptly and backed up slowly. His eyes landed on mine before they drifted to the letter on the bed behind me.

I lifted the shampoo bottle. "I was out, so I grabbed some from your bathroom."

Ian searched my eyes which I was sure were filled with guilt and his jaw ticked to confirm as much. He took a step back and let me through and Disco took the liberty of barking at my feet, doing her master's bidding. In the safety of my bedroom, I shut the door, my heart pounding and raced to my bathroom and shut the door leaving two closed between us and still I didn't feel safe. I paced while the hot water ran, in a fit of self-loathing for invading his privacy, before I stepped in and let my skin burn beneath the hot stream.

Something inside me mourned the loss of his relationship while the other part of me longed for the same sentiment. Even more disturbing was that I would want that sentiment from *him*. I was jealous of his ex-wife and had absolutely no reason to be. And since I'd read the letter, I was more curious than ever about the reason behind his sudden presence in St. Thomas. With the stunt I'd just pulled, I was positive I'd distanced myself further from any answers.

It was wrong, so wrong. And he didn't deserve my prying eyes. He said he hadn't felt anything about his wife for years, but if that were true, why would he have an open love letter on his bed?

I shampooed my hair and let the water run as I tried to build up the confidence to leave my bedroom. If he was angry, he had every right to be.

I lathered on some tangerine lotion and threw on shorts

and a cami. I half expected him not to be there when I emerged from the bedroom and walked down the hall. He was standing in the kitchen staring at the foil on the counter.

"Did you read it?"

Straight to the point. I should have been prepared for it, but I wasn't. I swallowed hard and took a step closer. "I'm so sorry. I had no right, I was really just getting the shampoo. Jesus, I'm sorry."

Gray eyes scoured me. "What did you think?"

"Think?"

I was equally unprepared for that question. "I think…" I frowned as he turned and pressed the broil button on the oven. I spoke up. "I can do that."

"Answer the question."

I exhaled unsure if I was ready for the wrath that would follow any answer I gave. "I think you were in love."

"I was a twenty-two-year-old soldier who could have died any minute. Do you think that was real love?"

I bit my lip and took a step forward. "I don't know. But the man who wrote that seemed sure of it with his words."

"Words mean nothing." Ian whistled, and Disco came running with one of my flip-flops in her mouth. Ian released it and set it on the counter.

"You don't really believe that. You can't possibly mean that."

His face was impassive. "I'm leaving in the morning. She'll need to stay with you."

"Ian—"

"Enjoy your dinner."

Four hours later, the fish sat untouched in the pan on my stove. From my hammock on the porch, I watched the dark waves roll in and leave their foam. I searched the beach every few minutes for any sign of him. His things were still in my house and though it was wrong, I was dying to see if there were any more letters in his room. But I couldn't concentrate on anything but the fact he was leaving and when he did, we would be on bad terms, or no terms. It was much later when I heard the creak of the porch steps and broke from my sleep. I stood as he paused on the bottom step.

"Please don't leave angry with me."

He exhaled and looked up at me, I could see him fight the scold on the tip of his tongue before he swallowed it.

"I'm truly sorry. I regret it. I crossed the line and violated the only thing you asked for." I stood shivering in the air, but it was the emotion that was winning. "Please don't leave angry with me."

"Koti, what do you want from me?"

I want you to be happy. I want you not to hate me.

"I want you to say when you come back someday we will still be friends."

He pressed his lips together and took another step up the porch gripping the railing. "Friday, okay?"

"What?"

"I'm going to see my daughter, I didn't say I was leaving for good."

"Oh," I felt my cheeks flame.

I pushed my unruly hair away from my lips and looked at the blanket I left on the hammock before his eyes implored mine.

"You were out here the whole time?"

"No." *Yes.*

Some sort of understanding crossed his features as his eyes

slowly raked over me, leaving nothing untouched. A breath passed between us and turned into two and then three until the static between us became too much to handle. I opened my mouth to speak but found myself weak with want. Ian beat me to the punch.

"I'm sorry."

I took a step back as he caged me on my porch. "For what?"

"For what I'm about to do to you."

In an instant his lips were covering mine, my small moan of surprise was cut short by his tongue. All too easily, I wrapped around him as he opened the door behind us carrying me in. I moaned as his lips found my neck and I clawed at his shoulders through his T-shirt.

"Are you on birth control?" His voice was pure sex.

"Yes," I hissed as his fingers dug into my waist when he slammed me into the wall of my hallway and ground his thick cock into my center.

"Damn," I whispered as his lips and tongue covered every inch of available skin. He ripped at the strap of my cami as if it was a nuisance to get to my nipple and once it was free, he covered it with his lips and tongue. I was dripping wet and could already feel the accelerating pulse between my thighs.

"I've been dreaming of fucking you for a month," he murmured into my neck. "If you don't want this, say it now."

"Don't you dare stop," I rasped out before his lips again claimed mine. Our tongues dueled, ravenous and coaxing until he let my legs down and pinned me to the wall by my wrists, his breaths coming out heavy as he pressed his forehead to mine in an attempt at restraint. I wasn't having it.

"Ian?" I whispered as I fought against his hold pushing out my middle to rub against the straining cock in his pants. "Don't stop. Use me. I don't give a damn. I can handle it. I want this and

I'm damn sure going to use you right back."

His eyes opened then, full of fire and heat and I sucked in a breath. It was as if something had awakened inside him and my fear of it matched my elation. He lifted me easily and pulled me into my bedroom ripping at my shorts until I was free of them. He sat on the edge of my bed and dragged me toward him. Palming my breasts, he watched my reaction to his every touch. My chest rose and fell with heavy breaths. *Everything* felt heavy and I succumbed under his potent gaze. What lay beneath was hellfire and I couldn't wait to tango with his demons.

Rattling with arousal, I gripped his hair in my fingers as he showered my navel with his lips and tongue. "I want you so much," I confessed as he groaned when his fingers dipped into my panties finding me soaked.

"This is for me, Koti, make no mistake."

"Then take it."

He explored until I was drunk on him, and then pulled his soaked fingers into his mouth, tasting me and by his reaction to my taste, I could only conclude the man was starving. I'd never been so turned on in my life.

"Ian," I implored in an urgent whisper. Typically, my fear of pain overshadowed my arousal but, in that moment, consequence be damned. "Ian, please, I don't get turned on like this often, so—"

Before I could get another word out, I was jerked off my feet and onto the mattress before he spread me wide. Ian's mouth covered my entire sex. Darting his tongue between my lips, he worked me over my panties and then moved the cotton out of the way and wrecked me with his fingers and tongue. Arching my back, I gasped out my surprise and he flattened me back to the bed with his palm. He devoured, his thick digits moving in and out, stretching and coaxing while filthy words poured out of him between savage licks. The whole of my body coiled as he lifted my lower half so that my knees rested on his shoulders while he drove his tongue in deep. Inside I began to come apart as he lapped me up and groaned in reward when I detonated. I'd never had an orgasm that fast. Still shaking from my release, his cock was at my entrance before I had a second to recover and then I was full, so incredibly full. I screamed at the severity of the feel of him. He stretched me wide and I moaned with every stroke. Dark, cloud-filled eyes watched my every reaction as he fucked me like it was his last time. I shrieked as he drove in deep and he rewarded me by shoving his fingers into my mouth.

"Suck," he commanded. I did what I was told, while he drove in, again and again, his fingers muting me, his body going rigid under my touch. Picking up speed, he pumped into me at a maddening pace as I held on for dear life. Biting down on his fingers, I bucked, meeting his thrusts, before I started to unravel. "Look at me," he demanded as I leaned up and kissed his chest.

He wrapped my hair in his fist and twisted my head, demanding my eyes. Mouth parted, I spread my legs wider knowing the hell I'd pay for it the next morning. He sank in deeper, his body shaking, while he slammed into me one last time and exploded, his mouth capturing mine in a devastating kiss that lasted long after he'd spilled his last drop. Pulling away we stared at each other, wordless, eyes searching before he collapsed on me, his weight welcome as I wrapped around him without a second thought. We spent the next minutes quietly exploring with lazy fingertips before we drifted to sleep.

When I woke up, he was gone.

twenty

Koti

Friday, I rushed through my workday and raced through the store picking up ingredients for a new recipe I thought Ian might like, only to find the driveway empty when I arrived home. Discouraged, I unloaded my groceries in the fridge. In my hammock surrounded by my candles and the whisper of music, I watched the cabbie struggle with Mrs. Tartar's luggage. When she was set to leave, she spotted me, walked over and thanked me. She looked refreshed and had a slight tan brewing. Though I didn't feel like smiling, I returned hers. My island had done wonders for her. She would be returning to wherever she came from with a clear head, if only for a little while. In bed that night, I heard the door open and fought the urge to greet Ian, even when he lightly knocked on my bedroom door. I ignored it because of the happiness I felt. I was traveling down a rocky road with him and I didn't have a single leg to stand on. He didn't come back for *me*. He came back for his reprieve. And I needed to face facts. If I hadn't spent so much time watching him, thinking about him, I wouldn't have found myself in that situation. Taking the amazing sex out of the equation was a given. He told me that night was just for him. Instead of hanging on to the hope it could lead to more between us, I decided to believe him. Because the truth was, at that point, I wanted more, which was ridiculous. Despite his progress, the man was still a minefield. One wrong step and I knew I would never find all my pieces. He didn't need to feel guilty or sorry about what happened between us. I told him I could handle it and I would... just as soon as I could stop fantasizing about him.

Perspective was everything. So I was a little fascinated with him, slightly infatuated and highly attracted, big deal. I felt that way about my first crush. Ian was in a no-fly zone. I wasn't desperate, but the feelings that brewed beneath the small friendship we'd formed already spoke volumes. And I already had far too many thoughts of him. More than ever, I needed him to stay on his side of the fence, because that's where he wanted to be. That's where he needed to be. I was sure he regretted that night and I didn't want to see it on his face. So, I would ignore the lingering soreness that I still felt from the stretch of him. I would ignore the beautiful feeling of being excited for the first time in years about a man. I would ignore the threatening feelings that were trying to make themselves known. I would ignore it all.

I could not have Ian Kemp, it didn't matter if I wanted to love him or not.

The next morning, I was up at the crack of dawn. I slipped out of the house only to be met by Ian on the beach. Soaked with sweat, he was doing sit-ups as Disco ran between his legs. He saw me right away and flashed me a panty-soaking smile, "Morning."

His spare tire was now a flat and his muscular arms glistened next to the sparkling water. He shined, God how he shined.

"Hey. Did you have a good trip?" I was already taking small steps toward my Jeep.

With furrowed brows, he watched me fail at a sneaky retreat. "Yeah, it was really good. Off to work so early?" He glanced at his sports watch. "It's six thirty."

"Yeah, busy day. So, you had a good trip, that's good then. You can have your house back, she left last night. I'll, uh, come back and make sure you get a schedule of the days we need the house. You are free to take the room when it's booked, of course."

"Okay."

"Have a good day." Disco was at my feet and even when Ian whistled for her, she refused to come.

"Go on, you little shit. I'm trying to make a clean getaway here." The dunce refused to cooperate and instead growled at the tassels hanging off my sandals. Hesitantly, I picked her up as Ian met me halfway. "I'll get her a leash," I said without looking at him because my resolve had already slipped tenfold by the mere sight of him.

"Probably a good idea." He plucked the puppy out of my arms. "Unless you want to finally take ownership of your dog."

"No, no. She's all yours."

I didn't bother to look for his reaction as I all but ran to my Jeep. Turning the ignition, I screamed out a little when The Beastie Boys blasted through my speakers. I turned it down and was out of breath as Ian approached, his forearms on my door. I buckled my seat belt. He looked me over before he spoke.

"Well I was hoping things wouldn't be awkward after the night we had, but apparently that's going to be impossible."

I snorted. "Don't get a big head, Ian. It was incredible, don't get me wrong but I'm having an off morning."

You are a total basket case.

"Okay, so if this isn't about the other night, then what's going on? Are you having a moment?"

I looked at him, *crossly*. "A moment? No, Ian, I'm not having a *moment*," I grit out.

Well, not that kind of moment.

"This is not an attack, then?" I hated how proper he sounded with his distant tongue and exceptional manners.

"Yes, I'm in hysterics, can't you tell?" I deadpanned.

"Well, you're acting strangely."

His face darkened slightly as he looked back at my house. "What's with the blush? Did you entertain last night?"

His jaw ticked as he glanced my way with prodding eyes. I had to suppress the slight satisfaction I got from his question.

"No, why would you think that?"

"I'm at a loss here," he said, resigned. "Have a good day."

He was only feet away when I barked at his back. "Hey, you, you know what assuming makes you, right?"

He belted out a laugh as he turned back to stand in front of me. "An asshole?"

"Exactly. And for your information, I've only had a few attacks since I got here, and I don't sleep around."

He winced. "I'm sorry. That was horrible of me."

"Yeah, well, I'm *handling* it."

"I was just concerned. We are friends now. I think it's safe to assume that, right?"

Feeling humiliated and remorse for my bite, I nodded. "Yes, we're friends."

I hated that he saw my weakness. I hated that was his first assumption. Even if it was an innocent question or asked out of concern, it stung.

More so, I hated that he would even think I could be intimate with anyone else.

"See you later?" he asked, pushing the hair off my forehead.

I met his gaze and saw nothing but warmth. "I'm sorry I'm

on edge. Maybe I do feel a little weird about us sleeping togeth-er. It's been a long time for me. And when I've done the casual hookup thing, I usually don't see the person after."

"No friends with benefits?" He grinned.

I grinned back. "You're my first."

He leaned in on a whisper. "You're mine too. I was married forever, remember?"

"Really?"

"Really," he said leaning in. "And I promise to make sure you benefit."

Goosebumps trailed over my skin and I shrugged. "I don't think I would *hate* it."

He chuckled. "Are you free tonight? I'll cook."

I nodded, and he leaned in and pressed a promising kiss to my lips. "I look forward to it."

I drove away cursing my stupidity.

Way to keep him on his side of the fence, Koti.

twenty-one

Koti

"**YOU WHAT!?**"

Glaring at her, I put my purse in my desk drawer. "This is exactly why I didn't tell you. Are those tears?" I laughed. "You are such an idiot."

"I'm just so happy. You finally got laid." She pulled me into her, pressing her huge boobs against my neck.

"Would you stop! I can't believe you're getting emotional because I had sex."

"Come on, I'm taking you to breakfast."

"No way, we have a full load today."

"And I'll take care of it. You're getting the day off."

"Jasmine, it's Saturday. We have a shitload of houses to flip."

"I've got them. Believe it or not, I did this all by myself before you came into the picture. I'm still the boss. Now get your purse and come on."

"God, you act like I graduated college or something monumental. This is *not* a special occasion."

"Did you orgasm?"

My face flushed.

"Oh, God. The man gave you multiples, didn't he?"

Grinning, I nodded.

"Oh, my God!"

"Would you chill out. The therapist down the hall is going

to file another complaint."

"If you ask me, she could use some multiples. She has resting bitch face. Not only that, she made her own reserved sign for her car. Like she actually went to Lowe's and bought the shit and made a sign. That's pathetic. Come on, we're going to celebrate."

"You're nuts."

"And you're glowing."

"You've seen me the last four days of work and haven't said a word about my glow." We piled into her convertible and buckled up.

"Better late than never. I'm hungry anyway, okay. Just stop being a killjoy and start from the beginning."

Jasmine grinned from ear to ear as I got most of the details out of the way before we pulled up to Pungy's Bistro. Their banana waffles with brown sugar syrup were my favorite and she knew it.

"I love you," I sighed with a mouthful of waffle.

"So tonight, he's cooking?"

"Yep." Swallowing half a glass of orange juice, I hesitated while she studied me.

"You really are glowing. Not that you'll believe me."

"Can I ask you something without you getting offended?"

"Sure," she said with a frown. "You can ask me anything."

"When you are done with a man or dating one, how do you keep your feelings out of it? I mean you do *date* some of these guys."

She sat back and grabbed her coffee cup. "You know I'm in love with someone else."

"That's the trick?"

"It is for me. I know that doesn't help you."

"I just... There's so much about him that I like. Aside from his beastly entrance, the man is truly worth a damn. I just don't know if I can separate the two."

"You might not be able to with him."

"I don't want to analyze. I'm acting like I've never done this before, but with him, it feels like I haven't. Does that make any sense?"

"Perfect."

"It feels so different with him."

"You may need to face the fact that you might already be in love with him."

"No, I'm not, not yet, but if I spend more time with him, I will be. I know it. So, I guess the question is, do I go in and break my own heart or ax it now? He can't stay. He has a daughter back in the States."

"Then you know there's a time limit and you work with what you have."

"Even with the risk?"

"Is he worth it?"

"Yeah, yeah, he is."

"I can't tell you what to do, but I will tell you even though I hate Steven, I don't regret falling in love with him. I never felt that way before or after. He's probably ruined me, but I would do it all over again."

"Why are we so damned stupid?"

She shrugged. "Built that way? But I look at it this way. Some people go their whole lives without that type of connection. Wouldn't you rather have it? And with a man like him?"

"Hell yes."

"Multiples."

"Sign me up."

"You can do this, Koti. Try to do what you said you were going to and use him right back."

"You never told me the good stuff," Jasmine scorned as I gathered my clipboard to turn one house I refused to compromise on. I'd been waiting to meet the renter for months.

"The good stuff?"

"Yeah, how did you orgasm?"

"First, it was his tongue and then from inside. I didn't even know that was possible."

"You poor thing, you got blasted."

"What?"

"Blasted. You can come both ways. He rubs your G inside with his penis or stimulates the clit outside. You can have both at the same time too."

Fire spread through my lower half as I imagined the possibilities.

"And I see today we're getting educational," Toby chimed in from the door of our office before he chuckled and looked over at me. "And I guess congratulations are in order?"

"God," I buried my head in my hands and muffled a "Hi, Toby."

"Happy Saturday, ladies," he said carrying his water bottle in and making the switch.

"See you later, Jasmine," I said in an attempt to make a quick exit. "Call me if you need anything."

She waved me off as she drank Toby in with a crocodile smile. God bless the poor man, it was only a matter of time.

Warm wind whipped through my hair as I blazed a trail through the roads I'd come to know. After a year in St. Thomas, I really had no choice but to take on the 'Hakuna Matata' attitude. Len sang "Steal My Sunshine" as I pulled up to the rental and parked my Jeep. I opened three sets of glass double doors from the living room to the patio and let the ocean air filter in while I laid out a bottle of wine and one of Banion's bouquets on the countertop. Half an hour later, I greeted two pale-faced couples. As soon as they pulled up, the driver—a tall, thin, wiry man with thick brown hair—jumped out and held out the keys over the hood to the laughing passenger who I assumed was his wife.

"Oh, hell no, I'm not driving here," she said with a guilty smile.

"Did you know it was left side versus right here!?" He exclaimed as she winked at me in greeting, mid-argument with her husband. She knew, all right, she knew because I told her. The U.S. Virgin Islands were formerly owned by the *British*. It's kind of like renting a car in England, but... not. Same driver's side but you drive on the opposite side of the road. With steep mountain cliffs and neck breaking turns—not to mention impatient natives—for those unprepared, it's pretty much the scariest experience ever from the airport to their destination.

"I can arrange for a driver for the rest of your trip," I piped in as all four of them looked my way. "Hi, I'm Koti."

A woman close to my age came toward me and gripped me in a bear hug. "Oh, this place, Koti! It's even more amazing than the pictures."

"Hi, Kelli. Wait until you see the inside." I whispered, hugging her back. I greeted the two men pulling bags from the trunk of the rental.

"Guys, I know you're anxious to get settled, but if you can let the bags wait a minute so I could show you around, I would appreciate it." The men reluctantly let the bags go and followed me down the tinted cement shell concrete stairs that sat surrounded by lush tropical plants. When I opened the door, they all gasped in unison. At the time I took the reservation and spoke to Kelli, I wanted to make sure she got the best rental we had. She had just survived her second round of chemo and deserved the oasis she was about to spend a week in. The tears that shimmered in her eyes as she assessed her piece of the island did it all for me. She lifted a grateful gaze to mine before she raced out onto the marble porch at the back of the house and tackled her husband, who had already covered half of the top floor. His smile matched hers and in a simple maneuver he gripped her from his back and pulled her tightly to him. Excited whispers were exchanged between them as he held her like his lifeline and his eyes conveyed everything he felt for her. My chest swelled with admiration while another part of me rejoiced in their excitement.

It was my favorite type of rush, sharing my peaceful island with those who deserved some peace of their own.

But I'd never had life be so ugly as to dish out cancer.

Kelli's eyes found me again and I pushed a tear away with my finger in an attempt to mask it as she mouthed "thank you."

The other couple, who Kelli told me was her best friend and husband, stood on a separate porch and rapidly spoke while they pointed to the lone mountain nestled across their lawn, made of deep blue water.

"That's Hans Lolich," I pointed out, "And it's for sale. Thirty-five million and it's yours."

The couples roamed the house taking in their rented oasis and kept their eyes glued past the cliffside back patio that stretched the length of the large two-story villa. It took me several minutes to get their attention, but I had to admit I loved watching them run around like children who just arrived at their first carnival.

"Okay, guys listen up." For the next few minutes, I showed them around the house and explained as much as I could get through to them, when their thoughts were on their first drink and a dive in their private pool.

Once I had them settled, and we'd said our goodbyes, I made my way out the front door and left the keys on the mahogany table next to it.

"Hey!" I turned to see Kelli close the front door behind her, her hands clasped on the knob. "I know you rented this house to me for under the normal weekly rate." I saw her audibly swallow and had to fight emotion to keep my tears from coming. She needed this trip. I'd heard it in her voice when she made the reservation, the defeat, the need to be excited about something, *anything*. It was rare that I spoke to a client for more than a few minutes, but Kelli and I spoke for the better part of an hour when she called. After my talk with her, I spent a day or two trying to imagine what it was like having poison shoved into my veins while I fought for my life and counted on others to try to save it.

Living in St Thomas, away from the life I knew and being disconnected, actually helped me become more in tune with those around me. I haven't always been a *person's* person. In fact, the New Yorker in me had grown immune to brushing shoulders with millions of other people, indifferent to the presence of other wandering souls. I was completely apathetic and I was positive the old Koti Vaughn might have shied away from the hug Kelli gave me earlier. My hope was I had evolved from that narcissistic New Yorker.

Even if my involvement with her elation was small, the smile on her face was my reward.

Saluting me, Kelli squinted from the bright sun as she spoke. "Thank you, Koti."

"You deserve to be happy."

She laughed and gripped her arms. "You know, I was just thinking that the other day. I looked in the mirror at the woman who used to run a 5k in twenty minutes and asked myself—what if there comes a time when I only have twenty minutes left. The answer was so simple."

"And what was it?"

"Be simple and do whatever the hell it is you have to do to make yourself happy."

"I think you're right." Except I knew she was, I'd been living as a simpleton for months.

She gave me a knowing grin. "*And* I'm not the only one who deserves it. New York lost a gem. Thank you again." I may have overshared a little when she called. It was cheaper than therapy and more rewarding when we shared the common bond that reality, sometimes sucked.

But sometimes reality shifted the clouds and let in a light so bright, it was impossible to ignore.

My island was that light for me, and I had a feeling it could be hers too.

She winked at me before she slipped into the light blue, double-wide doors.

On the drive home, I meditated on her words. I'd been so nervous about the prospect of having feelings for Ian, I'd nearly lost sight of the fact that our newly rekindled friendship was a gift. The truth was, being with Ian made me happy. And I would enjoy it for as long as we had.

twenty-two

Koti

I climbed my porch steps and paused when I heard the first few keys of the piano sound. The baby grand that sat in the living room hadn't been touched in years, well, not by the fingers of an experienced pianist. My dad used to play when I was a little girl, often entertaining our friends in the penthouse. Opting to see if any more music would come, I stood waiting at the front door. My jaw dropped when a melody began to fill the air. I couldn't put my finger on the song, but it sounded familiar. After a few bars, I managed to slip into the house unnoticed. Mesmerized by the sight of him, I picked Disco up before she could make a sound. He missed a key or two, but quickly recovered, his timing was that of a practiced musician. It took every bit of strength I had to remain idle as he blew me away with his talent. While watching him, my new 'live for the moment' confidence was being obliterated away note by note.

Don't overthink this, Koti!

No matter how hard I tried to forget Ian Kemp once he left me, I knew no matter how much time passed, or how our relationship ended, I would never forget how I felt watching him play that piano.

Thunder sounded in the distance and rain began to hit the roof of the house and trail down the windowpane next to me while the rest of the afternoon sun faded under the cover of the clouds. With the room dimmed, I smiled at the sight of lit candles. Ian had created his own bubble.

Inwardly sighing, I sat back on the arm of my sofa and admired my view. He grimaced, once or twice and then sank into the music, his posture relaxing slightly while his chest flexed under the white T-shirt that covered him. When the last note was played, he sat back, rubbing his hands on his thighs before he looked up and spotted me. I was sure I looked insane gawking at him, but he just grinned.

"Hi. I know that was horrible."

I shook my head. "Hi, back. That was beautiful. I know that song."

"I played it in my last recital, it's "Clair de Lune" by Debussy."

"Accomplished pianist too, huh? Is there anything you can't do?"

"Lots of things," he said, standing before he glanced at the large wall clock past my shoulder. "You're home early."

"Slow day. The boss told me to take the rest of it off. How long did you play?"

"Just through grade school."

"That was grade school level?"

"I was a bit advanced."

I harrumphed. "You think?"

He ignored my compliment as he stalked toward me, his eyes darkening.

"So lucky me," he said moving to stand in front of me before he took a squirming Disco from my arms to grant her freedom. "You're home early and it's raining," he murmured leaning in, "what shall we do?"

I swallowed. "I was thinking we could start our book club?"

"Sure," he said with a smirk, pulling my purse off my

shoulder and tossing it on the couch behind me. "After."

"After?"

"After," he whispered, crushing me to his chest before capturing my mouth.

Hours later, I lingered next to a hot running shower, my whole body vibrating as I stood in a daze, my hair a sex afro. My abdomen was screaming, and I winced at the pinch I still felt from his size. The man fucked like Tarzan.

"Hey," he said in a raspy voice behind me. I turned to see him darken my doorway and took a step back. "I, uh... I can't do it again, sorry." I jumped into the shower and ducked under the stream as the door open and he joined me. He chuckled as he turned me to face him. "What's with the brush-off?"

The banging began below, and I knew I was in a world of shit. I winced as I ducked for the shampoo.

"You're hurt?"

"I'm sore."

"I'm sorry," he said, tilting my chin. "I'm a little rough."

"A little," I said with wide eyes.

"Shit, I really hurt you?"

"No, I mean I'm hurting, but it doesn't really have to do with the sex. I mean it does but..."

"Koti, spit it out," he said impatiently. "I'm feeling like an asshole here."

"I have a condition that can make sex painful at times, well after sex." I glanced at the tile floor. "Sometimes during."

"You were hurting during?" he asked confused. "Those screams?"

"Were orgasms," I assured. "Ian, you're fine. It's called

endometriosis. That's why I was on the hammock that day crying. It's awful to endure and a shitty subject, so let's not talk about it."

He let out a breath and gripped my shoulders. "Be honest, did any part of that hurt *during?*"

"No, I swear. I like you but not enough to hurt myself."

"Okay, so what do we do?"

I laughed. "What do you mean, what do we do? *We* do nothing. I just have to deal with it."

I lathered up his hair while he studied me and gave him a faux hawk. "Sexy."

"Yeah?" He poked his head out of the shower and looked in the mirror. "I like this look on me."

"Me too," I murmured pressing a kiss to his throat.

He looked down at me with a grin, as suds slipped down his temple.

I was so in love with him.

He gathered me to him and slid his hands down to where I ached. I leaned back into his frame as his cock hardened. "I'm sorry. I'll take it easier on you."

"Don't you dare," I said fisting his thickness between us. "Don't. Please don't do that. I can honestly say this is the only time the pain has been worth it." Every single tooth he had was displayed with his answering crocky smile.

"Don't smile at me like that."

"So, what you're saying is I'm the best lover you've ever had."

Hell yes.

"I never said that, but thanks for blasting me, pal."

"Blasting you?"

"It's an inside joke."

"Ah," he said, lathering up. "Will I ever be privy to this

information?"

"Doubtful," I said, rubbing the soap over his chest and down his forearms. He clasped our hands and kissed the back of mine. "I'm starving. Hungry?"

"Sure." The ache in my belly began to roar as I pressed my lips to his before I stepped out of the shower. Once dry, I frantically searched my cabinets. "Shit."

"What?" he asked, toweling off. I took a second to admire him. "You look great, Ian. Not that you didn't look good before, but, you really look so… great."

His eyes softened. "Can't find anything for the pain?"

"You're shit at taking compliments, you know that?"

"I'll run to the chemist and fetch something."

"No, you don't have to do that."

"Then you can just suffer," he said rolling his eyes.

Half an hour later, I was curled up in bed with my heating pad when Ian strolled in with two bags. "Did you stock up on Advil until the apocalypse?"

"I've got it all." He emptied the bag onto my bed. "Lift your shirt and lower your broeks."

"Broeks?"

"Panties."

I smiled. "Sexy."

He cut a hand through the air. "Just do it."

I did as I was told, and he stuck a patch above my pelvic bone, opened a box and gave me four pills and a bottled water to take them with. "That heating patch should do you good, the pharmacist said we can change it every four hours. You can take four of these pills in one go if you need to."

Stunned by his kindness, I nodded toward the other bag. "What's in there?"

"Chinese food—and a shit load of it—ice cream, and two movies. Come on, we have to go to my house since you've decided to live past century." He held his hand out to me and I winced as I stood. He pressed a kiss to my temple. "I'm sorry."

"Damnit, Ian, don't. Okay? This isn't going to change, and I don't want it to interfere with our..." I nodded in embarrassment, "you know."

"Quality time?"

"Exactly," I said giving him a forced grin. I prayed for the pills to kick in as we walked to his house. He pulled me as close as I could be as we devoured the food and watched our favorite movies from when we were kids, *Raiders of the Lost Ark*—his—followed by mine, *Jaws*.

"Remember when we watched these?" he asked as he loaded *Jaws* into the DVD player.

"Of course."

"You were so young, I didn't know if you remembered a lot of that summer."

"I remember *all* of that summer."

He gave me warm eyes. "Me too."

"You were a hot-headed ass."

"You were a total crybaby brat," he smarted back before he pulled me into his lap. Sometime later, I woke up cradled to his chest. He was staring at my lips in the dim light of the house, the movie flickering over his features. His eyes fluttered closed and he turned his attention back to the screen. I pressed a kiss to his Adam's apple and drifted back to sleep.

Ian

Heaven or hell, I wasn't sure which I was dwelling in. I was leaning more toward the former. I'd spent my week on stand-by waiting for Ella after school to spend every moment I could with her. I applied for a few teaching positions for the fall. My life seemed to be back on track. I was feeling a little more like myself, aside from the new freedom I felt. I was running out of reasons to continue flying back to St. Thomas and I fucking hated the fact that I felt like I needed any other excuse than the one laying in my arms. The truth was we were on a slippery slope. At the same time, I still had so much hatred for Tara, I couldn't be civil to her for any amount of time. My plans for the summer were mine to make. I was a free man. Ella was going to summer camp in Washington. I had the summer. I could give her the summer. I studied her gorgeous face in the flickering light and got fixed on her lips. She stirred awake and gave me a small smile. I turned my attention back to the screen and felt her lips on my Adam's apple. My chest ached in that moment at the idea of leaving her.

I could give myself the summer.

twenty-three

Koti

I sucked my banana pop on the love seat flipping the pages of my new book. It was an incredibly hot day, and my AC was working overtime to cool the house. Our book club had commenced a few hours prior. Ian sat back on the couch opposite of me, his feet crossed and propped on the other end. I'd been stealing glances at him every page flip since we started reading. Shirtless in his faded palm tree swim trunks, he looked completely relaxed as he turned through the pages of a mystery novel.

Slurping on the sweet deliciousness of the freshly made frozen concoction, I managed to get through a chapter before I stole my next glance. To my surprise, his eyes were hot on me.

"Are you feeling better?"

"Yes, much."

"You have beautiful lips."

"Thank you."

"Get over here and put them on my cock."

"Whaa?" I sat up, my clit pulsing with the low rasp of his voice, my mouth watering at the idea. I couldn't look away. The whole situation was a train wreck because the New Yorker in me wanted to castrate him, while the feminist in me wanted to tell him to go straight to hell; but even as I feigned offense, I was strangely more turned on than I had ever been in my life.

Ian wore an infuriatingly sexy smirk. "I can see you fancy the idea as well."

He was right, and a part of me hated it. Breathless, I rubbed my lips together as he zeroed in.

He slipped his shorts down enough so his ready cock sprang free. He was so hard, pre-cum dripped from the tip. He took it in his hand and pumped a few times as I found myself gravitating toward it.

"You're serious?"

"It's sex and no one tops me in the bedroom, Koti, ever." He wiped the tip of his dick with a finger and held it out for me. "Come here."

I sank to my knees on the carpet looking up at his bedroom eyes. The man turned me on like no other.

"I'm going to need a view, *Miss* Vaughn.

Taking his cue, I unhooked my bikini top.

"Now, *that's* a view."

I was dripping. My eyes half closed with arousal as I sucked his finger eagerly before I moved to brace myself above him, one hand on the couch the other gripping his thick dick.

I was just about to wrap my lips around him when he spoke. "Do a good job, and I'll make sure you benefit."

"Jesus, Ian."

He gripped my hair in his fist and leaned down on a whisper. "Suck it."

God, why was I so turned on? I wrapped my lips around him down to the base as his fingers threaded through my hair. Pulling away with a pop, I grazed his tip with my teeth before I swallowed and took him in again.

"Perfect," he gritted out, gently guiding my head down. He never pushed, but lifted his hips, fucking my mouth as I pumped and sucked.

"Jesus, those lips, give them to me," he demanded, pulling me up by my hair, my scalp screaming as he smashed his mouth to mine. Our tongues gave and took as I straddled him on the couch rubbing my covered seam along his dick and moaning into his mouth. He ripped himself away and stared down at me as we both panted. "You aren't done, I just need to feel you right now,"

"Ian," I breathed as his eyes trailed over my chest and further down before they flit to mine.

"Get rid of those fucking bottoms." He yanked at the strings on the sides of my bikini until I was bared.

"How wonderfully convenient, these strings of yours, now bring that beautiful pussy to my mouth and ride my face."

"You're filthy."

"It's only going to get worse after I taste your beautiful ass," he promised as he lifted me up to feast, diving in like a madman. I stared down at him with my mouth open as he cradled my ass with his hands and pressed into me. Flicking his tongue expertly, he ate me until I was writhing in his hold. My arms began to shake with my weight as I got closer to the brink. Fiery gray eyes flit to mine after a leisurely lick. "Let go, I've got you."

"Ian," I rasped out, as he dove in, sliding his nose against my clit and thrusting his tongue inside. Breaths coming fast, I ground into his face and was rewarded with another groan. He pulled my clit between his lips and sucked hard until I began spasming uncontrollably in his hands. Licking me mercilessly, he refused to let up until I had soaked his chin. He pulled away and wiped it as he lowered me to sit on his bare stomach.

His illicit whispers lit my skin on fire. "I'll be at your mercy anywhere but in the bedroom."

He thrust two fingers up into me and I rode his hand, tilting my head back as he captured my nipple in his mouth.

"You are so damned beautiful," he murmured, before trailing his tongue from one side of my neck, across my chest to the other. I began to quicken as he sped up his fingers and without warning replaced them with his waiting dick and thrust into me. I shuddered on his cock as he cursed, bit his lip and closed his eyes. I bucked and slid my clit against the thick ridge of him as his eyes opened and lit the rest of me into an inferno.

We were nothing but movement then, lips and teeth gnashing as I jerked my hips down greedy for more.

"So tight," he murmured before pushing up so my knees lifted off the couch and I was impaled. I fell forward while he held me in the air, rubbing me back and forth, so all I could do was hold on.

"Come for me."

And I did, I imploded as he bit down on my nipple and reddened my ass with his palm. I'd never been touched like that and never felt so out of control. I cried into his chest as my orgasm lasted a small eternity and then rode him hard and fast until I saw him start to crumble. Mouth parted, he groaned, his hands palming my ass, his body glistening. I jerked my hips again as he let out a "Fuck, Fuck," before he collapsed back into the couch. Eyes closed, a slight smile played on his lips before he opened them and met my gaze. Wordless, we both sank into our connection. Moving to kiss him, I slid down his body and settled my lips on his.

Happy and relaxed, we settled into a warmth-filled silence until I heard a voice sound on the side of my house.

"Don't drag my suitcase through the sand, it's expensive!"

I shot off the couch like I was still on fire. "Ian, that's my mother."

He stood as if he didn't have a care in the world and casually pulled on his shorts. He had his second arm in his T-shirt hole as he walked down the hall toward his room when a knock finally sounded at the front door. I thanked God we'd shut it in an attempt to keep the cool air in.

"Jesus, it's hot out here. Knock again," my mother said as I managed to get my bikini tied.

Looking toward the direction Ian fled, I ignored the front door and ran down the hall. Opening his door, Ian looked at me puzzled as I raced up to him and kissed him, *hard*. He chuckled into my mouth.

"Like that, did you?"

"As soon as they leave, we're doing that again."

"Okay, puffer fish."

"Don't call me by my pet name after that kind of sex, it's weird."

"Would you *go* already? They're definitely going to know I was fucking you, *now*."

My clit pulsed at his vulgarity. "God, I love the way you say that." Biting my lip, I roved my eyes down his sexy form and that earned me another chuckle.

He slapped my ass. *"Go."*

"I'm going."

"Koti?"

I stopped at his door just as another knock landed. "Yeah?"

"It was amazing and we will be repeating that, *repeatedly.*"

We shared a smile before I looked toward the front door. "This is going to suck."

He reached out and gripped my hand.

"Everyone is a glass house, it's up to you to decide who to give the rocks to."

I nodded.

"Go."

"So beautiful," I heard him whisper before I closed his door.

"So, Ian," my father said as he sipped his beer, "my daughter failed to mention you were staying here. What brought you to St. Thomas?"

I glanced over at Ian and saw the hesitation on his face and so I gave my parents a half-truth.

"He's a teacher, so he's here to spend the summer prepping for his fall schedule."

"A teacher," my mother said perched upon one of the barstools, her golden hair slicked back into a tidy bun, her makeup flawless even after a stint in the heat. "What do you teach?"

"He's a professor actually, he teaches linguistics," I said on a redundant search for approval, for no other reason than I didn't like her tone. Ian gave me a pointed look that said he didn't need my help and I hoped he recognized the answering apology on my face.

"No need for the third-degree, Mom. We aren't dating. He's just staying here because we rented out the Kemp house this week."

Her lips tightened. "I'm not giving the third degree, I'm curious." Tension filled the air as Ian eased into conversation quickly telling them about his career.

"A former Marine. Thank you for your service," my father added thoughtfully before he looked at me. I kept my eyes down as my mother went on, using Ian's career success as an excuse for an unwelcome subject about my future.

"Did Koti tell you she worked as a real estate broker in New York? She was one of the best."

"She did," Ian confirmed as he took a sip of his beer.

"She had a huge future."

"Mom," I warned. She looked around the beach house she hadn't visited in years. "It still looks the same doesn't it, babe? Nothing's changed. I guess our girl is safe enough here." My father shot her daggers as he took another sip of his beer.

"Ian, I'm sure you have things to do." With the tension thickening to choking level, I had to give him an out. "Don't feel obligated to hang around."

Ian didn't move, his eyes challenged mine. Thoughts of what happened between us swirled around my newly aching head. I tried to read him but was disappointed when he flicked his eyes to my mother. "I have nothing pressing."

"How long will you be staying?" I asked my parents as casually as I could muster, and my mother took immediate offense. Before she could open her perfectly painted lips and let words through, my dad piped in.

"Only a few days, and we'll get a hotel tomorrow, we apologize for the intrusion."

"It's not an intrusion, Dad, this is your house."

Uncomfortable silence followed until Ian swooped in and saved the day turning to engage him. "Koti told me you used to work with some pretty big bands."

Conversation flowed easily from that point as my dad spoke about his days as a sound engineer and threw in a few stories including the one of how he met my mother.

"She hated me, it was so obvious."

"I didn't hate you," she chimed in.

He gave Ian a wary look. "Oh, she hated me, and I've never had to work so hard for anything in my life." My mother smiled, genuinely smiled at my father and a part of me sighed. Though I'd painted her the big bad wolf at times, and she was hard on me, she was a lot of other things. A loving wife being one of them. My parents clasped hands and my dad winked at her. They had a healthy marriage. It had been full of everything a union should be, mostly because my dad worshipped her, and she needed that worship. They met at a time where their hectic lives were winding down and I could always see their genuine appreciation for each other. I was a bit envious. And I saw Ian notice the same. My parents had wicked fights, mostly due to my mother being hardheaded in regards to me, but my father stood his ground and when he did, she seemed to respect him more for it. He'd done it a lot, especially where I was concerned. I'd almost missed the change of conversation until I felt all eyes on me.

"What?"

"I was just telling Ian how you tried the piano."

"Yeah," I said wrinkling my nose, "never got the hang of it. Ian plays beautifully."

Ian's flattered smile was brief, but I caught it. "I'm horrible."

"I don't think so."

My dad's eye darted between us and Ian looked at me with a mix of curiosity and something I couldn't put my finger on.

My father smiled at me with pride. "This little woman has great taste in music, though. I think she got that from me."

"I have your flat butt, that came from you."

"Maybe" he laughed. "And my business sense."

"Not sense enough," my mother jabbed and everyone at the table ignored her.

She eyed me curiously and then let her gaze drift between Ian and me. Ian ignored her scrutiny and kept his beautiful grays on me, filling me with much-needed warmth. My father stepped in, offering us a reprieve from her silent interrogation. "Let's go to bed, Blair. It's been a long day."

"I'm fine," she said as she looked at me pointedly. I was too tired for the conversation she wanted to have and to answer the questions in her eyes, questions even I didn't have the answers for when it came to me and Ian.

"*Now*, Blair."

My mother's eyes said it all as she reluctantly bid us good-night and followed him upstairs.

Ian didn't miss a beat before speaking up. "Jesus, you're that uncomfortable with your own mother around?"

"I'm tired," I moved to stand.

"Stop, look at me." I turned to look up at him feeling the zing of his touch while electricity rode through my body and sent a shock wave to my core. He peered down at me. "Koti—"

"Please, just don't. This isn't fixable, no matter how you see it—she's not going to let up, *ever*. I've been down this road so many times I could drive it blindfolded. So whatever suggestions you have, just know I've tried it. And I have to agree with you to some degree. When it comes to her, words mean nothing."

Ian peered down at me as I bit my lip and shook my head. "Whatever you're thinking, don't tell me."

"You have no idea what I'm thinking." His fingers drifted up my arm slowly until they reached the strap of my cami. Eyes intent, he toyed with the material between his fingers before he gently pulled it down. His breath hit first sending goosebumps up my spine. I tilted my head back as soft lips landed and I sank into him. His teeth grazed my shoulder as his tongue darted out. I soundlessly moaned as he gripped the side of my neck with his palm and blazed a trail from the nape to just below my ear. I kept my moan internal as I gripped his hand, leaned into his mouth, and let out a word filled whimper. "Please."

"She doesn't hold a candle to you."

I attempted to pull myself away, but he held me firmly in his grip.

"What?! Why would you say that?"

"She is beautiful, Koti, but you are so much more," he

whispered, continuing to explore, "so soft," he murmured, his scent consuming me. It took all my strength to fight him.

"You kissed me because you decided I was insecure about my mother?"

"It's apparent you're insecure about your mother, and I haven't kissed you, yet," he assured as he palmed my face in his hands.

"Look, I don't need your reassurances." I pulled away from his hold and faced him head on.

"Fine, my mistake," he whispered heatedly. "But I'm going to tell you how beautiful I think you are and what you do to me." He inched forward, his breath hitting my neck as he spoke low. "Before you let me, and even though I was angry, I thought about touching you every day for a month. You were a dream." He pressed his lips against my neck and I let out a soft moan. "The most perfect dream," he whispered. "I thought about the feel of your lips, my tongue in your mouth, my cock stretching you, the look in your eyes as I invaded you. I thought about sucking your tits while I buried myself deep enough, so you would never forget I was inside you. I thought about your ass and how red it could get under my palm. At night as I lay in bed, I thought about nothing *but* you. I'm so fucking hard for you right now it physically hurts, and I just had you hours ago."

Without an ounce of fight, he tugged me toward him by pulling my arms around his neck. I licked my lips as his arousal brushed my stomach. Mouth parted, my panties soaked, I threaded my fingers in his hair. Leaning in, he pushed the hair away from my ear as he whispered the rest of his seduction. "And even though I've had you, I've touched your skin, and buried myself so far inside you that you won't forget, you're still a dream for me, so beautiful it hurts."

We shared a breath and I could feel the frustration and need rolling off him.

He pulled back, demanding my eyes before our mouths met, his tongue diving deep as he fully tasted me. Between his confession and his perfect kiss, I was at his complete mercy. He thrust his tongue deep and I felt his every word match his desire. Returning it with the same fervor, he pulled away when I began to get aggressive. "I want you so much right now."

"So, take me to bed."

He shook his head. "It wouldn't be appropriate."

"Like you care."

"It's my respect for your father and nothing more."

"Okay."

He ran a hand through his hair. "I'll make myself scarce."

"You don't have to."

"Koti," his face twisted in regret. "I want to. I have to."

"Oh," I said, feeling my heart sink a little at his admission. But there were unspoken rules and he was holding us both to them. This was a family matter and highly personal. He wasn't mine to claim, he didn't want to be involved and he was making it known.

"I can't do this with you." That admission left a crack in my chest.

"I know."

"Damnit." He ripped his arms away and instantly I felt cold. "I can't. I'm sorry."

"I understa..." but before the words left my lips, he was through the door to his room and I felt the finality as he softly shut it behind him.

Could Ian and I be more?

I had my answer.

twenty-four

Koti

"**W**hat's wrong?"

Jasmine peered down at me as I entered the office mid-afternoon the next day. I explained I would be late due to the unexpected visit from my parents.

"I told you, my mother is here, need I say more?"

"She can't be that bad."

I shrugged. "She's not unless she decides to bring up my future, and she *always* does. I can't believe I was dumb enough to miss work to have breakfast with her, it was a massacre. My dad had to practically peel her off me so I could get to my Jeep."

"She needs a hobby," Jasmine frowned. "You aren't a project."

"Tell that to her," I said as I sat defeated in my chair. Ian was gone when I woke up, no doubt on another run. I spent most of the night tossing and turning and hadn't slept a single minute. I still felt his lips regardless of his words, but that was the scary part. No matter how transparent he was about our situation I'd ignored it and only saw him. And *oh*, how I wanted him in every way.

"If it's okay, I'm going to knock off early to deal with the inevitable fall out, so they can leave."

"Of course, you can take the day. I told you that on the phone."

"I had to get out of there for a little while. I need to prepare."

Her eyes rolled over me in concern. "You think it will be that bad?"

"I do, but I'm tired of running away from the conversation. It's time."

"Well, call me if you need me. I'll drop everything." She gave me a quick hug before the phone rang. It was on the tip of my tongue to tell her what happened with Ian. To wait around and see what she had to say on the matter, but inside I knew the truth. He'd laid it out for me and I knew it. I'd be asking Jasmine to give me hope, which would be pointless. He would never be mine to love.

On the porch with my parents later that day, my mother sat expectantly. "So, you won't come back and you're determined to stay here? Why?"

Ian had made himself scarce as promised and I couldn't help my wandering eyes as I searched the beach every so often for a sign of him. The renters had left that morning and I was sure he'd resumed residence at his house.

"I'm happy here."

"You're wasting your life," she argued, "your potential."

"I'm saving my fucking life," I snapped before my father shot me a warning look.

"Easy, Koti."

I swallowed the knot in my throat. "I'm happy here. Why can't that mean anything?"

She glanced at my dad for backup and got none. I could already see the war brewing that she would wage on him later.

"It does mean something. It means a lot that you've finally

pulled yourself together and now you can come back swinging."

"This isn't a resurrection, Mother. I'm not coming back for another round, I've accepted defeat as far as that goes and I wish you would too. I can't hack it out there, not in that world and not in that atmosphere. I have limitations, and I'm learning to deal with them."

"I can't believe you're hiding behind that excuse," she said incredulously. "We all have our stresses."

"You've talked to my therapist, Mom. You know I have it a little bit harder than that."

"It's an excuse."

I was on my feet instantly. "You have no idea what it's like to feel like you're drowning while life goes on around you, while people smile like they don't have a care in the world, while you're struggling to breathe! You have no idea!"

My mother bared her teeth. "Calm down."

I took a deep breath. "That's just it, Mother," I said with defeat, my bones aching from the emotions she stirred. "Sometimes I can't calm down until I'm so weak I can't move. You made an imperfect daughter—deal with it already. I'm tired of trying to explain it to you."

She looked at my father for more backup and he finally stepped in.

"Blair, listen to her. She's happy."

She shot daggers at him. "We agreed."

"We also agreed to hear her out." My father let out a heavy sigh as he looked over to me. His rehearsed question coming out as an obligation. "You won't even consider coming back?"

"No, Dad. I love New York but it's too hard for me. I won't go back to live in a place I can't breathe in. This is my life. I'm happy with it. The sooner you two accept it, the better."

"I'm selling this house," my mother stated plainly. "You can hide somewhere else."

"I was hiding in New York, Mom. *This* is who I am."

"We spent all that money on education, prep schools, what the hell was the point?" She argued, ruthlessly reminding me of the trouble she'd gone through to raise me.

"Maybe it was so she could figure this out on her own. Jesus Blair, give her some credit. She suffered for all those years just to please us, can't you see that?" My father had taken a side and from the look on her face, it wasn't the right one. "And you're not selling this goddamn house."

I felt the earth shift as he defied my mother and my pulse began to kick up.

"What in the hell did you just say?" She paled as he leaned forward, his face defiant.

"You heard me. Her happiness comes first, just like yours has for the last thirty-four years of our lives. I won't let you alienate our little girl. This whole situation is *your* doing."

Oh shit.

"Mom," my voice was shaking. I could feel the rattle begin in my brain. "Look at me, please."

Hurt and anger coursed through me as I pleaded to keep the situation from escalating further. "Please don't fight. I never wanted to disappoint you. I love you both so much. Please don't do this."

She looked over to me as I begged her once again to try to understand. "I will never live up to what you want me to be. Ever. This won't change. I'm not changing my mind and I can't change yours. Don't ruin what you have with daddy because you think I failed you. He didn't disappoint you, I did. But I can't let your ridiculous expectations ruin another minute of my life. If you can't be proud of me this way, please just leave."

"Blair, let's go."

Blair Vaughn stood five foot, nine inches of relentless beauty and never-ending expectation "The hell I will, we aren't done talking."

Twin tears rolled down my cheeks as I looked at my mother and accepted our fate. "*I'm* done, Mom. Please try to understand. *I'm* done."

"We're leaving. Blair, go get your bags."

"Daddy, you don't have to leave. Please, can we please just try to enjoy our time together?"

"We aren't done discussing this!"

My father turned on her, his eyes cold. "Now, Blair, damn you! This is the last time you make our daughter feel unworthy of your love. Do you hear me? This is the last time. She's a grown woman and old enough to choose her own happiness. Give it up and go get your things. We're leaving!"

My mother swallowed as incredulous tears built up in her eyes.

"Now, Blair, go!"

We both jumped at the anger in his voice. Her eyes flitted to mine and I saw the rest of our ties start to snap. "Mom," I called after her as she slammed the front door shut behind her.

Unable to handle the idea that I'd caused a rift between my parents, I pleaded with my dad who was shaking as he stared at the ocean. "Daddy, I'm so sorry."

He took a few steadying breaths before he pulled me into his arms. "I know. Jesus, Koti, I feel so responsible. I should have stopped this shit years ago, I'm so sorry."

"I hid it, Dad. I hid it from you both. This is just the way she is, she'll never get it and that's not your fault either."

He pulled back and searched my eyes. "I'm proud of you anyway. Always. I hope you know that. I'm so proud of you. I'm so sorry you had to save yourself, but so proud you did."

We cried together on the porch as my mother slammed her way through the house.

Licking the tears from my lips I apologized again, the guilt of what was in store for him hard to bear. "I'm sorry, I just can't cater to her anymore."

"I know. Just be happy. I know it's hard to believe, but I think a majority of this is because she wants you home."

"Daddy," I said tearfully as I pulled away, "I *am* home."

I sat on my porch hours after my parents left. My father's tearful goodbye on the forefront of my mind. There was a rift between my mother and I that may never be repaired, at least not in a way it would mend anytime in the foreseeable future. Though I was finally okay with it, I knew it had just broken his heart and ripped his family apart. And the sad part was, only the two of us knew it to be true. My mother would forever maintain this was my fault.

"Hey."

Ian walked up to the bottom step and looked up at me.

"Hey."

"Your parents left?"

"Yeah. Feel free to move about the cabin." The smile I offered was weak. "Sorry about that impromptu visit. They won't be back."

Ian winced. "That bad?"

"It always was."

He made his way on the porch and sat on the hammock.

Unexpected anger surfaced. "I don't need you to be here to tell me it's okay."

"Then I won't tell you it's okay."

"How's this? I don't *want* you here. And you didn't want to be here, remember?"

Ian flinched, pulling himself up from the hammock. He nodded, sliding his hands in his shorts before moving toward his house.

"Ian?"

He stared at the sand but stopped walking.

"You need to be out by Thursday. You can take the room."

"I can get a hotel."

"Don't be ridiculous."

"I've invited some friends to the island."

I wiped a tear from my eyes. "It's fine, I have the space."

"Koti..."

"It's *fine*."

He nodded before he disappeared down the beach.

twenty-five

Ian

It was fun while it lasted, right?

Fuck me. I was an unbelievable asshole. She'd been there to hold my hand and I'd practically burned hers when she needed mine. That sort of guilt was exactly what I'd been trying to avoid. For once in my life, I didn't want to be responsible for anyone else's well-being and I should have been satisfied she'd let me off the hook. But that wasn't what bothered me. What bothered me was that I wanted to be there for her. I wanted to sit next to her and hold her hand. I wanted to kiss her worries quiet and pull her back into our bubble. Stomping down the sand with thoughts of her had me rattling with disquiet and threatened the peace I'd only just found. I glanced at her house in the distance with no idea what state she was in. If the devastation on her face and the quiet tears she was trying to hide were any indication, she was in a world of hurt.

"You're a son of a bitch, Ian Kemp," I muttered as my phone buzzed in my pocket. Reluctantly I answered. "Hi, Mom."

"Hello, darling. How are you?"

"Good, I'm good."

"I'm calling because I'm afraid we're going to have to cancel our trip to see you. Your father has developed a case of the shingles. Terrible. He's hurting something awful."

"Shit, I'm sorry."

"I am too. I was looking so forward to seeing you. Maybe we can meet you and Ella next time you come home?"

"Sounds good. Give my best to dad."

"Not so fast, son. Tell me how you are *really*."

"I'm fine."

"Bullshit."

I chuckled because a curse out of Rowan Kemp was rare and sounded totally out of place.

"Tell me what upset you."

"I can't. Just trust me that I can't talk about it yet. Soon. Okay?"

"Okay?" My mother was a warrior, solely devoted to her love of family. I couldn't imagine life without her support and as I looked at the lifeless house next to mine, I was saddened for Koti that she hadn't experienced the same.

"Mom…"

"Yes?"

"I just want you to know I love you. And I'm a lucky bastard to have you as a mother."

"Oh, God. You aren't going to hurt yourself, are you?"

"No, of course—"

"Ian, don't do this to me, to Ella. Don't do anything rash. You have so much waiting for you here."

Though untimely because of her worry, I couldn't help my laughter. "I obviously need to tell you these things more often. Of course, I'm not going to do anything like that."

"Promise me, Ian. If things get so bad you have those thoughts…"

"That worry is unnecessary I assure you, but I promise. Take care of Dad and I'll call you soon."

"Liar, you never phone."

"Once a week, that's a new promise."

Her sarcasm leaked over the line. "I'll believe that, sure."

"I'll make you a believer."

"How are you and Koti getting along?"

"Fine," I said with a grimace. "We've been doing a lot of catching up." Though wildly inappropriate while speaking with my mother, I couldn't help to think of the look in her eyes when I had her clinging to me just a day before.

"You know we saw her last year. The poor thing looked malnourished. She's so beautiful though, don't you think?"

"I do," I said as gravel filled my throat. "Very beautiful."

"Yes, a little bit dazzling."

"Dazzling…" I faltered as Koti walked out of her house and began to light her candles before reggae started drifting through her speakers.

"She's such a beautiful spirit. Maybe you could take her out sometime? From what your dad and I saw, she doesn't venture out much."

"If you saw her, I think you would agree she's come a long way since the last time you were here."

"That's so good to know. So… do you think you two might be starting up more than a friendship?"

"I've got to go, Mom."

"Oh, come on! I'm an old lady, tell me something good. She finds you attractive, doesn't she?" she asked in a conspiratorial whisper. "Are you two flirting? Tell me anything."

"Ella made the honor roll."

"You are a right shit."

"You're cursing a lot." *Much like the other woman in my life that I seemed to bring out the worst in.*

"It's hot as hell here, it makes me crazy."

"Don't get me started on Dad's geographical choice to migrate."

"Adam was worth it. Did you know your brother is seeing a waitress at a bar called The Hooters?"

I chuckled. "It's just Hooters, Mom. No 'The' before it."

"He won't let us meet her. We offered to go. I think your dad and I might pop in as a surprise."

"I'm pretty sure Dad will enjoy it."

"Really, do they serve good food?"

"The best," I said, smiling. Adam was about to be humiliated.

"Right then, it's settled."

"Let me know how it goes," I said doing my best to conceal my smile.

She was too sharp. "What aren't you telling me?"

"Nothing Mom, enjoy *The* Hooters."

"If you say so. I'm sure I will. Love you, son."

"Love you."

I hung up and made my way toward the house. Koti read in the safety of her hammock and didn't bother to glance my way when I stepped up on my porch to let Disco out.

She couldn't avoid me forever, and at the same time, a few days apart might give us both perspective. We were only in danger of becoming closer.

Thursday she would be forced to make conversation, to look at me, to talk to me.

Thursday.

twenty-six

Koti

Scrubbing my stove, I was nervous in a way I hadn't been in years. Ian and I had barely looked at each other since my parents left. Well, I'd barely looked at him. I knew I was being a little childish. He told me he didn't want to get involved and I understood it to a degree but being a friend with benefits required him to be a friend. I couldn't help my anger at his decision to leave me hanging knowing my whole story. Pushing past it for the greater good, I decided to try and put my hurt aside to make the trip the best I could for Ian and his friends, even if I was irritated with him. Two sharp knocks at my door had me pulling my rubber gloves off. I opened it with a smile only to have the wind knocked out of me by the sight of him. Disco barked at my feet as Ian's scowl and shitty greeting quickly erased all my good intentions.

"They're pulling up and you don't have any clothes on!"

"I live at the beach. These are my clothes."

"A bikini isn't clothes. Get something else on, *now*."

"Hello to you too. I agree the house looks nice. I've been cleaning all day. You're welcome."

"It's appreciated

"Could've fooled me."

"Koti," he said in warning. "We don't have time to argue."

"Then let's not argue."

"Damnit, woman."

I eyed my waiting coverup dress on the couch and thought better of it.

"Don't bark orders at me, I'm doing you another favor."

The creak of the screen behind him put a stop to our argument.

"S'up, fucker," the guy at the door greeted as Ian turned to face him grinning from ear to ear.

"How the hell are you doing, Kemp?"

The man caught sight of me as they hugged and cleared his throat. "Sorry about the profanity, ma'am." The man was tall, with shortly-cropped brown hair and gorgeous dark blue eyes. "I'm Julian Drake."

I smiled. "Koti."

"Ian, you didn't tell us you had a new girl."

Ian glanced between us and I let him sweat a little before I spoke up. "We're just friends. Ian's parents own the house next door, but it's rented at the moment, so you guys are shacking up here."

Julian did a full sweep over me with appreciative eyes before he looked back to Ian. "Did you go blind?"

"Shut up," Ian snapped. "Where are dumb and dumber?"

"Getting their bags out of the car."

"I've got your dumb and dumber, dickhead," a guy said, climbing the porch steps and looking back at the ocean. "Nice spot." He grinned at Ian. "Ian Kemp, you *ugly* bastard."

"Doug, you piece of shit." They clapped backs and he grinned wider as he looked over at me. "Damn, I see things are good for you, Kemp."

"I'm Koti," I offered as he kissed my hand.

"I'm Doug and you must be his new lady."

I shook my head adamantly. "Nah, Ian's more of a big

brother to me."

Ian cleared his throat, gray laser beams directed at me until he was struck by a duffle in the back and let out a loud "oomph."

"What the hell, Drew," Ian grunted out, as he turned to face his attacker.

"You poor bastard, you just keep getting uglier," he said, as Drew hugged Ian before eyeing me. "God, please tell me she's my birthday present."

Ian cringed as I spoke up on my own behalf. "Sorry pal, I'm more of a *Navy* guy kind of girl."

All four of them looked at me with matching scowls before Drew spoke up with a shit-eating grin. "Beautiful *and* a ball-buster. I'm in love."

Ian smacked him playfully in the back of the head. "I see you haven't grown much. I'm assuming it's the same sad case for your dick."

I bit my lips to hide my smile. All four men spoke animatedly as beers were passed from the fridge and I sat on a stool with my wine in hand, the odd girl out. After half an hour of feeling like a fifth wheel, I decided if I was going to make it through the weekend, I would need backup.

"I could kick your ass for giving me a last-minute invite," Jasmine said under her breath as she walked up the porch steps. "A house full of Marines? And you were going to keep this from moi?"

"Hell yes, I was," I said, grabbing her bag. "Try to behave yourself."

"Oh, well yeah, that's impossible."

She stepped into the room where four gorgeous men sat

around my kitchen island shooting the shit.

"Jesus. Okay, let me pick out Ian. Oh God, he's not hand-some, he's Bradley-*fucking*-Cooper hot. What the hell have you been hiding from me?! I'm decreasing your pay."

"You can't legally do that."

"You're a real asshole. God, Koti, he's so beautiful."

I sighed. "I know." *A beautiful self-absorbed asshole.*

"Who's the tall one with the blue eyes?"

"Julian."

"Dibs."

"There's no one else here to call it."

"Dibs anyway," she said retrieving a bottle of tequila. "Hey fellas, the party has officially started." All four men turned to see Jasmine in her Salma Hayek getup and all jaws dropped, includ-ing the jaw of the bastard I was sleeping with. I narrowed my eyes as he cleared his throat.

Two of the guys whistled as Ian searched for shot glasses. I moved to the kitchen to help him.

"In here," I said as he stood behind me and grabbed the glasses from the cabinet I couldn't reach. He pressed into me and I smelled a hint of his cologne and damn near fell into his frame.

"I'm sorry," he whispered.

"You seem to have the need to say that a lot."

I stood encased in his arms, his smell unavoidable, my body coming alive with every brush of his chest.

"I'm dying to touch you, but I'm afraid you'll slap me."

"I should."

"Don't complicate this, Koti. Please."

"Oh, you've made yourself clear." I pushed at his arm and he kept me trapped as he leaned down and whispered. "I'm just asking for you to understand."

"I understand just fine. But you're the one who blurred the

line. A friend would have been the first to show up for me for that shit show. But don't worry, I have one of those and she's enough. I don't need you to go thinking I need you."

"Then why are you so pissed off?"

I turned in his arms as he kept me locked in place. "It's simple. You're a prick and you don't deserve my friendship *or* the benefits."

"Fine," he said taking the glasses from the counter. "Is this typical of you? You can't accept an apology and just move on. And you claim to be a grown-up."

"I'm seconds away from kneeing your crotch, crocky. Trust me, you don't want to meet the pissed off New Yorker."

Ian's eyes went cold and he stepped away. Everyone seemed oblivious to our exchange, except for Jasmine and Julian who watched us quietly and then scattered back into conversation as soon as we joined the rest of them. I poured everyone shots as Ian took out a few trays of food he'd bought from the deli earlier that day. He hadn't bothered to show up at my house until he saw the taxi drop the guys off. He'd avoided me all week and with each day I grew more resentful of the fact that he wanted it that way.

Hours later, all four guys and Jasmine sat at my kitchen table with cigars and played poker. Jasmine was holding her own, thumping a cigar in the air and taking man-sized tugs as her and Julian eye fucked. Ian glanced at me every so often as I kept busy cleaning and airing out the house of the pungent smell. I felt like an old lady, drinking my wine off in the corner as everyone laughed and took shots. I had piped in here and there, but it was Jasmine who remained the life of the party. I was happy to give her that title as my spine prickled with nervous energy.

Not tonight. Come on, not tonight.

I kept busy, drinking a little more wine than I should as the music got louder and the voices more animated.

"Guys!" Jasmine shouted. "Listen!"

The guys looked between each other, a few leaning in.

After a few seconds, she harrumphed. "It's "Roxanne""

The Police were playing the well-known song as she nudged Julian's shoulder. "Let's play the game." She looked over at me with a 'please' on her face. "Koti! Will you get us some fresh beers?"

"I'll get them," Ian offered, ashing his cigar in the tray and glancing my way. I kept my eyes on his and didn't let them stray until Jasmine squealed. "Hurry!"

Ian brought the beers back and passed them out and Julian spoke up. "Okay, so how does it go?"

"Easy," Jasmine said, pouring more Patron into shot glasses. "Every time he sings Roxanne, you have to take a drink."

The guys all grinned at her, amused, and she rolled her eyes. "Yes, the rules are *that* simple. You G.I. Joes won't be so smug when you realize how hard it is to keep up. Now, get ready. And don't stop tilting those beers until he stops."

She lifted a shot and as soon as Sting got to the chorus, all the beers were tipped, except for Ian's. He was glaring at me openly now, his eyes focused on my hand fidgeting with my necklace. I broke out in a mild sweat, as they all downed their beers.

"We need more, Koti? Please," Jasmine said, trapped behind the table with Marines on either side of her. I nodded and quickly did her bidding before the next chorus. They all kept up with the song, downing four beers each, along with the free-flowing shots Jasmine poured. When a new hand was dealt, Ian excused himself, sprang from his seat and stalked toward me.

"Stop with the grudge, Koti. I said I was sorry."

"Okay," I said with a shrug. "You're sorry. It's fine. I'm not saying anything."

"No, you've just been standing alone in the facking kitchen all night."

"I'm taking care of your company."

"No one asked you to."

"Well, this is my house and I'm hosting. It's fine. We're good. Just go enjoy yourself."

"Fine, Eish! I'm so over this," he hissed taking his seat and giving me one last eye full of 'you're the asshole' before he turned his attention back to his friends. An hour later, I was scrubbing my countertops in an attempt to drown out the noise when the familiar pang hit me.

"Come on, not now," I begged as one of the guys—I think it was Drew—yelled out a loud bark and the music was turned up. Jumping out of my skin, I took long breaths. "It's just a party. Jesus, Koti, calm down."

But I couldn't as my chest began rising and falling rapidly. The blood drained from my face as I rushed out of the house without trying to direct any attention my way.

Yards away from the house I sat on the cool sand, closed my eyes, and began to count.

One, two, three, four, five, six, seven.

"Koti?"

"Not now, okay. Please just leave me alone."

"Jesus, it was a dick move. I've apologized. I don't know what else to say!"

One, two, three, four, five, six, seven.

"Koti, damnit," he barked moving to squat in front of me. "Look at me."

One, two, three, four, five, six, seven.

"Ian, I'm having a moment, okay. Please, please leave me alone."

Air burst out of me as I began hyperventilating.

One, two, three, four, five, six, seven.

I breathed in sync with the sound of the waves and barely heard Ian's pleas to try to help.

"Tell me what to do. Can you tell me how to help?"

I concentrated on my breathing and was only faintly aware when he sat next to me.

One, two, three, four, five, six, seven.

In.

Out.

In.

Out.

In.

Out.

The music stirred me back to life as all the energy drained from me. I concentrated on my breathing again until all I could hear were the waves. After a few moments, Ian spoke up.

"Are you okay?"

"I'm fine."

"What triggered it? The noise? Fighting with me?"

"Yes, that or the fact that I've been on edge all week because of the fight with my parents. Or high tide. Ian, it could be anything," I said as my body began to shut down and my limbs felt like lead attached to me.

"So, you're okay now?"

"Yep."

"That was a good one?"

I laughed ironically. "If there is such a thing, yes, that was a smaller one."

His voice was stone. "Okay."

He stood and made his way toward the house.

"What's pissed you off now, Kemp?"

"Nothing, I'll get the party outside. I'll build a fire."

"Fine."

"Fine. Well, that seems to be the word for the day."

"It's a good word," I smarted toward his back. He turned on me so quickly I stumbled in the sand.

"I didn't want this! I spent fifteen fucking years catering to another woman's happiness and most of it was miserable. Just for *once* I wanted to think about me! And only me! But no, I've spent a majority of my night with my best bra's worrying about you, and how you feel, and if you're angry. If I've said the wrong thing or if you'll ever speak to me again!"

My eyes bulged. "You do hear what you're saying, right?"

"I know how selfish it sounds and that's the point!"

I swallowed as he took angry strides toward me. "You just couldn't take an apology, so we could move past it. No! Instead, you make me feel terrible for *existing*. I can't win! I didn't want this! I don't *want* to care about your feelings more than my own. I don't *want* to be responsible for your moods. I just wanted some damned freedom!"

"Whoa," I said, my head spinning with his wrath. Incredulous, I shook my head.

Three points to a good argument, Koti!

"Number one. Whoa. First of all, Tiger, you came to my island to implode and I rearranged everything to suit you. Number two, *for* you. Number three, because of the way *you* felt and what was happening to you. Which was what? Did you get bent out of shape over a hangnail, because *everything* seems to set you off."

His jaw ticked as he took another step toward me.

"It would do you good to mind your mouth about things

you know absolutely nothing about."

"Only because you won't tell me!"

"That's right I won't and that's my choice."

"Whatever. And by the way professor, your oh-so-polite way of telling me to shut up, isn't going to fly. I left my parents' in New York and even they don't hold that right anymore. I shut up for NO MAN!"

"No, but you would never tell your parents that, would you? Instead, you hide!"

"Oh, you go to HELL!"

"Right back at you, love!"

We were chest to chest as I stumbled with exhaustion.

"I'm not going to coddle you from the truth, Koti."

"Well, thank God for that, or else it would be a shame to see your soft side seeing as you're about as subtle as HITLER!"

He gripped me tight to his body as I pushed at him with clenched fists. In an instant, his lips were on mine and I bit them so hard I knew I'd punctured skin. He ripped his mouth away and lifted me to wrap my legs around him, before kneeling on the sand. Our next kiss was savage and filled with need. I ripped at his thick hair as he thoroughly fucked me with his tongue un-til his will won, limp in his arms as he dove in and touched every part of my mouth. I pulled away scratching his shoulders.

"I hate you so much right now."

He gripped my hair with his fist. "Feeling's mutual at the moment."

"What are you still doing here?" I said between kisses. "Just fucking go home!"

"Oh, how I want to, but I can't seem to stay away from you." Gliding his tongue over my chest he pulled away. "I need to, I do. I need to go," he gritted out.

"I know," I said truthfully.

"This is going to fuck us both."

"I know that too," I said, defeated, reaching between us and pulling his cock from his shorts, before he captured my mouth again. He snatched my dress away from my chest and sucked my nipple into his mouth.

Words fell away as we collided on that beach, our need for the other beating our senses away.

I sank onto him and we both groaned.

Licking the shell of my ear, his whisper had me halfway to the brink. "Fuck, I missed you."

I agreed into his mouth as he slid his greedy tongue against mine.

"I need more than this," he said, agitated as I struggled on his lap for friction I couldn't find. He stood with me still connected, the darkness in his eyes highlighted by the porch light as he carried me to the side of the house. With every step, his cock throbbed deep and I whimpered at the feel, biting his neck. Once hidden, he pressed me against the wall of the house and I gave him a grin. "You've got a thing for the side of houses, don't you?" He thrust into me so hard, it temporarily cut off my air supply.

"This will have to do until I can properly make it up to you."

"Fuck me," I rasped out, my heart banging in my chest.

"You just love to piss me off," he grunted before he drove in hard, with zero mercy as I gasped, clutching onto his neck. "No," he pushed at my chest, "lean back against the house, I want to see those beautiful tits bounce as I fuck you."

I could hear my arousal as he buried himself, pumping so hard I saw stars.

"Ian."

"This pussy is going to ruin me," he swore as he tore through me with pure vengeance. "So perfect."

"Please don't stop."

"No choice, love, this is going to be short and sweet. And I'm damn sure going to make it hurt as a warning. Stop fucking flirting with my friends or I'll redden your ass."

"I've barely looked at them."

"That's enough," he said as we both managed a laugh between us, before the feel of our connection took hold.

Heat spread across my ass as his palm connected with a few slaps before he spread me wider with both hands and thrust up, making us both call out to the other. I sank back against the house without much to hold onto. He was keeping me up with the sheer force of his thrusts. I came hard and fast just as he drove in one last time emptying himself into me.

He partially collapsed against me before kissing me so fiercely I had to pull back to draw my breath. Seconds after we recovered, I gave him a lazy smile before rubbing my palm down his jaw. "I guess you're forgiven."

I got nothing back aside from the show of emotion that surfaced in his eyes. Recognizing that look as fear and trepidation, we drew the same unspoken conclusion. We were no longer safe from attachment.

It was too late.

Way too late.

twenty-seven

Ian

When we stepped inside the house, the party had calmed considerably. Drew and Doug were cooking up some half-assed concoction in the kitchen and Julian and Jasmine had disappeared.

"He's a good one," I promised, kissing her hand. Both Drew and Doug looked to me with raised brows. "Yeah, she's with me and it would do you good to keep your comments to yourself."

Koti turned to me with a sheepish smile. "I'm going to go to bed." I leaned in and took her lips. "I'll be there soon. The pain pills are in the cabinet and," I winced, "sorry in advance."

"Don't be," she whispered with swollen kissable lips. "I'm not. I'll keep your side warm."

My side. I had a side?

My heart began to pound with that declaration. She leaned up on her toes. "Don't overthink it, professor."

"Right."

"If I'm asleep, wake me up with your apology."

"Won't you be hurting?"

She gave me a warning look.

"Okay."

With one more kiss, she disappeared into her bedroom.

"Some big brother you are," Drew said, as they both broke

down in a fit of laughter. "You fucked her so hard against the house we thought there was an earthquake."

I couldn't help my grin. "Mind your business, domkop."

"Domkop?"

"Idiot."

"Then say idiot. We don't speak South African."

I rolled my eyes. "*Domkop.*"

"Whatever. I think the entire island heard you two," Drew said, taking a bite of his sandwich. "She's truly beautiful, man. Congrats."

Ignoring his comment, I gestured toward the beach. "Come on, let's let the house rest."

We built a fire fit for a king between the three of us and began the task of draining the cooler we packed.

"So, what's the story between you and Koti?"

I glared at Drew as Doug sat back on the sand, threatening to pass out.

Throwing another piece of wood on the fire, I did my best to throw them off. "What are we, girlfriends? It's none of your damned business."

Drew looked at me pointedly. "We don't hold back. Never have. That's the deal. And why are you suddenly living in St. Thomas?"

"I'm interested to know that shit myself," Julian said as he joined us around the fire.

"That was fast. Did you even use the gentlemen's rule?" Doug said in a slur.

"They always come first," Julian assured. "And don't ask me shit. I like her."

All eyes drifted back to me. Drew spoke up first.

"What's the story, Ian? Will we be sending Christmas cards to St. Thomas?"

Toying with the cap of my beer, I pressed the wavy metal into my thumb and gave Drew a pointed look. "Let's not pretend you know how to spell."

The guys laughed, and Drew gave me the finger, but the heaviness of the question lingered in the air. They knew me well, *too* well. That kind of bond only came with spending months together in the desert.

"I'm here…" I swallowed because it was the first time I was going to say it out loud. "I'm here because Tara told me that Ella isn't mine."

Julian got deathly silent as Drew cupped the back of his head. Doug was already snoring.

"Jesus, man, what the fuck?"

"Yeah." I took a drink of beer. "So I came here to blow off some steam."

"Damn." Drew's eyes bulged. "Can she take her from you?"

"No, she wouldn't do that." Panic ripped through me at the thought. "Well, I don't know what in the hell she would do. If she went that far in the first place, who knows what she's capable of."

"Isn't she like sixteen?" Drew asked. "She got pregnant when? Our second year overseas?"

"Yep," I said, taking another swig. "She's just turned fifteen."

Drew spoke up. "You got fucking Jerry Springered. God, I knew I didn't like her for a reason."

"You loved Tara," I pointed out. Julian, Drew, and Doug had been groomsmen at my wedding.

Julian remained quiet as he eyed me over the roaring fire.

"What, Drake? No words of wisdom?"

"Sorry, man, I'm still trying to wrap my head around it."

"Me too," I said, retiring my bottle for another.

"How long are you staying here?" Julian asked.

"Not sure."

"What does that mean for Koti?" Drew asked.

"Not sure about that either, but you need to keep your hard-on to yourself, fucker," I said, throwing a handful of sand his way.

Julian spoke up. "I've got your back, whatever happens. Whatever you need, man. I'll be there."

"Same here," Drew offered.

"Me too," Doug said before he resumed his snoring.

Sharing a laugh, we tossed some beer on Doug and dropped the subject before we spent the rest of the night bullshitting until the sun peaked on the horizon. Drunk and exhausted, I showered off the sand and climbed into bed with Koti, on *my* side.

"Have fun?" Koti asked as I pulled her to me and kissed her neck.

"Mmm," I answered, shifting her leg to rest on my thigh and stretching her ready pussy with my fingers. Cupping her perfect tit, my cock grew unbearably harder as I brushed over her nipple with my thumb.

"You must be exhausted." Reaching back, she ran her fingers through my hair. Her soothing touch a balm to cure the ache of needing her. "Aren't you worn out?"

"Not yet," I promised, placing tongue-filled kisses on her neck before biting into her shoulder.

"Ian," she rasped out, as I pressed into her wet heat sliding in nice and slow in an attempt to save her from any more pain. "God, you feel so good."

"So do you, beauty," I whispered before I tilted her face back toward me with my finger and kissed her.

She felt too good, too right, but I was done dwelling on it. I had her now, I had her until I couldn't have her and that had to be enough.

I gently fucked her, our eyes remained fixed on the other. Memorizing every gasp, every moan, I kept us connected, until I couldn't take another second and spilled into her. After we'd both come down, I pulled her closer to me as I drifted to sleep.

twenty-eight

Koti

That morning I woke up to the feel of Ian's arms around me. Deciding it was dangerous to bask in the sensation of being surrounded by him, I opted for a shower. By the time I tiptoed back into the bedroom, he was awake and sitting at the edge of the bed. Wordlessly I walked over to him when he stood, his eyes covering every inch of my exposed skin before they met mine. He gently pushed the wet hair away from my shoulder.

"I'm sorry I hurt you. I don't want to."

"What *do* you want from me, Ian?"

He paused, his thick brown hair a mess, his eyes etched with concern and tenderness.

"For the moment, it's simple. You. And I want that to be okay. So, you tell me, is that okay?"

I'd already decided to roll the dice with Ian. There was no decision to make. He was worth it and so I nodded, giving him permission to break my heart. He kissed me long and hard before I pulled away. "You need a toothbrush, crocky."

He chuckled before he tossed me onto the bed, his hard-on proudly displayed an inch from my face when I sat up. "Jeesh, you're like a teenager with a new toy." I motioned toward his erection.

"I know," he said, waggling his brows. "But I have no time

to be your pleasure prince this morning. We're going deep sea fishing today. Want to come?"

"My pleasure prince?"

"Yep," he said, leaning down to ruffle my hair like he did when we were kids because he knew I *hated* it.

"Your ego gets bigger and bigger every day."

"Hey, I'm only gloating based on your screaming reviews. So, would you like to join us?"

"Join you out in the deep sea with only a life preserver if shit goes south? Uh, no thanks, but have fun."

"You'll be heavily guarded by four Marines."

I scoffed. "Four ex-Marines *way* past their prime."

"Ouch." He scowled at me from where he stood and then looked down at his stiff cock. "Hear that, buddy? She's trying to shoot us down. We're not having that are we?" He made his way towards the bathroom, his perfect bare ass on display before he shut the door. He ticked my every box both intellectually and sexually. He was attentive and warm and had a huge capacity for love, which he proudly displayed whenever he spoke to his beautiful little girl. He was the perfect man to steal my heart, and I had zero doubts once he was done with it, it would never be the same.

Breakfast had been served by the time I got to the table. Everyone was munching down on freshly made eggs and crisp bacon, but when I went to grab a plate, I noticed Jasmine was missing.

Julian's eyes met mine. "She's taken the dog out."

I walked out onto the porch as Jasmine jumped out of the hammock wiping at her eyes.

She dropped Disco on the porch who came running toward me. I picked her up and gave her a kiss. "Morning, baby." Dispensing the puppy in the house, I moved to where Jasmine stood.

"Why are you crying? Did Julian do something?"

She shook her head adamantly and then smiled, which quickly turned into a grimace that had my heart splintering when she started crying again.

"Jasmine, please tell me what's wrong. It's physically hurting me to see you like this."

"I just can't stop doing this. I need to stop. I'm stopping."

"Stopping what?"

"Being a slut, that's what! I don't *know* that man," she said, pointing toward the house. "I don't know these men I'm sleeping with. I don't know why I can't stop doing this or why I even started. Before Steven, I'd only slept with four men. I'm almost forty-one!"

"I thought you were thirty-nine?"

"*See*, I'm a liar too." She cried harder and I couldn't help my laugh.

"Babe, it's okay."

"No, it's not. It's not fun anymore. It hasn't been for a while. If my prince charming is out there, he missed the map."

"Are you sure this isn't about Julian? Did he hurt you?"

"No, if anything he saved me."

"What do you mean?"

"I mean for the first time in forever, I got an inkling. Like 'maybe if he didn't live in fucking Iowa, I may have a shot at something real and amicable' type inkling."

"That's amazing."

"Yeah, except I'm not moving to Iowa to test chemistry. I mean, who the hell chooses to live in Iowa?"

"Hey, Midwesterners are the *best* kind of people and our nicest clients."

"True," she sniffed, while tying her hair up on top of her head.

"So, you're done and you're going to hold out now, good for you. It will happen, Jasmine, and at least you know it's possible."

"Also true."

"Okay then. No more tears." I pulled her back down into the hammock with me and we started swinging.

"I don't know why I'm crying," she said with a sigh.

"You think you really like Julian?"

"Not to that extent."

"Maybe you're lonely and you're admitting it to yourself now."

"Probably."

"Well, you don't have to be lonely. You can come over anytime. And at least now you know what you *don't* want."

"I'll still be a pervert."

"Just a pervert who isn't getting any," I said, nudging her.

"That's probably going to worsen my condition."

"I can live with that."

"Here I am crying, and you're the one with real penis problems. God, I love him for you already. He could not keep his eyes off you all night. I swear it was so beautiful to see the way he looked at you. Maybe that's what has me crying. Maybe I'm jealous."

"That's a good thing—not you being jealous—but wanting it for yourself. Though I really don't think you have a reason to be."

"Well, you were too busy cleaning to see it. So, I'm guessing you two had it out?"

"Oh, we had it out." I grinned.

"Sounded like it," she grinned back. I threaded her fingers with mine.

"You are the best, you know that? I couldn't have ever gotten my shit together without you. You will too, you know. You'll get there."

"I think I'm there. And maybe I'm crying because the party is over."

"Julian's the last one, huh?"

"Tonight's my last night. And I'm glad it's with him. Nothing's going to top that ass for a while. I'm cutting my losses."

"Really?"

"God, yes. He was so good, he knocked me out."

"*Damn.*"

She pressed her lips together to hide a guilty smile.

"What?" I prompted.

"He's just turned thirty-one."

My eyes bulged. "I didn't realize he was that much younger than the rest of them."

"Me neither, he's seems more mature. I'm officially a cougar."

"That was your first younger guy?"

She nodded as the door opened and Jasmine looked to me to check her face for traces of weepy black streaks. When I nodded to let her know she was in the clear, we remained in the hammock as Ian greeted us.

"So, we're off." He looked mouthwatering in board shorts and a T-shirt that stretched over his new build. Gray eyes implored the both of us. "Julian said you won't join us either, Jasmine. You two sure you won't change your minds?"

"Nope, we're going to hang out here—girl stuff."

He nodded unsure of how to leave me. Making it easy, I stood and planted a wet kiss on his lips. Smiling into my kiss, he gripped me tightly to him and deepened it before he pulled away. I smoothed his cheek with my palm before I leaned in on a whisper. "See you later... pleasure prince."

Rewarded with another smile, I sank back into the hammock as Drew, Doug, and Julian stomped down the steps. Julian paused halfway to the alley and gripped Jasmine's hand over the railing. "See you tonight?"

"Sure."

"Have fun, fellas," I called out as they made their way toward Ian's truck. We eavesdropped as they packed their coolers.

"So, you're going to see her tonight?"

I think it was Drew who asked.

"Hell yes, if she'll have me."

Jasmine and I shared shit-eating grins.

"She doesn't know you well enough to deny you," Doug said. "But it's nice to know someone's getting laid around here."

"You're married, dude."

"Exactly, like I said, it's nice to know *someone* is getting laid."

"It can't be that bad," Drew said as the truck doors collectively opened.

"She won't even let me take my socks off in bed anymore."

Julian spoke up next. "Have you seen your fucking feet, man? Get a damned pedicure already, or hacksaw or something. Get a little man care going on."

I covered my mouth as Jasmine gripped my thigh.

"What kind of pussy gets a pedicure?"

Two of them spoke up in unison, "I do."

Ian spoke up next. "Don't look at me, no one touches my feet. But hey, do any of you guys know what blasted means?" The truck doors slammed as Jasmine and I sank into the hammock with tears of laughter pouring down our faces.

twenty-nine

Koti

Later that night, four sunburned and drunken Marines came barreling through my front door with victorious stories about being captains at sea. Doug, I had learned, was always the first to pass out and went straight to his guest room. Julian and Jasmine made themselves scarce as Drew and Ian faced off in a game of dominoes. Games seemed to be the guys bonding medium. I pretended to read my book while spying on their progress.

"You are a sloppy drunk, figure it out," Ian slurred.

"I'm working on it."

"Working on losing your ass," Ian said. "You already owe me fifty for the bet on the boat. You need to go ahead and cough it up now."

"Put it on my tab." He snickered at Ian as he popped open another beer.

"I best not have to clean up after your ugly ass tonight."

"Calm down, Mom, I can handle another beer."

Drew downed his beer in spite and Ian looked my way and gave me a drunken smile. "Hey, you."

I couldn't help my giggle. "Hey back."

Drew leaned over the table and spoke in nothing close to the whisper he was aiming for. "You two are soooo cute. You're sleeping with a supermodel, we get it."

"I can hear you, Drew," I said, turning a page.

"Well, I hope you take it as a compliment. Hey asshole, here's your fifty. I'm out."

"It was earned," Ian said, pocketing the money as Drew gave me a wave goodnight before turning it into the bird for Ian. I laughed as he retreated while Ian sauntered over to me, close to rearranging the furniture with his drunken sea legs.

"And it's time for bed for you."

His perma-smile only got wider. "I'll agree to that."

"Not that kind of bedtime, professor."

He pushed his lips out in a pout which was so unlike him, and I laughed.

"I've been meaning to talk to you," he said as I pulled his arm around my neck.

"Oh, yeah?"

"Yeah. I think you're stronger than you think you are. Much."

"Ian, please don't try to fix me."

"I'm not. I swear, I'm not."

"Did you Google anxiety and now you're an expert?"

"Give me credit, I know it's more complex to understand than watching a YouTube video."

We stumbled down the hall and he pulled away from me, pointing an index finger at my lips.

"Hey, did you know miraculous things can happen more than once? It happens. It happens every day to someone who says *never*. I mean you think you know. You're sure of it and it all falls apart or fades away and you can't remember when it happened. Do you understand?"

I shook my head. "No clue."

"Pity, try to keep up. It's not simple, any of it. Not one part of life is simple. There are no arrows to guide you that help you make one fucking thing simple. Every important decision is complicated because it leads to more decisions. You decided to step into my life, instead of sipping tea."

"Coffee," I said with a smirk.

"A beverage," he said in drunken agitation. "Anyway, emotions are a horrible catalyst for making decisions that matter. And some choices aren't yours, they float away on a cloud of emotions and come back made *for* you. Committing to how you *feel* is a recipe for disaster." He stumbled into my bedroom and I followed, tempted to kick him right in his smug ass. To my horror, he continued his reverie.

"All of it's ridiculous and cruelly unnatural for a realist."

"That's, uh, sad, Ian, if that's your outlook, and horribly put by someone who claims to be an educator. It's a good thing you don't teach philosophy, professor."

Ignoring my comment, he struggled with his sneakers as he began to undress.

"Free will is a bitch, puffer fish, and half the time it's got both signals on which can only confuse you further."

"Ah, the ponderings of a drunken sailor."

"Marine," he said, looking up at me pointedly, "and don't you forget it."

"Right."

He ripped off his shirt and glared at me. "You aren't taking me seriously."

"Oh, I'm listening."

"Good, you should."

"I was taught young to listen to my elders."

"Cute, that's the second time you've made fun of my age. I'll be reddening your ass for that."

"I look forward to it."

"So, I'm finally free to be a little selfish and I intend on enjoying every moment of it."

"Haven't we already had this conversation? I'm on your side and kudos to you."

"Look, I know *this*," he said, sitting on the edge of the bed. "I've been through *this* before, so I know this mystery, the need, the goddamn ache in my chest."

"Ian—"

He slowly raised his head, his glossy eyes boring into mine. "You're so beautiful." It sounded agonizing coming from his lips as if it were a burden for him.

"So are you." The irony was his beauty was just as much of a burden for me.

"I'm smashed, Koti."

"I've gathered that."

"You really are the most…" his voice turned hoarse, "what's inside of you is a heart that is dying to live, and your head is too afraid to let you do it fully, the way you deserve. It's the most tragic thing I've ever seen. You're a prisoner of your own making."

"Gee, thanks," I said, crossing my arms despite my ache to touch him.

"It's not your fault."

"Good to know."

"But what your mind won't let you understand is you can't control a single fucking thing. Control is an illusion and all your home remedies for coping aren't ever going to change that."

"I'm aware. This isn't news, Ian. In fact, it's redundant, and it changes nothing."

"Exactly, because anxiety stems from emotion, it doesn't listen to reason."

He wasn't saying it for me, to help me understand, he was explaining it to himself, so *he* could understand *me*.

"What's your point?"

He laid down and threw his arm over his face. "The point is—I don't believe in miracles, but I'm falling for mine."

And with that, he passed out cold.

I stood stunned as I watched his breathing. Never had I thought he was capable of feeling for me the way I did for him. But I had to remember they were the ramblings of a drunk and confused man. Even so, his confession filled me with a warmth that I didn't expect.

I took off his other sneaker and once I was sure he was comfortable, made my way to the kitchen. Julian was closing the fridge door with a water in hand. "Advil and a bottle of water before bed and you'll never have a hangover." He grinned, and I returned it.

"Have fun today?"

"Too much. I love the Virgin Islands, you're lucky to live here."

"Jasmine told me you live in Iowa."

"Yeah, I run a farm with my dad. He's getting ready to retire."

"Do you like it?"

"Love it, wouldn't dream of living anyplace else. I've seen the world and I like my version best. But yours doesn't suck. Want me to grab you something?"

"I'll take a water." Sitting on the other side of the island, I thanked him when he passed me the bottle and took a long drink.

"Ian got drunk early, try not to hold it against him."

"Does he always get so philosophical when he drinks?"

"Only when he's got something to think about. Today I'm thinking it was you?"

My cheeks heated slightly, but Julian was easy to talk to and far from hard to look at. He was shirtless and had an incredible build. I was happy Jasmine's last fix was with a man that hot, and for the most part he seemed to be intuitive and kind.

"He's a stand-up guy, but a bit opinionated and a little arrogant."

Raising my pointer and thumb, I showed Julian an inch. He pushed my fingers wider apart and we both laughed.

"Did you know his wife?"

Julian nodded. "I was his best man."

I left the question open because I was dying to know if his presence here had anything to do with her.

"He didn't tell you why he was here, did he?"

Intuitive Julian. I liked him.

"I bet you're the peacekeeper of the crew."

"Yep, Drew is the clown, Doug is the "always up for it" guy. I'm the peacekeeper and Ian is the thinker."

"I love that you guys still keep in touch."

"Ian's passed on most of our trips over the years, but he surprised us all with the invite out here."

"Why do you think he passed?"

"His daughter. Always Ella. He's a helicopter dad and won't miss anything when it comes to her. None of us blame him."

Finishing my water, I stood and threw it in the trash.

"I will tell you this. He's not here because of his ex-wife."

I nodded.

"But he's been through hell because of her and the damage she's done is going to fuck with him for some time."

"Thanks."

"Sure."

"As long as we're giving fair warning, you should know Jasmine's in a… strange place."

"We've been talking most of the night."

"Okay, cool," I said, relieved to be off the hook. "Well, see you in the morning."

He pushed off from the counter. "Night."

I got halfway to the hall when he spoke up. "Koti?"

"Yeah."

"Thanks for having us."

"Of course. I had fun."

"And just in case you need to hear it from someone who knows him, you won't be easily forgotten."

But I would be forgotten, at least that's the way I interpreted it. Unable to think of Julian as spiteful or having any reason to hurt me, my new hopes, even with Ian's confession of falling, were obliterated. Though I was confused, I refused to ask Julian for a better explanation. I'd already shown too much vulnerability when it came to Ian. I'd given Julian a rock to my glass house and he'd used it.

"Night, Julian."

"Night."

thirty

Ian

HI, Daddy.

Hi, brat.

Pain ripped through my chest and threatened my smile as I stared at my daughter on the screen. How many of his features did she have? Were any of her traits, the ones I thought were mine, his? Her smiles, especially those I earned, were those as hard-pressed to get from him? Did she suspect anything? Tara obviously hadn't told her.

You look happy.

I am happy. It's beautiful here. I can't wait for you to come.

Next week?

Yes. I'll be waiting at the airport. Are you sure you're okay with flying alone?

She rolled her eyes and I cut my hand through the air to tell her that was not okay. It was a sign of disrespect and she got away with little in the way of that.

Sorry.

Forgiven.

Her beautiful smile faltered by the presence of someone coming into her bedroom.

Mom's here, she wants to talk to you.

Later. I want to know how things are going. One more week until school is out. Are you excited?

Hell yes.

Language.

I reprimanded her even though I often let her get away with calling me an asshole. It was a long-running joke between us.

Do you love Koti?

No. Why would you ask that?

You can't lie to me, Dad. You look happy and she's behind you, staring at you.

That's because she's fascinated by sign language.

You should teach her.

I will.

Good.

What else is new?

Mom keeps asking me if I like Houston. I don't want to move; all my friends are here.

I'm working on that.

Work harder.

Easy, brat. I'm not going to let her move the two of you without a fight. But that's our business.

My business too.

True. But trust me to handle it.

She signed okay, but I could see the fear in her eyes which only infuriated me. It was only natural for Tara to move on and build a new life for herself, but her selfish choices were always an issue when it came between our daughter's happiness and her own.

Are you getting excited about Washington?

Yes. They had us start writing to our camp roommates to get to know them before we went. I have a pen pal, her name is Melissa and she goes to The School for the Deaf and Blind in South Carolina. She might be going to DC next year too for the program so we can be friends.

Do you think you'll like her?

I think so. Not sure.

No boys.

Dad!

If you roll your eyes again, you'll be grounded.

Fine. But Jessica gets to date.

I'm not Jessica's father.

Why are you so hard on me about this?

You know why.

I'm deaf, not stupid.

Exactly.

Then why can't you trust me? What if I like a hearing boy?

No boys period. Let's talk about something else.

She blew her bangs out of her eyes and nodded. *Are you staying in St. Thomas for the whole summer?*

Yes, and you know you can come here with me instead of Washington. I would love it.

She was already shaking her head.

That was a quick decision. Don't worry about my feelings being hurt. I bulged my eyes and she laughed. That sound would forever be the best sound of my life.

Sorry. I just don't want you hounding me. You are the fun police.

Have I lost my little girl already? I finished signing slowly. My devastation unintentional.

Daddy? What's wrong?

Nothing, baby. I'm just sad you're growing up so fast.

Mom keeps telling me she wants to talk.

I shook my head. *I'll call her later. I'll see you at the airport.*

Can't wait. Love you.

Love you so much. Be safe and get to me in one piece, okay?

She rubbed her chest with the sign of the P. *Promise.*

You are my heart, Ella Danielle Kemp.

You are my heart, Daddy Asshole.

I laughed as the screen cut off and then spoke to the sun-kissed beauty behind me.

"Ella says you were staring at me during our whole conversation." I glanced back at the island where Koti stood peeling potatoes, her cheeks reddening.

"I love to watch you two sign, it's fascinating."

I drew my brows and stood. "That's the only reason?"

"Yep. Love *it*," she said, toying with me. Everything about her from her chin-length, gold-spun hair to the tip of her polished blue toes made my veins ache. I wanted to possess her. Her silver-blue eyes bled me and often. It was damn near physically painful to be so attracted to her. The warmth I felt when I was with her was something else entirely.

"If you really want to learn, I'll teach you."

"Really?" My heart began to race at the appearance of her smile. Nothing affected me quite as much as the sight of it.

"We can start tonight after dinner. I'm going to teach you exactly as I was taught. There are strict rules."

"I'm up for it. I learned the alphabet for sign language in grade school. I still remember it."

"That will help," I made my way toward her and saw her falter slightly when she read my posture. "You'll have to do your part, study on your own, and use the workbooks."

"I will, I swear. We have a few deaf renters come in once in a while…" she subtly smiled in an effort to hide her anticipation as I drew closer. "I can't wait to be able to talk to them. Oh, and I can sign to Ella next week!"

"It takes time to master this language like any other and there's slang to learn too."

"Okay."

I could feel the rattle in her posture as I slipped in behind her and leaned in a whisper. "It could take you months to be conversational."

"Bring it on," she said as her skin heated beneath my fingertips.

"After." I pulled the peeler from her hands and set it on the counter.

"After." She repeated, leaning against me and slipping her hand between us to brush it over my ready cock.

"After." Turning her in my arms, I covered her mouth with my own.

Koti

After turned into a couple of hours of rough exploration by my nutty professor. The man was a God in the sack and though some days were filled with the painful effects of his aftermath, I couldn't stop myself from my new addiction. He was a thorough lover with endless imagination. I smiled as I waited outside my front door playing with Disco. Ian demanded that we conduct class just as he would anywhere else and had been adamant about treating me as he would any other student. Restless with anticipation, I waited the five minutes he asked for to ready himself for our first class.

When I walked into the house, I saw he had rearranged the furniture putting his dry erase board where my coffee table usually sat.

"It's getting hot out—"

My sentence was cut short by Ian's stomping on the hardwood floor and the shake of his head.

I took his cue and zipped it. He pointed to the couch as he stood next to the board that read "My name is Ian."

Once seated, he waved at me in greeting and I waved back. I could see a repressed grin lay idle on his lips before he wiped it away and replaced it with what I assumed was his teacher mask. He lifted his hands and signed.

Confused, I shrugged. He looked at me expectantly and signed again.

I gave him wide eyes.

Ten minutes later, we were in a lock of wills. He kept placing his hand to his chest, then crossing closed pointer and middle fingers on each hand before rapidly spelling out a word. I'd been working on that word the whole time because it was all of the language I knew but his fingers were moving so fast from letter to letter I couldn't read it. The last letter was an N. I was sure of it. A light bulb went off and I jumped in my seat excitedly with an "Oh, damn, how did I not get that!?"

Ian stomped his foot again and shook his head, eyes narrowed.

He signed the same phrase, this time slower so I could follow.

My name is Ian.

This time I lifted my own hands repeating his movements.

My name is Koti.

He nodded and made a quick sign, which I assumed was the word good or yes.

Over the next hour, we remained in silent conversation as I stayed puzzled half the time before I began to catch on. By the time class was over I'd learned to introduce myself and ask, "How are you?" Also a few basic signs, how, who, why, when and where.

"That was pretty good," he said as he erased the board.

"That was incredible! You learned sign language this way?"

"Yes, my teacher was a deaf woman named Billy, and she was incredible."

"It seems impossible to learn this way, but it's really kind of amazing."

"She could read lips and talk, but speaking was forbidden

in her classroom."

Excited, I jumped on him, he laughed at my unexpected enthusiasm and caught me easily, gripping my ass and holding me close to him. "I love it!"

"Really?"

"Yes, so much. I can't wait for more. Do we have to stop today?"

"Yes. It's easy to forget the signs. I want you to practice them all night and all morning. It may seem trivial to you, but you'll understand why later. Okay?"

"Is this like the *Karate Kid*, where you make me wax on, wax off and then show me some kick-ass moves?"

Ian chuckled. "Something like that."

"Well, I'll make you proud, sensei."

His eyes shone with something that resembled adoration and my heart warmed with the hope of it. "I suspect you will, puffer fish."

Our matching grins disappeared as he leaned in and took my lips, kissing me with a lazy and seductive tongue.

"About what I said the other night while I was smashed."

I gave him a side-eye. "You actually remember that?"

He winced. "Some of it?"

I shook my head. "No more. No more fighting, no more misconception, no more judging, speculating, worrying, none of it. I'm having a great time and so are you. That's all we need to know. Let's move on already."

He let out a breath of relief. "Music to my ears."

"Same here. Let's leave it at the egg comes first and have some more fun."

"What if I said the chicken came first?"

"Well then, I would have to burden you with coming up with proof, professor."

"I have no proof."

"Then we can debate about it during our swim like adults."

"Swim?"

"Let's go swimming and after," I waggled my brows, "we can *after*."

"Aren't you hurting?"

"I'm good. Actually, I'm great. I'm growing into a huge fan of sex after years of being on team abstinence. Also, sex between us requires little communication which, if we're honest, we seem to suck at."

"Good point," he said, smiling down at me. "But I think we're getting better."

"Agreed," I said, as he let me on my feet.

"I'll get my suit on."

I took his hand and moved toward the front door. "That won't be necessary, professor."

thirty-one

Koti

Anxious, I checked the roast in the oven for the second time in ten minutes. Any second, Ella would be walking through the door and I wanted more than anything for her to like me. Even if Ian and I didn't have a future, some part of me hoped for a lasting friendship. I lost everything when I left New York and severed ties with everyone I thought was close to me, but Ian and I were a different kind of close. He understood me like no one else in my life ever had, including Jasmine. He knew me intimately and touched me in ways I needed. He knew my secrets, my fears and asked me constantly what my hopes were, to which I had no reply. I never thought past getting through my days when I arrived on the island. And now it seemed I had a whole different life in front of me. I didn't tell him my hopes because the truth was I wasn't sure. For the first time in my life, it wasn't mapped out, which was both amazing and a bit terrifying. But I had learned I didn't need big dreams and accomplishments to matter. And his question was more geared toward my happiness, I knew it without him telling me. So, when it came to hopes, I would let them evolve just like I had when I set foot in St. Thomas. And maybe before he left, I would have something to share. Even when our time ended, I hoped to remain a part of his life, even if it meant I would have to witness him living it with someone else.

His friendship was a rare gift when it came to acceptance. While a part of me knew I was in love with him, a larger part of me knew that for some reason, when I was six-years-old I was gifted with a best friend who later turned into a soulmate. We spent the first month together at odds, but the last few weeks had been some of the most blissful days of my entire life. When I knocked off work, I raced home without a clue as to where our night would lead. It was different from the predictability I learned to count on every day, but oddly the new routine felt just as safe because of Ian.

And the fact that I had never been in love played a large part of the reason for my happiness. I tried not to dwell on it due to the impending heartbreak, but the truth was I had never experienced the constant pounding heart, desire, the elation, the need, the torturous want, the playful comfort. All of that, from the time I was in my teens, was stripped from my life by my ambitious schedule and the aftermath of trying to keep up with it. There had been boyfriends, a few of them memorable but never had I ever felt such an attraction to a man. I'd never in my life been inspired the way I was by Ian. His ability to make me feel everything with a single look was unparalleled by any before him.

I was weeks away from thirty years old and had just found my first love.

And my soulmate.

But not my forever.

The front door opened as I lit a candle, and Ian and Ella appeared. I waved my hello frantically and Ella rushed to my side. We both hesitated briefly before we hugged.

I took my time signing my greeting.

I'm so happy you are here.

She began frantically signing as her father corrected her

while talking. He made a fist with one hand and slid spaced fingers over it toward him.

"Slow, Ella. She's only been doing this for two weeks."

She turned back to me and signed with the letter S rubbing her chest.

Sorry.

I signed back.

It's okay.

She spoke then. "We can practice more while I'm here."

"I would love that."

"Can I see the puppy?"

"Of course." I moved to the bedroom where I had locked Disco in so I could mop the floors and jumped out of my skin when Ella shrieked. Ian had told me Ella was unbelievably loud at times. I shook my head at my foolish reaction and Ian gave a wink. "It's okay, beautiful. She startles me too at times."

"You aren't allowed to talk when you know she can't hear you. It's disrespectful."

"I can't call you beautiful in front of her."

"Doesn't matter."

"Right. It's bad manners. You must have a good teacher."

"He's the best." I managed to sign that part and Ella caught it.

"Who is the best?"

"Your dad, for teaching me."

She lifted her hands. *I'll be a better teacher.*

"I bet."

I poked her shoulder to get her attention as she fawned over the dog. *Do you like...* I took my time spelling out pot roast because I had no idea what the sign was. I was only halfway through the letters when she nodded.

"You knew what I was signing?"

She nodded again. "Of course."

"Wow. I hope I get that sharp with the language."

"You will," Ian assured.

We sat at the table as Ian and Ella went back and forth signing while talking at the same time so I could understand their conversation. I felt oddly emotional as I watched their interaction. It was like watching the most important part of Ian in those moments with his daughter. Their love was palpable, their relationship completely unique. They were close, as close as two people could be within the boundaries of a parent/child relationship. Although close with my own father, we never talked so candidly. Ian had told me that deaf people don't often beat around the bush and can sometimes come off as brash or rude, but most were just naturally and brutally honest. Since my classes with Ian started, I'd been learning a little about the deaf culture and it had only piqued my curiosity.

"You are such an asshole, Daddy," Ella said, leaving me with wide eyes to gauge his reaction. Ian didn't seem offended in the least which made me laugh. They both looked at me with matching grins.

"What?" Ella asked.

"You just called your dad an asshole. And while I agree, I'm surprised you get away with it."

"Not nice," Ian scolded me before he looked at Ella. "Do you want to tell the story?"

Ella nodded. "If I speak funny, tell me, okay?"

"You sound perfect." I signed the word good.

"Don't lie, Koti, that doesn't help me grow."

I sat shocked but then nodded. "Okay, you sound pretty damn good for someone who's never heard a single sound."

She immediately turned to Ian. "I like her."

"Me too," he said, his eyes darkening as he looked over at

me. I felt the blush creep up my cheeks.

Ella picked up on the chemistry. "You two are more than friends. When are you going to break it to me?"

I choked on a sip of water as Ian shook his head and spoke. "Tell the story, brat."

"Okay fine." Ella turned to me. "He wanted dad to be my first sign. He spent a long time trying his best to make me do it."

I stuck my thumb to my forehead the rest of my fingers pointing up at the ceiling and then pulled it away a half inch.

"Close, you don't have to touch your forehead with your thumb, but yes, that's the sign for dad."

I nodded.

"From what Daddy says, I wasn't good at lifting my thumb up to reach my forehead and instead of having my finger straight out… I'll show you." She took my hand and closed my thumb and pointer in a circle while leaving the other fingers open and spaced apart.

"This is the sign for asshole, isn't it?"

Ella laughed so loudly next to me I fought myself to keep from jumping in my seat.

"Yes. I've been calling him an asshole since I was little, and he got used to it."

"It was the only time I was ever happy she couldn't talk," Ian said with an embarrassed shake of his head.

"But you made sure I knew how to say it," Ella said with a giggle.

"Yes, I did." He was a proud dad, it leaked out of his every pore. I briefly wondered what it would be like to raise another human being. I never imagined it for myself, but Ian had done it. And from what I could tell, he'd done it well.

"So, are we sleeping here?"

"Yes, Grandma's house is rented for the rest of the summer,"

Ian answered. I tried to concentrate on his signing as he spoke. They were both too fast. Ian noticed my frown before he slowed down, which earned him a smile from me.

I loved his patience, the way he cared for me and those around him. He may have wanted to be selfish, but that was one thing Ian wasn't. And because I couldn't handle another second of watching him without expressing exactly what I loved about him, I excused myself and cleared the dishes. Ian spoke up.

"Ella's got dish duty. That's a rule."

At your house. I managed to sign. "She's on vacation."

Ian's jaw ticked and I did damage control. "Just for tonight."

He nodded and gave her a pointed look. "Wipe the table. And don't forget your manners."

She nodded before she turned to me. "Thank you so much for dinner"

"You are most welcome."

She then tilted her head at Ian. "Sir, may I be excused?"

"Yes, brat."

Ella joined me at the sink. "Marines," she cooed in what she thought was a whisper. Her father slashed his hand through the air and I gave her big eyes and brought her to me in a protective hold while she giggled.

Ian narrowed his eyes at me as he made his way toward his bedroom. "Don't encourage her."

Ella helped with the dishes anyway and we made small talk as she told me about the camp in Washington D.C. She planned to go to college there, but they had an early entrance program that she hoped to get into for her last two years of high school. I was sure that Ian had a future somewhere in D.C. In an attempt to mask the sting that threatened I told her of my common love for the *Outlander* books. She squealed in excitement and agreed to join our book club during her stay.

Minutes later, Ian returned with a brand-new iPad with a bow on top.

Ella squealed with delight.

"I wanted you to have it while you were here. I loaded it with age-appropriate books. Do not even think about downloading that smut I caught you with last month."

"Yes, sir! Thank you, Daddy!" She wrapped her arms around him tight as he hugged her with his whole being. Something about that had my emotion spilling over. I couldn't get over the appeal of the several sides of Ian Kemp and I loved every single one of them.

Jesus, Koti, get a grip.

Excusing myself for the second time, I grabbed my book and made my way onto the porch. Lighting candles, I turned on my music, Bob Marley's "Three Little Birds" and sank into my sanctuary. Minutes later, I looked up to see Ian on the porch staring at me with confusion.

"What are you doing?"

"Uh, reading?"

"Do you feel out of place?"

I sat up. "Not at all. I just wanted to give you time alone with her."

"Okay."

"I shouldn't... we shouldn't give her the wrong impression. We discussed this."

He glanced at the front door. "I know, I just thought tonight you would hang out with us."

"Ian Kemp, are you pouting?"

"I might be."

"Get your ass in there and spend time with your kid."

"Fine. But are you coming to the beach tomorrow?"

"Sure."

"And tonight, when she goes to bed, I'm going to sneak into your room and lick—"

"You will do no such thing. There will be no licking of anything."

"We'll see about that."

"I'm locking my door."

"Don't threaten me or every door in this house will be without locks within the hour."

"Behave yourself." I shooed him away as he glanced back at me from the front door.

"Koti, I don't mind you spending time with us."

But I mind, Ian, I'm falling for both of you.

"She already suspects foul play. Do you want to be the one to explain friends with benefits to her?"

"No."

"There you go."

"But that doesn't mean I can't discreetly *lick* things."

"Go lick a banana pop."

thirty-two

Koti

Magens Bay was a beautiful horseshoe shaped beach with white sand and turquoise water. It was the most bustling tourist attraction of St. Thomas and one of the best spots for water play in the Virgin Islands. Ella had Disco clutched to her as she raced toward the sand while Ian and I set up a camp that consisted of an umbrella and a few foldable beach chairs we'd purchased from the store on the way over.

"Do you come here much?" Ian asked, tossing a towel on his chair.

"Not really. I mean, what's the point? We *do* have a beach in our backyard."

"True, but you hardly leave home. Don't you get out at all?" His question was innocent, with an edge of curiosity mixed in.

"My first six months here I went hermit, but Jasmine helped me snap out of it a little. I went out a few times and will on occasion, but I'm to the point it doesn't appeal to me."

"Sign of old age, huh?"

"I turn thirty in a few weeks."

"That would be what, twenty-four years ago that we met?"

His sentiment took me by surprise. "Wow, I didn't think of that. That makes you the oldest friend I've ever had," I teased before cowering under his glare. "I mean the longest friendship.

Jasmine's the oldest friend I have anyway."

He looked down at the sand between us. "Too bad we didn't keep in touch."

"We might have been decent pen pals, but here we are anyway."

"Here we are," he said, his eyes meeting mine. "I had to stay away from you the last time I saw you."

"What?"

"When you were seventeen. I was already married, and you were…"

I sat up in my chair. "I was, what?"

He glanced down at his lap, attempting to hide his smirk with a few of my favorite fingers covering his mouth. "Can I be perfectly honest without ruining whatever favorable opinion you may have of me?"

"You're still so proper, crocky. Of course."

He raked his teeth over his bottom lip sending a shiver down my spine regardless of the heat. "My whole body tensed when I saw you. I know it was wrong, but there was no way I could stand to be in the same room as you if I stayed. I left St. Thomas a day early and wanked that night thinking about you when I got home."

"So *that's* why you didn't say hi. Professor! I was underage!"

"And I was married. Does it make a difference that my marriage was over for me by then?"

"Wait, you were only twenty-five, that was only a few years after you got married, right?"

"I'd just had my birthday and I needed a break from Tara, things were at their worst, so I'd flown in to check on the house for my parents. My mom was recovering from a minor surgery and there had been a storm. I made a few repairs and hired a contractor to take care of the rest. I was about ready to leave when you were coming in."

"I wish you would have stayed."

"Too dangerous for me. You were wearing your ridiculous gold sandals and a white sundress with tiny gold flowers all over it. Your hair was tied up, and you had on bright red lipstick."

My mouth parted as he leaned in.

"I'll never forget the way you looked that day, you took the breath right out of my body."

"I can't believe you remember what I was wearing."

"I remember every detail including the swish of your skirt when you got out of the SUV. I thought about nothing but smearing that lipstick for months."

"I remember feeling the same thing… I kind of had an instant crush on you the minute I saw you. I wish you would have talked to me."

"I couldn't. I knew I wouldn't be able to resist temptation. And seeing you when I got here was much, much, worse."

My heart lit up. "Well, I couldn't tell by the warm reception you gave."

"And I've apologized sincerely and repeatedly by mouth and orgasm."

It was my turn to bite my lip. "Forgiven."

"Fuck, I'm a lucky bastard to be able to touch you now. I mean it, Koti. I have no clue how you remained single all these years but am I damn glad you are at the moment." Utterly turned on, his eyes rested on my lips before they trailed the length of my body. "Lucky. Fucking. Me."

I didn't know how it was possible, but his words managed to fill me up and sting all at the same time.

"Yeah, well you're temporary," I said nudging his arm. *"Your* bad." I was only partially teasing.

He looked at me with unamused gray eyes. "I can't believe

you locked me out of your bedroom last night."

I laughed as I lathered some oil on. "You checked?"

"Of course I checked. I had things I wanted to lick."

"Serves you right with your daughter in the house, pervert."

I looked over at Ella who looked adorable in her newly purchased pink bikini, her blonde hair soaked from the sea as she and Disco hurdled the incoming waves at the shore.

"This is nice." Ian cracked a beer and held it out to me.

"Agreed," I stood shaking my head at his offered beer. "No thanks, I'm going to go get in the water."

He raised a wicked brow. "Going to put on a show for me?"

"Such a pervy professor."

"I was just thinking about the last time you wore that bikini." He playfully tugged at the string on my hip and slid his teeth over his lip.

"Maybe you should slow down yourself on that drinking. Pick out some music, I'll be back, and we can make some sandwiches."

"Yes, ma'am."

"Damnit, stop with the bedroom eyes."

"I have no clue what you're talking about," he teased as his darkening gaze smoldered me into a puddle.

"And don't watch me as I walk away."

"Not a snowball's chance in hell."

I 'harrumphed' as I walked toward the surf before I braved a quick glance over my shoulder. Ian had already zeroed in on my ass and I shook it a little before I gave him a wink.

Eat your heart out, professor.

Ella and I chased Disco through the waves until I was dying of thirst.

I waved to get her attention before I signed to her.

Thirsty?

She shook her head, "No thanks, but you're doing well with your signs."

Thank You. I'm trying. I shook my head in frustration, unable to sign the rest of what I wanted to say.

"If you don't know the signs, speak to me."

"It's reading them that's the hardest part."

She waved a dismissive hand. "It takes time. You'll get it. You have come a long way already."

Thank You. I nodded toward Ian to let her know where I would be.

"I'll be up there in a little while." She picked up a soggy Disco and inspected her an inch from her face. Disco rewarded Ella with a lick on the lips that had her giggling. "I love her soooo much," Ella said, giving me a smile.

I ran my hands through her soaked fur. "Me too."

I pranced toward Ian hoping his eyes had been on me unable to think of anything else but his confession as I played in the water. I loved his attention and reveled in it knowing I shouldn't. Pushing all shitty thoughts aside and preparing for some more flirting, I paused when I saw Ian in his chair feet away, his face buried in a towel. I wouldn't have thought anything of it if his entire body wasn't shaking. Cautiously, I approached him.

"Ian?"

He shook his head keeping the towel in place as I took a seat next to him and reached out to touch his thigh. His cries were soundless, but I could feel the pain rolling off him.

"Ian, what's wrong?" After another minute of watching him in soundless agony, I tried again. "Please talk to me."

His body shook a minute longer until he spoke low. "Where's Ella?"

"She's playing, she can't see. Ian, please," though I didn't know why, my heart was cracking. He finally lowered the towel and his red-rimmed eyes met mine as his face twisted.

"Please," I said as I pushed a quick tear away. "Please," I whispered, taking his hand. He squeezed it back so hard I winced as he pulled me closer to sit next to him shielding himself from prying eyes.

"She can't see us. No one is watching."

"She's..." his face twisted again as he puffed out incredulous air and began shaking again. "Jesus, I can't breathe."

"Take your time," I said softly.

"Fuck, Christ, this hurts so much," he said, his body trembling with emotion as I sank in the sand, my heart plummeting with the ache in his voice.

"I don't want to say it out loud. I feel like if I acknowledge it, it makes it true."

"Makes what true?"

He took a deep breath and blew it out, closing his eyes. I jerked back at the presence of tears trickling down his face. Unable to help myself, I moved to sit next to him, partially covering his body with my own to embrace him as much as I could without being obvious. "I'm here. Whatever it is, you can tell me."

My eyes were starting to fill with the sheer heartbreak etched on his face, though I had no idea why.

"She's..." his swallow was audible, "I didn't father Ella, she's not mine, not my biological daughter," he managed to get out before he pressed his chin to his chest and a gasp escaped him. "Fuck," he sat up and again pulled a towel to cover his face. Shock filtered through my body as I glanced around us. We were yards away from prying ears.

"Ian, there's no one around, it's okay."

"Fuck, it's so *not* okay." He pulled the towel away. Devastated, tear-filled eyes met mine. "The day I found out was the day I showed up here. I lost it. I totally fucking lost it."

I held my breath, unable to believe what he was telling me.

"The minute I found out I was going to be a father I felt like something clicked. It wasn't planned, I'd only been dating Tara for months, but it didn't matter. It was the greatest moment of my life and now I feel like it was a lie and it was. It's been taken from me."

He shook his head, his face coated in disbelief and hurt. "Koti, that little girl's first sign was daddy, and it meant *everything* to me. I've been there for every single step, every hurt, every heartbreak, every milestone—she's my whole fucking life." He shuddered as he tried to stifle his cries and more tears spilled from his eyes. The ache to touch him ripped through me as I inched forward, and he shook his head. "Don't, please," his misery paralyzed me as despair trailed down his face and he wiped it away with the back of his hand. "I know firsthand how much blood doesn't matter. I know, I have an adopted brother. It means nothing to our relationship. Adam is my brother in every sense of the word. But I can't help it, I feel like I've been robbed."

"I understand, I don't see anything wrong with that."

"I do. It's wrong thinking. Because I think other things too. I could've done things so differently. Married differently, and I know how wrong it is to think that way, I know it, but I feel robbed of years where I had choices and maybe could have had a different life."

"That's the twenty-two-year-old pissed off you talking, and you have the right to be furious about that. You're mourning what could have been if she hadn't lied to you. You *could* be living a totally different life right now."

"Ella became my life and I don't regret it, I probably would have married Tara anyway. I'm just… I still have my little girl, that's all that matters." For the first time and in front of me, he bled freely as I sat shocked and leaned in to whisper.

"She is yours in every way, you know that."

He nodded several times in agreement. "I know, I'm just fucking wrecked. I can't believe it, after all these years. How could she do that to me? When I devoted my life to her, to them both… how?"

"Daddy!" Ella called as we both snapped our heads in her direction. "Watch!"

He nodded as she picked Disco up and her paws started frantically moving before the wave swept through. "See? She's surfing!"

Ian and I nodded as she pranced away with her new prize tucked in her arms.

"Fuck," Ian said, wiping his face. I felt his raw heart bleed between us, helpless to come up with the right words.

"I don't know what to say. What she's done is unforgivable. I'm so sorry."

"Don't be, I can't be sorry. I refuse to do this pity party shit any longer, I have her," he said as he nodded toward where Ella stood in the ocean, a picture of health and happiness. "I have her."

"She is beautiful, kind, well-mannered and has a heart of gold. I'm so taken with her already. You have every reason to be proud."

Worry creased his brow. "Her mother is threatening to tell her the truth. She's back with the asshole who fathered her."

"Jesus, really?"

He nodded, and fear replaced devastation. "I don't know what this is going to mean. She's just turned fifteen years old, so it could result in an ugly custody battle if Tara presses it. And I can't find it in me to be civil to her long enough to discuss it."

"I know I'm prying, but will you tell me why you burned all those photos and kept the letter?"

"I didn't keep it." He sat back and ran a hand down his face before his eyes met mine. "I hadn't used that luggage since I left her. I'm assuming she put it in there while I was packing the day I told her I was leaving and I've only just found it. She didn't want the divorce and I assume she stuck it in my suitcase to try to stir up some nostalgia for feelings that hadn't been there in over a decade." He took a long sip of his beer. "It was just another attempt at manipulation. I found it while rifling through my bag the night I came to stay with you. I did read it. And all it did was prove what a fucking idiot I was to feel that way about her in the first place."

He shook his head in aggravation. "It's just that she played me so well. She played me, and I let her because I loved her so fucking much. And then she broke me... *twice*."

I ignored the sting in my chest though I had no right to be jealous of his ex-*wife*. "You *did* love her."

He gave me a sharp nod. We sat watching the commotion around us before he spoke again. "I'm not entirely proud of the way I've behaved. She phoned weeks ago and I told her I never loved her."

"You lied to hurt her?"

He nodded. "I did. I loved her so much that my disappointment killed me when she didn't turn out to be the woman I thought she was. She doesn't deserve to know and will never know the extent of my love."

I stayed mute, too afraid to lose the rest of his confession.

"She..." he swallowed, "when we found out about Ella's disability, Tara's behavior ruined our relationship. It's really that simple. She wouldn't accept the fact that Ella wasn't a candidate for getting cochlear implants. Her attitude just completely ruined her for me. She acted as if we had a defective baby and refused to learn how to sign until every last specialist had told her there was no chance. I couldn't understand Tara then, I felt like I had married someone else. It ruined us and because I felt so strongly about it, I let it ruin us. I couldn't forgive her, and I never looked at her the same way again."

"I'm so sorry."

"Don't be. I stayed married, but it was pointless. After a few years, we were two zombies and our marriage the apocalypse. But I stayed with her for Ella's sake, until I couldn't take it anymore."

"For a majority of your marriage?"

"Well over a decade," he said before taking a long pull of his beer, his eyes on Ella.

"No wonder you don't want to risk going through that again. I hate that I'm saying this, but as your friend, I totally understand why you don't want to get involved."

"And what about the woman I'm sleeping with?" he asked, eyeing me intently. "What would she say?

"I don't think she can fault you either."

He leaned in as if to kiss me and then glanced Ella's way.

"I can't blame you for being selfish about your freedom, Ian. I really do understand. But I hope you know if it came down to a custody battle, Ella would choose you. She would. I have no doubts."

He nodded. "I pray she does."

"You fight, you fucking fight her so hard. I'm having a terrible time believing a judge would ever grant her full custody based on a lie she kept up for fifteen years! Did she tell you purposefully to hurt you?"

"No, it was a coincidence I found out. She could have pulled that at any time, but she didn't. I think she knew it would destroy me. But now that I've found out and she's with Daniel, I think she wants to use paternity as an excuse to bring that fucker closer to Ella. Not only that, it seems like she wants me to be okay with it."

"What the fuck is wrong with her?!"

"I know it's screwed up. Let's..." he shook his head sighing, "let's let this go for now."

"Why?"

His grin at me seemed out of place. "Because you're yelling."

"I'm pissed for you!"

"I can tell."

"She's a horrible person!"

He nodded. "Seems to be the case."

"If she was here, I don't think I could hold myself back from beating the dog shit out of her!"

He gave me a beautiful grin. "So, *this* is the angry New Yorker? Cute."

"What a bitch!"

"Come on, Koti," he said, brushing some hair away from my face. "Let's drop it."

"Okay... okay, fine. But for the record, I hate your ex-wife."

"That makes two of us."

I pressed my lips together as the hairs rose on the back of my neck. It took me three beers to calm down.

"Easy killer," Ian said as I finished my beer, taking healthy gulps. "You know sun-drunk is not fun."

"I'm aware." I wiped my mouth with the back of my hand as he chuckled.

"Such a lady. Still mad?"

"Yes." Reaching out I ran my palm down his jaw. "But I'm glad you told me."

"Me too."

I frowned as I looked at my chipped blue toes. "I owe you an apology. On the beach that day. When I threw that sand ball at your head. I told you we didn't need you reproducing your kind of crazy. I'm sorry for that."

"Koti, I've been such an asshole, I deserved much worse from you." He reached out and gripped the back of my head, pulling me forward and kissed me on the temple and then chanced a kiss on my lips.

"Thank you," he said softly. "For listening, for being upset for me, and for understanding."

I sighed as Ian popped the top on two fresh beers and handed one to me. "What a mess we are, crocky." I clinked my bottle-neck to his.

"Rather be in the thick of the mess with you, puffer fish."

He brushed his knuckles along my thigh and I leaned into his touch.

"Ian?"

"Mmm?" We both got lost in the contact as my breathing picked up and his eyes pooled with desire watching my reaction to him.

I licked my lips. "Try my door tonight."

Sometime after midnight, I heard the click of my bedroom door followed by the lock. My body tensed as the covers were slowly pulled away from my waiting skin. I was on fire with need and already moaning before his lips brushed my ankle. I spread at his urging while the low rumble of his commands filled the room. He sank between my thighs, his eager tongue lapping up my arousal as I gripped the sheets next to me. We'd spent the majority of our dinner eye-fucking each other until it became too much, and I was forced to step away from the table. When Ella offered to take Disco for a walk, Ian had cornered me at the kitchen sink, biting into my shoulder and brushing his cock along my back with promising words.

"Fuck," Ian said pushing into me, I was dripping as he drove his way in, forcing us both to stifle our moans as I scratched at his back. "Easy," he whispered as he drove in again, his control lost a second later when I spoke.

"Fuck me." Gripping him closer, I crossed my legs around his back spreading wider.

"You're perfect," he grunted out before pulling me to ride his lap.

Moonlight shone just enough through the window to allow me to see his eager lips close around my nipple. A light shadow crossed over his face, his eyes closed as he sucked hard. The sight of it had me riding him harder before he gripped my wrists to slow me down.

"We've got all night. We are *taking* all night."

Helpless without the ability to cling to him, he forced me to gain the friction I needed by pumping my hips. That led to a whole new kind of ecstasy for us both. Our breaths came out fast, bodies covered in sweat and lust, we worked ourselves into a frenzy until he let go of my wrists and we collided, *hard*. Time didn't exist, though we stole those moments and breathed for only the other. Our bodies molded in the most beautiful way as he took away my fears and I absorbed his hurts.

"You're still dangerous," he whispered before we collapsed in a heap, our mouths refusing to separate until the moon disappeared and the stars faded into the morning sky.

Ian

Ella's glee-filled shriek warmed my heart as she pulled out her gift. "Thank you, Koti!"

"You're welcome. I got a set too so we can snorkel together, and I got one for you too." Koti tossed the bag my way.

"Thank you," I said, pulling the mask from the package.

"Welcome," Koti said, an intimate smile passed between us for a split second before she addressed Ella. "Your fins are on the porch." Ella raced to the screen door, letting it smack closed. I yanked Koti to me and kissed her soundly on the mouth, sucking on her lower lip before I kissed her just long enough to thank her properly.

"Every day you're getting worse. You're going to blow our cover."

The truth was, I couldn't help myself. No matter how hard I tried, I couldn't resist her. That need was a far cry from the only one I had the day I'd landed on that island. Then I only wanted isolation, now it was hard to imagine being there without her.

She was dangerous for me in every way. I was addicted to her warmth, her kiss, her body.

Not only that, the more time she spent with Ella, the more I was drawn to her. She didn't treat her like a kid, but a friend, which I respected. She wanted no part of authority and respected those boundaries as well. After her first few days in St. Thomas, Ella made it impossible for Koti to feel left out. She refused to do anything without her. Their fast bond made Ella's trip much easier to manage. I didn't constantly have the need to cater to one or the other. If I was honest, it was one of the best times I'd had with Ella. Our first vacation away from Texas just us, father and daughter, a new definition of family.

Except Koti really wasn't a part of it, so she played friend to *both* of us. I couldn't help but get a little sentimental at the sight of Koti when she slid on her mask.

"Now there is a familiar sight."

She grinned and pushed her chest out. "Except *this* time, I have *miss* tits."

I groaned. "Don't remind me."

She bounced from flipper to flipper. "You were all hot and bothered over my mother then, ewww."

"Hey, she was a retired supermodel and I was fourteen, sue me."

"Whatever happened to your chipped tooth?"

"The miracle of modern dentistry."

"You should have kept it, you were a lot cuter with it."

"Was I?"

"Your freckles are gone too, shame, and a lot of your accent. I would say I improved and you went downhill." Throwing my head back, I laughed as Ella came barreling through the front door with her flippers attached.

"Let's go!"

We all made our way down to the beach as Disco avoided the water, barking at the tide. After a day of sun and snorkeling, the girls settled by a fresh fire I constructed, marshmallows roasting.

"This is the life. That's how you say it right, Koti?"

"Yes. That's exactly how you say it."

"I wish I lived here," Ella piped. "Do you ever get tired of it?"

"Never. And I'll never leave."

"Do you ever go back to the States?"

"Technically, St. Thomas is the US."

"You know what I mean," Ella snorted.

"I haven't yet. I'm not a fan of flying, but I will."

"Will you come see me at my new school?"

I slashed the air with my hand, my eyes all warning and Ella went immediately on the defensive.

"Sorry, Dad, but I like her. She's *my* friend too. And you could let her sleep at our house since she let us stay with her all this time."

A moment of uncomfortable silence passed before I spoke up.

"True. Koti, you're welcome to come to Texas anytime."

"Thanks," she said, with a laugh due to my discomfort. She'd been true to her word and hadn't made any part of our situation awkward. A part of me hoped our time together meant more to her than a fling because it was becoming the case for me, but I knew I couldn't have it both ways.

"Or we could come back here, right Daddy? I'm sure Grandma won't mind."

"Right." I stared at the fire as the girls stuffed their mouths with s'mores and compared their chocolate-covered faces. I gazed at my daughter who was the perfect picture of innocence and the woman who sat next to her, who didn't deserve the shit cards she was dealt but looked just as pure sitting next to her. Inwardly I sighed as I snuffed out the fire and followed them in the house. Our nightly book club had begun, but it seemed I was the only one serious about reading as they giggled back and forth comparing notes about *Outlander* while snacking on grapes.

"Jamieeeee," Ella snorted. "He's so hot."

"He totally is," Koti said, with far too much enthusiasm for my taste.

After several minutes of listening to their fawning over

a fictional man, I lowered my book and gave them a pointed look. "Would you two shut up." I picked up my novel in an attempt to resume my reading. A second later, I was smacked in the head with a fistful of grapes. I glared over at the two of them who feigned innocence and hid my grin behind my book.

thirty-three

Koti

Stevie Nicks sang "Edge of Seventeen" as I pulled into the small parking lot singing along at the top of my lungs. Banion greeted me with his usual thousand-watt smile. "Yank, you look fresh."

"Not from the boat?"

"Nope, you've finally got the island glow."

"Finally, huh?"

"Yep, or something else making you happy. You got a new man?"

"Nope." And that was the truth of it. "New friend. And I've known him since I was a kid."

"Oh well, he gay?"

I laughed through my reply. "No."

"Well, then he's a blind yank. You were bones when ya got here."

"I know."

"All fixed up then?"

I nodded, my smile disappearing. "My parents came and *went*."

He looked me over, his skin darker from days of endless sun. "Not such a good time?"

"Not at all."

He shrugged. "Things happen the way they are supposed to

happen, nothing you can do."

"Yeah."

"Something else bothering ya?"

"Nope."

"So, this friend is nothing more? I think you pretend. I will wait here with a bottle of your banana rum," he joked as he handed me three fresh bouquets.

A month had passed since Ella left the island and Ian had managed to get back to the States twice. Each time he went I got a taste of missing him. Wanting to believe it was good exercise for my heart, I spent my days alone venturing out of my house, keeping dinner dates with Jasmine. I'd even graced her infamous wine bar again, got drunk off my ass and ended up dancing until the wee hours of the morning. I may have accidentally slipped up that night and borrowed Jasmine's phone to FaceTime my soon to be ex non-boyfriend.

He appeared on screen with a scowl. It was, after all, two o'clock in the morning.

"What in the hell are you doing, Koti?"

"Just wanted to check in with you, crocky."

"It's late."

"Or early, don't be such a pessimist."

He groaned as I tilted the phone down giving him an ample shot of my cleavage. "Try to use your nice words, I might be in the midst of missing you and you're going to fuck it all up."

He grinned then as he sat up in bed. "I might be missing you too. A little. But I have to say there are perks of sleeping in my own bed."

"Yeah, like what?"

"I don't get slapped in the head every night."

"That's active dreaming, totally unintentional."

"I don't have a dog trying to lick my balls in the morning."

"That's not her fault, they look a lot more fun than they are."

He lifted a brow. "I'll grant you that."

Ziggy Marley sang "Drive" over the radio as I stood and swayed my hips.

"So, I take it Jasmine finally talked you into another night out."

"Are you proud of me?"

His smile had me melting on the spot I was swaying in. "Very."

"Well, I didn't do it so you would be proud of me. Believe it or not, I love to dance."

"Then we should dance together."

Stopping my hips, I stood at a nearby stool at the bar. "You dance?"

"God, you act like I'm the Grinch."

"If the Whoville hat fits."

He shook his head, giving me that dead stare I'd grown to love.

"I'll be back in four days. I'm trying to tie some things up here."

It wasn't my place to ask what things, so I didn't. "K. See you then. Night."

There was a pause on his end as his eyes swept my face, the silence conveying more than we were allowed. "Night, beauty."

Ian's bag was left abandoned on the porch as he pressed me against my back door taking turns between nipping and biting at my neck.

"This dress, *damn*," he said as I smiled against his kiss.

"You like it?"

"I hope you aren't wearing this out."

My deep red backless sundress dipped so low you could see the divot at the top of my ass. My tits were bared on either side by a thin strip of material. Tilting my head back, I gasped as he discovered I wasn't wearing a thing underneath.

"You *better* not be wearing this out of the house."

"Chill out, *Dad*."

He turned me then lifted my dress and proceeded to redden my ass with his palm as I laughed. He pulled me into his arms and lifted me so I was cradled to his chest. "You look beautiful."

Ignoring the sting of tears, I slid my palm down his stubble-covered jaw. "You need a shave."

Rubbing his chin against my skin, I moaned as he made his intentions known. I would be covered in his beard rash by the time he was finished.

"Such an animal."

I began to sign.

Fuck me, Ian.

His eyes bulged. "Where did you learn that?"

"Your precious informational channel—YouTube. And don't get thinking I'm back online. It's not happening."

"Damn, you got my hopes up, I was thinking maybe you had plugged back in and joined the land of the living."

"Never."

"Who doesn't have a smartphone in this day and age? It's baffling."

"Me."

"You." He threw me on my bed and began to undress. The man was in amazing shape and my body started to flutter with anticipation.

"Pull your dress up and spread your legs."

I didn't hesitate a second.

"Show me more."

I reached between my legs and did his bidding.

"Hold it there."

"Ian... hurry."

"Not this time," he said with slow piercing gray eyes.

Once he'd shed his shoes, he tugged at the clasp on his

watch. In his slacks, I moaned as he kept his darkening gaze on me. I loved it when he wore a suit home. Something about him in dress attire did it for me.

"Are you wet?"

"Come find out."

"Show me," he said, leaning against my dresser and slipping off his shoes.

"Please," I begged, dipping my fingers in my center, so he could hear that I was ready. His cock jumped in his pants.

His eyes trailed down my body and jumped to meet mine. "I'll never tire of you, ever."

"I missed you. Please, *please*, Ian. I want you."

He was still partially clothed and driving me out of my mind with his control. His hair was combed neatly and gelled. He looked so sophisticated, so well put together—dashing—I could only imagine the fantasies of his students and felt a pang of jealousy as the idea struck.

I began to writhe on the bed, a completely different woman than I was before he'd become my lover. Never in a million years could I have dreamed of having the appetite I did then. Not every time was painful, but I would risk it every day for the slightest feel of him. It was hopeless, I was addicted to him and hopelessly in love.

"Say it again."

"I want you."

"Again."

"I fucking want you," I said as he remained where he stood. "Please."

When he didn't move, I sat up. "What are you doing?"

"Again."

"I want you."

"Again."

Anger began to surface. "What are you doing?"

"Again."

"Go to hell."

Moving to the edge of the bed, he stopped me from my retreat as tears sprang to my eyes.

"Fine," I sighed as my tears fell. "I *need* you, happy?"

"No," he said before kissing me within an inch of my life. When he pulled away, I was emotionally raw.

"Damnit, Ian, this wasn't supposed to happen."

He nodded. "I know."

"This isn't good, is it?"

"No, but you aren't alone."

I ripped his hair as he tilted my neck and bit and sucked until I was begging again.

I unzipped his pants freeing his cock, pumping it between us.

"Every time I see you, I feel so relieved. Like I'd been living in some sort of dream and then I come back and you're here," he put my hand over his chest, "and I can breathe again."

Emotion bounced between us as he slid into me, stretching me full while my throat burned with emotion. When we'd both come, he pulled me to his chest as the room began to darken with the setting sun.

"This is the best I've ever felt," he whispered, "ever."

"You're my first, Ian."

He paused his movements. "What?"

"You're the first man I've ever had this sort of connection with." I sat up and looked back at him with a smile. "You're the first man I've ever felt this way for. I never got this far with any-one because… you know. I just couldn't, so you're my first."

His eyes searched mine before he slowly pushed inside me again. Words failed us as we moved in sync, our hearts pounding out the words we weren't allowed to utter. We broke in a breath-less mess and he pulled me against his chest, his heart hammer-ing against my ear as I ran my nails down his skin.

"How was Ella?"

"I didn't get to see her, she's in Washington for the next week."

"Oh?"

"Yeah," he whispered. "Would you be terribly pissed off if I slept?"

"No, of course not."

"I was so busy getting things sorted I didn't get much done and this drunk crazy lady managed to call me on the one night I managed a few winks."

"Sorry."

"I loved watching you dance. It was…" he swallowed, "it was good."

"Good?"

"For lack of a better word. I'm sleep deprived, remember?"

I kissed his chest and pulled away. "Room's all yours."

He pulled me back and kissed me soundly. "Sit tight for a bit, okay?"

"Okay."

Seconds later his breathing deepened and for a solid day, he slept.

thirty-four

Koti

I greeted my new renters with a smile as they exited the cab both wrinkled and exhausted from a day of travel.

The husband pulled the sleeping little boy from his car seat as he roused wrapping his chubby arms around his father's neck. "Come on, buddy."

The baby glanced around, his beautiful green eyes meeting mine before he buried his head into his father's neck. "Come on, Noble, can you say hi to the lady?"

I waved at him and he giggled as his father extended a hand. "You must be Koti, nice to meet you. I'm Cameron and this is my wife, Abbie."

Abbie greeted me with a warm smile. "Nice to meet you. Wow, this place is truly beautiful."

"I'm hoping the surprise was a good one?" I'd been planning the trip with her husband for the past few weeks.

"I still can't believe he pulled this off," she said, glancing back at her family with love-soaked eyes. "We, uh, didn't really get to have a honeymoon. I got sick on our first try."

"Morning sickness?"

"Yes, it's the worst. Do you have children?"

"No," I said, staring at their beautiful little boy who wore a T-shirt that read *Woo King*.

"No kids yet, someday?"

Someday?

"Well, my little man was definitely worth it," Abbie said, kissing his hand before she scoured the rental with a smile.

Pangs of envy hit in that moment as Cameron leaned in and kissed his son on the forehead. "Ready to go swimming, buddy?"

He nodded and nestled further into his father's arms.

Realization struck, even with all the families I'd checked into rentals over the past year, it was the first time in my life I wished for a family of my own. My own baby boy with eyes the color of his father's.

Shocked at my personal admission, I walked the beautiful family through their beach house. Abbie ambled with me as Cameron chased Noble through the expansive living room. "Noble, stop. Don't touch that, buddy. Why you little…" he picked the baby up easily and tossed him up over his head, catching him as he squealed. "Gain, Dada, gain!"

Abbie took a step out onto the long back porch where she was met with the sight of thousands of miles of expansive ocean.

"You can get to the beach from the first level," I said as she looked back at her husband with utter love. Abbie's excitement was infectious. "This is incredible, baby!" She yelled to Cameron who answered back with a pride-filled grin. "Happy you love it, babe."

I chimed in. "You won't get used to the view and that's a good thing."

"I just can't believe we're here," she smiled. "I didn't realize how much we needed this."

"You'll be a new woman by the time you leave. Cameron's scheduled a massage for you in a few hours, there is a week's worth of groceries in the fridge. He's also opted for concierge service and a driver for the length of your stay. My number is in the book on the table." Abbie stood, eyes glistening, her smile growing with every word I spoke.

"Happy?"

"Ecstatic."

"Awesome. There are two keys to the house on the foyer table. And please don't hesitate to call if you need anything."

Cameron joined us standing by Abbie's side with a newly animated little boy wiggling in his arms.

"Thank you so much, Koti, I couldn't have pulled this off without you."

"You're welcome and welcome to St. Thomas."

I left the smiling family with a new kind of ache in my chest. I was just about to head back to the office when Jasmine called.

"Hey buddy, did you get the Bledsoe's checked in?"

"Yep, all set."

"We're done for the day if you want to knock off."

"Are you sure?" I asked with a smile.

"Yes girl, go play with Ian. But just keep your phone on for calls. I have a date tonight."

"Really? With who?"

She paused. "Jasmine, with who?"

"Toby. Am I crazy?"

"Of course not, I kind of figured that was going to happen."

"Really, you see us together? He's so…"

"Bold? Confident? Perfect for you?"

"If you thought that, why didn't you say something?"

"I wanted you two to figure it out for yourselves."

I pulled up to a stoplight where a Jeep, the same style as mine waited with me. I glanced over to see I had the attention of the passengers, a group of teenage guys.

"Let's just hope he doesn't come out in an apron or want me to R. Kelly his ass."

"What?"

"Pee on him or some freaky shit."

The guys burst into laughter as I hung my head. "You just embarrassed me at a stoplight," I hissed as I smashed onto the gas the minute the light changed.

It was all I remembered aside from the crunch of metal.

thirty-five

Ian

Ignoring my phone, I ran through my list of lectures and made notes. Looking around the expansive beach house, I basked in the serenity of Koti's bubble. As soon as she got home, I was going to cook her my favorite meal and spend the night making her moan. I wasn't taking a single fucking minute of our time together for granted. After making sure I had everything I needed I glanced at the clock. She would be home any minute. Warmth spread as I thought of the way she'd woken me up that morning, her lips wrapped around my cock before she lifted herself to sink on top of me. We didn't utter a word, just reveled in the connection as I pulled her to me so we were chest to chest, hearts pounding as she slowly rode me until we had no choice but to break the silence with words of praise.

There was something to be said about the sex we had, but the connection we shared was what made it so fucking incredible. Koti was a safe haven, and I drank with greed from her never-ending fountain of beauty and warmth. There was always an understanding in her eyes, kindness of her words. Our relationship was effortless, she was a relatable friend and an incredible lover. She gave and gave, and I took without hesitation because even though at the heart of it, I felt selfish, I felt like she too was thriving on letting me have my way. Anything else would have

been unacceptable, I knew that I cared too much about her to
hurt her. If I felt for one second over the last month we shared
that she had suffered in any way, I wouldn't have returned to St.
Thomas. There was no benefit in making her confess she needed
me the night before, but my desire to know if the feeling was
mutual was too much.

Because I needed her too, and as dangerous as it was to
get that admission, I didn't feel so alone in my ache and maybe,
just maybe, my confession that I needed her the same would be
enough for us for the moment.

My phone vibrated again, and I picked it up to see a local
area code.

"Hello."

"Ian, it's Jasmine."

My heart sank as every nerve in my body fired. "No, oh
fuck, is she all right?"

"She's been in an accident. Some asshole t-boned her at a
light but thankfully he wasn't going that fast. She's got a rash
from the airbag, but she's okay. I'm bringing her home now. She
just didn't want you to worry."

"Why didn't she call me?"

The silence confirmed my worst fear. "She had an attack?"

"Yes," Jasmine confirmed with a whisper, "and it was nasty.
They gave her some meds and she's a little loopy."

"Okay."

"Just don't walk on eggshells, okay, or she'll know I told
you."

"I won't."

"Ian, at some point you *aren't* going to be there, right?"

Pressing my lips together I tried to push away the burn in
my chest. "Right."

"I hope you know what you're doing."

On the defensive but feeling like a bastard, I answered. "I don't want to hurt her."

"But you're going to. And if I'm being honest, I think you already are."

Pacing the floor, I let out a sigh of relief when the front door opened. Koti appeared with a small red rash on the side of her nose and a larger stretch of it covering her chin.

"So today sucked," she said with a laugh. "I'm slightly medicated."

In an instant, she was in my arms. "I'm so sorry." I pulled away.

"I'm totally fine. Airbags fucking hurt though just so you know, stay as far away from the wheel when you drive as you possibly can. I feel like I got punched by a heavyweight."

"That bad?"

"Not on Vicodin and Xanax," she said with a laugh. "I'm feeling pretty damn loose, professor, tonight might be a good time to experiment."

I rolled my eyes.

"Look at you, rolling your eyes. I do remember you grounding your daughter for that."

"Are you okay, really?"

She paused when she read my expression. "She told you, didn't she? That asshole."

"Why can't I know?"

"Why should you know?" She ran her hands through her longer blonde hair. She'd been growing it out since I'd arrived at the island. I hadn't told her, but I loved it that length. I hadn't told her I loved a lot of things. "Because I'm the man waiting for you, that's why."

Ignoring me, she took a seat on the barstool by the island. "You're cooking for me?"

Her smile was forced, but I went with it.

"Yeah, I wanted to surprise you with my favorite dish from when I was a boy."

"What is it?"

"It's called Boboties. It's spiced meat with egg custard and topped with raisins."

"That sounds... interesting. Let's do this, I'm starving. All I've had to eat today was flying metal with a side of glass soup."

I frowned at her indifference, feeling her rattle with nerves across from me. "Not funny."

She held up her thumb and forefinger about an inch apart in front of her. "A little bit funny. My Jeep is totaled, well, my *parents'* Jeep. I don't even own a car, how am I going to have a baby?"

I froze the workings of my hands and faced her. "You're pregnant?"

She must have realized her slip. "No. God, Ian, no. I'm sorry, I didn't mean to scare you," she waved her hand like any drugged person would.

"Why are you talking about a baby then?"

"I just, in the future if I *wanted* to have a baby, I don't even own a car. I'm too poor to be a mother. Never mind, I'm rambling."

I pressed for more information, high on pills or not, I had to know.

"Are you thinking about a family?"

"I just saw the cutest little boy ever and it made my ovaries ache, that's all. Don't get weird."

"I'm not being weird, *you're* being weird."

"I'm high, what's your excuse? And why aren't you cooking,

crocky? I'm starving!"

"On it, your highness."

A beat of silence passed. "He was beautiful though—the baby, Noble—he was perfect. Shy, and just so... they were happy, you know, it wasn't forced or fake, you could see how happy they were."

I began slicing some onion. "It's okay to want a family, Koti."

She laughed without an ounce of humor. "Yeah, uh, I'd be a great mom. 'Hold on honey, mommy's having an anxiety attack in the pantry because I can't handle making a hundred cupcakes for your class tomorrow.'" She spun on the stool animatedly delivering her own self-deprecating blows as my chest cracked for her.

"Thousands of people with anxiety have children, stop it."

"I full-on had a meltdown because I wasn't sure if God existed today. Do you think it's okay to subject your child to that?"

I set the oven temperature and leaned over the counter. "You were in a car accident, it's okay to feel—however the hell you want to feel—after something like that happens. Stop hurting yourself with lies."

Imploring eyes sought mine. "Are you afraid to die, Ian?"

"No."

"Why?"

"It's a part of life I accepted when I was a soldier and I grew immune to death, as tragic as that sounds."

"Where did they go, Ian? When your friends died, where did they go?"

"I don't know."

"Then how are you not afraid?"

"Because if it's nothingness then we aren't aware of it and if God exists, we have to assume it's a place far better than the one we're standing in. Those are the two options, right?"

"Guess so. Well… there's hellfire and damnation for being faithless."

"See, I'm of the belief that if there is a creator so divine, he wouldn't have the capacity to be so cruel to those he created."

"That's comforting."

"Good, then take comfort you'll either be blissfully in paradise or completely unaware you no longer exist."

"You make it sound so simple."

"I'm sorry that it is for me."

Her face twisted to mask the sob she was holding. "I'm not sorry for you. I'm happy you aren't afraid. You're so smart."

"As are you."

"And still so polite," she said as tears made their way down her cheeks.

"I have to believe there is a place for us because I want there to be for my daughter."

Koti nodded, "I understand. I want that for her too."

"And I want it for you," I told her truthfully.

"Thank you."

I moved around and gripped her shoulders. "Koti."

"Yes, Ian?"

"Are you okay?"

"No," she sniffed, more tears budding in her eyes. "I'm not okay. That scared the shit out of me."

"I know, so let me put my tea down and be responsible for you, just for tonight, okay?"

"Coffee," she corrected as her voice cracked.

"Coffee," I whispered.

thirty-six

Ian

Three weeks later…

I whispered through a halo of blonde hair. "Hey, beautiful, wake-up."

"I should probably tell you those are fighting words."

I chuckled and kissed her until she roused from sleep.

"Would you please let me recover? Surely there's no skin on your penis after that last round."

This time I couldn't help my laughter as I gathered her to me and lifted her from the bed.

"Ian," she sighed, kissing my neck and wrapping her legs around my waist. "I can appreciate how sexually starved you must have been after going without, trust me, I love sleeping with you." I made my way down the porch steps and onto the sand. "Sex with you is my favorite hobby, but there are necessities that need priority as well. Wine, s'mores, and sleep."

Setting her on the beach, I smiled down at her and turned her to face the ocean. "Shut your drivel, woman, and look."

Her grin disappeared as her mouth parted. "Oh, my god!"

She sank into my frame as we stared at a moonlit sky. The islands below easily seen due to the sheer size of it. Thousands of stars littered the sky leaving us momentarily speechless.

"My God, now this is a good excuse to wake a girl up."

"I thought you would appreciate it."

"I used to be such a huge fan of the stars," she sighed. "So much mystery. I believed all that hoopla about mythology until my science teacher told me they were balls of fire. It was kind of like finding out Santa wasn't real."

"Sucked the magic right out of it?"

"Exactly. Like why can't we leave certain things a mystery?"

"Some would argue that those balls of fire in relation to where we stand are important."

"I don't *want* to know if some asteroid is coming for me."

"You're safe tonight."

"I feel safe." My stomach dropped as she settled further into me and I reveled in the feel of her warm skin.

She turned in my arms more beautiful than anything I'd ever seen in my thirty-eight years.

"This is wildly romantic, Kemp. Are you feeling okay?"

"Got a little moonstruck is all. I remember skies like this when we camped after a safari in South Africa."

"I can't imagine how amazing that was. Growing up there must have been incredible."

"I'll be a Saffa till I die. I can't believe my parents moved us to Texas. I'm still pissed."

We both laughed.

"That's the way it is, right? You think you'll end up one place and you end up on a different planet."

With both hands, I pushed the hair away from her face. "I loved this planet."

Even with the white noise of the waves, I was sure she could hear me swallow.

Her eyes watered as she looked at me for the truth. "This *is* an asteroid, isn't it?"

She searched my eyes before she hung her head. "When do

you leave?"

I choked on the answer. "Tomorrow afternoon."

She turned in my arms again to face the sky, seconds later I felt one of her tears fall on my hand as the rest of me shattered with the weight of it.

"I understand why you didn't tell me. I'm not angry."

"I want to stay. If that makes any difference at all."

"Of course it does."

Minutes later, in an attempt for any conversation other than the suffocating silence, I leaned in to whisper, "I have a favor to ask."

"Sure."

"Can you look out for Disco?"

She sniffed. "Of course."

"Thank you."

Agonizing seconds later, she finally spoke.

"So," she said as she took a deep breath. "I'm assuming you pulled this all together last minute to break it to me gently? Did a FaceTime with NASA to lasso the moon?"

I chuckled though I was already aching. We stood wordlessly a moment longer as she clutched my arms.

"I'll be okay. I don't want you to worry about me. I know Ella needs you."

"I know you will."

"You know I would live on your planet if I could."

I gripped her tighter to me. "The invitation stands."

"This sucks. Of all the beaches in the world, why did you have to have your breakdown on mine?"

"I'm not at all sorry we happened."

She sniffed again. "Me either."

"Koti, look at me."

"I can't. You can't make promises and I swear to God, that's all I want to hear from you right now so… just give me a minute."

"Okay." That minute was agony as we felt the reality come crashing in through the dream we'd existed in for months. An eternity later, I turned her to face me and kissed her tear-stained cheeks.

"You're making breakfast due to the deliverance of shitty news."

"Deal."

I brushed the tears away from her eyes as she looked up at me.

"Please be honest. Would you stay here with me if you could?"

"Without a second thought."

She sniffed again before I took her lips.

When we pulled away, she gave me a sad smile. "That's good enough."

"Koti—"

"There's nothing to say. Not tonight."

I nodded.

"Take me back to bed?"

"Let's go."

thirty-seven

Ian

I watched her sleep, tracing her skin with my fingers. She stirred slightly, her hair askew and then turned to face away from me. The pain that tiny move caused was unbearable. No part of me wanted to leave her. No part of me wanted the life that waited. I'd taken a job and sold my house to move into a rental. My future idle and dependent on Ella's. Decisions had been made, life was in order, my daughter was waiting. I had to leave. Koti stirred, and again I was graced with the sight of her face. She slept restlessly most of the time, her beautiful form flailing at all hours of the night. I'd been on the receiving end of some seriously rough hours but had grown used to it over the months on my side of her bed. The only time she fully stilled was when she lay on my chest. I pulled her into my arms to give her more peaceful minutes of sleep and she went instantly lax. I whispered my apology while she slept.

"What have I done to us? I'm so sorry."

I let it happen. She played a part too, but in the end, I'd given her every part of me. She knew my every side, the small details, and I knew hers. We shared the things that made *us* significant and I'd allowed it, knowing how much it would hurt to lose it.

Aside from my little girl, life had never gifted me anything so beautiful. I knew every inch of her golden skin, had drowned in the icy-blue pools of her eyes and basked in her warmth. I'd pulled every sweet sip from her lips. We'd become magnetic and inseparable and I let it happen in my selfish haze knowing it would rip us to shreds to lose it.

She was my golden shore after the shipwreck that was my life and she'd loved me with her whole heart, only to let me break it.

"Ian! Where are you, Ian!" she cried as she raced around the house.

"Over here, Koti," I said, gathering wood in the alley for the fire I was building us.

"I'm leaving. Mom says we have to leave early. I can't do the bonfire with you."

"Okay, it's okay, don't cry."

"She's making me go to the school camp, so I can make friends. I don't like those girls. I told you about them."

"I know. But you're easy to like so just let them come to you, okay? Remember what I said?"

"Have fun anyway?"

"Right."

She hiccupped as her chest heaved with her upset. "You're my best friend. Don't forget me just 'cause you get bigger, okay?"

"I won't. Besides, we're neighbors. I will probably see you around sometime next summer. Right?"

She nodded and nodded. "Maybe you'll come back, and we can be best friends again."

I rubbed the top of her head and she pushed it away with a smile.

"Of course."

"Okay, and you'll make me s'mores again?" She was still crying but trying her best to be brave for me.

"Banana pops too."

"Promise?"

"I swear it."

She hugged me tight with her whole little body and let go just as fast. "Bye, crocky"

"Bye, puffer fish."

"Forgive me," I whispered as I sank into sleep with her one last time.

Koti

Ian's duffle bag fell heavy on the porch as I swayed in the hammock with Disco in my arms. Seconds later, Ian knelt at my feet and rubbed his fingers through her fur. His voice alone was enough to threaten the strength I'd mustered up.

"I was just thinking earlier this morning about the first time we said goodbye. Do you remember that?"

I cleared my throat. "Nope, must be the one that got away. So, here's the way I see it." I stood and let Disco down at his feet. "We can do this the easy way or the hard way. I'm taking the easy route."

Pushing up on my toes I pressed my lips to his briefly and smoothed his cheek with my palm. "Go be happy, Ian. And do me a favor, take one small piece of advice from your muse?"

He bit his lip and nodded.

"Do whatever the hell it is you have to do to make yourself happy."

I was fighting hard and losing as my throat burned with each passing second. "Okay?"

"I will."

"Okay. And by the way," I said, rambling on as I took the steps off the porch, "you're a good friend. The best. And if you ever get back to St. Tho—"

I was pulled from the sand and crushed in his arms. Tumultuous gray eyes burned through me as he leaned in. "I choose the hard way." His mouth crushed mine in a soul-stealing kiss and I felt the rest of me break beneath him. He pulled away, his eyes shredding me as they filled with regret. He didn't want to hurt me, and I drew comfort that it hurt him just as much.

"I'm fucking miserable about leaving, but I would never ask you to give up your life for me. But if you ever find yourself in need of a change from the routine. Come to Texas."

I nodded as tears collected in my eyes, unable to speak for fear of begging.

"Kissing you feels like a free fall, touching you makes me ache, and being inside you is so damn addicting. I'll miss that, and our talks, our friendship. I'll miss your bubble, Koti because that's where I want to be, where I want to stay. And if it weren't for Ella—"

"I understand," I said around the ball in my throat. "I do. I swear. But watching you fall apart and put yourself back together was a gift. I'm so amazed by you."

"Thank you."

"Don't thank me. It's ridiculous. We're like a bad movie line, aren't we? We'll always have St. Thomas," I rasped out.

"Jesus, I feel like hell."

"Me too."

"I already miss you."

"Me too."

"And because I'm a complete masochist, I can't help but mention I've fallen madly in love with you."

The world started crumbling beneath my feet as my stars were stripped away one by one. Swallowing a sob, I briefly showed him my pain. "Please go. I don't think I can do this with you much longer."

He nodded and picked up his bag. "Okay."

He made it halfway down our sand alley when I stopped him.

"Bye, crocky."

He turned to me with a sad smile. "Bye, puffer fish."

Tears streamed down my face as he walked toward his truck before once more glancing back at me.

I whispered my plea to the wind. "Maybe you'll come back, and we can be best friends again."

He nodded as if he'd heard me and I fell apart where I stood. He took a step toward me and I shook my head.

"Go," I begged.

Shoulders slumped he got into his truck as I croaked out his name, but it was silenced by the wind.

And then he was gone.

thirty-eight

Koti

Three months later…

"**M**orning babe," Jasmine chimed as she put her desk phone on speaker and some melodic hold music filled the office."

"Hey," I said, trying to clear my head to start my workday. I'd had an attack last night and Disco had peed on the bed next to me. It had been a shit morning and I didn't at all feel like sharing. The pattern I'd started years ago had begun to recycle. I'd been having more attacks than usual, and I knew the reason. No one was to blame, but I'd never been so emotionally strung out. Horrible thoughts of Ian with someone else kept racing around my head as I attempted to fall asleep each night. I couldn't really blame myself, it had been months. There was a chance he was dating, or worse might be developing feelings for someone else. But if he felt a tenth of what I was feeling, maybe he wasn't living at all.

"You're a wreck. Call him."

"Why? Why do I have to be the one? I don't even know if he's feeling it on his end at all. Maybe I was imagining it."

"He told you he was madly in love with you. He didn't leave because he wanted to. He left because he had to. There's a difference. You didn't get left."

Brown eyes stared down at me as I swallowed. "I'm

forwarding the phones to my cell. You look like shit and I don't want you greeting the renters this morning."

"I know. I'm so sorry. I was up late last night."

She slapped the top of my computer screen. "Look at me."

Gazing up at her, I did my best to keep my chin from wobbling.

"Do I look upset?"

"No, well I really can't tell, you look kind of scary right now."

"That's because I'm mad at you for thinking I would be upset. You've held my hand for the last year and a half."

"I just want to stop missing him. God, just one day, I want this to go away. I don't know how you handled it."

"Not well, remember, I had sex in a backhoe?"

"That's not even funny now. But I'm glad you're happy with Toby."

"Don't send out wedding invites yet, we're taking things so slow, sometimes I think we're just friends."

"You still haven't had sex with Toby?" I couldn't remember the last time I'd even asked her for an update, what was even odder was that she hadn't offered one.

"Nope. I'm holding out. You and Ian were an amazing influence on me. And Julian is still calling."

"Really? Julian, huh? Well don't use me as an influence, look at me now. And your corn-fed man was the one that told me Ian would dump me no matter what. I don't know if I'm his biggest fan."

She tied her hair up before pouring some coffee. "Julian is brutally honest. Sometimes it gets on my nerves, but mostly I love it. And you need to call Ian. I think half of the problem is you're still hoping he'll come back or you'll get back together. And that's what's eating you alive. You need some sort of closure."

"I think the fact that I haven't heard a word from him is

closure enough. What if he's moved on and I end up embarrassing myself?"

She pulled her roller chair over and took a seat next to me. "Then you know, and you get to move on too."

"I don't want that."

Her eyes watered in sympathy, which only made me feel more pathetic. "I know baby, and it's killing me to see you hurt, but you've got to do something. Tell him how you feel. Are you still glad you took the chance?"

I didn't hesitate. "Yes."

"Then take one more. Call him and see how that goes."

"And if it's really over?"

"Then you won't be alone. I'll be here, and you can start sharing your new war stories."

"This is the worst."

"I know." She leaned in to hug me. "You can do this, Koti, you are so much braver than you will ever know. Every chance you take shows how much you've grown."

"God, I love you. I know this is strange, but I'm so glad I had a panic attack in that Mexican restaurant. What if you hadn't found me in that corner? I hate to think we wouldn't have met."

"I think life would have made sure we found a way."

"You think so?" I sniffed as she pulled away

"I'm sure of it. I'll always be your Mexican."

Ian

Three months of agony because I made the same decision I did fifteen years ago. It would always be my daughter, DNA or none, she was mine. I was taught early that blood didn't matter. My adopted brother was black, and when we got him, I was old enough to know better than ask questions about why he was different. My parents were careful with me the first few months, going out of their way to coddle me when we adopted him. I was never upset, in fact, that extra attention irritated me. Adam was the one who felt the most anguish, growing up in a home where he constantly felt the difference.

Blood didn't matter, skin nor eye color, or native tongue. What mattered was what that person meant to you. If my ex-wife had charged her sperm donor with the task of raising Ella, I would've been free to be whatever I wanted, I would've known that Tara was a liar and a cheat, and I would've had my choice of lives. But that wasn't what happened, and at the end of my selfish tirade, I found myself grateful for her deceit. It made me Ella's daddy.

And so, while I've never fathered a child, I was a father, a daddy, a dad, and on most days, she deemed me an asshole. My range of titles stemmed from trusting the one thing in the world I know to be true for so long, and it was the one thing that could never be taken away from me.

Hurt or not, I was never going to let that happen.

And then I think of Koti and our summer by the sea and how that was the life I wanted. With her. I didn't want to be waiting in the wings while my daughter lived her life. I wanted to be with the woman whose smiles lit up my soul, whose voice soothed the bullshit, whose heart was made of flesh and gold. I wanted to whisper to her that I love her every night before she drifted to sleep. To be her comfort when she got nervous. I wanted to ease her mind and make her laugh, make her come, make her mine. But that was the selfish part of me who still brimmed with anger about a life I didn't get to choose.

The father I am says there is no choice. That man remembers the chubby hands reaching for him along with the alligator tears. He remembers the first muddled sounds she made that were solely for him. She needed me and I needed her. Ella would always be my purpose in life.

The ache will eventually recede. I'll find a woman to keep my bed warm. And Koti would—

I cut myself off mid-thought. It shouldn't hurt this fucking much.

We hadn't spoken. Nothing to say. What can we say? I made my choice. She doesn't want to leave her life and my job as a father binds me to where I need to be. It was never supposed to start, and it was never going to last. We both knew it.

Doesn't matter you're in ashes, you love her, you miss her.

My throat burned with emotion as I tipped my coffee and stared at the green expanse of my new backyard. It wasn't the view I wanted.

She has my view and soon enough someone else will have my ocean.

My phone buzzed on the counter and I ignored it, sure it was my mother. Thinking better of it, I caught it just before it stopped.

"Hello," I said, looking at the screen and freezing when I saw her name.

"I love you," she whispered softly. "Ian, I love you."

I closed my eyes. I could hear the waves crash. I imagined her on her hammock staring at her toes.

"I should have said it when you were here. I would give anything to see your face right now, to see if it even matters to you."

My heart sank. "Of course it matters."

"I hate this. I hate it here without you."

"I'm in hell," I said my voice sandpaper. "I won't put on a brave front to spare you."

"Have you ever?" I could hear her smile, but it was solemn. "I don't want to leave, Ian. You know I've accepted my limits. I don't want to throw all this work away. I won't be the woman you love. I would never ask you to leave Ella, I just want you to know how not okay I am. Because I miss you and even though I was supposed to let you go, I can't."

"I'm not okay either."

"This is horrible."

"Agreed."

"Can you… will you come ho… back?"

"If I come back, we start this all over again when I leave. I don't think I can handle it twice."

She sobbed quietly as my heart shattered along with my coffee cup against my kitchen wall.

She sniffed as I wiped my eyes. "I'm sorry I called you. I'm so sorry. It was selfish."

"I still can't regret it. You are the true love of my life. You should know that."

That was the wrong thing to say. It took her minutes of silence to speak again.

"I'll be here, okay. I'll be here, Ian. I'll wait as long as you need me to. I'm being selfish so I can pay for it that way. If I wait for you, will you come?"

"Koti, don't waste your life on love's obligations. Things may change for you."

"Do you think you will still love me?"

"I know I will, I'll never stop loving you."

"Then I'll wait."

"I can't ask you for that."

"You didn't."

"Koti, this is ridiculous. You've wasted enough time."

"The stars are back, Ian, because of you, they're back. I

don't see them the same way. Do you still want to be here?"

"More than anything."

"I'll wait for you."

"No. That's ridiculous."

"Why? Why is it so ridiculous? I waited my whole life for you. I can wait a little longer. If you feel the same, ask me to wait."

"No. I could never ask that of you."

"Ask me."

I fought the words on the tip on my tongue. "No."

"Please ask me," she sobbed. "You said you loved me."

"I do. More than I ever thought possible. But this is a foolish notion. It's your heartache speaking. I love you, I do and that's why I refuse to let you do this."

"It's not foolish to me."

I sighed. "You're still so young. We're talking years, I won't be able to come to the island often, and you won't leave."

"For you, I would try."

"Then come now. Right now. I can't leave, I have to teach. Be with me."

"Ian."

"Right. That's what I thought."

"You know how hard it is for me."

"That's why I'm not begging you to do something you aren't capable of."

"What are you saying?"

"I'm saying I won't ask you."

Silence. And it might as well have meant death.

"Koti, please don't take it the wrong way. You have to understand, I put my life on hold for so long. I don't want you to feel obligated to do the same for me."

"How am I supposed to take it? You're telling me to let you

go when I'm telling you I'll wait. Because I think you're worth it. I guess I'm alone in that too."

"Don't put words in my mouth."

"You've said enough. Goodbye, Ian." Her voice broke as did our connection.

"Koti!"

I hit redial and got her voicemail.

After several tries, I left my first message.

"Answer the phone!"

And then rang her again.

"Koti, I can't ask you. Don't put me in this position please."

And the day after.

"I've never been so fucking miserable. Please just try to understand."

And the day after that.

"You're being childish."

And the day after.

"If I were there, your ass would be purple. God, but I'm not there and I'm dying to purple your ass. I miss you so much. I can't come to you now just to leave you. Please believe me, I have no choice. You might not understand it, but I do, and I know in my heart asking you to wait is wrong. I won't bother you again... but please call me back."

Koti

Trailing my fingers down the piano keys, I tried in vain to keep the tears from surfacing. Before he left and after our signing lesson, he'd played for me daily while I lit candles and uncorked some wine. We'd taken great care of our bubble before it burst. Disco came running at the sound and when she realized it was me, she resumed the wait of her master in front of the screen door.

"Come on, baby girl, please," I begged as I sat with her on the floor. Her missing him kept her alert. Any sound other than the noise inside the house had her scrambling for the door. Even after months away from him, her loyalty and unyielding love hadn't faltered a single day.

"I know how you feel, but we have to get our shit together. Hey... who want's *bacon?*"

She didn't move, and I was out of cards to play. That morning it seemed she was suffering the worst of it as if the realization struck he was never coming back. I started my mourning the minute he left the driveway. My days spent wiping away tears every time I woke up and realized he wasn't there to share a smile with and the fact that I would never again wake up to see his.

The devastation remained as the weeks passed and I couldn't bring myself to call him back. I was at my breaking point. A mental list full of my new hopes weaved between my racing thoughts and the irony was, those hopes for my future all included *him*. There was no one else I wanted to share my life with. He was never coming back for me—for us—and I agreed to the heartbreak. I'd allowed it in.

Ian was it for me. And he was gone in every sense of the word.

We agreed on a clean break, but I never agreed to stop loving him because that would be too much to ask of a woman who was finally using her heart for something other than pumping blood through a string of years filled with anxious days.

Though I knew I loved him before he left, I didn't realize how deep it ran. I didn't realize the extent of my love or how hard I would love him, or how much it would break me to lose his daily affection. I didn't realize how his presence would linger in my house or how I would forever sleep on the opposite side of the bed waiting for him to return to his side.

My love hadn't faded, my tears weren't anything more than fresh reminders on recycle. The pain of losing him wasn't lessening as the days and weeks passed, my insides only grew heavier with ache.

His presence and our relationship had restored my faith in the possibility of a different life other than just managing my disorder. His absence took that faith away when he left me with nothing but a house full of memories and days filled with longing. We'd only had a few months to love each other, but that love would have to be enough to last my lifetime. I understood Jasmine and her hesitance to move on. I understood her stubborn heart and crumbling morals. I understood the unending pain and the scars love could leave.

I finally understood, and I fucking hated it.

I grieved him with every breath.

"So, this is what a broken heart feels like, huh, girl?"

Disco began to cry again, the same sorrowful whimper that started months ago as I pulled her into my arms and cried with her. For a moment in time, I lived in a dream with a man who could read my thoughts, whose attention took me to unbelievable heights, whose touch set me on fire and filled me with hope. I had the love of a good man, the best of love stories.

I found the one person in the world who understood me and loved me wholly as I was.

Love stories aren't always perfect. They can wreak havoc on the heart and distort the soul. I'd gotten lost in love and found the reality at the end of it where I lived in the truth.

Not all love stories come with happy endings.

thirty-nine

Ian

Two Months later

I sat Ella's cocoa down on the wiry table at the park and took a sip of my coffee as she fed the birds the rest of her croissant. Once seated, she took a sip and commanded my attention with lifted hands.

Dad, you're still sad.

I'm fine.

You're lying.

I'm okay. How is school?

Please go. I'll be okay. I miss her too.

I put up my hands and she covered them with hers.

"Dad," she said. When it was just the two of us, she saved her voice for when she wanted to make her point. "You were happy with her."

Her speech was close to perfect. Her structure still lacked a little, but I'd never been a prouder father. Her voice was a gift, as was she.

"You sound beautiful," I said as she read my lips.

"I do not. I won't ever sound good. But one day a man will love me like you love her. Do you want me to be without that man?"

I lifted my hands. *No.*

"Talk," she commanded.

"No, I want you to have love."

"And I want that for you. This is not the time to give up." She swallowed and looked around us still a bit self-conscious from talking in public. "I'm going to the Washington program soon. You don't need to be here anymore."

I shook my head as she stomped her foot on the pavement. "Listen to me!"

She was loud, but I didn't flinch. She was showing me what was in her heart.

"You are a good dad. But I'm growing up to be a woman."

That time I couldn't help but laugh at the ironic tantrum.

I took a sip of my coffee. "And I haven't missed any of it and I don't intend to."

"You get on my nerves," she huffed.

"That's not nice."

"I don't want to be nice. You need to go. Mom is here if I need her."

"Good for her."

I still wasn't speaking to my ex-wife. I wasn't sure if I ever would. Daniel had buckled under the pressure of her expectations in their first few months of dating and left Tara holding the bag, especially when she told him Ella was his. I'd been spared a custody battle and because he was the piece of shit he was, Ella had been spared too. I got no satisfaction from any of it aside from the fact that my daughter didn't have to deal with the heartbreak I had.

Ella lifted her chin in defiance. "Go to her."

"No."

"What if Koti loves someone else now?" The burn in my chest scattered, singeing every part of me as Ella pulled an envelope out of her purse. Inside was a small square picture of

Koti. Pain radiated through me as I fixated on the perfection of her face. Had she moved on? Everything inside me ached at the thought and at the same time, it was exactly what I'd asked her to do. The picture had been taken a month ago and if her smile was any indication of her progress, she was in far better shape than me.

"She writes to me all the time. She loves me. She loves *you*. This is the good love you said you wanted me to know about. The kind you and Mom didn't have. Dad, *listen* to *me*."

I choked on the lump in my throat. "I'm listening, baby. I promise."

"Good." Tears sprung up as her passion flew out of her mouth. "I won't let you keep *me* from that love."

"I understand, but this is different."

"No. I'm almost a woman!" She seemed more intent than ever on making that clear.

"There are plenty of things you aren't old enough for."

She rolled her eyes dramatically. "Dad. Go to her before it's too late."

"I can't leave you. I won't."

"I'm leaving *you*, Dad!"

My head snapped up as she lifted her hands. *I'm leaving you. I'm sorry. It's time for you to find your new life.*

I lifted my hands. *You are my life.*

"No," she spoke again. "Koti too."

Shocked at her admission and the weight of what she was saying, I couldn't help the build of emotion that swam in my eyes. At the sight of it, Ella flew into my arms and spoke directly into my ear. "We can both be happy. I promise. I know you love me. Go be with her. She still loves you too. I know it."

Praying I could whisper back, just once, to my little girl she pulled away as we both righted ourselves. I wiped my face of more tears.

You are the best thing that ever happened to me. I want you to know that.

"I know," she said plainly.

I laughed at that as she took her seat and spoke again. "Do whatever the hell you have to do to make yourself happy. We only get one life, Daddy."

A small group of women walked by staring wide-eyed in our direction before they spoke up to encourage her.

"Damn right, baby!"

"You tell him, honey!"

I raised a brow in an attempt to hide my smirk. "Where did you get that?"

She signed back.

An asshole I'm proud of.

Ian

One week later...

I pulled into the driveway and took a deep breath as I studied the identical houses. So much time had passed, yet the sight remained as much the same as the feeling in my chest. I'd abandoned her here months ago, and the last time I'd spoken to her, I'd given her no reason to wait for me. No reason to believe I would ever return. Exiting the cab of the truck, I glanced around the darkening sky. Koti always made it home by sunset, and I was losing my window by screwing around. All week I'd run in circles in an attempt to settle things in the States, so I didn't have to leave her again in the near future. If by some miracle she took me back, if I had any place at all in her life, I was going to make damn sure I was able to be there. It took me a majority of the time to find someone to cover my class load, the rest I spent subletting my apartment. If Koti didn't take me back, I would be a gypsy. That fear had me on the sand making headway toward her house before I could even begin to think about the right words. I'd phoned her, but her number no longer worked, which only had me scrambling faster to get to her. At Ease Property was on hiatus according to the answering service and the number I had for Jasmine had long since been erased from my phone from her one time calling me. I was at a dead end in reaching her and had only one option.

I breached the clearing of the alley only to be disappointed by the sight of the ocean without her standing in front of it. The loud clatter of wood on her porch had me jumping out of my reverie.

"Can I help you?"

I scoured the guy questioning me from head to toe. Tall, dark, built, and decent looking. Instantly, I hated him.

"I'm looking for Koti Vaughn."

"She's not here."

Rage boiled through my veins as he gave me a subtle smirk. I wasn't in the mood for bullshit and it seemed the opposite for him. He positioned a large piece of wood over one of her windows and began nailing it in.

"Can I ask what in the hell you are doing?"

"Uh," he said with a furrowed brow. "I guess you could say I'm paying penance.

"Are you a friend of Koti's?" I asked, my tone full of accusation.

"Something like that," he said, giving me another disgusting fucking grin.

"In case it isn't apparent, I'm not in the mood for this. Where is she and what are you to her?"

The guy smiled showing me every single one of his white teeth. "I've never met Koti man, chill out."

"Then can I ask why you're on her porch boarding up her house?"

"A favor for her friend, Jasmine," he replied. "It's a long story, but made short she asked me to board up this house and the one over before the storm comes."

"Storm?"

"Big cell, hurricane headed straight for the islands. I don't know when you got here man, but you better turn around and get out fast. It's going to start tomorrow."

"I've been busy all week, haven't bothered to look at the news."

"Did you miss every TV screen on the way here?"

"Shit," I said, wiping my face.

"It's everywhere."

"Can you give me Jasmine's number?"

"No," he said. "But maybe she'll pick up if I call her."

"Maybe?"

"Like I said, long story."

I rolled up my sleeves and picked up some of the boards. "That's my parents' place next door. I'll get this done and come back and give you a hand."

"Thanks, man, I appreciate it. Tell you what, I have a jet leaving at six. You help me out here, and I'll make sure you get out of here in one piece."

"Where's Jasmine?"

"Iowa."

"Iowa?" I grinned. She was with Julian.

"Want to tell me what that grin is about, brother? I've been begging for crumbs for the last few months."

"I think it's best that I don't tell you for now."

"Fair enough." He swung the hammer as I got to work boarding up my parents' house. Once I finished, I helped to finish boarding up Koti's place. Every nail planted felt like more of what I didn't want. I choked down the emotion of being on the island without her as I did everything I could to board her house up. Wherever she was, I was sure she was terrified.

When we were finished, the guy held out his hand. "I'm Steven."

"Ian," I offered, shaking his hand.

"I'm not sure this is going to help these houses, but let's get the hell out of here."

"I'm not leaving without Koti."

"She's not here in St. Thomas. Sorry, I thought you understood me."

"And you don't know where she is?"

"Nope. Let's get on the plane and we can give Jasmine a call."

"Sounds good."

Two hours later, I was seated on a luxury jet when Steven put a cell phone in my hand.

"Hello?"

"You stupid ass men. I swear to God, I'm glad you found Steven, you two idiots deserve each other. If I was there, I would rip your damned balls off. You ASSHOLE!"

Steven chuckled across from me in his seat. "She's a live one."

I covered the mouthpiece. "I can see why you're so smitten."

"I'm so fucked," he muttered, sinking back in his seat before he closed his eyes.

"It's good to talk to you too, Jasmine. I've missed you as well."

"Your 'I'm a gentleman' crap won't work with me, and you damn well know it." I heard a muffled, "Is that Ian? Let me talk to him."

I would know Julian's voice anywhere and heard Jasmine's response to his request in the form of a painful grunt and a relenting, "Okay, baby, okay no need to get all batshit. Jeez!"

Jasmine responded to Julian by screaming in my ear. "I'll show you batshit. You're on my side. My SIDE!"

"You're right, I'm on your side." Seconds later, Julian's voice was on the line. "Hey, man!"

"What in the hell have you gotten yourself into," I muttered as Jasmine's voice rang out.

"I heard that you Australian asshole!"

"It's South African," Julian corrected. I chuckled as the phone was dropped, another grunt sounded and then Jasmine came on the line breathless.

"You don't deserve her."

"I know. But I love her, and I swear to God, I'll do everything I can to make it right."

"It's probably already too late."

"What do you mean?"

"She went back to New York. Ian... you really fucked up."

"Too late for what?"

"Her parents own a Fifth Avenue apartment. I'll text Steven the address, and that's all you're getting from me."

"Fair enough. Thank you. Out of curiosity, what's the situation with this guy, Steven?"

Steven opened one of his eyes across from me and sat up as if I'd thrown him a bone.

"He's just as screwed as you for the moment."

I chuckled again. "That bad, huh?"

"Tell her I'm coming to get her," Steven spoke up.

"Tell him I'm being taken care of," she shouted back. "Good luck, Ian, you're going to need it."

"Jasmine, I know you're pissed, but before you go, will you just tell me if she's okay?"

"She got her heart shattered by an asshole who knew better, is about to have her home destroyed by an act of nature, and is currently living with her mother, what do you think?"

"Jasmine, please tell me what I might be too late for?"

The line went dead, and I cringed in my seat.

Steven let out a sigh. "She's gotten a lot tougher since I left." I recognized a bit of a southern drawl as he spoke.

"Left? You're the ex-fiancé who left her in St. Thomas?"

"Yep," he said, rolling a tumbler of whiskey in his fingers. "Biggest mistake of my life."

"Why did you do it?"

"I had my reasons. None were good enough, hence the penance she's making me pay. I know she's with someone else right now. I'm biding my time and sooner or later she's going to have to hear me out."

"So, she's taking her revenge by making you board her friend's house?"

"Amongst other things," he said dryly. "It was my pleasure to do it. I'm not the total bastard she paints me to be."

"I'm afraid I may be the bastard she's accused me of being," I said, taking his whiskey and tossing it back. "My apologies. I think I needed it more than you."

He motioned for the attendant. "Don't worry about it, man. Plenty where that came from."

I looked down at the islands as they slowly disappeared from view and briefly wondered how the sight of it would change when I returned.

"So where can I drop you?"

"As close to Fifth Avenue in New York City as possible."

Steven grinned. "Looks like today's your lucky day."

I watched the expansive darkening sea fade as we drifted through the sky. "Hope so."

Dark clouds laced the sky as I walked toward Fifth Avenue, my thoughts as muddled as the sounds of the bustling city. We'd had a layover in Atlanta for a day and a half due to a string of storms from the approaching hurricane. I spent the night in one of Steven's mansions. Jasmine, in her wine-induced tale of woe months ago in St. Thomas, had failed to mention that Steven owned half of the media in the southeast. I liked him well enough and he'd been kind to lend me the use of his plane to get to New York. Despite that, Julian had my loyalty. I couldn't fault Jasmine for her indecision. Steven had a certain likability. Julian, if he had real feelings for Jasmine, was in for a fight.

Racing thoughts multiplied as Jasmine's words had me panicking.

Too late?

For what?

Had she found someone else?

And how long had she been in New York?

I couldn't breathe, and maybe that agony was the penance I deserved, still, the idea of seeing her had my flesh burning. Needing her wasn't the plan all those months ago, but each of my steps was purposeful, a way back to the truth of the fact that I did. I needed her. And she had to know that I was half a man without her. I had nothing rehearsed, no great speech planned of what a screw up I was to think we could treat our time together as a fling, that it hadn't changed my life, my dreams, me.

All thoughts slipped away as I saw her exit the building feet away from me. My wind knocked out from the mere sight of her, I scoured her from head to heels. She was dressed in a sleek black power suit, a curtain of long blonde hair shielding her face. The wind graced me by pushing it away so I could get a glimpse of her. She was painted perfectly, her eyes lined with black, her lips colored in deep red. My whole body spiked in awareness as she surveyed the street in front of her, stunning me motionless. Her head held high, she was the perfect picture of a Park Avenue princess. I'd never seen her in more than a smile and a bikini, and although it was my preference, for a moment, I was a bit intimidated by how incredible she looked. She glanced in my direction not seeing me before slipping into a waiting town car.

"Koti!" I chased after her as the car began to pull away. *Months*, I'd waited months to try to mend the gap between us. Fear of every color clouded my vision as did jealousy I didn't have the right to feel. Rain started to pour from the sky as all of my hopes began to fade.

What if her heart was no longer mine?

My veins screamed at the idea as I spit out the threatening defeat. There was no greater pain in life than losing love. Koti's own brand of affection had smashed through the brick and mortar of my resurrected heart. Rights be damned. I wanted her, she belonged to me and I to her, so much so my soul bled in that street streamlining in her direction. I managed to hail a cab just as her town car passed me.

"Follow that car, please."

The cabbie gave me a disbelieving grin in the rearview. "Are you fucking *serious*, man?"

316 | KATE STEWART

I pushed my drenched hair away from my eyes. "I'll give you every fucking dollar in my wallet, *man*. Follow it!"

Taking off like a shot, I sat back in the cab as the sight of her swam in my head. Absolutely nothing about her appearance resembled the woman I fell so much in love with.

Was I too late? No, it could never be too late, no matter what the case and I was desperate enough to breach anything between us. Repaying the favor, no matter what it took, I would break down every wall she built, even if I helped to resurrect them. I would never love another woman, of that I was certain. My fate was in her hands and I would make it known. We had something time and geography couldn't touch. Regardless of my mindset, fear scorched me everywhere making me nauseous. Seconds after the cabbie pulled up behind the town car, Koti dashed into the building as I looked up at the sign in bold letters next to the front door. C. Zanders-OBGYN.

"Hey man, is this your stop or what?"

All the blood left my face as I stared after her.

Too late?

I shoved all the promised cash into the cabbie's glove covered hand as blood filled my ears and my heart slammed against my chest.

Confused thoughts multiplied while I caught the door and held it for a woman with a stroller. She thanked me as I waited for her to move past before I rushed down the corridor. I stopped in the lobby searching for the floor. After a trip in the elevator, I stopped outside the office door and tried to collect myself.

Was she pregnant? Half of me boiled in thoughts of betrayal at the fact that she'd hidden it from me while the other half of me begged that was the truth of it. Jasmine had been cruel with her warning and maybe I deserved the state I was in, but I couldn't let it last a minute longer. The waiting receptionist gave me a kind smile.

"I'm here to meet Koti Vaughn. She has an appointment today."

"And you are?"

"Her husband?"

"Is that a question?"

I cleared my throat. "No, I'm her husband."

She picked up a file and eyed it. "Says here she's single."

I swallowed as the older woman with dyed fire red hair narrowed her eyes but couldn't contain the threatening smile on her lips.

"Is this a good story?"

"Not sure," I said hanging my head as droplets of rain hit her desk. "But I'm begging your pardon for lying and for your mercy. In the most unromantic gesture imaginable, I'm about to barge into her appointment and demand she marry me."

Her eyes widened. "In an OB appointment? You're serious?"

"Quite serious, yes."

"Love your Australian accent."

I held my bite. "Thank you."

"Down the hall, last door on the right, but if anyone asks you found it on your own."

"Thanks again."

"I hope she says yes."

We shared a smile. "Me too." I raced down the hall and burst through the door just as Koti sat down in a hospital gown tying it in place behind her. Shock, confusion and then anger transformed in seconds over her beautiful face.

"What in the hell are you doing here?"

I couldn't wait a single second longer. "What in the hell are *you* doing here? What is this? What am I too late for?"

"Ian, you can't be here."

"The hell I can't," I said, closing the door. "Tell me what this is."

"*This* is none of your damned business. Get out, I'm not decent."

I raised a brow. "I've seen you in far more compromising positions with a lot less on."

"How did you know I was here and you were too late for... Jasmine?" Without confirmation, she closed her eyes and shook her head. "I'm going to kill her."

"I just took a ride with her ex, Steven on his plane. Seems to be some unfinished business there."

"Yeah, well she has three men madly in love with her."

"Three?"

"Toby, the water guy is in the running too, may the best man win."

"Wow."

"Yeah, wow. Great talking to you, can you please leave now?"

It took every bit of strength I had not to sweep her off the bed and into my arms. I loved her sass more than I should, but even in a hideously loud hospital gown with bright orange flowers, she had me at her mercy. Still, panic more than anything strangled me at the thought she could betray me in a way I could never forgive.

"Are you pregnant?"

"Knock, knock," the doctor said, entering the room and looking at me in surprise.

"Hi there, didn't realize she had company. I'm Dr. Zanders," she introduced herself and I shook her hand. Koti spoke on my behalf before I could get a word out.

"He was just leaving," Koti offered before looking pointedly at me, *"now."*

I gave her a menacing smile. "Not a chance, puffer fish."

Dr. Zanders laughed. "I thought you were single, Koti."

"I am."

I cut in with an answer of my own. "She's not, I assure you."

Koti straightened herself on the bed in an attempt to muster as much dignity as she could in her gown. "You assure wrong. This isn't cute, Ian, you need to leave."

"No. Fucking. Way." I stood, my chest heaving as I looked her over. If she was pregnant, I would have to find a way to forgive her, every part of me hoped it was true, but a larger part of me was boiling mad... She wasn't showing, at that thought my chest sank at the idea something could be wrong. I turned to the doctor who seemed to be enjoying our back and forth.

"So, this is just routine then?"

She nodded. "There's no need to worry. Hysterectomies are *very* common. I perform about ten a week."

I felt sick as I tried to swallow the threatening bile. Not pregnant. Most definitely *not* pregnant.

I turned to face Koti who was staring at her red painted toes. Wrong color, wrong place, wrong news. I didn't know if anything would ever be right again.

Fighting a hundred different emotions, I spoke up to try to save face. "Dr. Zander, could you please excuse us for a moment?"

"Sure." She made her leave as I stared at the woman who owned me and refused to look my way.

forty

Koti

I wondered what color coffin Jasmine wanted, or if she wanted to be cremated, either way, I hoped she was enjoying her last day alive with Julian and that she'd broken her abstinence streak because she was a dead woman.

Seconds after the door closed, Ian stalked over to where I sat, pulled me to stand and grabbed the clothes I had laying over the chair and threw them on the bed toward me.

I stood arms crossed as he gathered my shoes throwing them my way as well. "This is like the opening of a bad joke. Your ex-boyfriend walks into your OB appointment. Care to tell me the punch line?"

Furious gray eyes met mine. "I'm still madly in love with you. Get dressed."

Trying to ignore the shock at the sight of him and his words, I shook my head.

"That's unfortunate, *crocky* because I've moved on." He looked gorgeous in a form-fitting button-down that matched his eyes and slacks. His hair was a little longer and even more unruly and it looked dead sexy on him. He was in even better shape than when he left the island and I tried my best not to stare too long. It hurt me to see him that way. It hurt me to see him at all. But I'd done my share of mourning over the way he'd left me with no trace of his love, of us.

"Moved on?" His eyes drank me in before he moved toward me. "Sorry if I don't believe you. And I've been chasing you all over to find you doing this? The surgery is not happening, get dressed."

"Sorry, Ian, I'm not that scared woman you left bleeding in the sand anymore. Things have changed. I've changed."

"Well now, *that* would be unfortunate, but fortunately I don't believe you on that either."

"This needs to happen."

I refused to believe the genuine fear that covered his features. "*Are* you sick?"

Ignoring him, I shed my nightgown as his eyes greedily took in my naked form. Eat your heart out, buddy. He wasn't the only one who'd been working out. It wasn't a lie, things had changed, I just wasn't sure if I was happy with all of them.

"Answer me, Koti," he commanded. "Please."

I sighed out my answer. "No, I'm not sick."

"Are you at risk of anything?"

"Well... no more than usual." Pulling my panties on, I could see desire stir in his eyes. I pretended to ignore that too.

"Then it's not happening."

"It *is* happening, tomorrow morning and you need to *leave*." I moved to grab my slacks and he stopped me with a hand on my arm.

"Not a damned chance."

I ripped myself away feigning indifference to his touch. "How about you answer some questions for me. Like, why are you here?"

"Because I came to tell you I was an idiot and I want another chance with you."

"That's not going to happen."

"Oh, it's happening."

Hand on my hips, I faced him head on. "Are you taking ste-roids now? Who in the hell are you to tell me what's happening?!"

"I'm the man in your life."

"You're the man who left me!"

"And I've paid for it in every imaginable way. You remember the hell I told you I didn't believe existed? I've been living in it because I can't stand life without you. And you aren't having this surgery."

"Ian, I'm having it. It's what's best for me."

"Why?" He shook his head, calling bullshit. "Because you're mad at me?"

"Still an egomaniac? It's sad to see not much has changed for you. Not everything revolves around you. Endometriosis is painful. Trust me on this."

"And there's a possibility the pain can lessen with childbirth."

"Did you YouTube that fact on the way over here? Good for you."

He narrowed his eyes. "No, I read up when I was on the is-land, making love to you every night and fucking you every day."

I swallowed as he took a step toward me.

"You were holding out to have this surgery because you thought there might be a chance for a family someday. You en-dured the pain because you were hoping for a child. Tell me that's not the truth." I stayed mute as his furious eyes bore into mine, his jaw clenched. "If I thought for one second this is what you really wanted, I would walk away, but it isn't. You don't want this surgery. You want to have babies, in St. Thomas, *my* babies. Now finish dressing, damnit, I'm here to take you home."

"There is no home." I pulled on my blouse and started tug-ging on the buttons, fighting my tears I turned away from him. "It's gone, *both* of our houses."

"What?"

I glanced at him over my shoulder. "Jasmine just called to let me know Banion's okay. He can't even get to our street. It's all gone. St. Thomas is in shambles."

His face paled. "Thank Christ you weren't there when it hit. But it's *still* our home."

I smiled ironically. "No, that was never my home."

The doctor poked her head in the door. "Koti, I have another appointment and we didn't really need an exam today. This visit was more for Q & A, so if you have any question feel free to call me on my cell. You can grab it at the receptionist's desk. Good to meet you..."

"Ian," he offered, his tone ice.

"Good to meet you, Ian."

"She's not having the surgery," he said matter-of-fact, "but we appreciate your time. Nice to meet you as well."

Dr. Zander smiled at me, her eyes alight with mischief. She was enjoying the volley between us far too much.

"I'll see you tomorrow," I told her. "I'm sorry about this."

"She won't be here," Ian said, fuming as he glared at me across the bed.

The Dr. spoke up with a smile on her face. "I'll wait for your call, Koti."

Once the door was shut, I turned on him, my anger spilling over.

"You have no right to speak on my behalf and you need to leave."

"And you need to wake the hell up. You aren't making this decision because it's what's best. It's an emotional call, you're still angry with me for leaving and you want to give up. I won't let you."

"It's my decision."

"The hell it is! Get your things we're leaving!"

"I'm not going anywhere with you!"

"You don't belong here."

"I don't belong on an island in the middle of the damned ocean, either. I'm not sure it's here, but I'm figuring it out."

"Jesus," he said taking a step closer, his eyes accusing. "What happened to you?"

"I woke up, and I needed to grow up. I can't live in my parents' vacation rental for the rest of my life, it's not practical. I'm staying in New York for now. I'm going back to work for a small firm after I recover. It's major progress, you should be happy for me."

He crossed his arms. "Are you kidding me?"

I fastened my belt while he fumed on the other side of the bed.

"Look, I've been battling this my whole life. I'll manage. You don't have to worry about me. I've got new plans. The house is gone, there's nothing to go home to. Jasmine's considering moving back to the States as well. It's just not home to either of us anymore. Things change. I took a cue from you, it's time to be responsible. *You* of all people should be proud of me."

"Proud of you? Aikona! No facking way." Ian's face turned crimson as I slid into my heels.

"Thank you for your concern, but I assure you I'm fine."

He narrowed his eyes and strode toward me until the back of my knees touched the bed. I tried not to react to a whiff of his scent. He towered over me as I stood to my full height, thankful for the few inches of advantage my stilettos gave me.

"You want to have this surgery? Fine, tell me how this decision came to pass? You just woke up and decided to change the course of the rest of your life, to give away your chance of having a family, why?"

"I'm in pain!" I defended.

"Bullshit, Koti."

"No, what's bullshit is me having to explain myself to you. You don't have a say in my life. Not anymore."

"The hell I don't. I'm the father of your future children so I damn sure do have a say."

Instant tears filled my eyes and I turned to look out of the window watching the bustling traffic and a woman with a stroller move toward Central Park.

"That's rich. I haven't seen or heard from you in months."

"Doesn't matter how much time has passed, we're still in love. I felt it the minute I walked through the door, I'm not playing the denial game with you, or any game ever, for that matter. That isn't who we are. We're closer than two people could ever be. I still love you, probably now more than I ever have. And I have loved you. Maybe in different ways and in different degrees over the years but I have loved you. You want to know what I'm doing here? I came to tell you that you're worth it. And I've been stupid and selfish, and I want to spend my life with you."

I turned back to glare at him. "News flash, egomaniac, I can live without you."

"I know."

"You left me with nothing."

"I know."

"I don't *need* you anymore."

"Maybe you don't, but I still need you."

He hung his head as I stood shaking with fury.

"That's funny, I remember begging for any sign that you might. I remember telling you I would wait for you and getting nothing."

"So, what's this then? The final fuck you to our relationship? Tell me something, Koti. That day you dreamed of having a baby, the day of the accident, what color eyes did that baby have?"

"Ian, stop it. Okay, stop it!"

"They were my eyes, weren't they? You never wanted a family, you never dreamed that far ahead until we fell in love."

I stayed quiet.

"They were my eyes. I'm the man you pictured having a child with. I'm here to tell you I want the same."

"Please," I pleaded. "Please stop. That's not the life I was supposed to live, remember? It's not realistic. It was a childish move to run and throw it all away. As much as I hate to admit it, my mother was right."

"Bullshit, that's your *mother* talking. I won't believe that of you. You were happy, and I destroyed it with my selfish shit and now you've used it as an excuse to move on the *wrong* way and in the wrong direction."

"Who are you to judge me? You don't know what it was like being in that house without—"

He took a step forward closing all the distance between us. "Without what? Me?"

"Just leave. I don't want you here. How can I make that any more clear?"

"You could stop lying, not have tears in your eyes, not be searching for my lips to kiss you and itching for me to reach out and touch you. I see it all because I know you that well. I watched you and worshipped you for the best months of my life. I *know* what you need because I loved giving it to you and I will touch you the way you need me to and kiss you the way you want me to, but I need you to stop lying to me... right now."

"So what, because you finally showed up I'm just supposed to get on my knees and be grateful you came back. Go to hell. It's too late."

His eyes closed painfully and when they opened, I could see them swimming with emotion.

"Maybe it is too late for us, if that's what you say, I have no choice but to believe you, but this life you're living now *isn't* you."

"No, this *is* me, the side you don't know and the part you've never met, just like there's an entire life you lived before me, that I don't have a clue about. These are our real lives. St. Thomas was a dream. What happened on that island was beautiful and magical and a once-in-a-lifetime thing, but it wasn't real or sustainable, and it was always going to end. We both knew eventually we would have to get back to reality. After you left to face yours, I decided to do the same for myself. *This* is who I am, that time on the island was a much-needed *break*. I was never supposed to be there."

"I know you don't believe that. That place, that beach, that ocean is ours, Koti, and maybe it's not the life either of us planned, but it's what I want now more than anything. We were happy there."

Anger won over ache. "You're still selfish. Words mean nothing to you because you don't listen. My life is here now, St. Thomas is over. Fucking me for a few months doesn't make you an authority on me. *We* are over. You made sure of it."

He continually swallowed, tears brimming in his eyes as he lifted his hands.

I love you.

I need you.

I want that beautiful dream back.

I can't live without you.

I tried, and I hated it.

I'll be there when you make mistakes, when you hurt, when you're scared.

I'll be there.

I'll marry you.

I'll want children with you.

We can live anywhere you want.

I'm lost without my love.

I need you back.

Tell me what to do.

If you don't want words, tell me what you want. Please. Please. Please.

Raw, I bit my lips to stifle the sob. "Stop. You broke my heart and you meant to. You can't take that back."

He gripped the sides of my face. "I'm late, but I'm here. And I'm sorry. I can't stop, I won't stop. I can't stay away from you any longer. I can't lose you again. And you can't lose the part of you that I know will be one of the best parts. You'll be the most beautiful and amazing mother. You'll give our children pure love and acceptance. Please don't do this. Tell me I'm not too late. Tell me your heart hasn't closed to me. Tell me our children are safe."

His tears fell rapidly down his beautiful face as my heart tried to claw its way out of my body toward the refuge of him.

"I have no place being a mother."

"You're the strongest woman I've ever met, despite your fears. I'd be so incredibly proud to have you mother my children. And as long as it's in my power, you won't be alone to ice those hundred cupcakes for the class. I'll be by your side through all of it. Every minute, good or hard. I want to be that man for you. I *want* to be there. I want our love story more than my selfish freedom. I want our life. I'm so sorry I ever made you doubt that. I'll never leave you again."

My walls began to crumble one by one.

"Please," he said, his eyes overflowing with love. "Baby, please be honest with me. I'm begging you. Be honest with me now before I do as you ask and walk out that door."

He searched my eyes as I swallowed hard.

"I know you still love me because I can feel it. I can feel it no matter how hard you're trying to fight it. I can feel your need for me, just like you feel mine. We're still in love, and I know we always will be. You are worthy of love and a life fuller than you can ever imagine. You're my best friend and I miss you. I miss laughing with you, I miss talking to you, I miss filling you with my cock and hearing your beautiful moans, I miss eating late at night in front of the fridge door, swimming naked and waking up together covered in sand. I miss fighting with you because making up feels so fucking good. I miss the Koti who can't stop laughing when she's had too much wine, I miss the way you hug my daughter with your eyes closed because you mean it. I miss the turned-on sounds you make when you're reading your romance novels."

"I make sounds?"

"Yes, that's why I never let you finish but a few chapters at a time, it drove me mad."

We both laughed despite our sagging hearts.

"I miss Disco and the way you loved her without trying to show me you'd grown too attached. There are so many things I miss, but your smile is the first. I'll do everything in my power to keep it there, to light you up the way you do me. I'm not just here because I miss you, because I need you, I'm begging for the beautiful dream of that life we started together. You think it's not realistic, but it can be a reality for *both* of us. We can go back and own that fucking life. No rules but our own. Our happiness won't ride on fulfilling anyone else's expectations, it will be a life catered to *us*."

A tear ran down my cheek and he brushed it away with his thumb.

"I just… couldn't think of a good enough reason to be in

330 | KATE STEWART

any more pain." I sniffed and tried to pull my face from his grip, but he kept me close.

"I'll be your reason, let our son or daughter be your reason and they will be worth it, I promise you. I promise you." He kissed my forehead, my eyelids, my cheeks and then stole my breath when he placed a slow kiss to my lips. I sank against the weight of it, my walls obliterated as my heart sprang free.

"It hurt so much when you left. I couldn't handle it without you. It was like everything I loved about being there evaporated without you to share it with. I didn't know it, but I think I was waiting for you before you came, and when you left, I could never love that place the same. I missed you so much, I felt like I was dying every day you stayed gone." He exhaled, closing his eyes before he kissed my tears away.

"I was a shitty boyfriend, but I'll be a better husband."

"I would have waited forever if you had asked me to."

He bit his lip and nodded. "I know."

"Why didn't you ask me, Ian? I hate you for it. You know muses don't just fall from the sky every day." It was my shitty attempt at humor, but I couldn't even manage a smile. "Domkop." I deadpanned.

He chuckled. "I'm swimming in regret. Please, Koti, please take me back."

"What about Ella?"

"She's fine. She's good, she sent me to you. The one thing that held me down set me free to love you because she loves you too. We both want you back."

"I'm so pissed at you."

"I'll fix this so you never have a reason to doubt me again. Say yes."

"To what?"

"To all of it, to everything. Be my life. Marry me and if you say yes, I promise the only thing I'll ever be selfish about again is you. Say yes and let's go back to our beach."

Three points to make a good argument, Koti.

Number one, you love him. Number two, you love him. Number three, you love him.

I didn't want to fight anymore.

"Yes."

"Again," he whispered hoarsely, his gray eyes pleading with mine.

"Yes, to all of it. I love you, Ian."

He let out a sigh as he gently took my lips, his slow kiss melting the space between us. "Let's go home."

"We don't have a home."

"Then we'll do what we do best, and this time together."

"What's that?"

"Start over."

epilogue

Koti

Eight months later…

Jasmine clasped a gold bracelet on my arm and stood back, tossing a piece of wavy hair off of my shoulder.

"You look so beautiful."

"Don't make me cry."

"I'm not trying to. Today looks good on you. I'd be jealous if I didn't have a hot ass man waiting on me."

"I wish he could have been here," I said, turning to look at my reflection. Most of my residual nerves of the day had faded as I took a sip of champagne. The last week had been kind and I was thankful. It had been weeks since I'd had an attack and for the most part, my body had been cooperating despite the stress of the past month.

But on the other side of my fear was a freedom I could never have imagined. In trusting Ian with my worries, in having him to lean on with my daily stresses, I found it much more bearable to deal instead of internalizing everything. It was incredible to me, the feeling of someone knowing me so intimately, he often knew just what to do, what to say so I didn't feel alone with my fears. I had a partner for the first time in my life. He never dismissed my anxiety or placated it either when I needed to work it out. Simply put, he was just there in any capacity I needed him.

"Maybe I'll get here someday," Jasmine said, fidgeting with one of Banion's beautiful bouquets.

"Oh," I said with a knowing grin. "I have zero doubts you will."

"I'd look ridiculous as a bride."

"Please," I said giving her an eye roll. "You're still fresh, I think Banion started to cry a little when I told him you weren't single."

"I *am* single."

I gave her a pointed look. "You are so *not* single."

"I'm undecided."

"And you're loving it," I said, kissing her cheek. "And I'm so proud of you."

Her eyes glistened. "If you want to run away, now is the time. I know a sucker with a getaway plane."

"I'm good."

"God, I know you are. But he's still lucky I didn't rip his balls off."

"I am too, I have plans for those balls."

My dad cleared his throat as Jasmine and I made bulging eyes at each other and I coughed out a laugh. "Sorry, Dad."

He gave me a soft look. "She's here."

I frowned in confusion before realization struck. "How?"

"Ian called her last night."

My mother and I hadn't spoken since I left New York with Ian. I knew deep down her real disappointment was that she finally had me back in her life and on her path. Her vocally expressed distaste for our new plans as I packed my things had led to a nasty fight. Ian had held his tongue until she insulted our relationship and he, in turn, had blown up by calling her an eleventh-hour mother. My dad hadn't faulted either of us for her

334 | KATE STEWART

upset when we left New York to pick up the literal pieces of our life in St. Thomas. Even as I wrestled with the fact that my mother and I would never see eye to eye, my heart made a decision that that day was as good as any to give our relationship another chance. It was, after all, a day of new beginnings.

I looked to Jasmine whose eyes shimmered with happy tears. "I knew she would come."

"Let's do this." I couldn't get to him fast enough.

Jasmine gripped my hand and squeezed before handing me my bouquet. "Let's get you married."

"Ready, Daddy?"

He nodded. "She loves you. Please try, if you can, to forgive her."

I hugged him close. "I already did."

My father put my hand in his as we made our way off my freshly painted back porch toward my finish line. Brilliant colors glittered the sky as the sun began to sink beneath the sparkling ocean's surface. Jars full of votive candles were scattered in the sand around the small arch lighting up our beach. Ian stood in wait for me looking gorgeous in a simple white button-down and slacks. Flowers of every color were strewn where I stepped as I was escorted toward my waiting groom. I smiled at Ian's family, Rowan, William, and his brother Adam as they stood in wait with matching smiles. Rowan's eyes overflowed the minute she caught sight of me. After sharing a tearful smile, I turned my attention back to Ian who mouthed "you're beautiful." Halfway down the aisle, Ella stepped away from her place beside her father and moved toward me stopping just a few feet away.

"Hi," she said simply in greeting.

"H h-hi," I whispered back with a nervous laugh.

"I love you, Koti," she said in the most sincere and perfect voice imaginable.

Instant tears sprang to my eyes. "I love you, too."

Seconds later, a change in music filled the air and Ella looked back to her father who did a short three finger countdown for her before she turned and began to sign the words of the song to me. It was a gift from Ian who stood behind her with a clear view as I tried to hold in my threatening sobs. Ella threw her heart into her every movement as she signed Calum Scott's "The Reason". Happy tears trailed down her sun-kissed cheeks as she told me of her father's love for me and pressed her hands against her heart swaying back and forth to the music she couldn't hear, but to words she could feel. Piano keys struck every chord in my heart as I looked past Ella to Ian who began to sign with her on the second verse. An ache of the purest kind poured from my heart as I watched my future happiness tell me of a love so incredible it was limitless, endless and ours. I crumbled in my father's hold as he looked on at me with shimmering eyes and faith-filled assurance. They swayed together as my heart over-flowed with love for them both. Ella stood back next to her father as Ian signed the rest of the lyrics. When the last of the notes had played, I resumed my walk toward my forever.

My mother was weeping freely as she stood and searched my eyes for forgiveness before her and my father agreed to give me away. I eagerly hugged her as she held me tightly in her arms and pulled back to tell me I was a beautiful bride. We shared a smile before Jasmine stepped in to take my bouquet while wiping the tears from her eyes.

Breathless and overwhelmed I turned to face my groom, my heart alight with love and acceptance I could never have dreamed up. Ian and I stared at each other, filled with uncondi-tional love as we promised our lives to one another, our hearts united in our place of peace, where we began the dream that had become our reality.

Later at the reception under our star-sprinkled sky, Ian pulled me onto the porch full of guests and we slow danced to Cyndi Lauper's "Time after Time".

"You made me choose the song," he whispered, "I think it's fitting."

"So fitting," I whispered. "I can't believe we just got married, crocky."

"I can't believe you wore those damned gold sandals," he said, pulling me closer and rubbing his nose against mine.

"Of course you can. You sure you're up for this? You ready to be a Home Depot dad again?"

"I'm up for whatever happens. I can't believe you're mine."

"I can't believe you're building us a house." We both turned to the framed skeleton sitting where our sand alley used to lay. The only thing finished was the expansive deck and that had only happened days ago as a request from a bride to a groom for her wedding day. The width of the house took up both lots that our houses used to dwell on. Ian planned to repurpose some of the wood from the old houses to add character. I think a part of him was just as sentimental that a cherished part of our childhood was gone, and it was his way of incorporating our past into our future. It had taken us close to a month to get back to the island and far longer to handle the desolation that surrounded us. The day we arrived in St. Thomas, Ian proposed to me in front of our wrecked houses amongst the scattered remains all over our beach. He wanted to turn one of our most miserable days into the happiest, and he managed it on bended knee with the question of forever and future promises pouring from his beautiful lips. We spent our days helping with the cleanup and our nights catching up. Our love paved the way through the endless wreckage that once was our paradise. We lived off love in the worst of conditions and nearly a year later, we were beginning to see some semblance of our dream. The day we broke ground on our new house, I started to plan our wedding.

I danced with my husband as Cyndi sang our love's lullaby thinking about the past year and the ones ahead of us.

"This is everything I had hoped," I said, feeling tearful. "Gah, I'm so emotional lately."

Ian's smile deepened. "You think maybe that's a good sign?"

"No," I said with a sigh. "Dr. Z said it will probably take a while with being on birth control so long and then there are my asshole ovaries."

"Have faith, beauty," he said. "We have time, plenty of time."

"I know, I'm not worried about it. I just gained a teenager."

"She's just agreed to stay for the summer, and she keeps eyeing that kid who lives a few streets over," he shook his head, "let the good times roll. Remember new wife of mine, no boys, those are the rules."

"I have equal say now and you just made it so. I think it's time for her to date."

Ian winced as if I'd punched him. "Are you kidding me? No way."

"She's plenty old enough and she's probably going to start with or without your consent. So, you might as well give her a little freedom."

"Are you purposefully trying to give me a fucking heart attack on our wedding night?"

"Don't die just yet. I need your sperm."

He scoffed. "How romantic."

"And I'm horny. We should go fuck while everyone is dancing."

Ian's eyes bulged. "Do you hear yourself right now?"

"What? Like your mouth isn't ten times worse. Besides, it's the hormones," I whispered. "We can make all the sweet wedding night love later. Now come see to my needs, *Pleasure Prince.*"

I yanked at his hand as he laughed loudly behind me. "Oh, my God, woman, I love you so damned much."

Behind his back, I signaled Ella the okay as she pulled her island crush toward the dance floor and mouthed. "Thank you."

Giving her the thumbs up, I smiled inwardly as Ian stomped enthusiastically through the sand toward our half a house. Minutes later, my back against the wood frame, my dress was around my waist, Ian drove into me as I bit into his shoulder to stifle my moans.

"I could do this forever with you," he whispered as he cradled me in his palms, holding me tightly to him.

"That's kind of the point of the day," I whispered against his neck, "we get to do this forever."

He pulled back to gaze down at me, slowing his pace as he thrust in, the feel of him too much and not enough. There was nothing funny about the look in his eyes.

He stopped his movements and leaned down kissing me so tenderly, tears surfaced.

"My beautiful wife," he dipped in. "I never thought I would be this happy."

"Ian."

"I love you so much, baby," he said making me ache and filling it all at once. "So much."

Connected on every level, he gently pushed in again filling me over and over as I clung to him, our labored breaths mingling as we sank into a slow rhythm until I came apart, my body shuddering as he kissed me again and again, his tongue tasting, taking, savoring as he slid it gently against mine.

His body tensed as I leaned in and whispered, "I love you." He let go then, his frame shaking as he let out a long breath. He pulled back as we stared at each other in wonder, neither of us taking a single second for granted. It was a testament to what we had to look forward to, a collection of minutes, hours, days, weeks, months that would turn into years of the same love we both thrived on. His excitement matched mine as we shared our happiness with a smile and then sealed it with a kiss underneath the stars we unveiled for the other.

Koti

Eleven months later...

Ella smiled between us sensing our shared secret before her eyes lingered on her father who gave her a reassuring nod.

She lifted her hands. *What's the news?*

Ian grabbed my hand and we beamed at each other before we both turned to Ella. "We're pregnant."

Ella's smile disappeared, her face twisting in agony as she lifted her hands to sign.

Excuse me.

She shot up from the table unaware her water glass had spilled. I managed to catch it before it hit the floor and shattered and looked up to see Ian try to stop her with a hand on her arm while she tried her best to pull away. When she finally managed to get free, she began frantically signing.

"No," he spoke and signed in unison, "You're signing too fast. Slow down or speak."

Her face twisted as her broken voice sounded out breaking

both our hearts. "Congrats, *Ian*, you finally get a child of your own."

"What?" Ian paled as I sucked in a breath.

Tears flooding her eyes, Ella leveled us both with her next words. "I know you're not my father."

Ian flinched as Ella faced him head-on.

"I'm deaf, not stupid, remember? You've been telling me that my whole life. Hey, *Ian*—"

"Stop calling me that!" He was smashing his hands together as he signed, pain twisting his features.

"Fine, *Dad*, how could you think I wouldn't know? Haven't you ever seen a picture of Daniel?"

Ian closed his eyes and I could feel the shatter in his chest from a foot away.

"I look just like him!" She was screaming, her voice faltering in heartbreak as she continued. "I have his face, his eyes! I'm not an idiot. All those months ago when you were sad, when you first came to St. Thomas, I saw you crying when you thought I wasn't watching. The minute I met Daniel, I knew why."

Ian slowly lifted his hands. *You knew this whole time?*

Ella slowly nodded. "So, it's true?"

Ian's tears were instant, the hurt on his face etched in every line. "I'm so sorry, baby."

Ella sobbed in our kitchen, her words coming out in an angry burst. "I hate her!"

Ian signed slowly. "You told her you know?"

"No, she was too busy kissing his *dick* until he broke up with her."

"Language!"

"It doesn't matter, I don't care about her or him. And now I'm losing you because you will have this new family without me. I know you got what you want now. A baby of your *own*."

"That's not why Koti got pregnant, not for that reason."

"You're too old."

"Now who's the asshole? And I'm not too old, I'm still in my thirties until tomorrow."

"Then why?"

"Because I love her, and I'm meant to be a dad."

"You got your wish." Her heart was breaking, and I could feel the pain radiating off him. Ella shook with emotion as her father cut the air with his hand furiously until she raised her eyes to his.

"You. Are. Mine," he whispered fiercely, as he signed slow and with the same emphasis.

"But I'm not. I'm not your daughter, I'm *his*."

I coughed back a sob standing on the sidelines, helpless and wanting to comfort them both.

"You are mine and you know it. Neither of us can help what your mother did, but we can move past it because of the truth, nothing will ever come between us. I love you as much now as I did the minute I found out you were coming. It was the happiest moment of my life."

Ella broke before us, watching his hands as Ian fought with emotion, on the verge of losing his own battle. He cut the air, again and again, stomping his foot so she could feel the vibration as Ella's shoulders fell forward in defeat. He moved swiftly toward her but remained inches away so she had no choice but to watch his plea. She lifted shimmering eyes to meet his before she followed his hands.

"I'm so proud of you. You are mine. Your sarcasm, that's mine, your need to fix things, that's me, your independence, me, your mean right hook, your love for superhero movies, that all comes from *me*. All of those things and much more. You are a reflection of me. And you will never be replaced."

"Daddy." She crumbled, and he stood where he was, his

eyes filling as his voice broke. "But I deserve to be happy too. You are the one who pointed that out to me. And Koti makes me happy and this baby is a blessing and you will finally have the brother or sister you've been asking for since you were five."

Ella cried harder as Ian stood strong, adamant on making his point as he fought his need to physically comfort her. "Look at me, little woman. I'm your father, your Dad, *forever*. Don't be afraid of this change, of this baby, or of losing an ounce of my love. Don't be afraid of *anything*, because you are mine."

He pressed both hands to his chest and closed his eyes moving his body back and forth. I muffled back a sob. "You are mine, since the day your mother put you in my arms and we got linked." He clasped his fingers together and pushed them toward her. "We are forever, Ella, nothing or no one can or will ever change that. Tell me you understand. Tell me you know that."

She nodded before she rushed into his open arms and broke inside them with relief. Ella's cries had Ian faltering as I coughed out my own tears. After a few minutes of their embrace, Ella lifted her soaked face from his shoulder and stretched a hand out to me. "I'm sorry, Koti. I didn't mean to ruin it for you."

Don't you dare be sorry. You didn't ruin anything. I love you and you are mine too.

She nodded as she moved from her father's embrace and nestled into my arms. After a few minutes, she looked up at me with stained cheeks and a sheepish smile. "I hope it's a girl."

"I don't," Ian coughed out with a sigh as I shook with laughter. Ella frowned sensing her father's smartassed comment and glanced behind at him before she looked to me for an answer.

"What?"

"Your dad is an asshole."

"That's not news."

My dreams and I spent the rest of the day playing in the waves on the shore in the backyard of our new home and later that night, two childhood friends held hands beneath the stars.

"Well that went wonderfully," Ian said with a chuckle. "Fuck, I think I had a small stroke."

"I think it went the way it was supposed to."

"I never wanted her to know."

"Ian, she's lived with it for a while. She just needed to hear from you what she already knew, that it doesn't matter."

"You think so?"

"I know so. Also, you're kind of incredible. Who knew the insane man with the shitty accent and bubble butt, would turn out to be Mr. Wonderful? Definitely *not* me."

He kissed the back of our clasped hands.

"I think I first loved you when I was fourteen. Not the way I do now, but I'm pretty sure I loved you even then."

"I loved you because you gave me sweets."

"I know," he chuckled.

I stopped and turned to stare at my husband whose laughter lines had deepened and only made him more appealing. I reveled in the sexy grays that framed his temple. I looked forward to every year I noticed those subtle differences because it meant we would spend those years together. "Ian, how lucky are we to have met at all?"

"Coming from different worlds, we had so many chances to miss each other."

I nodded. "Does this make you a believer?"

"It makes me a believer of *us*."

"Forever a realist."

"Not so much anymore."

"Why is that?"

He cupped my face and brushed his lips against mine. "Because I married my miracle."

I laid in bed gazing at the twinkling galaxy outside of our skylight window thinking of the narrow roads that brought us back together. Sometimes what's meant to be isn't written in the stars, instead, it's a journey on the path less traveled without a map of guidance, without certainty. Though Ian didn't fully admit it, I was sure he had to believe that every battle we fought in our separate lives—good or bad—led us to that beach, to a glimpse of the life we could share together, and that was enough for us. That brief blip in time was all we needed to decide on the life we wanted. In that moment, I was grudgingly thankful for a body that wouldn't cooperate and a mind that ran in circles, and I knew without a doubt my husband was grateful for the trials that led him to me because, without them, our stars wouldn't have finally aligned. Our lives would've turned out differently, and for me, that would have been the real tragedy. In finding each other, we also discovered the *why* of our journey.

Ian tenderly kissed my stomach while I whispered a prayer of thanks to the stars above with renewed faith.

Not all love stories come with happy endings, but some do.

THE END

Listen to *Someone Else's Ocean* playlist on Spotify:

Coming Soon! Jasmine's Story in—*Falling over Forty*

thank you

First and forever, I want to thank my readers. Four years after I published my first book, I'm still able to do something I love and it's because of you. Thank you from the bottom to the top of my heart.

A huge thank you to my Beta readers: Donna Cooksley Sanderson, Stacy Hahn, Sharon Dunn, Maiwenn Blogs, Patty Tennyson, Malene Dich, Christy Baldwin, Kathy Sheffler, Kelli Collopy, Sophie Broughton, Anne Christine, and Bex Kettner. Your infectious excitement makes it so easy to hand over a piece of my heart. Trusting you ladies is one of the best things I could ever do. You are so greatly appreciated and loved.

Thank you to my PA, Bex Kettner, for effortlessly doing the job you do and for being my rock. You are an amazing help to me and a top-notch friend. I love you.

Thank you, Autumn Gantz, for organizing the chaos and being the kick-ass friend you are. You are one of a kind and I'm so lucky to have found you.

Donna Cooksley Sanderson, wow, just wow. You are one of the brightest lights I've ever met. I consider your friendship a gift and one of the best I've ever been blessed with. Our talks are the best parts of my day. You are one of the best friends I've ever had, and I promise to always set my coffee down for you. XO

Thank you to my proof team-Donna Cooksley Sanderson, Joy Sadowski, Bethany Castaneda, Marissa D'Onofrio, Grey Ditto, for swooping in and saving the day.

Christine Estevez, my editor extraordinaire, thank you so much for the endless faith you have in me. It means so much. I'm so excited about our new adventure and friendship.

Thank you to my amazing family; Bob & Alta Scott, Angie, Kristan, Tommy, and Stephen. Watching everyone grow is such a gift. I love you all and our crazy dynamic. Not a day goes by where I'm not thankful to be a part of such a fantastic family. We are so lucky. I'm so lucky. I love you guys.

A huge thank you to my BFF, Erica Fischer, my inspiration for Jasmine and her and Koti's friendship. I'll never be able to express how much I love and admire you, or how knowing you has changed me and at times saved me. You and me until the wheels fall off, buddy, and even after. Thank you for holding my hand through the last fourteen years.

Thank you to my fabulous group—the asskickers. You ladies light me up daily and make my world a better place. XO

Thank you to Elizanne (Zanna) for all the help with the South African Slang. It was a blast getting to meet you.

Thank you to my hubby, Nick, for your never-ending understanding. You make deadlines bearable and life worth living. I love you.

about the author

A Texas native, Kate Stewart lives in North Carolina with her husband, Nick, and her naughty beagle, Sadie. She pens messy, sexy, angst-filled contemporary romance as well as romantic comedy and erotic suspense because it's what she loves as a reader. Kate is a lover of all things '80s and '90s, especially John Hughes films and rap. She dabbles a little in photography, can knit a simple stitch scarf for necessity, and on occasion, does very well at whisky.

Let's stay in touch!

www.facebook.com/authorkatestewart

www.twitter.com/authorklstewart

www.instagram.com/authorkatestewart/?hl=en

www.facebook.com/groups/793483714004942

open.spotify.com/user/authorkatestewart

Sign up for the newsletter now and get a free eBook from Kate's Library!
www.katestewartwrites.com/contact-me.html

other titles available now
by Kate

Room 212

Never Me

Loving the White Liar

The Fall

The Mind

The Heart

The Brave Line

Drive

The Real

Romantic Comedy

Anything but Minor

Major Love

Sweeping the Series

Erotic Suspense

Sexual Awakenings

Excess

Predator and Prey

Made in the USA
Middletown, DE
29 March 2021